# PRAISE FOR M.J. POLELLE'S
## *AMERICAN CONSPIRACY*

"A stellar novel of action, adventure, and intrigue. The twists of betrayal unravel at a perfect pace, and Polelle nails the details of this high-caliber political drama."

—Steve Berry, *New York Times* bestselling author

## PRAISE FOR *THE MITHRAS CONSPIRACY*

"An enjoyable thriller . . . Polelle rewards readers with uncertainty in every chapter. Leone's Rome is a dangerous place with a masked attacker around virtually every corner. And that's what makes it fun to visit."

—*Kirkus Reviews*

"Things done 'in the name of religion' have brought out both the best and worst of humankind. The 'whatifs' in this book are real possibilities—ancient legacies that may someday be uncovered and reshape the perceptions of the past and ancestral faiths."

—Dr. Steven Derfler, Emeritus Professor, Joint Doctorate in Classics and Archaeology (University Of Minnesota)

"A fast-paced thriller, very much in keeping with *The Da Vinci Code*. An enjoyable ride."

—The Wishing Shelf Book Awards

# AMERICAN CONSPIRACY

# AMERICAN CONSPIRACY

## M.J. POLELLE

LIDO PRESS

Published by Lido Press, Sarasota, Florida
www.mjpolelle.com

Edited and designed by Girl Friday Productions
www.girlfridayproductions.com

Cover design: Paul Barrett
Project management: Sara Spees Addicott
Editorial: Bethany Davis
Image credits: cover © Shutterstock/Konstantin L

ISBN (paperback): 978-0-9600863-2-0
ISBN (ebook): 978-0-9600863-3-7

Library of Congress Control Number: 2021907618

First edition

*To the memory of Jim Murphy*

*Imagine what would have happened if, God forbid, Barack Obama had been assassinated after becoming the de facto nominee? What would have happened in America?*
—President Joe Biden, August 23, 2019, on the
campaign trail at Dartmouth College

# CHAPTER ONE

**NOVEMBER 10, 2028**
**THIRD DAY AFTER THE ELECTION**
**CHICAGO, ILLINOIS**

After sixty throws of the presidential dice, the election of 2028 came up snake eyes. Media oracles had prophesied Franklin Dexter Walker the presidential winner by one electoral vote. During a Democratic victory parade to rivet the prediction in the public mind, a ball bounded through police barricades on Michigan Avenue. A girl in a wheelchair cried out for the ball. Detective Jim Murphy stooped to retrieve it and changed the course of American history.

The air cracked overhead.

The crowd screamed.

Looking like the old Soviet politburo on a reviewing stand, roly-poly politicians in black overcoats ducked for cover.

Murphy turned.

Walker lay bleeding on the ground behind him.

"They shot Walker," said the Secret Service agent in charge, fingering a loose earpiece. "Get the ambulance."

Scanning the surrounding buildings with upturned faces, the Secret Service agents ringed Walker.

Murphy scrambled to join the protective circle.

"This is on your head, Murphy," said the special agent in charge. "Get the hell out of our way."

The ambulance wailed as it made its way up the line of vehicles to stop near the candidate's limousine. Paramedics rushed FDW to Northwestern Memorial Hospital. The Secret Service and the ambulance left Murphy holding the ball in the middle of Michigan Avenue. He gave it back to the shaken girl and headed for the hospital.

At Northwestern Memorial, Murphy joined the crowd of hospital staff, media, and police milling around the ER for news about Franklin Dexter Walker. "Serious" was all the media relations department would say about the candidate's medical condition. The eyes all around the detective were saying, *You're responsible for this*. At headquarters they'd be saying: *It's Murphy's Law again in spades*.

And they'd be right. He had just passed the detective exam and was on his way up in the Chicago Police Department. Awaiting reassignment to the Bureau of Detectives from his current position as security specialist with the International Relations Department, he had screwed up his career path again.

"I wanna talk to you," said the Secret Service agent in charge, tugging at Murphy's sleeve. Murphy brushed away the agent's fingers and followed him into a small conference room down the hallway. Closing the door, the agent said, "Why were you out of position?"

"I wanted to get the ball for the girl."

He didn't add that she reminded him of his younger sister, who died as a child.

"And I wanna be Sherlock Holmes. That's no excuse." The agent removed his hand from the doorknob. "You should've taken the bullet."

"You don't know I could have stopped it."

"I've been around long enough. Forensics will back me up."

"And Walker should've stayed in the limo." He reached for the doorknob. "You know damn well he jumped out to grandstand without telling anyone. How could I know what shenanigans he was up to behind my back?"

"It wasn't your effing job to chase a ball."

"I don't take orders from you guys."

"Your brass is going to get an earful about your colossal blunder." He shook his head. "And to think you came recommended."

"I'm out of here." Murphy yanked the door open and tromped down the hallway.

"If Walker dies," the agent shouted after him, "your career's down the toilet."

Murphy paced outside the ER, waiting for the latest about Franklin Dexter Walker.

The CPD brass had picked him to join an elite security unit selected for physical prowess. He still aced the three-mile runs he had done at the police academy. Without breaking a sweat, he had kept pace with the limo gliding along the avenue. The Secret Service agents had huffed and puffed, jogging behind him. He earned the honor of guarding FDW fair and square in a city where things weren't always fair and square.

And then along came Murphy's Law and prompted Franklin Dexter Walker to do his shtick as the "walking" candidate by walking out of the limo right into a bullet. The detective collapsed into a chair and waited. He had failed the Chicago police and himself.

———

Franklin Dexter Walker was supposed to be with her before the altar as guests of honor at the Holy Savior United Church of Christ on Chicago's South Side for the four o'clock Wednesday afternoon prayer service. Clapping to the gospel music, Dallas Taylor, the vice-presidential candidate on the Democratic ticket, had had enough of Franklin Dexter Walker's quirkiness on the campaign trail.

In tune with the rhythm, her hips swayed under her butterscotch sheath dress with agitation more than with piety. She had promised the pastor her running mate would come to give thanks for support from the African American community. Taylor joined her voice in song with the churchgoers, undulating to the music and clapping hands.

"Is he coming?" the minister said, about to deliver the afternoon prayer.

"Any minute," she replied. "He promised." *But sticking to promises isn't his thing,* she thought. The Secret Service had code-named him "the Millennial," even though Taylor was younger. If she acted older, it was only because she was the responsible one on their unprecedented youth ticket. Being the eldest child in a low-income family of six children, she knew what responsibility was. She wasn't born with a silver spoon in her mouth like Franklin Dexter Walker.

While the minister delivered his prayer called "God Shed His Grace on This Land," she sat down and felt for the cell in her pocket. She had to call him right away. Her name on the ticket got him the presidency by a whisker. He wasn't going to blow off this congregation waiting to be personally thanked for its support.

Being the first African American senator from Texas and now the soon-to-be African American vice president meant she didn't have to take any more crap from him. Taylor slipped out her cell, trying to hide it in her lap, and checked with downward eyes for messages before texting him in all caps.

The usher built like a bouncer shot her a stern look. She put the cell away.

At the end of his prayer, the pastor introduced Taylor from the pulpit. Although it was music to her ears, the pastor was dragging out his praise of her accomplishments in the hope Walker would show up. But what he most dwelled on and what most pleased her was his recollection of her tap-dancing skill and all the awards she had won. Probably running out of things to say, he asked her to do a few of her basic moves in the Lord's praise. She objected that she didn't have the right shoes. Just a few moves, he insisted. The congregation seconded the pastor with a round of clapping.

*Love to,* her heart wanted her to say. But her head said: *Hell no!* If the media got wind of tap dancing in church, the tight-assed tycoons bankrolling their election would mutter something about inappropriate behavior. "Love to," she said, "but my foot's troubling me." It wasn't her foot troubling her. It was politics. And she hated herself for her acquiescence.

The buzz of her cell startled her. He could have texted instead of disrupting a church service. Walker was one of the most inconsiderate SOBs she had ever met. She'd give him an earful. She stormed from the front of the church into a side room and jabbed Accept on her cell.

"Why aren't you here, Frankie? Are you playing me for a fool?"

"I beg your pardon?"

"Who's this?"

"Dallas, this is Candace from Franklin's staff. He's been shot. He just came out of surgery."

"Oh my God; I'm on my way."

———

As heads turned to mark her entrance, a Chicago alderman gave up his seat for Dallas Taylor in the packed waiting room of Northwestern Memorial Hospital.

"*You*? Why are you here?" Taylor asked Detective Murphy as she slid into the seat next to him.

"Same as you, waiting for the latest on Walker."

He had pulled her over on Lake Shore Drive under suspicion of driving a stolen vehicle. Because of him, she was late for the last campaign rally before the election. If the waiting room hadn't been filled with reporters and local politicians, she would have taken another seat. Taylor didn't like being late or the person who had made her late.

"I'm going to report you for stopping me."

"I told you. Your car's description matched a stolen vehicle."

"My Jaguar's not the only one on the road."

"You were speeding and didn't pull over right away."

"But it wasn't stolen, was it?" She got up and folded her arms. "You disrupted an important political rally I had to attend."

"I had to run a license check to verify it wasn't stolen."

"You sure took your sweet time doing that."

"Like you took your sweet time pulling over and stopping."

"You forgot the most important reason for stopping me."

"What's that?"

"Driving while black."

"You've got to be kidding me."

"Don't give me—"

"Ladies and gentlemen." A representative of the Northwestern Memorial media department cleared her throat. "I have an announcement to make about the medical condition of Franklin Dexter Walker."

# CHAPTER TWO

*They will pay.* Sebastian Senex simmered watching the YouTube video of his mugging outside the Meridian Club. It wasn't enough for the hoodlum pack to rob him. The video showed a quivering old man begging for his life at the point of a gun barrel while the robbers laughed. The video went viral, forcing him into humiliated seclusion until the internet frenzy died down.

He had to save his city and his country.

Chicago had become number one in homicides even as it sank further into debt and decline on the borderline of bankruptcy. TV news stringers called "night crawlers" slithered out at dark through back alleys and streets in their vans to record the rising number of gang shootings. Some even paid the gangs to stage mock shootings on slow nights. Gangbangers edged beyond their territories to terrorize the downtown area like barbarians at the gates. Grandson gangbangers now accompanied their elders to apprentice the criminal craft. A hereditary class of gang nobility had been spawned out of the major criminal tribes infesting the city.

They increasingly outgunned Chicago law enforcement with armor-piercing ammunition. The police drew back from confrontation to avoid the risk of brutality complaints. A vigilante band of PTSD-afflicted veterans had risen up to organize sporadic counterattacks against the gangs. In the neighborhoods of Back of the Yards and Brighton Park, gangs increased their firepower with military-designed

AR-15 and AK-47 rifles. Abandoned buildings popped up like poisonous mushrooms in once solid neighborhoods. In one of history's ironies, the African American middle class was packing up and moving back to the South, to cities such as Atlanta, for safety and a future. An underclass of gangbangers and immigrant aliens gnawed away at the foundations of Senex's society.

Diagnosed with Huntington's disease at age sixty-five, the doctors gave him ten to fifteen more years to live. Now seventy-nine, he was on borrowed time, desperate enough to even try colonic irrigation and a chimp's diet of green and raw food to prolong life. Nothing worked.

His final hope was the Phoenix Project. Dr. Angelo Mora, his concierge physician and medical researcher, was about to discover the fountain of youth. He and his city did not deserve to die. Only the gangbangers did. The way he intended them to die would be karma in action.

He ran agitated hands along the tufts of white hair on either side of his bald crown. It had been nature's bad joke to give an aging atheist the tonsured hair of a medieval monk. He padded across the antique Persian rug of his penthouse in pink bunny slippers with fluffy cotton-ball tails.

If others knew about the slippers he wore in private during times of tension, they would call it early-onset dementia related to Huntington's. But he knew better. His mother had bought him such a pair when he was a child before a drunken illegal alien had killed both his parents in a car accident. Not even the bunny slippers calmed him this time.

He checked his Rolex. It was time. In his rage he almost forgot.

He stumbled against a Louis XVI walnut chair on his way to the medicine chest. From shelves crammed with prescription bottles, he popped pills manufactured by Promethean Pharma. He was the CEO and founder of Promethean Pharma, and he had the wonders of modern medicine available at the snap of his fingers. If anyone could cheat death, he was the one.

From the top-floor perch of his corporate headquarters in the nearby suburbs, he piled up astronomical profits from patented medications for deadly diseases . . . which the envious called obscene . . . and controlled city and state decisions in the shadows. Not bad for a somebody whose nobody father was a political hack from the Bridgeport neighborhood with a white-collar sinecure in Streets and Sanitation.

The somebody had chased the monkey of success and caught it. He had a fortune in the bank to prove it, but he was bored. He needed Dr. Angelo Mora to keep his body alive and another monkey to give him a reason to live. And that monkey was political power on a national level. The politics of national salvation got his juices bubbling up again through the black mud of rising despair.

He clicked the TV remote to watch history in the making. An ambulance and police cars flashing red and blue lights blockaded the emergency room entrance to Northwestern Memorial Hospital. Police officers held back a knot of pedestrians trying to get as close to the door as possible. The announcer killed time repeating what already was known about Walker's shooting until the network had more news.

Franklin Dexter Walker deserved what he got for threatening to take over the pharmaceutical industry. FDW was out to ruin him and was a traitor to his social class just like FDR. Walker had sucked up Promethean Pharma's campaign contributions when running as a wannabe politician for the Illinois legislature. He then turned against his benefactor. If the turncoat had his way, he'd ruin Promethean Pharma and destroy those who had made America great. And the election results opened the door to that disaster.

The new generation of whiners and leftists led by Franklin Dexter Walker accelerated the fall and decline of Senex's Chicago and his America. Walker's success over Senex's boy, Governor Brock Brewster from Ohio, was an unacceptable constitutional fluke. The Republican presidential candidate, supported by Promethean Pharma's thirty-million-dollar contribution through a daisy chain of anonymous and untraceable political contributions from tax-exempt organizations, should have won. At his suggestion, Brewster even picked Luisa Garcia as his Hispanic vice-presidential candidate to balance out the old, white male Republican running for president.

BREAKING NEWS: GENERATIONAL WARFARE! scrolled across the TV screen in red letters. The anchorperson reported that a Democratic youth PAC had scammed retired seniors living in gated assisted-living facilities operated by the New Pastures Corporation.

The business chain had been set up after the COVID-19 scourge to offer pandemic-proof fortresses for seniors.

"Fortresses, my ass," he yelled at the TV. "They're concentration camps."

Techies working for the PAC pretended to offer charitable assistance to resident seniors coping with technological challenges in the internet age. While those residents enjoyed a recreational escape in the la-la land of virtual reality simulators, the techies hacked computer passwords and "tuned up" computers with malware in a scheme to bilk unsuspecting seniors of their life savings.

The stolen funds had gone to the political campaign of Franklin Dexter Walker and Dallas Taylor. Key states might not have voted for them had the news broken before the election. The news story not only skyrocketed his blood pressure but confirmed his historic decision to make sure the election turned out the right way.

Don't trust anyone under fifty, his twist on the Age of Aquarius mantra, applied in spades to the Democrat ticket. Franklin Dexter Walker was a demagogue who had fired up feckless youths into a wave that would carry him into the White House. Many of the young had resented the social restrictions required by the COVID-19 pandemic to protect senior citizens with social distancing and the use of masks. Never again, the more radical of them chanted at rallies.

Stand-up comedians from Generation Y and even Generation Z joked openly that any new outbreak of COVID would be an ideal "boomer remover." Some academics suggested that infectious diseases should be given leeway among seniors so that nature could run its course more quickly. Unless the elderly hurried up and died, the economy would stagnate, they said. Baby boomers were clinging on to their jobs and refusing to retire. These young radicals now treated the Greatest Generation and their children like trash.

This was madness and the way to national destruction. Every society needed the wisdom of elders like him. Without the dominance of this demographic class, the country would be reduced to government by photogenic adolescents. Youthful scammers adept in the dark arts of modern technology would fleece the Greatest Generation and their progeny of its wealth and reduce it to senile irrelevance.

The vigorous image of the youthful Democratic candidate plaguing Senex's mind stirred a venomous envy. George Bernard Shaw was right: Youth was wasted on the young. Even though the resources of Promethean Pharma had not been enough to stop this young socialist rabble-rouser in the political arena, he had known what would. The TV anchor stopped his marking-time prattle.

A spokesperson for Northwestern Memorial Hospital took the podium for an announcement: Franklin Dexter Walker had died on the operating table.

The news brought Senex to his feet and set his hands clapping. Breaking out a bottle of Dom Pérignon, he did a short jig in his bunny slippers and drank himself into a stupor of self-satisfaction. The enfeebled criminal organization called the Chicago Outfit was not up to the task, but one up-and-coming organization was. He and people like him had once made the city work like a machine where every cog stayed in place and the center held. They were on their way to making things work once again for the entire country.

Before going to bed, he texted: *Congratulations Signor M. P. . . . Mission accomplished.*

# CHAPTER THREE

With Detective Jim Murphy long overdue to meet him at O'Hare International Airport, Commissario Marco Leone of Rome's Polizia di Stato called Murphy's cell. Franklin Dexter Walker's assassination must have thrown the Chicago Police Department into turmoil. No wonder the Chicago detective hadn't met him. Leone left a voice mail saying he didn't want to cause problems and would take the metro to his Loop hotel. After he had a good night's sleep, he could contact Murphy to sort out the details of the Rome-Chicago police exchange program.

Dragging his roller suitcase in one hand and the roller dog carrier with Mondocane in the other, he rattled his way toward the Blue Line to begin his American adventure.

He paused to practice English by reading a dedication plaque honoring Butch O'Hare, the World War II hometown hero, after whom the airport was named. The hero's father had been the lawyer for Al Capone. Leone knew nothing of the hero, but Capone had made Chicago world famous. The city offered, he imagined, premonitions of light and dark, saint and sinner, a synergy of contradictions that made him feel right at home.

Before boarding the Blue Line he bought a newspaper. On the L, as they called it, he sat near the window and plopped the carrier cage with the orange-and-white dog on the seat next to him. He cramped his suitcase against his legs. Mondocane barked. He fed him a tidbit.

The dog barked again, probably knowing he had the upper hand in extorting treats. He fed him another tidbit. Mondocane fell asleep.

As the train pulled away, he fought through his jet lag and the foreign English words to decipher the lead articles in the local newspaper. In addition to the assassination of a presidential candidate, a financial crisis had overtaken Chicago. A credit-rating agency had reduced city bonds to junk status. As best he could make out, the state of Illinois had appointed an oversight committee to handle Chicago's finances in a last-ditch effort to avoid municipal bankruptcy proceedings. The news made him feel even more at home. Rome and Chicago had more in common than even the great fires that nearly destroyed both. Try as he might, the jet lag got the better of him. He drowsed until he heard a voice asking him to move the carrier cage.

A bearded man in a torn T-shirt and knit cap swayed before him in patched trousers and mismatched sneakers. "I wanna sit down." He shivered, holding a partially zipped duffel bag.

Leone removed Mondocane's carrier. The man sat down, trying to stave off sleep. "'Scuse me," he said with a tooth-missing grin as he bumped into Leone. "The CTA's my living room."

"Where ya from?" the man asked.

"Italy."

"Do you need help with anything?"

"No. Thank you."

"Great, lovely city, but you gotta be careful."

As the train sped in a rocking motion toward downtown, the man fell asleep. Leone slipped a few dollars unnoticed into the duffel bag. The man woke with a start at the next stop and jumped out the car door onto the weathered wooden platform just before the door slammed shut.

Wooden frame houses with rickety back stairs needing paint jobs whizzed by as the train picked up speed. Space . . . that struck him. Open to the world, the city sprawled out with breathing space between buildings and wide, grid-patterned streets. How unlike Rome.

Like a consumptive not long for life, the train rattled and clacked down under the earth to become a subway train with the screech of metal on metal in the narrow confines of a dark tunnel linking one stop to another. This was not the Line C subway, built new and gleaming and noiseless in Rome. Surely, this pioneering subway system was a marvel in its time. But that was over a hundred years ago. Weren't things supposed to be new in the New World?

A voice from behind hawked white sox for sale. He turned. The sock peddler stepped over a body lying in the empty rear of the car.

"Sox for a dollar a pair." Next to a sign that prohibited soliciting on CTA trains, the peddler stood in the aisle, opening a box filled with pairs of white athletic sox for Leone's inspection.

Leone had heard of the Chicago White Sox. Was wearing white sox before a game a fan tradition? He had to learn more about baseball if he was to fit in. Before he could decide whether to buy, a conductor shooed the peddler off the train at the Washington stop.

"Pardon me," Leone said to the conductor. "There is a man lying on the floor."

"He's drunk," the conductor said. "Security'll take him off at the Monroe stop coming up."

"That is where I descend for my hotel."

At the Monroe stop, three security guards boarded the train car and waved passengers away while they contemplated the body. "I seen him before," said the squat woman in charge. "He's a regular drunk."

"I'm a detective from Italy. May I help?"

"I'll be." The security woman put her hands on her hammy hips. "Mighty nice of you, sweetie, but we can handle this."

"Better not touch him." The bearded security assistant shook his head. "He might sue."

The other security assistant poked the body with the tip of his boot. The body twitched and slurred an obscenity. "He's drunk all right." He looked at Leone. "Let the foreigner take him off. He wants to help."

"Get out of my face." She pushed the male assistants aside and grabbed the body by the back of its torn jacket. Leone and the two security men tagged behind as she dragged the supine body onto the underground platform like a beached fish. She jerked the derelict into a sitting position while explaining to the detective how he could find his hotel. "Welcome to Chicago," she said, with a warm smile across her face.

# CHAPTER FOUR

Jim Murphy sat with his big sister, Katie, at the rectangular bar of Dugan's Irish pub on Halsted with his pint of Guinness. Tiny bubbles crept up inside the glass and merged into the top layer of creamy white froth. He thanked her for leaving work early at the Good Samaritan Blood Bank to cheer him up, even though it wasn't necessary. The mirthful chatter on a Friday afternoon around the crowded bar of "the only Irish pub in Greektown" sounded walled off from him and distant.

"Haven't you had enough, Jimmy?" She rotated her glass of shandy beer on the bar with both hands.

Only she could call him Jimmy. It didn't sound dismissive when she said it.

"Enough? This is only my second beer."

"That's not what I mean. Stop beating yourself up." She took a sip. "It'll blow over."

"No, it won't. Because I'm involved in the assassination, they're keeping me exiled in the International Relations section of the Chicago Police Department." Assignment to the department should have gone to a cop with a beer belly to mark time until retirement. "There goes my detective career."

"You're not just your career, Jimmy. You've done a great job with Santiago while taking care of Dad with his Alzheimer's. How many cops could carry on as well as you after their wives died?"

Why wasn't Santiago at home when he called earlier? Was his son mixed up with the gangs again?

A gulp of the jet-black, smoky beer slipped down his throat with a taste of bittersweet chocolate and coffee. The Guinness warmed his body like a woolen comforter easing the blustery weather outside and the bad memories inside. "Aren't you tired of still looking after the screwup?"

"What's an older sister for?" She turned stern. "It wasn't your fault."

"He's still dead. I was out of position."

"Remember our little sister? You thought you caused her flopping limbs because you played too rough." She gave a love tap with her fist on his shoulder. "Ninny that you were. It finally sank in she died of spinal muscular atrophy."

"She reminded me of our little sister . . . the girl in the wheelchair."

"Let it go, Jimmy." She put her hand over his on the bar counter. "Heard from our brother?"

"Mr. Big Shot phoned to announce he's flying into town tomorrow from DC. Won't say why."

"Like you, he only wants what's best for Dad." She took a deep breath and pursed her lips. "Did you get into a donnybrook with him again?"

"How's the job at the blood bank?"

"They promoted me to director of quality assurance. We're making plans to stockpile blood in case there's another COVID outbreak." She sipped her shandy beer. "Guess even a spinster ex-nurse like me can have a second act."

"Good for you." He took a long, hard gulp of the Guinness. "Nice to hear you and Mr. Big Shot are doing well at least."

"Gotta go, Jimmy. You should have given up the guilt when you gave up being an altar boy." She slid off the barstool. "What does Big Sis always say?"

"Big Sis always says . . . you can't move forward looking backward."

"Now you got it." She kissed him on the forehead.

———

Upon his sister's departure, Jim Murphy telephoned and left a voice mail.

*Where was he?*

"Wanna nother Guinness?" asked the bartender.

"I'll pass on the black stuff."

"Still Two-Drink Murph. What kinda Irishman are ya?"

"A sober one."

Depressed and confused, he sank back into himself just wanting to brood over his memories. His wife had left him after delivering their only child, stillborn. At least they had another three years after reconciling before she died of breast cancer. Santiago was part of those wonderful years. Now that she was gone, he couldn't reach Santiago the way she had with her gentle touch.

Murphy and his partner had responded to a 911 call. They first found the fourteen-year-old Santiago in a housing project defending his mother against her boyfriend's punches. When the kid with cigarette-burn marks on his arm said he wanted to become a cop just like him, Murphy promised to keep in touch with the teen. He kept that promise by checking in on him when passing through, with money and candy bars.

Things went south from there. A shoot-out between rival Pilsen gangs took the life of the kid's mother. He had no other family. Murphy and his reconciled wife took on Santiago as a foster child, and then they adopted him. They saved him, and he in turn saved their renewed relationship through its ups and downs.

Murphy's cell rang. "Santiago? Where were you?"

"I just got home. Your dad's OK. Everything's cool."

"Kids teasing you again about my screwup?"

"No . . . not much."

"Where were you?"

"Just hanging out."

"Not with those hopheads I warned you about?"

"No." A sigh of exasperation over the phone. "I don't do dope no more."

"I'm coming home."

"You OK . . . Dad? With all those lies about the shooting."

"Sure, sure. See you soon, buddy."

# CHAPTER FIVE

On the way home from Dugan's on Halsted, Detective Jim Murphy pulled up his coat collar as he took a shortcut through an alley. Snow whirled in the night air, brisk and clean like a quality aftershave. Down the dark alley, a garbage can fell over and a female screamed. Through the veil of falling snow he made out two figures struggling on the ground. He ran toward them. A muscled male in baggy pants and a hooded pullover crouched over the sobbing girl. He had his left hand on her throat and the other up her dress.

"Stop it. I'm a cop." Murphy flashed his ID with outstretched hand. "Hands up."

The piss-amber light flickering down from the sodium-vapor alley lamp highlighted a five-pointed crown on the male's left bicep. The gang tattoo meant trouble. An uncomprehending face, probably dazed by dope, turned up to Murphy. The wimpy chin hair contradicted the thick jawbone.

The hands did not go up. The attacker poked the middle finger of his right hand against his own chest. He swiped the bottom of his chin with the finger and pointed it straight at Murphy.

The detective pulled out his 9 mm semiautomatic pistol.

"Hands up."

The attacker's right hand returned to the girl.

Murphy assumed the firing stance and took aim.

"Hands up, right now . . . *Las manos arriba ahora mismo* . . . or I shoot . . . *O disparo.*"

He let go of the girl and balanced up on his knees without a word.

"Go, go," Murphy ordered the girl. She crawled to the side of the alley. "Get away from my gun." She stumbled her way behind her protector.

The attacker reached with his right hand toward a pocket bulge.

The gun blast echoed throughout the alley.

# CHAPTER SIX

"The Millennial gets himself assassinated on your watch, and now this hooligan bawling police brutality in the hospital." Commander Jack Cronin of the Thirteenth District swiveled back in his office chair. "A fine mess you're in, my lad." He folded his hands behind his head. "Murphy's Law strikes again."

"I don't appreciate the dig," Jim Murphy said, "from the commander of what's called the unlucky Thirteenth because of its checkered past."

"Ancient history. Everything's now hunky-dory under my command."

"Why did you want to see me?"

"You're my godson, for God's sake. You should've come to me for help." He shook his head as if in disbelief. "I could've arranged somethin' for you instead of that shithole in International Relations while you studied for the detective test. To settle this shooting thing right away, I could've called in chips from department guys who owe me . . ." He sighed. "Water under the bridge."

An Irish bachelor in the tight-knit Bridgeport neighborhood, this patron with a Santa Claus complexion like his own had taken Murphy under his wing and guided him through the twists and turns of his fledgling career. Whenever Murphy had gained some advantage, his fellow officers would say: "Commander Cronin's your clout, right?" More often than not he did it on his own, but no one believed him. Everyone in the Windy City knew, or at least believed, that few got to the promised land without a bigger and better political sponsor to pull strings in the puppet show called Chicago politics. He wanted to do things his own way without the crutch of clout. He had. And now he paid for it.

"I'm resigning."

"What for, Jimmy?" Cronin's lower jaw dropped. His caterpillar eyebrows jumped.

"Only my sister calls me Jimmy."

"OK, OK . . . Jim." Cronin raised his hands in mock protection. "Look, Internal Affairs is goin' to clear you of the shootin'. He didn't die. Why resign?"

"The media will just call it another cover-up."

"You're overreactin'," Cronin said, running his hand through a thick shock of silky silver hair. "Jeez, the gangbanger reached for a weapon in his pocket. It was self-defense."

"Except it wasn't a weapon. It was his wallet with ID."

"You know the law. If you reasonably thought it was a weapon, you're home free."

"Still . . . the kid was unable to hear or speak." Murphy drew his hands over his face. "About Santiago's age. I almost killed a human being who couldn't hear or speak, who could have been Santiago."

"Has my godson gone bonkers?" The commander's face flushed. "You know as well as me he was sayin' *screw you* in gang sign language."

"I couldn't sleep last night."

"Get a grip." The commander stood and paced behind his desk. "Jeez!" He ran his hand through his hair. "You come from a line of outstandin' cops, your father and his father before him. That means making the hard calls and not lookin' back." He put his hands on his hips and lowered his voice. "Is it true your father's got Alzheimer's?" His hands slipped down to fall limp at his sides.

"Early stages."

"Your old man and I were once patrol partners."

"I know. Heard the stories enough."

"Yes sir, thick as thieves we were when he asked me to be your godfather." The commander slumped back in his chair. "Then for reasons unknown he wouldn't talk to me again."

Reasons unknown? Hardly. Cronin had helped the family through hard times by slipping money to Murphy's mother on the condition of secrecy. When his father found out, the old man exploded and forced her to return what was left and repay what was spent. The commander had punctured his father's male ego.

"Enough walking down memory lane. Why did you want to see me?"

"Will you reconsider resignin'?"

"Why should I? Even though I'm cleared of what happened in the alley, I'll have the black mark of the assassination on my back. Top brass will let me rot in the career sinkhole . . . International Relations . . . where I'll babysit foreign bigwigs visiting the city."

"Buck up." The commander came around the desk and placed his hand on Murphy's shoulder. He squeezed. "I wanted to see you because I got some grand news."

"I could use some."

"The alderwoman of the twenty-seventh ward, and first cousin of His Honor, the mayor, feels she owes you. And that she does."

"I don't understand."

"That was her daughter. The gangbanger tried to rape her daughter." He gave Murphy a cuff on the shoulder. "The lady and myself put our heads together, we did, and made a few calls. And what do you know, lad, you have been assigned to the Thirteenth District as a detective where yours truly presides as the beloved commander."

"Why didn't you ask me first?"

"You're welcome."

"Thanks anyway."

"No need for thankin'. You'd do the same for me." Commander Cronin grew serious. "As you know, somethin' strange is goin' on in the streets. Hooligans disappearing . . . drug pushers gone. I know you're curious and always liked puzzles . . . which is why you'll make a dandy detective." The commander sank back into his chair. "So . . . whaddaya say?" He extended his hand over the desk.

Cronin had always looked out for him growing up. He owed Cronin something.

"I'll give it a try." He shook the commander's hand. "See how it goes . . . but no promises to stay?"

"No promises."

Murphy's cell buzzed. He answered. "Damn . . . I forgot with all that's going on. I'm in the Thirteenth District now," he said into the phone. "I'll get right on it and call him to meet up somewhere and work out something for him to do."

"What's that about?"

"With everything going on, I forgot to call back that hotshot Italian detective who put down a coup. He's the first in our professional exchange program." Murphy got up to leave. "I left him stranded at O'Hare."

"Murphy's La—" The commander put his hand over his lips with a sheepish smirk. "What was the name of that eye-talian dick?" His hand slipped down to his chin, eyes looking at the ceiling. "Somethin' like Marco . . . Marco Baloney . . . or Macaroni, is it?"

"Marco Leone . . . He's police brass like you."

"Jesus, Mary, and Joseph." He ran both hands through his silver hair. "I warned upstairs to keep him out. Someone's threatening the death of him if he comes to Chicago."

"He knew the danger before he came."

"Hmmm. Police brass with balls." Cronin smiled, stroking his chin. "I'm startin' to like him already."

# CHAPTER SEVEN

"This isn't working." The voice coming over Dr. Angelo Mora's cell whined with panic. "This isn't the Ponce de León protein we want," said Sebastian Senex. "Weren't you supposed to be the hematology genius at the University of Padua?"

"My profound apologies, Mr. Senex." Mora stroked his goatee. "I agree with you. The CDF11 protein is not the answer. But please be patient. I have already worked through ten thousand of the approximately forty thousand proteins found in plasma and am about to—"

"Enough lecturing. I demand the other option."

"But I am so close to finding the Ponce de León protein . . . the fountain of youth." He rubbed his right knee to lessen its ache.

"And I'm close to death."

"Are you sure?" Mora wanted no misunderstanding. "Parabiosis is a crude shortcut with serious risks."

"I'm aware of that," Senex said. "I've made arrangements to try out your parabiosis procedure on guinea pigs, shall we say, before you use it on me. You will be provided two guinea pigs. We'll see what happens to the older one."

"Where will you get these . . . these guinea pigs?"

"That's not your concern."

"Forgive me."

"Your only concern is medical. Understand?"

"I do." He hesitated. "You will find the situation distasteful."

"Distasteful?" The voice quivered. "More than death by Huntington's disease? More than losing the ability to swallow, walk, or speak . . . or losing my mind?"

"I did not mean to—"

"Get started on the parabiosis protocol." The voice regained its composure. "And don't disappoint me again . . . unless you want to face a treason trial back in Italy. I can arrange that."

"I'll get started at once."

After the call to Senex, Mora limped to the Phoenix Project laboratory under the Promethean Pharma campus. Senex and he had set up the lab for parabiosis research under the pretext of trying to create artificial blood. Already late for a meeting with his assistants, he poked an authentication code into the keypad. The biometric door lock allowed entry. Making a right turn inside the tunnel to the laboratory, he twisted his right knee. Waves of sharp pain pulsated through the joint. He reached under his white lab coat to rub it.

Senex's threat to return him to the jaws of Italian justice aroused unpleasant memories that had never left. The so-called eminent surgeon at San Paolo Hospital in Milan had assured him the experimental knee replacement with a tantalum-and-zirconium metal implant was a medical breakthrough. The procedure combined the biocompatible qualities of tantalum with the wear-resistant qualities of zirconium.

Dr. Eminence had botched the surgery. Every day the pain in Mora's right knee recalled the malpractice. If Mora had not been forced to flee Italy, he would have settled scores with Dr. Eminence even though the surgeon was a fellow co-conspirator in Lucio Piso's coup attempt. Mora had barely escaped with his life in a shoot-out under the Baths of Caracalla with Commissario Marco Leone's special operations unit. The cost of the escape from the failed coup was shrapnel damage to his right knee. A friend of the dead Piso, Senex had extracted him from the reach of Italian law so he could help the ailing Promethean Pharma CEO cheat death.

Mora could never forgive Commissario Marco Leone for causing the knee injury and for crushing Italy's far-right coup. Leone's days were numbered as soon as the detective's plane touched down in Chicago.

He emerged from the dark tunnel into the bright light of the lab.

"Uno and Due, I see you have ordered your favorite pizzas for lunch," he remarked to his research assistants. The twin brothers fresh from Poland, Szczepan and Grzegorz Wojciechowski, squabbled about whether Pizzeria Uno or Pizzeria Due had the best pizza. Everything, including pizza, became grist for conflict between these two brilliant but moody blood researchers devoted body and soul to finding the fountain of youth.

The names of the twins also proved impossible tongue twisters for his Italian lips. During a night out on the town, he proposed christening them with the nicknames Uno and Due after the pizzerias in Chicago. What he proposed as a joke, the twins took to heart because of their love for the deep-dish pizza at these twin restaurants.

"Would you like some?" Due asked.

The sight of the deep-dish pizza piled high with crumbled sausage and cheese on a thick white-flour crust brought back heartburn memories of when they had welcomed Mora to Chicago with dinners on two successive nights at each of the restaurants.

"Heavens no," he said.

The older one, Szczepan, he called Uno, because that twin claimed Pizzeria Uno had the better pizza, while the younger one with the cheek scar, Grzegorz, claimed Pizzeria Due did. If it were not for that scar, he could scarcely have kept the two straight based on their appearances alone.

"We have a change in our research protocol for the Phoenix Project," he said. "We will explore the parabiosis option instead of looking for the Ponce de León protein."

"That would be a mistake." Uno stopped eating. "We should not give up on CDF11 as the Ponce de León protein."

"Researchers have had conflicting results with CDF11," Mora replied. "Subsequent research has questioned the preliminary findings of the Harvard researchers."

"Why this sudden change of mind?" Uno shook his head. "I don't understand."

"Promethean Pharma," Mora said, "will stop our funding unless we get results soon."

"Parabiosis is impractical for humans." Uno stashed the remainder of his dinner back in the refrigerator. "Even if you doubt CDF11, it

points to the biological region where the Ponce de León protein probably resides."

Mora could not tell them that CDF11 had failed to work on a
human—Sebastian Senex himself. Even though the assistants knew
the artificial-blood research unit was simply a subterfuge for the real
Phoenix Project, Senex did not want them to know their boss had
designed the project to save his own life.

"Hear me out," Mora replied. Anticipating dissent, he had come
armed with a review of the scientific literature, which he summarized
for his assistants. "Back in the 1950s, when young and old mice were
sutured together and their circulatory systems combined, the old mice
showed remarkable signs of age reversal. No one knew why, because
no one knew much about blood and nothing about the potency of stem
cells. The procedure referred to as parabiosis, meaning 'side-by-side
life' in Greek, was abandoned after the 1950s."

"Abandoned for good reason," Uno interrupted.

"Not so." Mora stared Uno into submission before continuing.
"Recently, scientists have replicated the parabiosis protocol with similar results. The old mice became rejuvenated. They had younger heart
muscle, newer liver cells, and better healing." He laid down his papers
on the lab table. "Conversely, the younger mice aged. Draw your own
conclusions."

"Parabiosis is dangerous," Uno said. "The possibility of an immunological reaction is—"

"Basically nonexistent." Mora waved a sheaf of paper. "An experiment at UCLA in 2013 showed that parabiosis partners are free of
harmful immune system reactions. Why do you think that is?"

Like a star pupil, Due leaped to his mentor's defense. "Because
the conjoined mice share a common blood pool, the antigens of each
mouse are not treated as invading foreign elements to be attacked by
the immune system of the other."

"Excellent." He liked Due, who always showed the deference to his
opinion that Uno lacked. "The risk of a harmful immunological reaction is greater with transfusions between separate partners precisely
because the antigens are not shared." He held the lapel collars of his
jacket.

"I also agree with Dr. Mora," Due said, "because we don't know whether there's only one silver-bullet protein responsible for rejuvenating older mice. More likely, it's some combination of proteins presently unknown in the blood, not necessarily one protein alone, that provides the rejuvenating effect of parabiosis."

"Bravo," Mora said. "Even if, hypothetically, there is only one protein that causes rejuvenation, parabiosis shortcuts our hunt by using thousands of proteins all at once instead of proceeding one by one." Mora picked up a basic treatise on hematology and slammed it on the table. "This book confirms what every trauma or transfusion specialist knows. Younger blood is better in every way than older blood."

"Why the hurry?" Uno asked. "The gruesomeness of parabiosis is not a practical solution for commercial use. Remember the decapitated rat experiments? Where two rats stitched together were not properly adjusted, one would chew off the other's head."

"Dramatic nonsense," Due replied. "Those were early experiments. We would use parabiotic dialysis with a state-of-the-art pump similar to a kidney dialysis machine."

"Exactly," Mora said. He went to a whiteboard and sketched the machine that Promethean Pharma had already specially ordered for the Phoenix Project. "Except that this blood-exchange machine uses catheters to connect two humans into a unified circulatory system."

"Nonetheless." Uno folded his arms. "The FDA claims the science of parabiosis is unproven. It will never get approval."

"I have it." Mora touched the side of his head. "Due will work on a parabiosis protocol with me. You, Uno, will continue the hunt for the silver bullet."

"I agree," said Uno.

"Me too," added Due.

"This is the only time you two ever agreed on anything."

# CHAPTER EIGHT

Back at Dugan's on Halsted, Detective Jim Murphy took Commissario Marco Leone's measure behind the joviality of beer-fueled small talk. Murphy clinked his bottle of Guinness against Leone's bottle of Peroni beer and swallowed a gulp of the thick, dark liquid.

"Welcome." He put down his bottle. "Any sign of COVID when you left Italy?"

"None." Leone sipped his Peroni. "Let us hope the Chinese can contain this reported new strain of COVID. They say it has mutated."

"Promethean Pharma says it'll have a vaccine. America has nothing to worry about."

"I think America does."

"If you say so."

*A know-it all.* As best he could figure out, the Italian commissario outranked his own detective status. That was reason enough for suspicion. Police brass were the same the world over. All talk and no longer streetwise. Those who lectured to those who did. He put down the Guinness. "I hear you commissarios rely on inspectors to do your work."

"Do not regular police help American detectives?" Leone's jawline tightened. "I work with my investigator. I do not inhabit what you call the ivory tower."

"No offense intended." Murphy held his right palm out, not completely regretting his indiscretion. "Shake?" Leone gave his hand a stiff pump.

He would have to get along with Leone. Since she had failed to prepare for Leone's arrival with a detailed plan, the head of Chicago PD's International Relations Department readily accepted Commander Jack Cronin's offer to make Leone a tagalong assistant to his godson, Jim Murphy, now assigned to the Thirteenth District.

The commander was happy, not because he was doing his godson a one-way favor, and they both knew it. The truth was that Jack Cronin was happy he had helped his godson and in the process banked a favor for a future favor in a city where account books of favors given and received had to be balanced to maintain the order of the political universe. The director of the International Relations Department was happy because the commander had taken the foreigner off her hands. Murphy was the only one not happy. He had a so-called "assistant" Italian detective with no police authority in the United States and likely to second-guess his every move on the streets.

Even so, he owed Leone civility. He had left the Italian stranded at O'Hare.

"Although I told you about the death threat against you, you still came." Murphy pulled an English-Italian dictionary from his leather jacket. "It took"—he thumbed through the Cs—"*coglioni* . . . to come to Chicago despite the death threat."

"Took balls?" Leone broke out laughing. "I understand. The idiom is the same in Italian."

"Why did you still come?"

"I was burned up with my professional routine in Rome."

"Burned up?" He stifled a laugh for fear of offending. "You mean burned-out, right?"

"Precisely." Leone sighed. "I was burned-out. I needed a change. To see America." Leone pushed aside the glass of Peroni beer. "This is not my first death threat. It goes with the position of commissario."

"Who would threaten you here in Chicago and why?"

Before Leone could answer, Murphy's cell vibrated a little jig on the bar counter. He answered and listened for half a minute, scowling. He clicked off the call and looked over at Leone. "Gotta go. Domestic abuse case in progress nearby." He plunked down enough to take care of the beers and then some. "University cop needs backup."

Leone tailed Murphy to the exit.

"Why don't you stay here?" Murphy said.

"You order me not to come?"

"You don't have to."

"I want to."

"Then let's get going . . . but I'm in charge and you observe. *Capish?*"

"Of course."

At the wheel, Murphy switched on the Ford Explorer's blue flashers and siren. The unmarked SUV hurtled down Harrison Street to the postmodern condominiums of glass and polished steel crowding out the red brick and stone houses of a Little Italy rapidly becoming Chicago's Littlest Italy. The Ford Explorer screeched to a stop behind a parked police car marked University of Illinois at Chicago.

A UIC police officer hustled from the stoop of a townhouse to the Explorer. "He's inside, Murph . . . threatening to kill himself and his wife."

"Did you try talking him down?" Murphy said.

"He doesn't think UIC cops are really cops. He won't talk to me."

Murphy winked at Leone and turned to the UIC cop. "The mope's got that right." Murphy punctuated his jibe with a jovial shove to the cop's shoulder. "I'll take care of it. But you owe me one."

Outside the open front door of the townhouse, Murphy negotiated with the suspect husband who introduced himself as a UIC professor of linguistics. Swinging a bicycle chain from side to side, the professor allowed Murphy and Leone to enter but demanded that the UIC "cop-lite," as he called him, remain outside. For that concession, the professor surrendered the chain to "cop-lite."

Murphy entered with Leone to see a woman cowering on the floor in a corner with a bruise on her arm. Murphy felt absurd trying to convince this egghead that the law did not allow one to "chastise" . . . as the egghead put it . . . one's wife with the bicycle chain, no matter what early English common law had to say.

The feeling of absurdity turned to anger when the professor ignored him and tried to engage Leone in a discussion about the phonetics of the Italian language. The egghead still had a living person who loved him in her own twisted way. He, on the other hand, had seen his wife die in his arms while wiping the sweat off her pained face with a cold cloth.

"Enough trying to teach some sense to the professor." Murphy faced the woman. "Did your husband beat you with a chain?"

Sobbing on the floor, she nodded her head without looking up.

"You're overreacting, dear," the professor said. "Remember. This gumshoe won't be around later, but I will."

"That's it." Murphy read the professor his Miranda rights and prepared to handcuff him. "You're under arrest for domestic violence."

"Don't arrest him," the woman cried out, staggering to her feet. "He didn't mean it."

"I'm taking you to the station for booking," Murphy said to the professor.

"Can I get my wallet from the drawer in the next room?"

"In and out," Murphy said. "And leave the door open."

"Should I not accompany him?" Leone asked.

"Not necessary." Murphy had a plan to teach the egghead a lesson, but he didn't want Leone to see it unfold. "Wait outside."

Alone with the woman, Murphy faced her. "If you back down, he'll do it again. We can get a protective order."

A drawer closed in the neighboring bedroom.

"No, no." Swaying side to side, she held her hands over her ears. "Let him go."

Murphy pounded his fist into the open palm of his other hand. If he pimped the professor enough with insults maybe he could provoke . . . watch his Irish temper, they said . . . maybe then his fist would slide . . . accidentally, of course, into the professor's face . . . or better, if, God willing, he resisted arrest . . . maybe it would slip again into his face and then again and again.

The professor came at him with a .38 Colt revolver pointed at his chest.

"I knew I could outwit a dumbo cop . . . even a real one at that."

Murphy saw his deliverance advancing toward the attacker from behind.

Leone wrapped his arms around the front of the professor's chest and threw him to the floor. "I suspected he would create difficulty," he said, picking up the .38 revolver.

"Thanks for saving my ass." Murphy clapped the cuffs on the professor. "I owe you big time . . . partner."

# CHAPTER NINE

At District Thirteen's roll call, Commander Jack Cronin introduced Commissario Marco Leone, standing along the back wall of the conference room with Detective Jim Murphy. "May Commissario Leone be an inspiration to you all." The commander sat down behind the desk at the front of the room. "He came to the aid of Detective Murphy who was bein' held at gunpoint by the perp. He subdued the perp by wrestlin' him to the ground."

The police captain seated at the table facing the commander's desk turned to the group and led a round of applause to honor the commissario. Several detectives let out whistles of approval. Wearing a Cubs baseball cap turned backward, a young undercover cop in T-shirt and jeans high-fived the surprised Leone.

"You're all no doubt wonderin' why I'm doin' the roll call today. We have a mystery in the neighborhood. And I need my detectives to solve the mystery."

He stood up and walked over to a wall map depicting Chicago gang boundaries dividing up the city like a Thanksgiving turkey. The biggest slices went to the Big Five: Gangster Disciples, Vice Lords, Black P. Stones, Latin Kings, and Black Disciples. For Leone's benefit, Murphy suspected, the commander repeated what everyone in the room but Leone knew. With more than six hundred lesser gangs than the Big Five, like the Asian Boyz, the Arabian Posse, and the Insane Deuces,

Chicago had become the gang capital of the United States, fueled by the sale of street drugs worth tens of thousands of dollars per day.

A new gang calling itself the Aztec Warriors had acquired military-grade weapons and used guerilla tactics similar to those of US special operations forces. The commander's hunch was that the leaders were hardened veterans returned from wars being fought by the United States in at least seven different countries.

The combined gang membership across the city was estimated at about seventy thousand. That was more than three US army divisions. With each new gang, the territory of the others became smaller. The resulting turf battles meant increasing homicides and mayhem on the streets. Even established gangs split and formed separate factions. They were biting and scratching one another like rats in an ever-more crowded cage.

The Big Five, reduced in power by police action, no longer had the ability to impose a truce, even if they wanted to. The commander concluded his overview of Chicago gangs with his perennial bit of wisdom: unorganized crime was now more of a danger to the life and property of the ordinary citizens than organized crime.

"Not like Windy City," Leone said. "More like Wild City." He turned to Murphy with a smirk. "I thought crime was organized in Chicago like our Mafia."

"Here in Chicago we call it 'the Outfit,' also known as the Mob and the Syndicate. It's been coming apart since the 1970s. The RICO Act devastated the leadership. Wiretaps and witness protection encouraged members to turn on one another."

Bored by the commander's recitation of gang facts known to every detective in the room, Murphy tuned out, ruminating about what Cronin had told him a few days ago. Rumor on the street was that Santiago had returned to gang life. *Not Santiago.* The commander never liked Santiago and was biased against him. Santiago was a common Hispanic name on the street. It had to be a case of mistaken identity.

Murphy had used every tool of persuasion he had learned in books and on the streets to prevent Santiago from returning to gang life. He was good at only a few things, but working with kids was one of them. They tapped him when a grammar school needed an Officer Friendly to explain police work. His old Bridgeport neighbors said he could charm the birds out of the trees. He had that Irish knack for gab that offset his otherwise too numerous deficiencies. Santiago had denied returning to a gang, and that was good enough confirmation of Murphy's parental skill. His son's rehabilitation was one of his few success stories.

"Any questions?" the commander asked, ending his gang report.

"Where's the mystery, Commander?" asked the captain. "This is old news."

No one knew how he got away with his cheek toward his supervisor. It had to be something he had on Cronin as leverage. He could get away with things no one else could.

"Just to see if you lads are awake." The commander grimaced, his normally pinkish cheeks flared into crimson. He loosened the knot on his tie over his white shirt. "The mystery is that gangbangers are disappearin' from the streets, and we're not sure why. Not even their fellow gang members know."

Things were at a strange pass, the commander continued, when gang leaders wanted the police to do something about locating their missing members.

"That's a problem?" the captain asked. "Good riddance, I say. One less gangbanger on the streets. Street cleaners don't worry about less trash to pick up."

Applause broke out in support of the captain's declaration.

"I'll have no more outburstin', thank you." The commander beat a tattoo on the desk before him with his pointer. "The problem is the gangs are blamin' each other for the disappearances. It's causin' friction, it is, and unless we do somethin', the violence is goin' to escalate."

"Is the roll call over?" the captain asked.

"It is over when I say so," the commander replied. He paced behind the desk. "We have to find out what's goin' on." Cronin sat down in his chair. "I'm lookin' for volunteers."

No one raised their hand. The rookie with the baseball cap started to but lowered his hand when fellow officers drilled stares into him.

Leone looked at Murphy for their answer. Murphy gave him a thumbs-down.

"Do you men of the Thirteenth District. . . and women . . . want the other districts to be shamin' you now?" The commander tapped his palm rhythmically with the pointer. There was no response to his question. "Dismissed." He threw the pointer on the desk and stalked out of the room.

# CHAPTER TEN

"They're bringing him back here any minute," Jim Murphy said. He resented his brother's eyes accusing him with that cold-fish stare. "Everything's OK."

"If a man with Alzheimer's wandering near the Indiana border is OK."

"Santiago was supposed to watch him." He blew out a breath. "They found him and are bringing him back. That's all that counts."

"I warned you about Santiago. Once a gangbanger, always a gangbanger."

"That's enough, Bryan." His brother wasn't going to suck him into another quarrel. "You surprised me, flying into town and showing up at my front door without notice. Why exactly are you here?"

"The Justice Department sent me and my team to investigate Walker's assassination. They needed their top guy here." Bryan set down his suitcase. "Only staying a few days."

"Where do you start investigating?"

"Looks like it starts"—a thin smile spread across his brother's face—"and maybe ends with you."

Nothing Jim Murphy ever did was good enough. Nothing would match his brother's accomplishments: college valedictorian, Yale Law School, clerk to a Supreme Court justice, and now deputy attorney general of the United States.

"I was out of position, OK?" Jim clenched his fists. "But he shouldn't have left the limo against Secret Service orders and become a sitting duck." He unclenched his fists and looked out the window for his brother's team's arrival. "You just got here and already you're in my face."

"Don't get your Irish up." Bryan set down his carry-on bag. "I didn't blame you."

"It's what you're implying."

"Methinks the lady doth protest too much."

"Get off my case, Bryan, with your hifalutin crap." He turned his back and poured a cup of coffee. His brother could get his own. "I think it best if you don't stay here."

"We'll see what Dad says about that when they bring him back."

"This is my house. Not Dad's. In case you've been too busy to notice, I'm taking care of him with his Alzheimer's while you're off fancy-free in DC."

"Dad belongs in DC at the skilled nursing home I mentioned."

Jim hurried to his cubbyhole of a den to cool off and slammed the door. He had a more pressing issue to take care off than to mix it up with Bryan. He called his contact at Missing Persons to find out if Santiago had turned up. It wasn't like him to leave home without an explanation.

Was Commander Cronin right? Had Santiago returned to gang life? *That isn't possible.* He had given Santiago everything he could in the way of counseling and tutors and fatherly love. His smartphone buzzed.

"How you doin', Murph?" asked the sergeant from Missing Persons.

"Lousy."

"Sorry, but no news. But we found your father and we'll find Santiago."

"Sure you will. Bye."

Something bad must have happened. Santiago must have been abducted. He and his wife had put too much love into Santiago even to imagine that their son would abandon his Alzheimer's-stricken grandfather to return to the streets.

From the den window, Murphy saw a familiar cop walking his father to the front door. He ran out the den past his brother to open the door before the doorbell rang.

"Is this your father, Jim? His ID says Patrick Murphy."

"It is." He went to hug his father on the porch stoop.

His father pushed him away. "Get your mitts off me."

Bryan came out and hugged their father. Patrick Murphy returned the embrace. The father pulled away. "What a sight for sore eyes. What is my wonderful son, Bryan, doing in Chicago?"

"Just some business." Bryan had agreed not to disturb their father with news of the Walker assassination. One of the few times Patrick Murphy ever cried was on the day JFK died.

"Who's this guy, Bryan?" Patrick pointed at Jim. "He keeps saying he's my son."

"I'm Jim, the Chicago cop, your youngest son."

"No you're not." Patrick shrank away.

"Where's Santiago?" Jim asked.

"You should know. You took him away. You invaded our house and held us hostage. Did he kill Santiago?" Patrick asked Bryan.

"Dad . . . ," Jim Murphy said. "Don't you remember? I'm your son, a Chicago cop just like you were." He faced Bryan. "Tell him, damn it; tell him who I am."

"He's disturbed enough." Bryan put his arm around their father. "I don't want to upset him some more."

The cop who'd escorted the elder Murphy home squeezed Jim's shoulder and took his leave.

"You never did back me up," Jim said to Bryan.

"You're getting paranoid." Bryan got into his brother's face. "You shouldn't be his guardian."

"Get out of my house. Before I throw you out."

# CHAPTER ELEVEN

From his Meridian Club penthouse, Sebastian Senex gazed down through the night onto the glowing grids of streets and expressways that made Chicago the city of straight lines. On the surface, the everyday course of city life ran true and direct without pussyfooting and meanderings, a plain-spokenness he admired. But that was the surface where salt-of-the-earth Chicagoans lived. Under the rectilinear rectitude lay a political labyrinth where movers and shakers cut corners in the shade to make the straight ways crooked.

Not for nothing had he named his secret organization of municipal heavy hitters the Hinky Dink Society in honor of the most colorfully corrupt alderman in Chicago's history. Michael "Hinky Dink" Kenna and his partner, John "Bathhouse" Coughlin, were kings of corruption in a city where myriad politicians had failed to dethrone them. No one could surpass their First Ward Ball of prostitutes and drunken carousers parading through the streets or the shepherding of bribed flophouse residents to vote early and often on Election Day.

The Hinky Dinks of the twenty-first century were more subtle. Under his leadership, this clandestine network of power brokers ran a shadow government manipulating city and county officials of both parties to do their bidding behind the scenes. The executive committee of the Hinky Dinks had urged him to get over his loathing of Franklin Dexter Walker. Getting involved in ideology, they said, wasn't good for business. Brewster would win the presidency, they assured him. No need to get obsessed with Walker.

They were woefully wrong in their smugness. FDW had just barely snatched the narrowest of victories in a rigged election. Unless stopped, he would have plunged America headlong into disaster. Senex had correctly decided to eliminate Franklin Dexter Walker without the knowledge of fellow Hinky Dinks. They didn't have the intestinal fortitude. By contracting for a targeted removal, he had not only neutralized FDW. He had also derailed the political plans of Dallas Taylor.

Because of her background, Walker's vice-presidential candidate was the more dangerous of the two millennials. Unlike Walker, born to a power conferred by privileged social status, she had proved her mettle by clawing and scratching her way out of a south Dallas ghetto through law school and onto the *Judge Dallas* TV show where millions watched her small claims court drama week after week until they admired her more than any Supreme Court justice.

She moved on to become a rabble-rouser in the House and then the Senate for leftist-liberal causes. Taylor had grown to be the darling of the progressive movement. She knew the secret of politics in twenty-first-century America: Notoriety and fame were equally valid entry tickets to the reality show called national politics. The two words blurred into one another. She had the entertainment skills to survive in that jungle of exhibitionism. She scared Sebastian Senex.

"Here's the confidential briefing memo," Senex's secretary said, entering his office. "Bryan Murphy emailed it this morning from the Justice Department."

He flipped through the memorandum. Not just anyone could have the deputy attorney general of the Justice Department send them documents not intended for outside eyes. He had done well to keep in contact with the former general counsel of Promethean Pharma, who became the second-in-command at the Justice Department.

Like Mora's lab mice, Bryan Murphy and all the other suck-ups with political aspirations were conditioned by his backroom power. He dangled the cheese of their career ambitions before them to get what he wanted. Once they had served his goals, they became dispensable. Aside from Brock Brewster, Bryan Murphy was the most promising of the mice. With careful grooming for high office, Murphy could someday replace Brewster. Brewster had muddled a presidential election he should have won hands down. He narrowly won the popular vote but was predicted to lose the election by one vote in the Electoral College.

Senex skipped over the blah-blah sections of the memorandum discussing the history of the Constitutional Convention of 1787 and the presidency. On page twenty-one of the report, he found what he wanted:

> *The United States has never before confronted the constitutional puzzle of what happens if a presidential candidate who loses the popular vote but wins a majority of the electoral votes dies before members of the Electoral College meet in their respective states to cast their official ballots.*
>
> *Must the electors vote for their pledged candidate even if he or she is dead? Or are electors free to vote for anyone they or their state chooses? Or may the party of the deceased candidate substitute another candidate for consideration by the Electoral College?*
>
> *The assassination of the Democratic presidential candidate has set the United States adrift without guidance from the Constitution.*

The political chaos worked to his advantage in sowing dissension among the Democratic enemy. The Democratic National Committee, controlled by entrenched political insiders, wanted to select a new presidential candidate to replace Franklin Dexter Walker. They rejected what they considered to be the unrealistic proposal of rank-and-file Democrats who desired an expedited virtual convention to select a new presidential candidate.

To rebut the charge of the party elders that not enough time remained until the Electoral College met in December, the party's grass roots wanted Congress to postpone the meeting. Some, called the "crazies," even suggested that Congress should cancel the election results and schedule a new general election with a new Electoral College and a delayed inauguration date.

The fundamental law of the land had no provision for a do-over. The Constitution invested the Electoral College with the independent and ultimate authority to pick the president of the United States. Pundits reminded the public that the Founding Fathers did not authorize a direct election of the president. The people of the United States through their state governments only elected the Electoral College. The college elected the president in the world's greatest democracy. Not the people.

Instead of staying on message, Brock Brewster suggested that since he and his running mate had won the popular vote, they should automatically assume office. That would undermine the Electoral College completely and challenge the legitimacy of past presidents who had lost the popular vote but won in the Electoral College. Brewster showed deplorable judgment in overplaying his hand.

If Governor Brewster had any political judgment, he would have known he was the odds-on favorite to be selected by the Electoral College anyway now that his rival was dead. Not many electors would have the audacity to vote against Brewster for president in favor of a last-minute replacement when Brewster had won the popular vote.

He would have to keep an eye on Brock Brewster.

# CHAPTER TWELVE

Even before his daily examination of the test subject, Dr. Angelo Mora suspected the parabiosis procedure would exceed expectations. Yesterday's exam had revealed the older subject's facial furrows smoothed down by collagen from the younger subject's blood. The bagginess around the eyes firmed up. The older subject looked younger.

Nodding to the strapping toughs outside, he entered the unoccupied building of a suburban industrial park gone to seed. Sebastian Senex had told him they . . . security assistants he called him . . . would help out with the nonmedical aspects. Mora was not to ask questions about them or whom they worked for. They had delivered the two test subjects to the hidden site in a warehouse with no questions asked: an elderly man and a belligerent youth under sedation with mouth taped shut.

He entered the portion of the warehouse set aside as a postoperative recuperation area. The older test subject sat up as Mora entered the cage that had been set up to contain the older and younger patients. He could see a question forming in the older man's facial expression.

"What's happening to me, Doc?"

"How do you feel?"

"Not tired like I was. I feel like a million bucks." He stretched his arms up and yawned. "He agreed I'd go free if I volunteered. Can I go now?"

The security assistants came into the room within hearing range. Mora hesitated but couldn't resist asking the subject, "Who said you'd go free?"

"The boss said he'd forget my unpaid juice if I did this." He gulped. "I kept my promise. Can I leave?"

So that's how it was. The Chicago underworld had supplied the subjects and the assistants.

Agitated, Mora twisted his knee, bending down to the cot where the subject was sitting. A bolt of pain shot through Mora's right knee. He rested on a chair near the cot and rubbed his swollen joint. Waiting for the pain to subside, he looked over the results from the liver and kidney function tests. The older man's organs functioned much more efficiently than before parabiosis.

Feeling better, Mora ordered the subject to stand. He held a stethoscope to the man's chest and listened. He pushed against different body parts to test resistance. The subject pulled on a hand dynamometer to test strength. Muscle strength had increased. Every day the subject's metabolic age grew younger at a slow but steady rate.

"I wanna go. I done what I was supposed to. Ask those guys guarding me."

One of the security assistants yelled at him to shut up.

He, the great Dr. Mora, was to biological science what Enrico Fermi was to physics. The two Italians were scientific pioneers. Fermi had ignited the first self-sustaining nuclear chain reaction in Chicago, while Mora had now found the fountain of youth in the same city. Someday Chicago would honor him as it honored Fermi. Maybe now Sebastian Senex would treat his concierge physician-scientist with the respect and gratitude he deserved.

He ignored the test subject who complained, "The boss promised we'd be square if I did this. Can I scram now?"

What he, the great Dr. Angelo Mora, would be remembered for was the brilliant use of modern technology and creative insight to revolutionize the parabiosis procedure from its crude beginnings. He'd had help from blood experiments conducted by Sigmund Rascher, a Nazi scientist, at the Dachau concentration camp. Rascher's descendant had handed over the unpublished records of the experiments for a modest fee. But the world didn't need to know of that help, so the original research was destroyed. He alone would be the discoverer of the fountain of youth.

"Pay attention, damn it, and answer me." The subject grabbed Mora by the shoulders. "I'm a human being."

"If you say so." He waved away the assistants coming to his aid. "My experiment worked. You became younger with young blood."

The two Chicago Outfit men blocked the subject's exit from the cage.

He turned to Mora. "Tell 'em to let me go."

"That's not up to me." He packed up his medical instruments.

"Let me go. I done what you and the boss asked. That was the deal."

"I'm also done." He washed his hands at the sink. "The procedure was a success. The rest is between you and whomever."

"Doc . . . ya gotta help me. Put in a good word for me."

Mora nodded to the two assistants. "I'm done."

"Whatever happened to that kid whose blood I received?"

"The guards say they're taking you to meet him."

At Mora's cue the security guards took the captive away to the basement to join the younger test subject. From where he stood on the ground floor, he heard a scream and the loud pop of what sounded like a hammer on metal coming from the warehouse basement. And then a moan and another loud pop of hammer on metal. The sounds didn't concern him.

He looked out the window. A truck marked PALIOS KOSMOS GREEK BUTCHER SHOP pulled up to the loading dock outside. The security guards hauled two sealed barrels up through the cellar door into the rear of the truck and drove away.

About to enter his own car on the way home, Mora felt a hand biting into his shoulder.

# CHAPTER THIRTEEN

A Chicago Outfit mobster took his hand from Dr. Angelo Mora's shoulder and spread-eagled him against the car hood before patting him down. He removed the doctor's tie clasp and examined it. He handed it back. Finished with the inspection, he made a call on his cell. "He's clean, Boss."

Moments later, a black Lincoln Continental glided into the parking lot from behind a tree line concealing a gravel side road. The driver in a chauffeur's cap opened the rear door. A man emerged in rumpled clothes.

Mora estimated the man's weight at three hundred pounds. The medical disaster in the making wheezed and caught his breath. His unruly salt-and-pepper hair ruffled in the wind. He had an engraved scowl on his round face, accented by black horn-rimmed glasses. He looked like a perpetually ticked-off owl. With a lumbering gait he stopped in front of Mora. "You got business with my son, Vinnie Palomba."

"Vinnie's your son?" Mora feigned ignorance out of caution. At Mora's request, the son had agreed to put out a contract for a hit on Commissario Marco Leone. This man was Dino Palomba, the feared boss of the Chicago Outfit.

"I wanna be sewed up for young blood." The voice rumbled from years of vocal cords marinating in smoke.

"How did you know?" Mora asked. As soon as he asked, the answer hit him. The boss of the Chicago Outfit must have learned of the successful parabiosis experiment through the two "assistants" he supplied to Sebastian Senex. Their number one loyalty was to Dino Palomba and not to Senex or himself.

"How soon can you do it?" the boss asked.

"Why do you want the procedure?"

"Why dayya think? You're the genius." The boss took a deep breath. "Look at me. I'm an aging diabetic playing hide-and-seek with death. My ticker's about to go. If you do this, I gotta chance to beat the odds."

"The procedure's dangerous." Mora fumbled his tie clasp back on. "The possibility of antigens—"

"Shut the hell up." The oval face of organized crime in Chicago turned crimson. "You do this, or Vinnie don't do the hit you want. I'll hit you instead. Got that, genius?"

"I understand fully, Mr. Palomba." He ran his hand through his hair. "We'll need—"

"Not your problem. We'll find the young guinea pig."

"When?"

"I got some business in Vegas to take care of this weekend. As soon as I get back. Got that?" Palomba rubbed his eyes with his knuckles. "My eyes are shot, my legs swollen and asleep. Sometimes I feel like I'm walking on hot, broken glass."

"I'll set things up here for your return."

"One more thing." Palomba shuffled his feet. "That Italian dick . . . Commissario Marco Leone . . . the one you put a contract on. He arrived in the city. Still want Vinnie to whack him?"

"I do." He could not have said the words more solemnly had it been his marriage vow.

"Vinnie will arrange to take care of it. But no backing out."

"I'll never back away from my revenge."

"You do the para . . . the whatsis on me, and Vinnie arranges the hit on Leone. Then we're even." Palomba offered a thick, waxy-looking hand. "And I'm not giving you nothing else. Just one hand washing the other. Agreed?"

He shook the stiff fingers of the mobster's hand. "Agreed."

"I'm curious." Palomba came closer. "Whadda Leone ever do to you?"

"He ruined me and his country." The memory of his narrow escape from Italy after the collapse of the Piso coup agitated him. "He broke Lucio Piso's political movement. I had a great future with Roma Rinata."

"Lucio Piso?" Palomba emitted a guffaw. "Thought he was another Duce." More laughter. "Piso was a goof."

"Lucio was my brother-in-law as well as my patient."

"Now that's different." Palomba nodded his head. "Avenging family. Reason enough to whack him. You didn't really believe Piso's crapola, did you?"

"Not at all." A lie was the best course. These low-life mobsters had no finesse. They had no social vision. Had he lived and taken over the government, Piso would have strung up mobsters like Dino Palomba. Mora had to sing their song to take revenge on Leone. "I just wanted to use Piso."

"If I was you, I'd be careful with your boss, that Sebastian Senex."

"If you permit me," Mora said, "may I ask why you are helping Senex?"

"Strictly business. He helps me from time to time. I help him. One hand washing the other. But your boss's head is full of hooey about making over the city and country, clearing the streets of scum . . . crazy talk. He even shouts and whispers sometimes. A wacko like his dead friend, Lucio Piso."

Senex's mental disturbances reflected in speech were due to Huntington's. Mora had nothing to gain by revealing this to Palomba. Flattery would be more productive. "I appreciate your wise advice."

"Quit the brownnosing." A hacking cough interrupted the boss. "Just be ready to do that para-thing when I come back."

Senex had warned Mora to get permission before communicating with business associates of himself or Promethean Pharma. His employer would not take kindly to the assassination of a celebrity law-enforcement official or the unauthorized medical treatment of Dino Palomba by an underling.

"You must keep the hit on Leone confidential. An employee almost ruined Senex early in his career with a side deal. If he finds out, he'll ruin me."

"You questioning me about secrecy?" A coughing attack cooled the rising bile in the boss's voice. When the coughing ended, he said, "My associates and I tell Senex nothing. For what he did to my father, he should kiss the ground he's still alive." He walked back toward the Lincoln Continental and turned. "Just be ready to do the para . . . whatever you call it . . . or else."

# CHAPTER FOURTEEN

Sebastian Senex closed the drapes in his penthouse den at the Meridian Club. The stray rays of sun sneaking in between the heavy folds added golden highlights to his burgundy smoking jacket rimmed with a black satin collar. Dr. Angelo Mora thought the smoking jacket amiss for a man who shunned tobacco and required the same of his employees.

"Before we set the date for my parabiosis procedure, I have some good news." Senex tightened the tasseled sash of his jacket with a twitching hand, most likely the result of Huntington's disease. "Dino Palomba died of organ failure in a Las Vegas hospital. It'll soon be all over the news."

Mora grew light-headed at his last-minute reprieve from administering the parabiosis treatment to Dino Palomba.

"Are you OK?" Senex asked.

"Never felt better." And well he might. If Palomba had died or been injured by the procedure, the Chicago Outfit would have retaliated against him. If Senex had discovered his unauthorized treatment of Palomba, his boss would also have had his head. Fate had saved him from this dual predicament.

He now had only one secret to keep from Senex . . . the Outfit hit he had on Commissario Marco Leone's head. Did Senex suspect? Is that why he brought up the death?

"Was Dino Palomba a friend?" Mora asked.

"Friend?" Senex snorted. "I detested him and he me. But we found each other useful."

Senex's face relaxed into the sly smile of a prankish adolescent. "There was this time," he said, pausing with a dreamy look. "A long time ago, the mayor appointed me head of the Municipal Crime Committee to investigate and expose organized crime. Dino Palomba's father and Vinnie's grandfather . . . the Outfit leader then . . . was gambling high stakes at a card game with cronies in a social club. Young and brash, I instigated and joined a police raid on the place.

"You should have seen the mobsters falling over one another trying to get out. We were feeling our oats shaking up the bad guys, so at my suggestion, the coppers made Dino's father drop his pants with the pretext of a search and seizure warrant." Senex's face resumed its normal intensity of the present day. "Lucky I'm not dead after that youthful foolishness.

"What I'm about to say," Senex said, "you'd better keep under your hat."

"Absolutely," he replied.

At times like this, whether due to Huntington's or his approaching demise, or simply to showcase his brilliance, Senex grew talkative. To draw Senex out further, Mora said, "I regret you think I would be less loyal to you than to Lucio Piso."

"You've been loyal, Angelo." Senex patted him on the arm. "I give you that."

Senex proceeded to explain at length his relationship to the Outfit. The death of Dino Palomba opened up the possibility of a fruitful business enterprise with Vinnie Palomba, Dino's son. As luck would have it, Daisy, Senex's daughter, a criminologist at the University of Chicago's new criminology program, had met the son when Vinnie was still an aspiring underboss in the Outfit. They both audited a class on campus about Dante Alighieri's poetry. They shared a passion for poetry and became lovers against her father's wishes. For Daisy, Vinnie had the jailhouse attraction of a bad boy operating outside of society's rules. For Vinnie, she represented a world of social acceptance he had never known and now wanted.

While Senex's daughter was promoted to associate professor of criminology, the mobster son was promoted to be the right hand of his father. Vinnie ran a front organization for the Outfit and in his spare time published his own postmodern verses. These poetic creations bewildered Dino, the father, to no end. The Outfit underlings tagged Vinnie with the underworld moniker of "the Poet." At first Senex tried to rupture his daughter's relationship with Vinnie.

All that did was make Daisy determined to remain in the relationship. It struck him that he could turn events to his advantage. The son and father were opposites. The son craved social legitimacy and recognition, whereas the father cared nothing for social approval beyond the narrow limits of the Outfit.

By the advent of what Senex called Dino Palomba's timely death in Las Vegas, Vinnie and his father had become estranged. Senex manipulated Vinnie's desire for social approval through his daughter's relationship with the Outfit's heir. He persuaded Vinnie to further the under-the-table interests they shared. They worked well together in a way he and Vinnie's father never could.

"Enough of the walk down memory lane," Senex said, breaking off the monologue. His face hardened. "I called you to arrange my parabiosis procedure." He checked his calendar. "I'm open next week."

"But we need the right donor."

"My new partner . . . junior partner . . . Vinnie Palomba has taken care of that." His hand began shaking. "His father refused to provide . . . shall we say . . . more experimental supply shortly before his death. His hatred for me overcame his greed." Senex held his shaking hand steady with his good one. "But his son and I continued our relationship behind Dino's back."

"We need better lab equipment. Your life is at stake."

"I've taken care of that."

"What about secrecy?"

"The Phoenix Project is our cover story. That trumped-up search for artificial blood is already top secret. We're just moving it off the Promethean Pharma campus."

"Where?"

"Shh." Senex put a finger to his mouth. "It's a secret."

# CHAPTER FIFTEEN

The cave doors slid open under a bluff in the hill country of north-western Illinois. Lying atop a reclining vinyl cot, Sebastian Senex woke from his drowsing. He fingered the lump of silicone and plastic to make sure it was in place. This medical port implanted into his chest resembled a black-and-blue welt rising from the skin. A central venous catheter circulated his blood into a whirring blood-exchange machine. The innovative device commingled his blood with that of the gang-banger donor on the other side of the curtain.

Dr. Mora had joined the donor to Senex so that their two circulatory systems became one. A moan broke out on the other side of the curtain separating him from the drugged youth. The curtain failed to contain the stench of body odor wafting over like wet dog dung. Though they had never met, Senex imagined the repulsive face of the punk plucked from the streets for his benefit.

Mora hobbled into the white-crystal cave chamber sparkling in the backlight of Promethean Pharma's generators. Onyx stalactites hung from the ceiling. They pointed to a stone floor leveled smooth by the hand of man. Senex lifted his head from the cot to peer over his feet at a cabinet crammed with lab equipment. Mora was putting on his white lab coat and checking over the equipment. A Hispanic guard slumped in a chair with his hat tilted over his eyes and snored.

A TV mounted on the cabinet wall showed Chicago police and fire-fighters escorting schoolchildren to protect them from neighborhood gangs. Shots erupted from an abandoned house. The police took cover and fired back at gangbangers holed up in the house. The children scattered up and down the street.

"Shut the damn thing off," Senex said. "Armed guards for school kids. What's this city coming to? Things have to change."

Mora clicked off the TV and came to the operating table. He hovered over Senex.

"When can I leave? Promethean Pharma needs me."

"Careful, Mr. Senex. You'll tangle the tubing." He buttoned up his white lab coat. "We'll have you out of here today."

"I can't stand that street scum. He stinks." He twisted his head up to face Mora as best he could. "Are you wasting my time?"

"Does this answer your question?" Mora held a mirror next to his patient's face.

"I don't believe it." Senex studied his reflection. The band of white hair along the side of his head now sprouted strands of pepper color. The loose skin folds on his face and around his eyes had tightened. A ruddiness lit up skin pasty colored before parabiosis. "I'm going to live. I'm going to live as long as I want."

"I need to confirm—"

"I know how I feel." He now had the power to turn back the bodily ravages of time. He just knew he was on the verge of cheating death. Suffering and death need not be part of the natural order of things. Through his control over Mora, he was now a god that conferred or withheld immortality from the rest of mankind.

"The scientific results are remarkable. I've been able to not only replicate the results from my earlier experiment but have bettered them." Mora looked over the notebook he had taken from the pocket of his white lab coat. "We'll need more booster procedures for the time being. Can we get more young donors?"

"No problem." Senex smiled. "My governmental contacts scanned prison records and other information for blood compatibility. We can meet your blood requirements. I gave a list of names to Vinnie Palomba. His crews will snatch the chosen gangbangers off the street."

"What's in it for him?"

"The gangbangers are muscling in on the Outfit. Organized crime can't afford losing market share. They want the gangbangers gone."

"Palomba will be curious about what we're doing."

"He thinks the blood's for our hush-hush artificial blood project."

"It's dangerous to underestimate the Outfit."

"Stick to your research. I know what I'm doing. I have contacts with the Sinaloa drug cartel. They provide the guards now, and all the Outfit does is dispose of the donors. The right hand won't know what the left's doing."

Moaning and scuffling broke out behind the curtain.

"He's coming out of it." Senex pointed his finger at Mora. "Now."

"First, I must detach your circulatory system from his."

While Mora disconnected him from the thug's body, Senex calculated the discovery had more potential than ever imagined. Not even a week had passed, and the results were already astonishing. Parabiosis was more than just his ticket to hyperextended life. It opened the way to untold wealth. Once he consolidated his political power, parabiosis could come out of the shadows. He'd establish a network of blood clinics where the young could sell themselves to rejuvenate society's seniors.

"You're disconnected, Mr. Senex."

"Lemme outta here," a voice cried from behind the curtain. "Untie me."

"Take care of him, Mora. He's coming around."

Mora nodded and held up a syringe. "I'll be right back."

The doctor went around the operating table behind the curtain. Senex could hear the protests of the donor and Mora's calm assurance. Fastened to the operating table, the donor wasn't going anywhere. Soon, the protests lowered to a whimpering and then silence.

"He's done his duty," Mora said. "He won't be a problem anymore."

"What did you give him?"

"A combination of heroin, fentanyl, elephant tranquilizer, a synthetic opioid, and my own secret ingredient." Mora showed him the syringe. "Instant death."

"Can it be traced back to us?"

"That's the beauty of it," Mora said. "Law enforcement will think it's just another drug overdose from a new combination of street drugs."

"Good work, Mora." Mora helped Senex into a wheelchair and rolled him to the locker room, where he dressed.

When Senex emerged, he saw the guard trundling the dead body out of the cave. "I'll bet the gangbanger kid was an illegal, right?"

"No," Mora said.

"But he sounded Hispanic."

"He was. They called him Santiago."

# CHAPTER SIXTEEN

"I know you're in there." In a sequined cowboy hat, Senator Dallas Taylor pounded on the oak door of Al Tweed, the chairman of the Democratic National Committee in Washington, DC. "Let me in, Al, or I'll blow the whistle on you all."

The door cracked open. Lowering her glasses down the high bridge of her nose, a secretary peeked through. "You're creating a disturbance. Please make an appointment."

"You can kiss my you know what." Taylor jammed her foot against the door and shoved it open.

"How dare—"

"Not another word." She strode on past the secretary into Tweed's private office and plopped into the guest chair next to the desk. The glossy, L-shaped rosewood desk looked like it had never been used for serious work. A framed photo of the chairman's wife stood on the left side of the desk.

"Good to see ya again, Dallas." Tweed's eyes widened. "Still looking hot, I see."

"Something cooled you off, though." She pointed to the photo. "Maybe the wife you hid from me until I found out."

"Things change." The DNC chairman sighed and plucked a Cohiba cigar from a cherrywood humidor. "I meant to tell ya."

"Sure," she said with an ache in her voice. He was slicker than a Texas slop jar. She could rail and rant at him, but she had made the bad choice. It wasn't the first. Besides, she needed something from him.

He stuck the cigar in his mouth.

"Still have that filthy habit?" She forced herself into lighthearted-ness. "Don't smoke me out."

"Won't light it . . . promise." He studied her for a few minutes. He removed the cigar from his mouth. "You're not here to catch up on old times." He shook his head as if in disbelief. "Ya want the DNC to stick you into the presidential slot on the ticket."

"The veep candidate should move up to the presidential slot."

"That was the old rule. It's up to the DNC leaders now."

"And you control them."

"We just see things the same way."

"The Democratic Party's supposed to be democratic." He wouldn't budge if she flamed him with her sharp tongue. "Look, Al, I know you can't call another convention." She flipped her hair and bit her lower lip. "But can't you at least have the whole Democratic Committee meet and make a decision? Not just the DNC muckety-mucks."

He reached for her. She pulled away.

"No can do." He pulled his hand back as though singed on a stove. "Too late to change the rules."

"The new rule gives you discretion to call the DNC together."

"Ya got me there. But we're talking about two hundred people get-ting together." He put the cigar back in the humidor. "Besides, grass-roots Dems are calling. They oppose a general meeting. Rumors of a COVID-28 bug blowing out of China got 'em spooked."

"You know better than to BS me with tall tales." Diplomacy would get her nowhere. The flimflam man in politics and romance wasn't going to budge. "I supported you when the Black Caucus wanted me to break off our relationship. It cost me plenty to stick with you until . . ." *You dumped me* remained her unfinished thought.

"I know, I know, Dallas." He held up his hands. "If it was up to me . . . but it's not. The party elders say the quickest way out of this mess is to substitute Roscoe Corker for president. They say you're too young. Corker came in close second in the primaries. Seems fair to me." He leaned over the desk toward her. "If ya take the veep slot for the team, that puts ya in line for POTUS next time."

"Roscoe Corker is Sebastian Senex's water boy." She stood up to leave. "He's an Illinois political hack with a closet full of scandals."

"Ya got your own issues." He opened the humidor top and then closed it. "It's not so much you're African American or a woman. It's that you're unmarried without a significant other. How we goin' sell that to soccer moms?"

"Corker can't keep his pants up whenever a woman's around."

"Come on. The man's an all-American war hero awarded the Distinguished Flying Cross in the Gulf War." He scratched his cheek with his finger. "In this business ya don't often get a war hero to run."

"He's got heart trouble. That cigar-smoking, whiskey-drinking, whore-chasing Chicago sewer rat looks like death warmed over."

"So what? He's the junior senator from Illinois. He looks and talks great on TV."

"Corker was your drinking buddy."

"He almost beat Franklin Dexter Walker in the primaries. Joe Sixpack likes him."

"The party can't afford another dead candidate."

"I'll make sure he watches his health."

"I worked hard for the party. I want the top slot."

"Wait your turn."

"Pie in the sky by and by doesn't work for me. I get it. Senex has his hooks into you."

"What did ya mean out there . . . y'all blow the whistle on us?"

"I know what you and your honey, the treasurer, got going."

"Whaddya talking about?"

"I did some checking." She surveyed the customized satin drapery and Andy Warhol original on the wall. "You two have been robbing the party till to pay for your hanky-panky trips."

"Don't say things you'll regret." Again, he grabbed a cigar from the humidor. "Anyway, Sebastian Senex made a generous contribution. Our financial problems are behind us."

"I know your game." Her hoop earrings bobbed as she fumed. "You're repaying Senex by picking Corker."

"Senex isn't the devil."

"Coulda fooled me." She wagged her forefinger at the chairman. "Senex is no Democrat, and Corker's one in name only."

"The party's a big tent. Ya know that." He frowned and reached for a lighter. "Ya keep talking that way, Dallas, and I 'spect ya won't get jack shit from me ever again." He sucked on the cigar. "And then there's the incident at the AIPAC conference ya might not want to get out."

"You wouldn't."

"Who am I to cast the first stone?" He lit the cigar. "Just don't throw the first stone, or you'll find yourself under an avalanche."

# CHAPTER SEVENTEEN

Detective Jim Murphy approached the damaged Palios Kosmos butcher truck abandoned in an empty field just off Stony Island Avenue in Chicago. Parched weeds and prairie grass poked through a light blanket of snow with a white plastic bag blowing in the wind like a baby ghost.

"What are we doing here?" he asked Commander Jack Cronin.

"I'm thinkin' this might involve the gangbangers gone missin'."

"It's outside our jurisdiction. Not our problem."

"But the missin' are mostly from our jurisdiction."

"Why did you want me to come?" He blew into his hands to warm them. "It's just a drug deal gone bad. The cop on the scene noted the needle marks."

"You're new to the Thirteenth District, lad. You've lots to learn," said Cronin. "Oh, before I forget. Senator Dallas Taylor called me to complain about your racial profiling on Lake Shore Drive . . . 'driving while black,' she called it."

"Her beef is bogus. I thought her Jaguar was stolen."

"Jesus, Mary, and Joseph." The commander removed his gold-leaf hat and ran his hand through his hair. "You lack discretion, lad. She's a United States senator . . . and anyway you were working security for the Millennial, not pulling traffic duty."

"I can handle it."

"It's already been handled. I'm thick with someone who knows someone in the Civilian Office of Police Accountability." The commander put his hat back on. "The complaint's been deep-sixed. Win-win for everybody."

"Not for me. I didn't ask you to do it the Chicago way."

"You're my godson." He winked. "I have a religious duty to look after you."

With the commander at his side, Murphy scoured the scene. Tire tracks in the snow indicated the truck had probably lost control on black ice going south and caromed off a utility pole into the field. Crumpled metal ran like a scar across the passenger side of the vehicle. Shielding his eyes from sun glare, he saw beyond the truck a line of cranes and an abandoned cement factory silhouetted along the horizon. First on the scene, the CPD cop in a patrol car had found no witnesses in the desolate landscape. Only a dead body in the back of the truck. Whoever drove it had reason to scram.

Murphy scrambled his way up onto the back of the truck. The commander hesitated to climb up after his godson. Cronin had put on a few pounds and always suffered from back problems. The patrol cop lowered the aluminum walk ramps for the commander to climb. Crates labeled Lamb Carcasses lined the long sides of the truck in unsteady piles. An opened crate prevented Murphy's movement down the center aisle. "I only see skinned lamb carcasses in an open box," he shouted back to Cronin.

While he moved the open crate blocking the center aisle, the commander talked outside to the patrol officer who had found the body. He then rattled up the walk ramp to the bed of the truck. "The copper tells me the body he found is in the crate behind the cab. Let's take a gander."

As Murphy climbed over a jumble of boxes, one tumbled from the top of another and dumped the corpse of a young man frozen stiff onto the truck bed. He bent over to examine the body. A gang tattoo of a crown on the back of the corpse. Needle marks on the left arm.

The commander came from behind and strained to flip over the corpse. The cheek under the right eye bore three teardrop tattoos. "Gangbanger tattoos. What's he doing so far from his territory?" Cronin exhaled a foggy stream from his mouth. "Looks like my hunch might be right."

"Or just a drug deal gone bad," Murphy said.

"Let's move to the front," the commander said, "to check out the other body."

They found a crate pushed against the rear of the cab. The officer outside had already loosened the top. "You do the honors," Cronin said to Murphy.

Murphy took off the top. He let out a moan.

"What's the matter, Jimmy?"

He looked away from the box and closed his eyes, too devastated to care the commander had called him Jimmy.

It was Santiago but looking older.

*What had they done to him?*

The commander looked inside the crate. "What's the matter? Needle marks in the left arm. Just another druggie gangbanger."

"He's not a gangbanger, damn it. Not anymore. And he didn't use drugs. I never saw needle marks on him when he was alive." He couldn't hold it in any longer. "That's my son, Santiago."

"Your son?"

"We adopted him."

"I'm sorry, Jim."

"That he's my son? That he's a gangbanger? Just come out and say it." He glared at the commander. "You'll never convince me he went back to the gangs."

"Don't worry," Cronin said. "I don't have any convictions left to sell you." The commander took off his hat and ran his hand through his hair. "I didn't know." He put on his hat and replaced the crate cover over Santiago's body. He put his arm around Murphy's shoulders. "We'll get forensics out here to finish the investigation. Let's go."

Before getting into the squad car with the commander, who insisted on driving, Murphy collected himself by studying a solitary crane moving rusted slabs of steel onto a scrap heap. *The bastards threw his son into a scrap heap.* The region had once been alive with steel mills. *The region is now desolate and dead . . . just like Santiago.*

Murphy got in. "I'm volunteering for your investigation."

"What made you change your mind?"

"They murdered my son."

# CHAPTER EIGHTEEN

**DECEMBER 18, 2028**
**MEETING OF ILLINOIS ELECTORS**
**SPRINGFIELD, ILLINOIS**

On a blustery afternoon, Sebastian Senex stopped checking the entrance to the Green Mill Cocktail Lounge for their overdue arrival. Holiday wreaths on the walls and Santa Claus figures on the bar festooned with miniature red light bulbs lifted his spirits. The neon Green Mill sign blinked green behind the empty stage where a jazz band played evenings. Hidden away in the dark and timeworn art deco hangout of Chicago mobsters long dead, Senex felt secure and snug in the green-velvet booth of the legendary bar lounge.

They said Al Capone liked the booth so he could keep an eye on both the front and side doors to avoid unwelcome surprises. He and Big Al had something in common. They both had Plan Bs. Chicagoans would someday remember him along with Big Al. They'd both be Chicago boys who had put the city on the world map.

He turned to a news report on the television set. Illinois presidential electors were meeting in the state capital of Springfield on the required date of the first Monday after the second Wednesday in December. With unexpected permission granted by the Illinois secretary of state, reporters with cameras circled around the electors about to vote for president and vice president of the United States after reciting the Pledge of Allegiance.

"This Electoral College pageantry is pretty much a formality," the TV anchor announced. "Each delegate has one vote for president and one for vice president. The Democratic National Committee has selected Roscoe Corker to replace the assassinated Franklin Dexter Walker as its candidate for the office of president. The twenty Illinois electors whom voters elected to support the now deceased Franklin Dexter Walker are expected to rubber-stamp Roscoe Corker for president and Dallas Taylor for vice president."

Everything was going as it should. He wasn't called Mr. Plan B for nothing. Since the election of Tweedledum-Republican Brock Brewster looked in danger, he had engineered the Tweedledee-Democrat Roscoe Corker to replace the deceased Franklin Dexter Walker. Corker would do almost as well as Brewster for him.

The Democratic presidential replacement had been his errand boy for a long time in the world of Chicago politics. That made him comfortable with a candidate who didn't resent being owned as long as he got his thirty pieces of silver.

Only two parties existed for him: the In Party and the Out Party. And he wanted to be with the In Party to get things done. Things change. So, down with Brewster if necessary and up with Corker. The public liked the derring-do personality of Corker the Gulf War flying ace with sex appeal.

Hidden campaign contributions ensured the support of the chairman of the Democratic National Committee for Roscoe Corker. Al Tweed appreciated the blind eye the head of Promethean Pharma turned to the chairman's periodic embezzlement of party funds. It didn't take much effort to persuade the DNC chairman to substitute the name of Roscoe Corker as the Democratic candidate for president.

The only reason Senex preferred Brock Brewster, his Plan A, as president was that Brewster agreed with him that the United States had to be saved from itself. Corker was too much of a political dimwit to know what he and Brewster were talking about.

"The Democratic electors," the TV anchor reported, "are ready to cast their votes for president and vice president of the United States."

One of the twenty Democratic electors, Roscoe Corker's personal trainer, voted first. Except for him, the electors were all political insiders honored by the Democratic State Central Committee for services rendered to the Democratic Party. The personal trainer commented that "sure as God made green apples" they'd all follow tradition and support the Democratic candidates chosen by the Democratic Party. The following nine came up one by one to deposit their votes in the wooden ballot box inside the state capitol building as soon as the elector chosen as chairperson called their names.

The remaining ten of the twenty electors greeted Dallas Taylor, who requested and was granted permission to enter the room. Taylor's appearance was a surprise in what was supposed to be a choreographed proceeding. At the request of one of the ten, the chairperson allowed a fifteen-minute recess for Taylor to converse with electors in a corner of the room. The screen cut to a commercial.

*What is she doing?* She didn't belong there. It wasn't in the script. He drummed his fingers on the table. Showboating as usual was his answer. Despite the publicity-seeking antics of Dallas Taylor, everything was going as it should just as the front door to the Green Mill opened.

———

Sebastian's daughter, Daisy Senex, sauntered through the door hand in hand with Vinnie "the Poet" Palomba. The new head of the Outfit sported a suntanned face in his Armani suit and mirrored sunglasses with red tint. The underworld rumor was that Palomba frittered away too much time in Nevada and wasn't taking care of family business the way his father had. Senex gulped the remainder of the Cognac hot toddy to fortify himself for the face-off with Palomba.

Unaware of her father's business relationship with Palomba, Daisy introduced him to her boyfriend. Palomba handed her a wad of cash with the suggestion she do some shopping before meeting up later. She tried saying that she'd like to stay but stopped when her boyfriend held a forefinger to his lips.

As Senex watched his daughter leave, the vignette confirmed what he had long known. She was a bright criminologist but docile and ditzy. At least she would never become one of those radical feminists who'd cross him.

"You look great, Sebastian," Palomba said, sliding into the special booth across from him without asking permission. "What's the secret?"

He leaned across the table and whispered, "Chasing dames." It was the kind of thing Big Al might have said.

"Yeah, right."

Over the past days, a warmth had spread throughout his body from what Daisy in her tai chi babble called the lower *dantian*, three fingers below the navel. Each day parabiosis reversed aging at a steady rate. Urges he thought long dead surfaced once again. He distrusted them. The pharmaceutical empire he had built could come crashing down if the urges made him vulnerable. An atheist, he found it paradoxical he shared the same fear of modern females as many in the Roman Catholic hierarchy. The new breed of women would want to take over the power to run things if he let them in. He couldn't allow that.

"Seriously, I try to live a healthy lifestyle." He wasn't about to share the magic of parabiosis with Palomba, whose youth he resented. He could be young like Palomba. Now that he had the answers, he wanted a do-over in the game of life. He needed the mulligan of parabiosis to continue chasing the monkey of success. He had caught the monkey in the rise of Promethean Pharma, but it had escaped into the world of politics where he would hurry after it.

"Shall we get down to business?" Eager to finish up with the Poet, he checked the front and back doors. He preferred not to be seen with the new leader of the Outfit. It wouldn't look good. "The glare of the neon sign bothers me," he lied, slipping on his own pair of sunglasses. He cleared his throat. "I'm concerned the police are now involved."

On the table Palomba spread his fingers, slender as a pianist's. "The truck accident was unforeseen." He looked directly at Senex, sunglasses to sunglasses, each man's roadblock to the soul of the other. "Shit happens."

*Who does this goombah gangster think he is talking to?*

"I don't pay for shit."

"Tough guy, huh?" Palomba laughed. "Lucky for you, I'm a kinder and gentler boss."

A joke of a boss was more like it. Palomba's father had kept his organization thriving. The son was not the father. He could be had. The man in front of him was too busy hustling bimbos like his daughter and writing postmodern poetry. "I'm concerned our . . . our street trash removal project . . . might be discovered."

"No need for code," Palomba said. "I'm not bugged, and this place is clean."

"I don't want you to think—"

"Why would I think you're wearing a wire?" Palomba asked. "My father checked you out."

"Good." He had the son's trust even though he never had the father's. "I just don't want anything to go wrong."

"Of course." Palomba's fingers reached across the table like tentacles. He put his hand on Senex's. "Don't worry. You're insulated. Even if something happens, my boys take the rap . . . not you."

*That's the way it should be,* Senex thought. *You are the expendables whose only function is to help the In Party stay in. We each use each other to get things done under the table. I can return to the surface life of respectability, but in the end, the whiff of crime will always hang around your head like the faint odor of sewer stench.*

"I have a problem," Palomba said.

"What is it?"

"The chicken feed you're paying us for disappearing the street punks is just walking-around money." Palomba waved off a waiter who asked if he wanted to order. "We're really doing you a favor. We're not worried about the gangs cutting into our business."

Senex called back the waiter and asked for another Cognac hot toddy. The truth was that the Outfit was very worried about its future. The RICO law, witness protection programs, and breakthrough eavesdropping technology had the Outfit on its knees. The code of silence was broken. Mobsters ratted out one another to save their own skins. Its sources of revenue were drying up so that it could no longer permit the street gangs to siphon away the take from criminal activity. The house of Big Al was tumbling down, and the only question was what would replace it. The Russian mafia? The Mexican cartels? Certainly not a poet named Vinnie Palomba.

"Why are you here?" Senex took off his sunglasses and drilled the Outfit boss with his eyes. "You didn't come just to reassure me."

"I want the bounty per head raised to what I suggested last month." He glared at Senex. "And I want your answer now . . . no more stalling."

"I'll do it." He offered his hand to Palomba. "Do we have a deal?"

Palomba took Senex's hand. "We've got a deal." Palomba checked his cell and slid out of the booth. "It's time to meet up with Daisy. But before I go, what's the real reason you're having me disappear gang members? And don't give me a civics lesson about a better America."

"You got me." Expecting this moment, Senex held up his hands in surrender and whispered into Palomba's ear. "We need blood for research. We're working on finding the holy grail of artificial blood. For that we need a lot of human blood."

"That checks." Palomba patted Senex on the back. "We know you have a special unit at Promethean doing top-secret research."

Palomba walked toward the door as if to leave but then turned. "C'mon, Sebastian, level with me. What do you take to look so good?"

"Blood." Senex paused. "The secret project is I'm really a vampire."

"Never took you for being a comedian." Palomba smiled. "If we ever fall out, I'll have to drive a stake through your heart."

———

After Palomba's departure, Sebastian Senex was about to make a call to Dr. Angelo Mora when the sound and images from the TV caught his attention.

"This is extraordinary, ladies and gentlemen. After talking to Senator Dallas Taylor from Texas, the Democratic Party's vice-presidential candidate, in what appears to have been a highly emotional conversation, five of the ten delegates remaining to vote have announced their intention to break ranks with the other electoral delegates from Illinois. They have reversed the order from what the national Democratic leaders wanted. They are instead casting five votes for Dallas Taylor as president and five for Roscoe Corker as vice president."

"They can't do that," the bartender said. "The voters elected them to support their party's candidates in the order the party wants."

"They sure can," said a patron. "I teach constitutional law at DePaul University. They call them . . . faithless electors . . . We've had almost two hundred of them since the United States first held presidential elections. Unlike other states, Illinois hasn't yet taken away their discretion to change their votes."

"I want another Cognac hot toddy," said Senex, wobbling to the bar for a closer look at the TV.

"Haven't you had enough, Mr. Senex?" the bartender asked.

"Don't you want a fat tip?"

"Cognac hot toddy coming right up."

"What a day," the TV anchor continued. "This switch could prevent any party from obtaining a majority of electoral votes. This election is probably headed for a final determination by Congress. This has only happened twice before in American history for a presidential election and once in an election for vice president."

"That's not right." The bartender snapped a towel at the TV set. "This is supposed to be a democracy."

Tweedledum Brewster or Tweedledee Corker. He had won either way.

# CHAPTER NINETEEN

Junk littered the triangular patch of earth outside his unmarked car under the expressway. Detective Jim Murphy called it his writer's room. Here he could work on his secret project free of prying eyes. The thump of overhead traffic prodded him awake as the digital dashboard clock flashed 11:47 p.m. in red. While Commissario Marco Leone visited a relative at the University of Chicago, Murphy had precious time alone to follow his private dream.

Near shift's end he hoped the rest of the night would be free of dispatch calls. He never knew when a call might come. Two nights ago, a mob of two hundred teenagers ran frenzied through the Loop in an act of "wilding" that resulted in purse snatching and theft from Loop department stores. Merchants demanded the police do something. But if they did the wrong something, cops feared finding themselves as defendants in a courtroom. So more police took to doing something. They did nothing.

As part of its initiation rites, a street gang in his surveillance area began to hurl rocks from the Jackson Boulevard Bridge at vehicles passing underneath on the Kennedy Expressway. The gang played a game of cat and mouse to see how many times they could evade the police. So far the score was gang ten and police six. The rock hurling picked up speed with each gang success of a wounded or dead driver.

The anticipation of a radio dispatch made his fingers fly faster over the laptop keys and . . . at least he liked to think . . . more creatively. He had a better reason tonight to throw himself into his work. Santiago dead in the truck rushed into his mind like a leak in a rowboat he had to bail out with the ferocity of his typing.

He turned up the heat while appraising the sentence on the laptop. *Sparky Squirrel was surprised how fat and grubby his Chicago cousins had become and . . .* And what? He blew into his hands. He rubbed his eyes. He tried as hard as he could to find the words he needed to finish the *Sparky Squirrel* children's book.

He couldn't tell his colleagues. They'd hoot him down. They'd say he should join the Evanston police, made up of pointy-headed officers with advanced university degrees. It was his secret. Someday he'd finish writing down the oral tale he had created and read to his little sister before she died. His dream was that someday children . . . like Santiago . . . when they were still young . . . would learn to read by reading his—

The cell beeped. The commander.

"I got the report."

"What's it say?"

"They found another crated body in the truck. That makes three. Your Santiago and the other young man. The bonus body was an older man indebted to the Outfit for unpaid juice."

"Did the Outfit whack him?"

"You're goin' to find out."

"I'll get right on it."

"Are you up to handlin' it? Santiago was one of the vics."

"That exactly why I'll find the piece of shit who did this."

"OK, but check in with me. I'm not wantin' you to go off the rails."

"That all?"

"One other thing." He paused. "They found a deadly combination of drugs in both young men. They call it gray death. And they both had needle marks . . . Santiago included."

Murphy refused to believe Santiago had returned to gangs and drugs. But if he said so, the case might be snatched from him. If Santiago wasn't clean of drugs and done with gangs, he wasn't sure what he believed.

He suspected the Outfit was involved or knew who was. Organized crime had the means. The Palios Kosmos butcher shop near Evanston was a suspected Outfit front company. The butcher shop had reported its truck stolen shortly before the police discovered the dead bodies in the abandoned vehicle. This plausible denial of responsibility was too convenient to be credible. Motivation also existed. The third body found had committed the mortal sin of reneging on a debt owed the Outfit. He was stuffed in a meat crate, not a car trunk, but the MO looked close enough. The Outfit resented the increasing insolence of Chicago gangs in challenging its urban turf. But he had nothing specific to go on.

He tried clearing his mind by returning to *Sparky Squirrel.* No use. Even at his most alert, he struggled to find the right words. He was too tired and too agitated. The cell beeped again.

"It's me. Bryan."

"Bryan?" He ran his hand over his face. Just what he needed. "Why are you calling? We have nothing to say to each other."

"You got that right." A pause on the other end. "I'm just calling to say I think it best if I don't show Santiago around the Justice Department on his school trip to DC."

"Don't worry your ass about that." He clamped his teeth on a forefinger knuckle. He wasn't going to let his brother get a rise out of him. "We found him dead on the South Side."

"What?" A long pause on the other end. "I don't know what to say."

"You might try . . . I'm so sorry to hear that." He blew out his sorrow in a long breath. He disliked his response. Sarcasm was his brother's thing. "Look, I've got trouble enough. I don't want to get into it with you."

"I'm sorry for your loss." Bryan's voice had the tone of someone asking for the bread at a boarding house dinner. "I liked him. I have no kids of my own. I—"

"Stuff the blarney. You never liked Santiago." He looked at the cell as if he could see Bryan's face and punch it. "'Once a gangbanger always a gangbanger' . . . Remember your words?"

"I was trying to protect you. I didn't want your hopes too high for his future."

"I . . . I . . . I . . . Everything you say revolves around you. It's not about you." The way their father had refused to recognize Jim as his son, even asking if he'd killed Santiago, overwhelmed his anger with sadness. "But maybe everything does revolve around you in our family. You're the wonderful son, and he says I'm not even his son."

"Cut him some slack. The man has Alzheimer's."

"Even before Alzheimer's we had problems."

"You were the fair-haired boy until something happened," Bryan said. "You want the truth? Now don't get mad at what I'm about to say."

He poised his finger to disconnect Bryan in midsentence if necessary. "Don't tell me how to feel."

"Dad changed when you began to screw up. Leaving the seminary, dropping law school. Almost failing out of the police academy."

He couldn't bring himself to disconnect Bryan. Those failures hadn't helped his relationship with his father, but there was something more, something earlier in the relationship.

"But look at the bright side," Bryan continued. "Everyone but Dad always liked you better. Mom, Sis, the neighborhood. I was the book nerd; you were the life of the party. Even Dad used to . . . until he soured on you. You were like the Cubs used to be . . . a lovable loser. You—"

*Enough.* He pressed disconnect.

The reflection of his eyes in the rearview mirror repeated his brother's accusation. He took a swig of thermos coffee and swallowed hard. How could he have missed the signs of Santiago's return to the gangs? He was so sure he could save Santiago. *What went wrong?* He had to redeem himself by finding Santiago's killers.

"Car 1221. Come in," crackled over the radio. "Intoxicated driver at Racine and Morgan. Crashed into utility pole. Nonresponsive to bystanders."

"Any ID?"

"Have license number from 911 call."

"Who's the owner?"

"Senex. A Sebastian Senex."

"On my way." He turned on the blue flashers and was off.

# CHAPTER TWENTY

Waiting to testify, Jim Murphy feared the fix was in. Where the clout is equal, justice prevails, the local lawyers said. It didn't seem equal in this case. Sebastian Senex had chosen an expedited bench trial before Judge Apollo instead of trial by jury for driving under the influence on a suspended license. Something was up. Was the Promethean Pharma CEO trying to pull a fast one? A corrupt or biased judge protected a defendant better than any jury trial guaranteed by the Constitution.

Unlike his classical namesake, the pug-nosed Judge Apollo had neither handsomeness nor a reputation for truth. The man owed his black robe to a judge-maker alderman and campaign contributions from a multimillionaire friend of Sebastian Senex whose restaurant had burned to the ground under suspicious circumstances. The judicial powers that be early on transferred him to traffic court where his incompetence would cause the least harm.

"Before the State puts on its case, I am dismissing the added charge of driving on a suspended license." Judge Apollo adjusted his robe. "Before this incident, Mr. Senex had three prior speeding convictions. Normally that would trigger an automatic license suspension. However, I reduce his last conviction to court supervision." He waved his hand like a magician's wand. "He now has only two priors, and the suspension statute doesn't apply." He relaxed into his seat on high. "Therefore, the only charge left is driving while intoxicated."

"Your Honor—"

"Objection overruled."

The assistant prosecutor sank back into his chair.

"Can he do that?" Murphy whispered to the prosecutor. "He wasn't the judge in the speeding cases."

"He just did it."

"What are you going to do about it?"

"Take it up to the Supreme Court, of course." The prosecutor whispered into his ear. "Let me do my job, will you?"

On the stand Murphy laid out in detail how he found Senex unconscious. He sent him to the emergency room of Rush University Medical Center by ambulance and ordered a hospital blood test to verify Senex's suspected intoxication. After Murphy's testimony, the prosecutor received permission for a brief recess. He took Murphy into the hallway and handed him the report of the hospital emergency room. "Look at this."

Murphy riffled through the report. The blood test profile confirmed Senex was illegally intoxicated at the time of the test. "So? He was drunk."

"Read the note at the bottom."

> SPECIAL OBSERVATION: ER team included visiting Dutch hematologist, Dr. Henrik Janseen, who specializes in age-related blood disorders. Patient's blood proteins remarkably indicate younger biological age than expected.

"You're the lawyer." Murphy handed back the report. "But I don't see how the note prevents the report from going into evidence."

"With Judge Oliver Wendell Holmes on the bench, who knows?"

"What are you getting at?"

"The guy on trial here." The prosecutor grimaced and bit his lower lip. "Just making sure he's the same one you sent to Rush. No mistaking a younger man for an older one?"

"Not unless somebody body-snatched him from the ambulance."

"Just curious." He motioned Murphy back into the courtroom. "The defendant does look a lot younger than his age."

Senex's high-priced lawyer had prepared a thorough memorandum of law for the judge to consider. The memorandum contended Senex's hospital blood sample had been unconstitutionally seized while he was unconscious. Thus, it could not be allowed into evidence.

The prosecutor counterargued that although the blood profile incriminated Senex, the physicians at Rush hospital had also used his blood for medical diagnosis and treatment under emergency conditions. They would have done so even if Detective Jim Murphy had not ordered a blood test to confirm the defendant's intoxication. Since an overdose of alcohol can cause unconsciousness and even death by respiratory depression, the ER team properly ordered a blood profile in the normal course of competent medical practice. Therefore, the blood profile test should be admitted into evidence.

Judge Apollo rejected the admission of the blood profile into evidence to prove Senex's intoxication. He quoted verbatim from the memorandum of law prepared by the defense attorney. The judge looked uneasy and told Murphy, "You should have gotten the patient's consent to the blood test if it was so important."

"Really?" The prosecutor crossed his arms. "How could the ER have obtained consent from an unconscious man?"

"They could have waited." The judge fingered his chin. "They might have waited till he woke up."

"Brilliant," the prosecutor said. "By then the alcohol in his blood level could have gone down or he could have died before regaining consciousness."

"Another crack like that," the judge said, "and you risk contempt of court. The report will not be allowed into evidence. End of story."

"If necessary," the defense attorney paused and continued, "we are prepared to put on our case, Your Honor. I would like to call to the stand Mr. Senex's personal physician and an internationally renowned blood researcher . . . Dr. Angelo Mora."

Murphy twisted his chair from the prosecutor's table and looked back into the audience. A dark-complected man, squat and stooped with thick glasses and a goatee, limped through the courtroom doors toward the bench.

"Wait a minute." Judge Apollo looked at his wristwatch. "It's lunch-time. Why don't you make a motion to dismiss the State's case for failure to prove guilt beyond a reasonable doubt?"

"Of course," said the defense attorney. "I so move."

"Case dismissed." The judge smiled at Senex. "You're a free man, Sebastian. Sorry for the inconvenience."

Senex looked over at Detective Jim Murphy. "Not as sorry as some will be."

# CHAPTER TWENTY-ONE

**JANUARY 6, 2029**
**ELECTORAL BALLOTS CERTIFIED**
**WASHINGTON, DC**

On the day set by law, Congress gathered to certify the results of the Electoral College. Sebastian Senex slipped into the front-row gallery seat next to Bryan Murphy. Their chairs overlooked the floor of the United States House of Representatives. A joint session of the Senate and House sat to certify the tabulation of electoral votes for president and vice president.

"Thanks for arranging this, Bryan. Couldn't miss this historic occasion."

"Only the best for my old boss."

Bryan was buttering him up because he wanted the support of his former boss when he left the Justice Department and ran for Congress. Bryan's lust for a political life would be Senex's hold over him.

"It's the least I could do after the trouble my brother caused you."

At the highest level of the wood rostrum sat the lame-duck vice president, acting as presiding officer of the Senate, with the Speaker of the House to his right. Tellers sat at the clerk's desk below, together with the secretary of the Senate and the clerk of the House of Representatives. The vice president looked up at the gallery where

US Capitol Police were dragging away protestors shouting demands for a second national election to replace the muddled results of the original one.

"Rabble," Senex muttered. He turned his attention to the wall behind the rostrum where the Roman fasces symbol of rods surrounding an axe appeared on either side of an American flag. What the country lacked in this time of uncertainty, he thought, was a strong leader who could pull the country out of the looming calamity about to take place just as ancient Roman dictators did during emergencies. Just as his dead friend, Lucio Piso, had unsuccessfully tried to do in modern Italy.

Everyone in the country now knew Roscoe Corker had only 265 electoral votes for president, Brock Brewster 192, Frank Hammer of the National Independent Party 76, and Dallas Taylor had gained 5. If the five defecting Illinois electors had voted as Democratic Party officials demanded, Roscoe Corker would have reached 270 electoral votes, a one-vote majority.

The decision of the five Democratic electors to reverse the order and cast their votes for Taylor as president and Corker as vice president meant that Corker was not the president-elect.

"Thanks to these turncoat electors, Congress may have to pick our next president and vice president." Bryan shook his head. "The country won't accept that."

"It's the fault of Dallas Taylor and her attempted socialist takeover." Senex felt his blood pounding his temples. "She caused this problem."

"It wasn't just her." Bryan waved to someone in the gallery. "The National Independent Party with their seventy-six votes also prevented Corker's election by the Electoral College."

"It was just her. She's behind the National Independent Party to stop Brewster from winning." He tapped Bryan's shoulder several times with his fingers. "I say Taylor is responsible for this mess. Professor David Chang, the veep candidate for the National Independent Party, is her friend and former professor. Get it? Just put two and two together. Without her backing and advice, Hammer and Chang would be nobodies."

"Never heard that, but if you say so," Bryan said. "You always had a better political sense."

"I do say so." He had to remind Bryan who was boss. "Don't forget that."

Taylor's conniving set Senex back on his heels. She had clouded the electoral vote to block Corker's path to the presidency. He couldn't let her snatch the monkey of political success away when he was so close.

Unless Congress stopped those maverick Illinois electors, no candidate would have a majority of electoral votes needed for the brass ring of the presidency. If the Kabuki ritual of certification went ahead without a hitch, the Constitution mandated that in the absence of a majority of electors for a candidate, the House of Representatives would elect the next president, and the Senate would elect the next vice president.

"Those clown protestors aren't the danger." He couldn't get her out of his mind. "The harebrained National Independent Party isn't either. It's a joke," Senex said. "Keep your eye on Dallas Taylor and her band of radical socialists."

Everything about that woman—her gender, her race, her personality, her style—offended him. She must have schemed the rebellion of the Illinois delegates as payback for the Democratic Party not slating her for president. "They'd welcome a governmental breakdown for their revolution."

Senex feigned interest as Bryan explained how the oral recitation of a state's electoral votes would occur in alphabetical order. All he cared about was the end result. The process bored him. The end was always more important than the means.

A teller started off by certifying the electoral result reported by the state of Alabama. The next of the four rotating tellers continued the process by certifying the electoral results from the state of Alaska.

"Would that be so bad?" Senex wondered aloud more to himself than to Bryan.

"Would what be so bad?" Bryan asked.

"Having the House elect the president."

"A perilous way to elect a president." Bryan clucked his tongue. "It's happened only twice before in our history."

"What's the problem?" Senex asked. "The Constitution provides for the House of Representatives to elect a president if no candidate wins a majority of electoral votes."

"The problem is the potential refusal of a losing candidate to abide by the results." Bryan held up a Justice Department memorandum prepared by his staff. "Andrew Jackson and John Quincy Adams carried on a blood feud because of a disputed 1824 election in the House of Representatives. Jackson alleged one of the presidential candidates, Henry Clay, made a corrupt bargain to switch his support to Adams in exchange for appointment as secretary of state by the Adams administration."

"Just normal horse-trading." A smirk spread across Senex's face. "I admire that."

"What if General Andrew Jackson, the popular hero of the Battle of New Orleans, had refused to accept the election results and marched on the Capitol . . . like an American Napoleon?"

"I don't have time for what-ifs." If the election were left to Congress, Senex would have a better chance of getting Brock Brewster elected president by the House with its razor-thin Republican majority. That was his Plan A after all. "Rocking the ship of state might shake the barnacles off." He could rock the ship to the right just as much as Dallas Taylor was trying to rock it to the left.

The electors owed him nothing. They vacated their offices as soon as they voted. He couldn't control these strangers now in the public eye the way he could members of Congress bought with untraceable campaign contributions and backroom deals.

He didn't have to settle for Roscoe Corker as Plan B. He still had a chance of getting Brock Brewster, his Plan A, into the Oval Office through the House of Representatives.

"Be careful what you wish for." Bryan's lips tightened. "The Constitution has stress points. It could sink the country if the stress is too great."

The droning on of the tellers as they called for election results from each state caused Senex to drowse until he awoke with a start to hear a teller announce:

"The certificate of the electoral vote of the State of Illinois appears to be regular in form and authentic, and it appears therefrom that Roscoe Corker of the state of Illinois received fifteen votes for president and Dallas Taylor of the state of Texas fifteen votes for vice president, and it further appears that the aforesaid Dallas Taylor received five votes for president and the aforesaid Roscoe Corker five votes for vice president."

An Illinois congressman objected that the refusal of the five electoral delegates to vote in accordance with the wishes of party leaders required their votes to be rejected. Since the objection was in writing and endorsed by a senator, as required by federal statute, the vice president suspended further deliberation of the joint session until the House and the Senate met separately to debate and vote on the objection.

"What are the chances they'll uphold the objection?" Senex asked.

"Not likely. Both chambers of Congress have to agree with the objection." Bryan reviewed the Justice Department memorandum. "The closest precedent is the 1872 election. Horace Greeley died after the popular vote but before the Electoral College cast its votes for president. Most of Greeley's electors then voted for different presidential and vice-presidential candidates. A joint session of Congress allowed those votes but not the three votes that remained loyal to the dead candidate." Bryan laughed. "Loyalty is not owed the Grim Reaper."

"Illinois law doesn't help Corker either," Senex said. "Illinois doesn't even require a pledge of loyalty. Electors can vote as they choose."

As they got up to leave, Senex arrived at two firm conclusions. One: Bryan Murphy had become one of his most useful political puppets. Two: the obsolete procedure for electing a president was a house of cards poised to plunge the United States into constitutional chaos.

# CHAPTER TWENTY-TWO

At a table nearest the forty-five-foot Christmas tree in Macy's Walnut Room, Jim Murphy waited for the overdue couple. Marco Leone had called to say he was running late, but could he bring a guest?

"Who?"

A surprise, his partner had replied. A crowd at the wine bar chattered holiday cheer along the west wall. That and the tree lights making the thousands of hanging ornaments sparkle softened his impatience at their delay.

He groped in his overcoat pocket for what he hoped he had remembered to bring. Pleased, he pulled out a blank sheet of punched paper. He liked snatching tatters of free time to capture inspiration for his children's book. He'd take the completed sheets home and add them to others in the three-ring binder his wife had once used for recipes. It reminded him of her and the creative encouragement she had given him. He put the pencil to his lips. He scrawled *Sparky Squirrel forgot where he had buried the nuts for his family. Big brother squirrel teased Sparky. What is the matter with . . .*

Leone was walking toward him with a younger woman on his arm. To avoid questions, Murphy broke off writing and stuffed the sheet into a pocket. It was his secret.

The bounce in the woman's step and the flounce of her red hair stirred interest. His Latin-lover partner sure didn't waste time in the City of Big Shoulders finding a girlfriend who looked like a daughter.

Robbing the cradle is what his mother had called it. Commander Jack Cronin was notorious in their Bridgeport neighborhood for serially dating younger bubbleheads. His Italian partner and Cronin had something in common after all. The only difference was that Cronin would not have waited so long to show off his trophy girlfriends.

"Jim, I present my American cousin, Nicole Garvey."

"Cousin?"

"Have I mistaken the English word?"

"Not at all, Marco." She removed her arm from her cousin's. "I'm a distant relative on the Italian side of the family. We discovered our blood relationship when I worked in Italy during the attempted Piso coup."

Of course. He now remembered her from the media reports about the coup and the history-shattering manuscripts she helped find in the Villa of the Papyri.

"Nicole, I present Jim Murphy, my colleague from the Chicago police."

She looked surprised when Murphy pulled the chair out for her. Her visiting professorship in archaeology piqued his interest. She was different from the women he knew.

"How did the Senex trial go?" Leone asked.

"Acquitted." Murphy shrugged. "Senex brought Dr. Angelo Mora to the trial. An Italian expert on human blood. Do you know him?"

"Can it be?" Leone looked up as though he were praying to heaven for an answer. "The brother-in-law of Lucio Piso and a coup supporter. My government is about to seek his extradition from the United States."

"He's in Chicago now," Murphy said. "Here's what I learned. Senex connived to expedite a special visa for Dr. Mora to work at Promethean Pharma. He's a renowned hematologist."

"I've heard about him too." Garvey folded her hands at the edge of the table. "Daisy, my colleague at the University of Chicago, is Sebastian Senex's daughter. She mentioned he works for her father at Promethean Pharma. Daisy . . ." The server stopped by the table to take their order.

After the waitress left, she continued. "Daisy said his secret project involves finding an artificial substitute for blood."

As a police officer, Murphy appreciated her discretion in preventing the waitress from listening in.

"What did you learn about the Palios Kosmos vehicle?" Leone asked.

"We don't want to bore your cousin with shoptalk."

"Hardly." She smiled. "I'd like to hear what my cousin does with his days."

"Well . . ." Murphy tugged at his ear.

"Oh, I get it." She started to rise from the chair. "On cue I'm off to the powder room so you boys can talk in private."

"You can stay . . . just keep it confidential."

"Mum's the word," she said, placing her forefinger over her lips and sitting back down. "I don't want to risk handcuffs."

"Palios Kosmos is a likely Outfit front," Murphy said, "but the company has the old stolen-car alibi."

"I think the Outfit, as you call it," Leone said, "is involved with the dead bodies in the truck."

"So do I, partner."

"Does this Outfit perhaps own the steel mill nearby?" Leone asked.

"Kinzie Steel?" Murphy laughed. "Guess again. Sebastian Senex bought the steel mill recently."

"Why?" asked Leone. "A drug company owning a steel mill?"

"Our American tax laws, my dear commissario." He paused to request a glass of water from the passing waitress. "Promethean probably wanted the operating steel mill losses to offset its pharmaceutical profits."

"Enough." Leone held out his hands. "Much about this country is sufficiently confusing without its tax laws." He broke apart a roll on his bread plate. "If I may change the subject, what is going on with the election? Can it be Congress will pick your next president?"

Murphy explained that since no candidate had a majority of the electoral votes, the House of Representatives would pick the next president.

"But was there not an objection to what you call . . . the faithless electors . . . the five from Illinois who changed their votes?"

"There was," Garvey said. "The Senate dominated by Democrats allowed the objection. But the House dominated by Republicans voted along party lines to deny the objection." She sipped from her water glass. "The objection failed because both chambers of the legislature must allow the objection."

"I am confused," Leone said to Murphy. "Your Congress is not supposed to be a parliament where the legislature picks and controls the prime minister." He shook his head. "Congress will decide the next president and vice president. Not the people of the United States. Brock Brewster won the popular vote, did he not?"

"Hey, Marco," Murphy said, laughing. "I'm a cop. Not a constitutional law expert."

"Only fifteen percent of the public approves of Congress," Garvey said. "Will a polarized public accept a House decision picking the next president?"

Murphy received a call from police dispatch. He and Leone had to leave immediately. He threw down enough cash to cover the bill and a tip. Garvey trailed behind. Catching up to them at the elevator, she held the three-ringed sheet fallen from his coat pocket.

Smiling, she handed him the sheet and whispered in his ear, "You forgot Sparky Squirrel's nuts."

# CHAPTER TWENTY-THREE

"Time's running out." Sebastian Senex paced alongside the sofa in the office of Clyde Pomeroy, Speaker of the House of Representatives. "You must get Brock Brewster elected president by the House before Inauguration Day on January twentieth." His nostrils twitched. Tobacco fumes had soaked into the drapes and rugs and stunk like musty socks.

"Our lame-duck president's got the House panicked," said the Speaker. "Because of the COVID flare-up over there, he's considering a travel ban on China. House members are reluctant to meet until the situation's cleared up."

"Don't give me that." Senex frowned. "The Chinese know how to do things. They got it under control."

"Patience, Sebastian." Pomeroy shifted his bloated belly on the sofa. "We have until January twentieth, twelve o'clock noon."

"Don't go Pollyanna on me." He stopped pacing. "It takes a majority of twenty-six states in the House to elect a president. You don't have twenty-six in the bag." He wrung his hands. "It took thirty-six rounds of voting in the House to get Thomas Jefferson elected. And Brock Brewster is no Thomas Jefferson."

"Don't worry." The Speaker placed his hands on the sofa and hoisted himself up. "Republicans are the House majority. It's in the bag for Brewster."

"Whataya smoking besides tobacco?" He jabbed his finger at Pomeroy. "States vote as a separate unit in this election. Individual representatives don't vote. It doesn't matter Republicans have a slight numerical edge in individual representatives."

"I'm the Speaker. I know that." Pomeroy put his hands on his hips. "One more thing I know that you don't is that Corker's worse off. He has fewer states lined up for him."

"So what?" he said. "If neither Corker nor Brewster gets a majority of states, the House might compromise on my enemy. Dallas Taylor."

"The House is limited by the Constitution to picking a president from the top three candidates in the Electoral College. That's Brewster, Corker, and Hammer in that order. With her pitiful five votes she came in fourth."

"You underestimate her."

"You're overreacting, friend." Pomeroy patted Senex's shoulder. "I have a plan to push Brewster over the top."

"No need to patronize me." He poked his finger into Pomeroy's chest. "Now tell me your plan?"

Senex had elevated Pomeroy from the position of part-time boxing coach at a small Illinois college they both attended into an ascending political heavyweight. He had bankrolled his rise in the Illinois legislature, election to the US House of Representatives, and then to Speaker of the House. He twisted arms to get Pomeroy where he was. The Speaker owed him.

"Wait just a minute." The Speaker's face brightened. "We almost forgot. I won last time, and I want the pleasure of beating you again."

"Not now, for heaven's sake." With the nation sliding into a political abyss, the Speaker wanted to play their silly game. "You know you're better at it."

"Now." Pomeroy folded his arms. "We promised to do this whenever we met after college. I'll tell you my plan . . . but first we have to do it."

Humoring Pomeroy cost nothing. Besides, he wondered whether his feeling of youth was just his mind playing tricks. He accompanied the Speaker to a table and took a chair opposite him. They joined right hands with elbows on the table in the opening movements of an arm wrestling match. Their muscles vibrated with tension. He held firm until Pomeroy's arm trembled and was slammed down.

"I'll be damned." Pomeroy rubbed his right forearm with his left hand. "I can't remember when you last beat me. Are you taking drugs?"

"Not on your life." It was no mental illusion. Time was running backward for him.

"You look great." Pomeroy rolled down his shirtsleeve. "What's your secret?"

Senex resolved not to share the fountain of youth with the Speaker. He needed more information from Mora and more time to decide how best to use the lure of resurrected youth to his advantage.

"I don't smoke coffin nails." He frowned. "You ought to get this place fumigated."

"That's not it. You never smoked and I always beat you." He put his hands on his hammy hips. "I wanna know . . . What's going on?"

"Get Brewster elected, Clyde, and maybe I'll tell you."

"Whaddya worried about? Even if the House were to reject Brewster, which it won't, you've got Corker as a Plan B insurance policy. Harebrained Hammer doesn't have a prayer."

"I like Brewster better. Besides, Corker's having health problems and seeing a cardiologist in secret. The deadlocked House vote is stressing him out."

"Once the newshounds get wind of his womanizing, he'll have real stress." The Speaker's heavy breathing settled down to normal. "Tell him to stop chasing skirts. Or he'll have a problem with Bible Belt House members."

"Let's get back to business." Senex straightened his shirt and tie. "The House has voted four times so far without electing a president." He stood up. "I want to know your plan . . . now."

"I have several." Pomeroy directed Senex back to the sofa where they sat down.

Senex could scarcely believe that the gold athletic trophies in a trophy case across the room belonged to this man gone to seed. At least Roscoe Corker looked trim and healthy on the outside, even with his bum ticker.

"I'm trying real hard for Brewster." Pomeroy held up his fingers, plump like breakfast sausages. "Since tradition says it takes a majority of state representatives to cast the vote of that state as a unit, it's become a recipe for stalemate in states where Republicans and Democrats are about evenly divided. So I tried to persuade the Democrat leadership that a simple plurality of representatives from a state should determine the state vote."

"Did they buy it?"

"No." The Speaker's shoulders slumped. "They wouldn't back off the tradition."

"A mere plurality would swing more states to Brewster. They're not stupid, Clyde."

"They might still agree."

"That's your plan?" Senex threw his hands up in the air. "That's your damn plan? Do you take me for an idiot?"

"It's not the only plan." Pomeroy sank back into the sofa and radiated a cat-ate-the-mouse smile. "I have a trump card up my sleeve."

"What?"

"Some Democrat representatives resent the Democratic National Committee chairman for steamrollering the selection of Roscoe Corker." The Speaker stumbled up to his feet by grasping the sofa arm. "The main player is the House Democrat minority leader who's been screwed over before by the DNC committeeman. We're simpatico. But he needs a sweetener in exchange for bringing his boys over."

"What's the sweetener? Money? If he does—"

"Nothing so crude." Pomeroy paused. "What I'm about to say can't leave this room or we'll lose them."

"Of course."

"He wants to save a military base in his state and another one in Virginia for his party whip. My inside source is certain the Base Closure and Realignment Commission will put them on the chopping block in its report to Congress." Pomeroy grabbed the lapels of his own suit jacket. "I suggested a deal. Know what it is?"

"He swings his boys over to Brewster and the bases remain open." Senex rubbed his chin. "I like it."

"Bingo." The Speaker and Senex high-fived each other. "If the minority leader and his whip keep their side of the deal, our Republican majority in the House will make sure those bases stay open for our Democratic brethren."

"Bipartisanship at its finest." He clapped Pomeroy on the back. "Let's do it."

"Not so fast." Pomeroy held on to his lapels. "The commission's keeping the final decision under lock and key until shortly before Inauguration Day. The minority leader doesn't want to make a final deal until he's absolutely sure the bases are on the chopping block."

"Clyde, I have to warn you. I don't like the delay." Senex studied the floor and looked up. "I want Brewster in the Oval Office by Inauguration Day."

"Trust me, Sebastian." The Speaker took Senex's hands into his. "Have I ever failed you?"

# CHAPTER TWENTY-FOUR

"Go on in." At the revolving door of La Gola Restaurant, Daisy Senex took Nicole Garvey by the arm. "He won't bite."

"Mobsters aren't my thing," Nicole said.

"He's not like his father." Daisy pursed her lips. "He writes poetry."

"That's nice." She didn't want to hurt Daisy's feelings. Uncertain what to do, she kept her hand on the restaurant's glass revolving door. "Is that what he does for a living?"

"Not really." Daisy's forehead wrinkled. "Something about insurance."

*Like the protection racket?* She held her tongue. "What about our shopping?"

"Double surprise." A smile returned to her friend's face. "You're surprised to be here, and Vince will be surprised I found out his birthday." Daisy had a schoolgirl's glow. "I really want you to meet him."

Why not? Marco and Jim Murphy with the square jaw and playful blue eyes had pumped her for information after their Macy's luncheon about Daisy's mobster friend. It wouldn't kill her to do them a favor, especially the partner with the square jaw and playful blue eyes. Any cop who wrote children's stories interested her. Information on Vinnie "the Poet" Palomba could be her entry ticket into the world of Sparky the Squirrel and his creator.

"You win." She pushed the revolving door. "Let's meet your boyfriend."

Inside the restaurant, Daisy asked for Mr. Palomba's table. The restaurant manager escorted them to a back room closed off with beaded curtains. In that back room, a pudgy, swarthy man with a limp and a goatee gathered his things.

"Dr. Mora," Daisy said. "How are . . ."

He brushed past her with a black fedora obscuring his face on the way out of the restaurant and out of sight.

"My, what's gotten into him? He's in such a rush." Daisy turned to Nicole. "That was Dr. Angelo Mora. You know, the one who works for my father."

Inside the back room, Daisy pecked the poker-faced Palomba on the cheek before sidling down to his right into the chair vacated by Mora. A carafe of red wine and an appetizer bowl of grilled calamari with lemon slices occupied the center of the table covered with a red-and-white checkered tablecloth.

Palomba motioned with a head jerk to a muscleman with a five-o'clock shadow seated to his left. About to shovel a forkful of food into his mouth, the underling left the room to Palomba and the two women.

"Vince, this is my friend and colleague Nicole Garvey."

"A pleasure." Palomba dabbed the corners of his mouth with a napkin. He set the napkin down next to a plate of golden-crisped chicken smelling of garlic and rosemary. The chicken came garnished with bits of celery and carrots over a bed of baked potatoes and peas.

"Please, have this seat," he said, indicating the one abandoned by the muscleman.

She sat, looking at Daisy who was transfixed by Palomba.

The restaurant manager entered full of apologies for the interruption. He held out a pocket notebook belonging to Mora. A waiter had found it near the revolving-door entrance.

"I'll return it to him," Daisy said, taking the notebook. "He was in such a rush he must have dropped it."

After the manager left, Palomba turned on Daisy. "Why did you interrupt my business meeting without notice?" A vein on the side of his head throbbed.

"It's your birthday." Daisy's face quivered. "I wanted to surprise you."

"I don't like surprises."

"I didn't know you and Dr. Mora—"

"That's enough." His tone vibrated with restrained anger. "I don't want to talk about him now." His face enshrouded itself in a fake smile. "Would you ladies like anything?"

Daisy shriveled in her chair. Her head shook no.

"I've lost my appetite," Nicole said, watching Daisy struggling to keep it together. What did she see in this overbearing mobster? Her friend acted like a soul sister to women who love imprisoned felons.

Daisy handed her boyfriend a gift-wrapped package.

He unwrapped it and held up a book. "A collection of Shakespeare's sonnets." He put the book down. "Just what I always . . . didn't want." He turned to Nicole. "You see, I'm a postmodern poet. I don't like rules, poetic or otherwise."

"How about manners?" Nicole asked.

"Not phony ones." He slid the book of sonnets across the table to Garvey. "I regift the sonnets to you."

His rudeness prompted her to consider leaving, but she knew that would upset Daisy even more.

"Daisy mentioned," Palomba said, "that you know Commissario Marco Leone, a relative, now in Chicago."

"A remote cousin I discovered in Italy," she said, seizing the chance for a conversational de-escalation. "Why do you ask?" Leone's partner with the square jaw and playful blue eyes might like to know whatever she could find out about Palomba's relationship to Mora.

"Daisy says he's a creature of habit," Palomba said. "What's his daily routine?"

The Poet's focus on the commissario put her on alert.

"First, Mr. Palomba, tell me all about Dr. Mora."

"I can tell you everything, Vince." Daisy took her boyfriend's arm as if trying to make him face her. "Nicole says Leone has his cappuccino every morning at the Conte Di Savoia import store on Taylor Street. It reminds him of Italy. You'd love knowing—"

"Daisy . . . stop." Competing sensations of pity and anger tongue-tied Nicole for a few seconds. "Revealing our conversations about my cousin makes me uncomfortable."

Palomba patted Daisy on the head. "Good idea. We mustn't make Nicole uncomfortable." He turned back to Garvey and sneered. "Daisy and I can talk later about your Commissario Marco Leone."

After shoving the book of sonnets back across the table to Palomba, Nicole stormed out of the room.

# CHAPTER TWENTY-FIVE

Seated on a plush red leather armchair in the Backroom Bar of the Meridian Club, Sebastian Senex knew the meeting requested by Vinnie Palomba spelled trouble. The torchère lamps with subdued light and shadows made the Backroom Bar Senex's favorite place for discreet discussions.

An oval coffee table topped with Carrara marble over hand-carved mahogany separated Senex and his visitor. Two snifter glasses of Cognac rested on the table. A fire crackled in the fireplace behind Palomba while an elevator-music version of "Frosty the Snowman" wafted into the bar from the dining room down the hall. In a red vest and club necktie, a bored bartender leaned against the bar counter.

"Made in Italy?" Palomba rapped his knuckles on the table.

"Only the best for the Meridian Club."

"How much?"

"I would never think to ask."

Palomba lifted the brandy glass to his nose. He closed his eyes and inhaled. He sipped. "Definitely not grappa." Scanning the room with hooded eyes, he fidgeted in his chair. Mouth open, he craned his neck to study the painted cherubs swirling on the sky-blue ceiling. "Nice digs."

"I think so." Palomba's kind didn't belong in the Meridian Club. Despite the longing written across Palomba's face, he hoped the mobster had the wit to know the Meridian Club was out of his league.

That silent understanding would save them both from embarrassment should club membership ever cross the mobster's mind.

Things weren't on the level in the city. They both knew that. But a gentleman at least had the couth to pretend they were. It was simply a matter of good taste and profitable discretion. Despite his poetic inclinations, the man across from him was no gentleman.

"Why are we meeting?"

"I want a cut."

"A cut?" Senex dug his fingernails into the soft leather arms of the chair. "We have nice cuts of prime rib or bone-in ham in our dining room."

"Quit the smart-ass talk." Palomba looked pained. "You're using parabiosis to rejuvenate yourself. I know you're buying up blood banks on the quiet. You want to cash in on making geezers young again, don't you?" He leaned over the table. "We're supposed to be partners."

*Daisy must have blabbed.* She was more involved with Palomba than he'd expected or wanted. Marrying the mobster was now in her plans. He would become the laughingstock of the Hinky Dinks if Daisy married the boss of the Outfit.

He had only himself to blame for telling her about his private plans for operating a chain of blood banks that rejuvenated seniors with young blood. Why had he thought she could ever be the photogenic front female for the blood-bank operation? She was the spitting image of her beautiful and shrewd mother, but he had overlooked a key difference. She was her mother in everything except common sense and street smarts.

In a moment of weakness, he had confided in her how parabiosis was saving his life in order to ease her constant concern about his health. He had to. She was falling apart with worry because of her dependence on him. Fortunately, he had not told her how he and her mobster boyfriend kidnapped and killed gangbangers. And Palomba certainly wouldn't tell.

"We're only partners in one thing." Senex waited until two tipsy club members had passed them on the way out of the Backroom Bar. "Street gang removal."

He should have sent his daughter on a worldwide boondoggle to study comparative criminology before she got in over her head with

Palomba. She was an overeducated and scatterbrained nitwit and always would be. That was the bitter truth he kept forgetting.

"Removal? Is that what you call it?" Palomba set down his Cognac glass. "I call it killing young gangsters for their blood." He laughed dry and hollow. "We're partners in blood, that's what we are, Sebastian, whether it's playing Dracula with gangbangers or going legit in a multibillion-dollar industry called blood banks."

"Careful what you say." Senex made sure the room was empty. "Anyone could walk through that door and hear us."

"Listen up and tell me if I'm wrong," Palomba said. "With the help of contacts in the United States Organization of Blood Banks, you have FDA and state licenses. Under the radar, you're buying up independent blood banks and incorporating new ones. You're planning a chain of blood banks run by you behind the scenes." He waggled his forefinger across the table. "Very naughty, Sebastian, to be so underhanded with your partner in blood."

"Come on, Vinnie. People don't make money on blood banks. Otherwise the not-for-profit Red Cross would be a Fortune 500 company." He pursed his lips. "Why would I do that?"

Palomba gave the evil eye to a nosy club member about to sit down at the next table. The stranger shuffled off to a barstool outside hearing distance.

"You'd do that," Palomba said, "because it's legit to create for-profit blood banks. You'd do that because you're dreaming of huge profits by selling young blood to the sick and the old about to die . . . people who will pay any price for a chance at survival."

"No way." His throat ran dry. He coughed. "You know blood banks don't pay for blood anymore."

"Don't try to con me." Palomba crossed his arms. "My lawyer says it's not against the law as long as any blood collected shows payment was made."

"But hospitals won't use paid blood." He tugged at the band of his Rolex watch. "Too many health risks."

"Sebastian, Sebastian. What am I going to do with you? Feed you to the fishes?" Smirking, Palomba shook his head. "We saw your articles of incorporation, your business plan. Cash-starved millennials and even Gen-Zers will make chump money by selling their blood, while you get to tout yourself as their friend when we both know you despise their guts."

No use pretending. Palomba had figured it out. He held up his hands as if in surrender. "OK, OK. You got it." He placed his palms on the table and leaned toward the mobster. "What do you want?"

"A fair street tax."

"What do I get for it?"

"Protection."

"I can crush competitors myself."

"Maybe, maybe not." Palomba examined his manicured nails. "Bottom line. We also provide insurance protection against damage to your blood banks . . . like fire or vandalism. Get it?"

"I'll give you twenty percent of net."

"Fifty. Not a penny less."

"Fifty percent? You must be kidding." Senex brushed his fingers across his forehead. "At least give me something besides property protection."

"I forgot to mention the dual coverage. It's also life insurance." Palomba got up. "Is your life worth the fifty percent? End of discussion." He walked out of the room.

# CHAPTER TWENTY-SIX

*La Gola Restaurant* appeared on the caller ID of Sebastian Senex's retro landline. The owner had returned his call for an answer one way or another. Senex hesitated before picking up. Either answer would be painful.

Out the picture window of his Meridian Club apartment, a tugboat chugged along the Chicago River like a toy against the current. He looked across the room at Daisy with suspicion. His luncheon with Vinnie Palomba had surprised and shaken him. He now had the Outfit to contend with before they muscled their way into his affairs. Either Dr. Mora or Daisy had betrayed his secrets to Palomba about the parabiosis procedure and his plan for blood banks. No one else knew.

He picked up the receiver.

"Did a Dr. Angelo Mora lose a pocket notebook at your restaurant?"

"Why, yes, Mr. Senex. I gave the notebook to your daughter. She offered to return it to him. That was the day she and a friend came to lunch with Mr. Vincent Palomba."

"Did Dr. Mora meet with Palomba at your restaurant on the same day?"

"He met with Mr. Palomba in our private Medici Room and passed your daughter on the way out."

"Are you certain?"

"Absolutely."

After hanging up, he felt light-headed and vulnerable. Mora, not Daisy, was the traitor. He bumped into a chair and steadied himself by holding on to its back. Mora could be dealt with when he no longer had need of the doctor's rejuvenating services.

"I was right, wasn't I?" Eyes red and puffy from crying, Daisy came over to him with handkerchief in hand. "Dr. Mora was in the restaurant with . . . with . . . Vince." She choked up and broke into tears. "I never told Vince. You told me not to tell anyone. Why didn't you believe me?"

"I had to be sure." He didn't want to add that he regretted sharing his confidences with her. In a moment of weakness, he thought she might have what it took to help him manage Promethean Pharma. But she was fragile, emotional, and feebleminded when it came to judging people. Even though Palomba had disrespected her at the restaurant, she forgave him. He had to resist confusing Daisy with her mother. "I'm sure now."

She held out her arms to hug him. He let her throw her arms around him. For a fleeting moment, when she touched him, he imagined his divorced wife with skin softer than the silk robe or the pink bunny slippers he was wearing. That was all her mother and Daisy had in common.

He didn't regret having a daughter instead of a testosterone-charged alpha son who might have challenged his control of Promethean Pharma. If only she had her mother's moxie, he would have let her manage Promethean Pharma, while he controlled her behind the scenes. Whatever his disappointment, he had to put up with her. She was blood and he knew how important blood was. But the double-crosser Mora was another matter.

"There, there, little Daisy flower." He eased her away. "Everything's going to be OK."

"You're not angry with me for making up with Vince, are you?" She hung her head. "It was my fault for surprising him at his meeting with Dr. Mora. He can get grumpy and depressed but he doesn't mean it."

"Of course not." He patted her head. "You make your own decisions."

"Thank you for letting me be me." She took his hand. "I love Vince. He reminds me of you."

He had the urge to strike her across the face with the back of his hand. How dare she compare him to that gangster? She would never change. Her safe zone was in the ivory tower.

"I shouldn't have told you about my spat with Vince. You have enough burdens." She was on the verge of tears again. "I should solve my own problems with Vince."

He looked out the picture window. A barge inched around the bend of the Chicago River and was gone. All the distant people scurried like ants around the little buildings, appearing and disappearing. "I'm sure Vince Palomba won't be a problem for you anymore."

"Vince isn't a problem, Daddy. I provoke him." She ran a forefinger down his chest and looked into his eyes. "Are you sure Dr. Mora's treatments are safe?"

"Don't worry your head, Daisy flower." He tousled her hair. "He's improved the procedure. I don't need parabiosis anymore. All I need are injections of what Dr. Mora calls the Ponce de León protein."

"Daddy," she said, holding his hands. "You look great. The lines in your face . . . almost gone." She giggled. "I understand now why Mother fell in love with you."

His misplaced cell chirped. He followed the sound to the sofa where he found it under the cushions.

"Mr. Senex. It's me. Angelo. Did you still want to see me?"

"No."

"You sounded upset. Is everything alright?"

"It is now."

"I could come over if you want."

"Not necessary. I found out what I needed to know."

# CHAPTER TWENTY-SEVEN

"You're correct, Señor Perez." Sebastian Senex closed the vertical blinds to block the afternoon sun from his executive office at Promethean Pharma in suburban Chicago. "I've changed my mind." Bands of sunlight sneaked through the slits to sparkle on his glass desktop ribbed in chrome and black oak.

He would do business after all with the North American viceroy of the reinvigorated Sinaloa drug cartel. Through the self-defeating theatrics of the El Chapo era, the cartel had emerged more powerful and more subtle in its North American operations. To his satisfaction, the cartel had shown its derring-do in the assassination of Franklin Dexter Walker. He needed Sinaloa for the reversal of fortune he had in mind.

"I will provide ephedrine for your meth labs."

"A miracle truly," Miguel Perez said. He folded his hands, standing tall and gaunt in front of Senex's desk. The bathroom-cleanser whiff of cheap orange-blossom cologne radiated from the Mexican and polluted the room. "Santa Muerte answers my prayers." The *S* in *Santa* escaped his mouth as a soft hissing sound.

"You're joking," Senex said, returning to his desk and sitting down. "You don't believe in that stuff, do you?"

"In what do you believe Me-es-ter S-Senex?"

"This." He tapped his chest. "Me and myself alone."

"Then why talk to me?" A sardonic smile creased his face. "What can I do for a god?"

"Why do you people embrace the cult of Holy Death? You should fight death tooth and nail."

"You gringos." Perez's upper denture slipped. He pushed it back up with his fingers. "My customers are s-slaves to s-street drugs. You are s-slaves to the most powerful drug."

"What drug is that?"

"Life."

The drug lord pressed a thumb to his upper denture and popped it out. He removed a pocketknife and poked away at food particles stuck in the denture.

"Please, Mr. Perez." Senex wrinkled his nose and squinted in disbelief. "Do have a seat over there on the sofa. It's more comfortable." He wanted this stomach-turning spectacle away from him. "There's a box of tissues on the side table to clean your dentures."

On the sofa the drug lord looked pathetic with graying hair betrayed by a cheap dye job. This man who pumped illegal drugs worth billions into the Chicago area was so miserly that he collected napkins, ketchup packets, and other condiments from restaurants. It was rumored this man, protected by bodyguards in gold jewelry, inserted cardboard pieces in his shoes to conceal holes in the soles.

No wonder he put up with ill-fitting dentures. *Get implants, damn it.* Didn't this peasant have enough pride to rage against old age?

"You want more than before . . . no doubt." Perez's voice rattled like gravel let loose in a neck set on broad shoulders and a bony torso. He rubbed his thumb repeatedly over the tips of his index finger. *"Mucho más-s dinero, no?"*

"The money's enough . . . but I want something else." Senex twisted a paper clip out of shape and let it drop. "I want the destruction of the Chicago Outfit . . . Chicago Mob . . . whatever you guys call it."

"I have long asked S-Santa Muerte for guidance on that matter." Heaving soft teakettle whistles through his dentures, Perez continued, "What you ask would require not only the interces-s-s-s-ion of S-Santa Muerte but that of S-Santa Ramon and Jes-sú-ss Malverde and perhaps even that of the Virgin of Guadalupe herself."

"Whatever it takes."

"But first." Perez wiped sweat from his brow with his handkerchief. "Why do you want to do this?"

"Because your organization proved its ability in . . . shall we say . . . solving my problem with Franklin Dexter Walker." He leaned toward Perez. "I like permanent solutions to problems."

"Most gracious of you, Me-ester S-Senex." Perez bowed his head. "But not an ans-swer to my ques-stion."

"Besides dishonoring my daughter, Vinnie Palomba plans to extort my business. This is the desperate gasp of a weak and dying organization. With a push from you and me, we can destroy the Chicago Outfit for good." He slapped the desk to emphasize the point. "The future is with Sinaloa if you seize the opportunity."

Perez clapped his hands slowly. "Bravo!" He rose unsteadily from the sofa. "But I don't get rich on fine talk." He came toward the desk. "What is the benefit to my organization? We already control the drug trade in the city."

"The Outfit has declared war on Chicago gangs. Selected gang leaders mysteriously disappear. The Outfit now attacks gang members and stops young Hispanic men trying to get ahead. Fewer drug deals are going down. The public and police are secretly pleased to see the Outfit decimate your street distributors."

"This is true."

"Dead and disappeared gang distributors can't sell your products."

"We can find new people."

"Not anymore. They're scared of an Outfit with its back against the wall. Street sales are way down and you know it."

"It is-s a problem."

"The bigger problem is that Sinaloa has decided to use its own street peddlers and cut out the middlemen. No more independents. That puts you and the Chicago Mob in direct conflict."

"I am impres-sed by your knowledge." Perez's face turned serious. "Will you help or do we battle alone?"

"While Sinaloa battles the Outfit on the streets, I will mobilize the politicians and businesspeople into a crusade against them. A one-two punch to the belly and the head." Senex mimicked his words with his left hand and then his right. As a boxing aficionado, Perez would appreciate his analogy.

"Agreed, then." Perez offered his hand. "But one condition."

"What?"

"We are allowed to ally with the Aztec Warriors."

"They say they're insanely brutal. That's good." Senex took his hand. "You may use the devil if it gets the job done."

"Some think them devils-s." Perez tapped his cell phone and said something in Spanish. Two bodyguards entered from the outer office to escort him away.

"One condition I have before you go, Señor Perez. Vinnie Palomba must be the first one eliminated."

"Of course. I learned that as a dirt farmer in my youth when I came across a snake. Chop off the head at once and the danger is over." Perez walked out of the office.

# CHAPTER TWENTY-EIGHT

Detective Jim Murphy tried yanking open his locker in the Thirteenth District. The lock wouldn't budge. He kicked the locker door. "Bastards."

"What is the difficulty?" Marco Leone looked up from shining his Bruno Magli black oxfords spit-and-polish clean.

"They glued my locker shut."

"How do you say . . . a cop prank?"

"This is no prank." It was the price he paid for refusing to join what corrupt cops in the unit called an escort service. For a kickback percentage, the service provided a cop to escort and protect drug dealers from being ripped off between street buys. When he refused to join, they made faces like a street john propositioning a woman and finding out she was a nun.

"Will you report them?"

"What good would that do?" He sat on the bench beside Marco to wait for the maintenance guy. "I have no proof."

After the maintenance guy drilled out the glued lock and opened the locker, Jim and his partner changed into their undercover cool-dude duds for a night on the town. He advised Marco to ditch the oxfords for Nike sneakers. Better for running if they had to chase someone in the Rush Street neighborhood of the city's Gold Coast. He and his partner had to take their turn doing the scut work of arresting high-priced call girls and brawling drunks, such as there were, in the cold winds that had tamped down street crime.

Luckily, these weren't the summer months when geezer sugar daddies in their fake hairpieces and swinging clothes swaggered about the swarming crowds on Rush Street with girls half their age. Crime rose with the temperature and skirts on those hot nights. He hoped this night would be as quiet as the last few in patrolling the triangular patch of park christened the Viagra Triangle.

As Saturday evening fell, they headed for Gibson's Bar & Steakhouse, the place to see and be seen, for a break from the freezing wind known as the Hawk blowing off Lake Michigan. His mood warmed basking in the restaurant's bustle and glow. The lobby vibrated with the loud chatter of the crowd cramming forward into the bar and dining room to flee the pall of a Chicago winter.

The light, warmth, and laughter around the bar provided the relief he needed from the streets splattered with dirty snow slush. Like moths to light, men hovered around a gaggle of young women perched on barstools in satiny dresses with legs crossed for maximum exposure. Inside the dining room, waitstaff dangled at tableside three-pound steaks raw and red like the crude but enticing energy of the city. He tensed when he saw who was at the bar.

"Hey," said Ansel, a District Thirteen detective in stylish jeans and sports jacket. "Whatcha doing here?"

"Wondering the same about you," Murphy said. Ansel's under-cover pose was pathetic. The bulge under his Harley-Davidson shirt from a police ID badge hanging on a metal chain around his neck was a dead giveaway. "You're not supposed to be here tonight."

"I got business." He licked his lower lip. "You going to rat on us?"

"After you damaged my locker, what would you do?"

"Before we get into it"—Ansel jerked his thumb at Leone—"I need your pal here to head south down the street a block. I got a call from the beat cop. Looks like a guy got mugged or is on drugs. He's wandering around, no coat, shouting in Italian and getting scrappy. The cop needs a translator."

Murphy nodded to Leone. His partner left to help out the street cop.

"This is your last chance, Mr. Straight Arrow. You join or we can't trust you." He pointed to the end of the bar where three tanned men stood.

They looked just in from Florida for a short visit. The clothes were all wrong for a Chicago winter. Two wore paisley shirts and colored slacks. He pegged the third as the alpha male in light-blue pinstripes and Panama hat.

"These guys need our escort, Jim." Ansel put his hand on Murphy's shoulder. "They've got a buy set up tonight, and they're carrying a shit-load of cash."

"Sounds good," Murphy said. He knocked the hand off his shoulder. "I'll escort them right to headquarters for booking."

"You douchebag."

"Unless you help me arrest these mopes, this douchebag's reporting you to the commander."

"I'd expect that from a rat fink like you." Ansel shuffled his feet. "Look, I'm shaking in my boots."

Ansel walked to the end of the bar, huddled with the three men, and pointed back at Murphy. The three came over. The alpha male punched Murphy from the front while the paisley shirts grabbed him from behind.

A chorus of screams and shouts rippled through the line of bar patrons.

Murphy broke free. He shoved the alpha male against the piano, setting off a cacophony of musical chords. The paisley shirts behind Murphy threw him to the ground and kicked him on their way out the door with the alpha male. Ansel shouted at them to stop as though he meant it. When they didn't, he announced to everyone in the room he was going after the assailants to make an arrest.

Murphy scrambled out the door. He couldn't see either the drug dealers or Ansel. The bite of bitter weather congealed his nosebleed.

Looking about to explode with bad news, Marco scurried up the street to him.

"Let me guess," Jim said. "The Italian doesn't exist and the beat cop doesn't know what you're talking about."

"You should be a fortune-teller," Marco answered.

# CHAPTER TWENTY-NINE

Three police from internal affairs raided the locker room of the Thirteenth District. They threw Jim Murphy against the wall and handcuffed him. While two grabbed his arm, the third rifled through Murphy's locker contents.

"Get out of my locker."

"Quiet," barked the internal affairs lieutenant. "You're under arrest."

Commander Jack Cronin appeared in the doorway with a leprechaun smile. "What's goin' on?"

"We're looking for your boy's cookie jar." Turning his nose away, the lieutenant examined a pile of rumpled shirts and shorts. His hand slithered under a pack of paper forms and through the pockets of a stored uniform like a snake on the move for prey. He tossed the locker contents onto the floor. "It's gotta be here."

The commander sauntered over. He tapped the lieutenant on the shoulder. "What might you be after now?"

"He's got crystal meth stashed here." The lieutenant kicked the pile of Murphy's personal possessions on the floor. "I know it."

"Mighty peculiar," the commander said. "I don't see meth anywhere."

"It's not here." The lieutenant banged the locker with his fist. He hung his head for a second before turning around and shouting at Murphy. "Where is it?"

"In your dreams."

The lieutenant lunged toward him.

The commander blocked the lunge. "I'm thinkin' it's time to end this charade."

"Why should I?"

"Because," the commander said, "I know why you think you know it's here."

"I guess I had bogus information." The lieutenant's face turned sheepish. "Sorry for the mistake, Detective." He turned to the commander. "Are we all squared now?"

"All squared," the commander replied, winking at his godson.

———

Back in the commander's office, Murphy listened to Jack Cronin explain that the lieutenant was a bad apple protected by higher-ups who had pressured the maintenance man to plant crystal meth in the locker. When the commander discovered the setup, he had the crystal meth removed but let the raid go ahead to blow up in the lieutenant's face.

"How did you know he was setting me up?"

"I have a stool pigeon in internal affairs."

"They're connected to the rent-a-cop corruption in our district, right?"

"No. It's me they're after." The commander grabbed jelly beans from a jar and jiggled them in his hand. "The internal affairs lieutenant always had a hard-on for me. His way of gettin' back at me was through you. He knew you were my godson and that I'd hired you." He popped jelly beans into his mouth, chewed, and swallowed. "Simple as that."

"I don't think so." He had put up with the code of silence long enough. "I know who set me up."

"And who might that be?"

"You have dirty cops in the Thirteenth District. The internal affairs lieutenant must be in bed with them." He straightened up in his chair. "They call themselves the escort service. They protect drug dealers from getting ripped off. I wouldn't be part of it. There's payback alright . . . against me, not you."

"You got no proof, Jimmy. We've been through this."

"Jim."

"Jim, it is." The commander stretched his neck. "As I was saying, no proof." He held up a helpless pair of hands. "I've heard the rumors . . . and that's all they are, rumors by coppers with axes to grind."

"We have proof. Marco and I saw Ansel at Gibson's. He pressured me again that night to do escort service." He turned his bruised face to the commander. "This is what I got for not going along."

"Let it go." The commander ran his hand through his thick mane of silver hair. "He denies knowing they were dealers. Customers say he tried to help you. He tried to pinch the muggers after they took off."

"He knew the muggers were dealers." Murphy sprang up from the chair. "He knew."

"You got no proof." The commander came around the desk and put his hand on his godson's shoulder. "I promise to transfer them for the sake of morale."

"They'd be getting away with it."

"What does your eye-talian partner say?" The commander folded his arms and looked out the office window. "Mondo . . . Mondo . . . whatever. It's a dog's life." The commander packed up his things to leave for the day. "Not so glum, my boy. A dog's life's not so bad . . . as long as you're top dog. And since I am top dog in this district, you've got nothin' to worry about."

# CHAPTER THIRTY

"I refuse to leave, Jim. That is that . . . as you say." Commissario Marco Leone laid the newspaper on the table next to the plate-glass window of the Conte Di Savoia import store on Taylor Street. "It's Sunday morning. I am off duty today." He lifted a cup of cappuccino in salute to Jim Murphy across the table and sipped. "Time to relax with this excellent cappuccino. It reminds me of home."

"Didn't you read this report from the Polizia di Stato in Rome?" Jim dropped it on top of the newspaper.

The report confirmed Dr. Angelo Mora was the neofascist brother-in-law and physician of Lucio Piso, the billionaire megalomaniac, who had tried to overthrow the Italian government. By the time Italian police fully uncovered Mora's role in the conspiracy, Marco had already left for Chicago. The report concluded: witness interrogations indicated Mora planned to assassinate Marco in Chicago.

"I did read the report."

"You're risking your life." Jim bolted up from the table, almost knocking his chair over. "A gangland war is breaking out between the Sinaloa cartel and the Outfit. Last week set a record for mob killings, the most recent one in this neighborhood. We've been finding dead bodies in garbage cans, car trunks, the Chicago River." He buttoned up his leather jacket. "You could be next, sitting here exposed."

"The victims are members of the Chicago Outfit or Sinaloa." Marco blew on the cappuccino before sipping. "I belong to neither."

"You're being stubborn." Jim's Irish was rising. "We know now Dr. Mora wants to kill you. Nicole told us Mora lunched with Palomba and that the Outfit boss showed a peculiar interest in your habits. Mora may have put out a contract on you." He screeched his chair back into position under the table. "But what do I know? I'm just a Chicago detective and you're the foreign big-shot brass."

"No need to worry, Jim." Marco put on his reading glasses.

"Your colleagues in the Polizia di Stato are worried. Why shouldn't I be?"

"All is well." Marco picked up the newspaper and glanced at the front page. "Now that the Polizia di Stato knows Dr. Mora is in Chicago, they will hasten to extradite him to Italy."

"And I'll be on a police pension and you in a casket before that happens."

"It is my decision." Marco poked his reading glasses at Jim. "If I cowered before every death threat, I would drink my cappuccino under the bed. I move not one centimeter to appease these criminal . . . dirt-bags . . . as you call them."

"Your call." Jim put on his cap. "I have to leave. I'm still on duty."

He rolled up his jacket collar and tightened his scarf as he braved the driving swirls of snow kissing his face. Taylor Street was empty except for an old-timer wiseguy hobbling down the street around patches of sidewalk ice. The aging mobsters in the Outfit were either dead, in jail, or coping with prostate problems. If his big-shot partner wanted to put himself at risk, so be it. The commissario had that mulish streak of stubbornness that Italian Americans on the force called *testa dura* . . . hard head.

The scrunch of day-old snow underfoot, he jaywalked Taylor Street to his unmarked beater car. At the car he turned around to see his partner absorbed in reading the newspaper right behind the plate-glass window. As if he knew he were being watched, the hardhead looked up and waved him away.

He took off a glove and blew warmth into his hand before reaching in his pocket for the car key. Not finding it where it should be, he warmed his breath with expletives. His partner's refusal to take precautions reminded him of gung ho cops whose bravado risked the lives of their partners as well as their own.

But Marco endangered only himself, and who could say for sure his partner was wrong? The street looked Christmas-card calm with a dusting of falling snow not yet sullied by traffic. Maybe yours truly was the one off base with unjustified anxiety triggered by the outbreak of criminal violence across the city. He found his car key in a back pocket. It was an omen. His day would go better.

As soon as he entered the unmarked car, a radio dispatch from headquarters broke the silence.

"Ten one. Emergency at La Gola Restaurant. Des Plaines and Roosevelt. Several shots heard. Officer down."

"Ten ninety-nine. On my way from Taylor Street."

"OK. Lemme know what we got when you arrive."

As he opened the car door to take off for La Gola Restaurant, a black Jeep Cherokee caked in winter grime cruised east on Taylor Street toward him and the Conte Di Savoia. A man in the front seat lowered the passenger window. The driver slowed to a crawl in front of the import store.

*Who opens a car window on a bitter-cold day like this?*

Running into the street, he fingered his holster.

The passenger stuck a handgun out the window.

"Drop the gun. Chicago police," he yelled, withdrawing his revolver.

The passenger fired.

Plate glass broke and crashed.

Murphy fired.

The shooter slumped against the dashboard.

The driver gunned the Jeep forward, squealing. It zigzagged eastward down Taylor.

He positioned himself for another shot at the fleeing car.

A Sunday-morning Wiseguy Tour bus rumbled westward toward him standing in the middle of Taylor Street.

The Jeep Cherokee veered over street center and smashed into the front of the bus.

The driver fled the Jeep. Murphy pursued the driver into an alley but lost him. The driver had escaped through one of the backyards. Murphy doubled back to the crime scene.

The shooter lay sprawled across the front seat of the Cherokee with his left hand over his chest. Murphy called for an ambulance. The

Wiseguy Tour passengers had exited the bus and formed a circle of gawkers around him and the Jeep. "It's the real thing. A mobster hit," said a passenger. "We're sure getting our money's worth."

He felt a tap on his shoulder. He turned.

Unharmed, Marco stood before him.

"You could've gotten killed," Jim said. His cell buzzed.

"This is dispatch. I said 'officer down.' Where the hell are you?"

———

Jack Cronin summoned Murphy into his office as soon as the detective returned from Conte Di Savoia. The commander sat transfixed by the images flittering across the TV. Uniformed police officers had cordoned off the area outside La Gola Restaurant with yellow tape warning in bold black letters: POLICE LINE DO NOT CROSS. Numbered evidence markers looking like tiny sandwich boards dotted the sidewalk and street outside the restaurant.

A TV anchor reported three men had been shot in a shoot-out outside La Gola Restaurant. In what looked like another mobster hit, two gunmen were seen fleeing the scene with a plastic cooler in a Dodge Charger Hellcat. A witness claimed that after the shooting, the gunmen huddled over Vincent Palomba's body and did something to his chest.

Besides the reputed Outfit leader, the attackers shot his bodyguard and a patrol officer. Ambulances transported the three to Rush University Medical Center where a hospital spokesperson would shortly issue a statement.

The commander swiveled around in his office chair. "Godson or not . . . you are responsible for this."

No use denying it anymore. The Murphy's Law ridicule fit him to a T. Some leprechaun must have cursed a Murphy ancestor.

"Let me explain. I had an impossible choice." Still standing, he grasped the back of the guest chair facing the commander's desk. "Marco was about to be shot."

"And Vinnie Palomba was really shot. If you had responded at once, he might not be in the hospital." Cronin took the police baton he had kept ever since his early days on patrol. He beat it methodically in the palm of his free hand. "If he dies, you put me in a tough spot."

"You're worried about Palomba?" Murphy white-knuckled his grip on the back of the chair. "Not about our patrol officer in the hospital?"

"That too, that too." Cronin jabbed the baton at him. "You disobeyed a dispatch assignment without even requesting reassignment."

"I didn't have time. I had to save Marco."

The image on the TV monitor switched from a diarrhea-treatment commercial to a spokeswoman for Rush University Medical Center announcing that Palomba's bodyguard was stable, but the patrol officer was in critical condition.

"Five days' suspension for neglect of duty." Cronin held up his hand. "If you weren't my godson . . ." He left the sentence incomplete. "You'd better get on your knees and pray no one dies."

"Why didn't you tell us Vincent Palomba's medical status?" a reporter asked the hospital spokeswoman on screen.

"Vincent Palomba suffered a nonlethal gunshot wound."

"Does that mean he's alive?" the TV reporter asked.

"No."

"Which is it?" the reporter pressed. "Dead or alive?"

"Dead."

"Cause of death?"

"His heart was removed from his chest cavity."

# CHAPTER THIRTY-ONE

After a bout with the punching bag in the back room, Jim Murphy ordered a Guinness in Dugan's Irish pub on Halsted while awaiting Katie. His sister had called to say she was running late. Her voice vibrated an excitement untypical of the placid personality that could sometimes annoy him. If she had a meditation mantra, it would be *I have things under control.* Something thrilled her. She wasn't coming just to commiserate over his suspension.

She entered in a flurry and took the barstool to his right. A burly bartender with a Slavic accent switched TV channels. He took her order for a shandy and scuttled off.

"What's with the new East European bartender," she asked, "in an Irish pub?"

"Same thing as an Irish pub in Greek Town. It's called diversity." He jerked his thumb in the bartender's direction. "Ivan's decreed no news tonight. Only the Blackhawks game, like it or not."

She put her hand on his arm. "Wanna talk about the suspension before I get to my news?"

Once a nurse, always a nurse. His big sister always put others' needs before her own. And he loved her for it.

"Nothing to talk about." He rocked the Guinness bottle back and forth in his hands. "I can't figure him out. Blaming me for Palomba's death."

"The commander's under pressure, Jimmy. Your police district is on the frontline of the war between the Outfit and the Sinaloa cartel. He needs a scapegoat."

"So much for Bridgeporters-gotta-stick-together." He took a slug of Guinness. "Something's not right. He's too upset by Palomba's death."

"His job's on the line." She glanced up at the TV soap commercial. "You know how you felt about . . . the Millennial's assassination."

"I do. I could've prevented the assassination." He rubbed the counter with his hand. "I didn't try to blame someone else."

"Unlike some people I know, self-flagellation is not his style."

"I didn't deserve five days suspension for preventing the high-profile killing of a foreign police commissioner." He fixed her with his eyes. "Imagine how Marco's death would've played out in the Italian press. Instead the commander's beside himself with the death of a mobster."

"You're talking a load of malarkey now, Jimmy." She removed her hand from his arm. "It was a love tap. You're lucky the wounded patrol officer is on the mend. Anyone else in your shoes would have gotten far worse . . . and you know it."

"The way he overreacted about Palomba's death." He shook his head as if to clear it. "It doesn't make sense."

"Chicago's never seen anything like this. Worse than the Roaring Twenties," she said. "It's all over the news about the Outfit crew boss found decapitated with a chainsaw." She sipped her shandy. "The Aztec Warriors are taking over."

"I don't think so." He took a handful of counter popcorn. "I think Sinaloa's behind this."

"Why?" With a compact mirror in hand, she attended to a facial zit. She saw him watching. She snapped the compact shut.

"The Aztec Warriors are ruthless psychopaths, but they're too disorganized to be the brains. Sinaloa used them in the past as mercenary shock troops." His attention drifted to a TV hockey player recycling through the penalty box, ready to commit another penalty. It reminded him of his revolving-door teenage confessions before Father Malachy. *Bless me, Father, for I have had impure thoughts.* "Sinaloa's using them to do the dirty work before moving in."

"Whoever it is," she said, "the Outfit's losing control of city crime."

"Enough about me." He pushed the popcorn bowl down the bar counter beyond his reach. "What's the news you're dying to tell me?"

"Sebastian Senex." Her eyes brightened and her voice perked up. "He's taken over Good Samaritan Blood Bank where I work."

"So? Nothing illegal there."

"I did a little checking. He's trying to take over other blood banks in the city. Highly suspicious, I'd say."

"Suspicious?" He rolled his eyes up. "Come on, Katie. It's not a crime to buy blood banks."

"That's not all." She looked around and then back at him. "Through a straw man, the Outfit tried to buy a blood bank for themselves."

"With the bloodbath on the streets, they'll need the blood."

The Blackhawks were hopelessly behind already in the first period.

"Get serious, little brother." She poked his arm the bossy way she did when they were children. "Breaking news. A relative identified the dead Outfit straw man."

"The guy found in an alley off Ashland two days ago?" She had his full attention. "Stuffed in a fifty-five-gallon drum?"

She nodded. "The deal fell through . . . and guess who bought the blood bank."

"Don't tell me." He closed his eyes and touched his forehead like a mock soothsayer. His eyes sprang open. "Sebastian Senex."

"You nailed it."

His cell buzzed.

"Hi, Marco. Anything on the Palomba killing?"

"I want to inform you." Marco paused. "Three Aztec Warriors have been arrested in a house of safety for the La Gola homicides."

"House of safety? Oh, safe house." He scratched his head. "What's the proof?"

"They took a plastic cooler from the crime scene."

"What's that got to do with the murder?"

"They were arrested in the act of devouring Palomba's heart from the cooler."

# CHAPTER THIRTY-TWO

Waiting for the latecomers to shuffle in, Sebastian Senex, the newly elected president of the Windy City Reform Council, scanned members and their guests packed into the dark-wood banquet hall of Maggiore's Ristorante. They nattered at tables covered with white tablecloths and sparkling cut-crystal glasses.

He no longer needed eyeglasses to discern the details of their expectant faces. Friends and associates increasingly remarked on his more youthful appearance. He put the text of his inaugural presentation on the lectern.

Clear skies lay ahead for him and Promethean Pharma.

Now that Vinnie Palomba was dead, only three persons . . . he, Daisy, and Dr. Angelo Mora . . . knew the secret of his physical regeneration. The way was open to reduce that number to only him and his daughter. Last week Mora had discovered the silver bullet of the Ponce de León protein in blood plasma by pursuing the lead of an assistant researcher.

He no longer needed the whole blood required by parabiosis treatments. If the trial period for the protein ended as Mora anticipated, he would no longer even need injections of the Ponce de León protein. At that point Mora believed his metabolism would be reset to a youthful age. And then Mora would become disposable.

Trusted scientists at Promethean Pharma could carry on once he announced to the world the discovery of the Ponce de León protein and the chain of clinics he would open in the Midwest. He would register the Ponce de León protein with a tangle of patents to protect his billions in profits. He would chase the monkey of success all the way to the bank. He might even buy the bank.

For a king's ransom, he would make the old young and the lame walk. With an army of graying baby boomers behind him, he would conduct a crusade against aging. He would become the true savior of mankind with the difference that he would establish his kingdom of eternal life here on Earth. Lest he be accused of mercenary motives, he would pay the Gen-Xers, the Gen-Yers, and the Gen-Zers for their blood. But no more than strictly necessary.

The nation's youth would no longer have to become squatters in abandoned buildings due to a lack of affordable housing and crushing student loans and slave-wage gig work. He would take their blood and turn them into private welfare recipients dependent on the stream of revenue from their periodic blood donations. The younger the blood, the higher the sum he would pay.

But today the topic of his inaugural address to the Windy City Reform Council was different. He looked down at the title of his prepared remarks laid out on the lectern: "Whack the Chicago Outfit for Good."

One bang of the gavel snapped the audience to attention.

After the usual formalities, he opened his presentation with a disinformation offensive that would have done the Russians proud. Chicago's organized crime syndicate, he alleged, had instigated the crime wave by kidnapping selected gang members in order to provoke a war with unorganized bands of poor and disadvantaged youth whose circumstances had forced them into a life of crime. The crime syndicate, known as the Chicago Outfit, and now in decline, had been reduced to fighting the gangs for a greater market share of lower-level crime in the city.

He made the lie more believable by making it bigger. He announced that the Outfit was planning to move into the lucrative but illegal procurement of human organs for desperate patients. The FBI had discovered (and he knew because he had planted them there) over a hundred organ transplant carriers in an Outfit social club. He forced indignation into his voice. As he hoped, horror and disgust spread across the faces of the audience like a contagion.

They did this, he said, not by buying organs, illegal though that might be under the National Organ Transplant Act of 1984. No! Instead the Outfit planned to not just simply kill gangbangers encroaching on its profits but to pluck whatever organs they fancied from the fresh corpses of the gang victims. Al Capone at least had some standards. The gangster's heirs had none! The lives of young Latinos and African Americans trapped in ghettos were disproportionately at risk. Minority lives matter, he boomed in his most righteous voice recently reinvigorated by Mora's blood therapy. He was on a roll to unimagined power and influence. Nothing could stop him now. He pushed away the microphone. He didn't need it. The voice of an old man on the verge of death had become the roar of a young lion.

The Chicago Outfit must be destroyed once and for all.

He ended his presentation and sat down to thunderous applause.

———

Itching to confront the new president of the Windy City Reform Council, Jim Murphy bided his time on the perimeter of admirers congratulating Senex on his presentation. Angelo Mora was the key to taking down Senex. If necessary, he could flip Mora against Senex by threatening not only to have him extradited to Italy but also to stand trial in the United States for the contract on Marco's life. While admirers shook Senex's hand after descending the podium, Murphy elbowed his way to the front. Senex eyed him with suspicion.

The mayor's administrative aide pushed his way through the crowd to Senex. The aide told him His Honor was on board with the crusade against the Outfit. Murphy knew that in the next election, Chicago's chief executive wanted to be the first passenger on the Senex Express in its anti-Outfit campaign so he could ride it back into office.

When the crowd dwindled away, he cornered Senex.

"Why are you here?" Senex shoved papers into his briefcase. "I won the traffic case."

"I'm investigating the deaths of young men abducted from the streets."

"You mean the dope-dealing gangbangers?" Senex tucked his brief-case under his arm.

"The three we found didn't have organs missing," Murphy said. "Like you said in your speech."

"Maybe if you guys found all the others still missing, you'd find organs missing. So who's to say I'm wrong?" A smirk formed at the corners of his lips. "Besides, I said the Outfit was planning to sell human organs, not that they're doing it now."

"You've got something to do with the missing and dead gang-bangers, don't you?"

"Where's your proof, Detective?"

"Dr. Angelo Mora for one." He positioned himself to block Senex's exit. "Does that name ring a bell?"

"He's an employee wanted by the Italian authorities for treason." Senex tut-tutted disapproval. "Had I only known his secret past, I would never have arranged his arrival in Chicago." He shook his head with a sheepish grin. "That's what I get for being too trusting."

"We know he's your right-hand man in secret blood research."

"It's not a crime to do scientific research or protect corporate trade secrets."

"It is if you kidnap and kill people to do it."

"You have no proof."

"When I turn on the tap, Dr. Mora will leak like a faulty faucet."

"You're bluffing. Why would he talk to you?"

"Mora will beg for a plea bargain. The Outfit shooter we arrested tagged Mora for the contract on the life of Commissario Marco Leone."

"The shooter's uncommunicative and in critical condition."

"Was. We got a statement yesterday after he revived."

"Behind my back." Senex blurted out to no one in particular.

He was either genuinely surprised or a remarkable actor.

"If Mora did try to arrange for your partner's assassination, he did it behind my back. I knew nothing about his plans." He straightened up. "My word against that of a neofascist traitor. Take your pick."

"Mora is only the beginning of the end for you."

"Get out of my way." Senex brushed past him. "You're confusing me with the Mafia. I'm a law-abiding citizen."

"God help you if you're involved in killing my son."

# CHAPTER THIRTY-THREE

"No need to ambush me down here. Make an appointment," said Clyde Pomeroy, Speaker of the House of Representatives. He panted his way along the underground walkway to the Capitol Building from the Cannon House Office Building. "I'm in a hurry. I have to organize another vote for president."

"Stop your play-acting. I saw the report, just out, from the Base Closure and Realignment Commission." Sebastian Senex grabbed Pomeroy's arm to stop him. "You lied to me."

"Let go." The Speaker pulled away. "I was duped. They changed their minds without telling me."

"A lie. My inside sources say the commission never intended to put those bases on the chopping block."

A Metropolitan police officer walked toward them. Senex let go of Pomeroy until the officer walked by.

"I'm trying to get a majority vote, but House members aren't showing up for a quorum," the Speaker said. "The Capitol physician is having temperatures checked before they enter the House. He's scaring them away. They're afraid infected Chinese got through the travel ban and are in DC."

"Why did you lie?"

"You knew Brewster was a long shot." The Speaker resumed walking toward the Capitol Building with Senex alongside. "Why be worried? Roscoe Corker is your Plan B."

"I didn't get you elected, Clyde, for Plan Bs."

"I have to rest. My COPD's getting worse." The Speaker stopped to wipe sweat from his forehead. "Thank God I'm moving to the Rayburn House Office Building tomorrow. Then I can ride the underground subway to the Capitol instead of walking."

"You lied to me."

The Speaker backed against the walkway guardrail and hung on with hands outstretched on either side of his body. His chest heaved in and out for air.

"You stabbed me in the back." Senex squeezed Pomeroy's shoulders. "Your plan was a sham from the get-go."

"No, it wasn't. I swear."

Senex glanced at the high school artwork on the wall behind the Speaker's head. The winning picture of a national competition showed a line of smiling men stabbing one another in the back with the caption: THE CONGRESSIONAL BACKSLAP.

He removed his hands from Pomeroy's shoulders. "You little conniver."

"Don't worry, Sebastian." Easy breathing returning, the Speaker moved away from the guardrail. He drew the palms of both hands down his face. "I'll think of something."

"You already have."

"What do you mean?"

"You purposely used the COVID-28 confusion as a pretext to further delay the House selection of a president before Inauguration Day on January twentieth. Your sham deal on military bases plus your parliamentary maneuvers as Speaker were all designed to postpone the election of a president."

"Why would I ever do that?"

Senex waited until a congressman hustled past, jabbering nonstop with legislative assistants in tow.

"Your plan all along was to snatch the presidency for yourself."

"That's preposterous."

"In talking to my lawyers and confirming it with Bryan Murphy at Justice, I learned that if the House doesn't elect a president by Inauguration Day, you become president under the Presidential Succession Act."

"You've got it all wrong." Pomeroy wiped his brow with the back of his hand. "If it's not Brewster, it's going to be Corker."

"No it won't." He took off his hat and clenched it with both hands. "You're playing out the clock so neither of them gets it."

"You got it all wrong, Sebastian."

"You lying weasel." Senex pushed the Speaker back against the railing. "You had no more intention of getting Brewster or Corker elected than I have to fly to the moon. You double-crossed me to get it for yourself."

"That's not true." Pomeroy licked his lips. "But even if it happened . . . but mind you, I'm not saying I would want it to happen . . . but let's say it just happens neither gets in and I do after Inauguration Day." He touched Senex's arm. "You know I'd do more for you, more than Brewster, and even more than Corker."

"You pathetic con artist." Senex started walking back to the Cannon House Office Building. He turned. "If you let Inauguration Day go by without the House picking a president, that'll be the last time you two-time me."

# CHAPTER THIRTY-FOUR

On a counter stool at 1:12 a.m., Detective Jim Murphy put down his pepper-and-egg sandwich in the White Palace Grill at the corner of Canal and Roosevelt. He peered out the plate-glass window into the winter night for the laggard insistent on meeting him but nowhere to be seen. Two drunks bathed in fluorescent street lighting on an icy sidewalk gave up their swing-and-miss brawl. Wet gobs of falling snow clung to their hair. They staggered away on Canal in opposite directions.

He returned to his stool to hear the only other customer down the counter slurping soup into a wild-whiskered face. In the lull of the night, a middle-aged waitress sucked ice cubes from a glass and fanned herself with a menu. The angry-bee buzz of his cell skittering along the slick countertop drowned out the gurgle of soup.

"Katie? What gives at this hour?"

"Bryan called. He's been drinking."

"What's new?"

"He's had enough, he says. He wants Dad in a DC nursing home."

"Without talking to me?" The die had been cast. "Over my dead body."

"Don't overreact, Jimmy. Bryan knows Dad got out again. He knows the home nurse quit. And I can't take more time from my job to look after Dad."

"I'll find someone. Dad's not going to any institution. Period."

"Bryan's ready to go to court."

"Let him."

"Think what's best for Dad."

Through the venetian blinds of the plate-glass window, he saw the familiar figure make his way on the slick street toward the seasonal canvas vestibule protecting the front door from a snowstorm blasting into town.

"Gotta go," he said. "We'll talk later."

Commander Jack Cronin entered. He brushed snow off his overcoat and dropped down on a stool next to Murphy.

The whiskered derelict to the left of the commander raised the dish to his lips and guzzled the remaining soup. He wiped his mouth and dropped a pile of coins on the counter before scuttling past them with coat collar upturned. The commander glared at him. The derelict pulled his scarf around his face and stumbled out the door into the dark. A piece of vestibule canvas came loose and flapped like a trapped bird in the gathering wind of an approaching blizzard.

"Know him?" he asked the commander.

"I pinched him years ago for robbery." Cronin rubbed his hands and face, still chilled from the outside weather. "That's a pinch he'll never forget." He blew into his hands before pretending to beat one hand with an invisible billy club held in the other. "Ah, for those days with different rules."

"You wanted to see me. I'm off duty and I want to go home." His suspicions about Jack Cronin overcame any inclination toward civility. "Let's get this over with."

"No wonder. The weather's brutal tonight."

"Stop wasting my time."

Red-eyed, the commander yawned. "Hard time sleeping lately."

"Why did you turn on me? And no BS."

"That's why I'm here." The commander looked out onto the street. "To try to explain."

"Start talking." Murphy rose from his stool. "Or I'm gone."

"I'm sorry, lad. Truly I am." Cronin turned his eyes back to him. "The Outfit called in some chips. I had to keep them happy. They wanted me to do worse to you until I sweet-talked them out of it. It's not somethin' I'm proud of." He traced a finger on the counter. "That's it in a nutshell."

The waitress went through the motions of cleaning an already clean counter around them until she was in eavesdropping distance. "Do ya want anything?" she asked the commander.

"Get me a Pancho Villa omelet."

"And deliver it in the back," Murphy added. "We need privacy . . . if you know what I mean."

"I can take a hint, honey," she said. "Just like being around you guys at night. The gangs come in about now and try to stiff me."

———

In the room at the back of the White Palace Grill, Murphy sat facing the commander with the Chicago mural on the wall over the commander's shoulders. In the center, Harry Caray, Michael Jordan, Jane Byrne, and Mayor Richard J. Daley played cards against a downtown Chicago skyline while Mayor Harold Washington and Richard M. Daley kibitzed above. To the left, his eyes ran over the poster honoring the Blues Brothers, Muddy Waters, and other cultural icons. Outside the perimeter of Chicago's icons, Al Capone smirked, martini in hand, like he knew the game was rigged.

"It was either go along or wind up in a car trunk." The commander wrapped his hands around a hot coffee mug. "I did what I had to do."

"Either Marco or you had to die, is that it?" He wondered how the muralist had captured the almost invisible wink in Capone's eye. "Don't serve me that crapolini. You took the first bribe, then the second, and on and on. You chose your fate one payoff at a time, one bribe at a time, until you locked yourself in. And I'm supposed to feel sorry for you?"

"Still the goody-goody, like your old man."

Murphy stood up halfway in his chair. "Keep my father out of this. He wasn't a dirty cop like—"

"Me?" The commander pointed to his chest and forced a hollow laugh. "The odd couple, we were. I always assumed he'd tell you I was . . . different."

"Corrupt, I'd call it."

"I'll tell you somethin' I'd tell my son." He folded his hands on the table. "There's good in the worst of us and bad in the best."

"And most of us know the difference."

"I can't undo it, Jim, but I gotta be honest." He lifted his head to look him in the eye. "I'd have to do it all over again. I didn't choose to be born in this city, grow up with the folks I did. I had to play the cards I was dealt." Cronin spread his fingers across the table and hunched over. "Ain't life grand?"

"Life is what you make it."

"Says the man who dropped out of the priesthood, dropped out of law school, and dropped out of position so a presidential candidate gets himself shot."

"I grew up in the same neighborhood you did. I kept trying to find my way, trial and error maybe, but I kept trying." He sighed, realizing maybe the commander was right. Maybe his godfather couldn't change now. Maybe that was hell. Living in wet concrete until it hardened with time and you couldn't get out. "Do right and wrong mean anything to you anymore?"

"If you weren't such a Holy Joe, you'd give me credit for improving morale, modernizing the Thirteenth District, cracking down on crime where I could . . . and, yes, not letting graft and departmental politics get out of hand."

"Oh, I give you credit alright," he said. "You really cracked down on crime. They didn't call you Mr. Billy Club for nothing when you walked the beat. You'd crack any petty crook to an inch of his life . . . when you weren't kissing Mob ass."

The commander's face reddened. "I ought to . . . What's the use?" His eyes watered. "You're right. And it hurts to hear you, of all people, say it."

"I don't want to work with you." He looked away. "I'm applying for a transfer."

"No need, my boy." The commander folded his arms. "I'm resignin' from the force. The FBI's hot on my trail. Maybe resignin' will satisfy them."

"Dream on, Commander." He waved the waitress away. "They'll want you to flip against the Outfit."

"I'm no snitch."

"The golden rule of corruption. Rats don't rat on other rats."

"They'd kill me."

"What about the Witness Protection Program?"

"They're bigger than the Witness Protection Program."

"Is that why the cartel is taking them down, piece by piece? Because they're so powerful?"

"I'm not a stool pigeon."

"Of course not." He tossed some bills on the table before leaving. "You're a rat."

# CHAPTER THIRTY-FIVE

Sebastian Senex and Brock Brewster had set down their food trays in the hospital cafeteria when Brewster's ringtone sounded. Brewster tapped his smartphone. He gasped as he read the email message. His jaw grew slack. His eyes widened.

"Put that thing away," Senex said. "We're eating."

"The Senate just selected Dallas Taylor as the vice president of the United States." Brewster shook his head. "I don't like it. The House hasn't selected a president yet. We're coming down to the wire of Inauguration Day on January twentieth, and she's already vice president. I don't like it one bit."

Of course he wouldn't. No president wants to be upstaged by a stand-in. But Brewster couldn't see the forest for the trees. The Senate had done them a favor by sticking Taylor into the dead-end office. The first vice president, John Adams, had called it the most insignificant office that mankind ever invented. Harry Truman put it more memorably: The office of vice president was like the fifth teat on a cow.

"Aren't you surprised, Sebastian?"

"No." He held up his two hands as though he had something in each. "The Constitution limits the Senate's choice to the two candidates with the most electoral votes. In the right hand, we have the Democrat senator from Texas being considered by fellow senators in a Senate dominated by Democrats. In the left hand, we have Luisa Garcia, your Republican veep running mate, who's not a senator and is a political lightweight, except for her Hispanic appeal." He raised his right hand higher than left. "No surprise to me at all."

"But what if the Speaker can't get me elected in the House before Inauguration Day?"

"It's in the bag."

"After what the Speaker did to delay the House election, how can you say that?"

"Let's say I twisted Pomeroy's arm a little. He's knows now I'm deadly serious about getting you into office by January twentieth."

"That still means I'll have a Democrat for my vice president when the House elects me president." He took a roll from the basket and buttered it. "She'll make trouble."

"Give her nothing to do. Let her vegetate."

"Thanks, Sebastian, for all your advice and support." Brewster picked at the watery meat lasagna on his plate. "But I especially appreciate your visiting my wife in the hospital. It really meant the world to her."

*Meant the world to her?* Senex laughed to himself. The ice-cube coldness in her eyes and the hardening furrows of her face shouted the opposite when he had entered the hospital room. She cut short the visit with the excuse of needing sleep although she had just awakened. Brewster the doofus was still in the dark about the affair between him and Brewster's wife.

Just as well, because his protégé, Brewster, wouldn't understand what a favor he had done by screwing Brewster's wife. Everyone knew she was a shrew who made Brewster's life miserable. The CEO of Promethean Pharma had molded her into a more pleasant and contented woman because of his amorous ministrations. If anything, Brewster owed him for making her a better woman.

When he refused to leave his own wife for her, Brewster's wife ended the affair without telling her husband. She took her revenge by doing everything she could to undermine her husband's political allegiance to him. Fortunately, Brewster treasured his allegiance with the CEO of Promethean Pharma more than a wife's advice.

He knew why Brewster wanted to talk to him over lunch. It meant he had sunk the hook into Brewster and had him where he wanted him. He just had to guide him into the net.

"Cheer up, Brewster." Senex slurped a spoonful of a not-so-creamy broccoli-and-mushroom soup. "She'll recover."

"Not likely, the doc says. Not with her stage-three multiple myeloma." Brewster's eyes looked bloodshot. "I don't know what I'm going to do."

"Buck up, man." Why had Ohio voters elected this wimpish ex-hedge-fund manager to the governorship? "Look on the bright side. Your wife's illness only adds to your appeal."

"Are you going to let her have the treatment?"

"What do you mean?"

"You know." Brewster wrung a napkin in his hands. "Everyone suspects you're taking something to look so young and healthy." He put the napkin down and leaned in. "Word's getting around. They say it has something to do with secret experiments at Promethean Pharma."

"Everything's been exaggerated."

"Please tell me about the treatment."

"Alright. I have had an experimental treatment." He pretended to be cautious about bystanders overhearing them. "Just keep our conversation confidential."

"What's the treatment?"

He feigned annoyance but relished Brewster's desperate curiosity.

"The procedure's a trade secret to keep it from business competitors. Besides, it's risky and highly dangerous."

"Not for you apparently."

"Her medical condition is different."

"She's hospitalized because she almost broke her hip. She has advanced osteoporosis. If she falls again, she could die."

"I don't know." He feigned indecision. "But if you two are willing to take the risk, I—"

"We are, Sebastian, we are." Brewster stood up and shook his hand across the table. "How can we ever repay you?"

"There is one thing."

"Name it."

"File a lawsuit to prevent Clyde Pomeroy, Speaker of the House, from becoming president if this mess goes beyond Inauguration Day."

"Why would I do that? Clyde is a friend." Brewster paused. "Anyway, you said my House election was in the bag."

"I always like to have a Plan B. Just in case the Speaker tries to double-cross us again."

"I can't do that." His eyebrows arched over unblinking eyes. "The Presidential Succession Act expressly puts the Speaker in the line of succession after the vice president."

"The Constitution trumps an act of Congress."

"Where does the Constitution say the Speaker can't assume the presidency?"

"My lawyers told me about Article One in the Constitution. It says you have to be a quote . . . officer . . . unquote to assume the office of the presidency."

"So?"

"The Speaker is a representative elected to the legislative branch of government. He's not technically an officer of the United States."

"Not everyone agrees with that interpretation."

"It's unconstitutional, damn it." He folded his arms and glared at Brewster. "Bryan Murphy of the Justice Department agrees."

"The Supreme Court has the last word," Brewster said. "Not Bryan Murphy or the Justice Department."

"You're missing the big picture." Senex pushed away the bowl of unfinished soup. "I will use Plan A, Plan B, or whatever it takes to stop the Speaker from ever becoming president. Got it?"

"I think you're overreacting. Clyde Pomeroy and I have always gotten along."

"Listen up, Brewster. The Speaker stabbed you in the back. He's only pretending to help you get elected. Where's your spine?"

"Don't confuse my back or my spine with yours. I never made any deal with him. And I won't fight your battles." Breathing deeply, Brewster rubbed the back of his neck. "My wife is top priority now . . . not the presidency."

Senex slapped his hand on the table. "I demand you file that lawsuit against the Speaker . . . or else."

"Or else what?"

"Or else your wife will never get my treatment."

# CHAPTER THIRTY-SIX

Seated on a burgundy sofa in the Backroom Bar of the Meridian Club, Sebastian Senex waited alone with his thoughts. He had miscalculated. Clyde Pomeroy, Speaker of the House of Representatives, was not the pushover he counted on.

Brewster's lawsuit to prevent Pomeroy from becoming president had sparked a counterattack. The Speaker had held a press conference several days earlier to announce his withdrawal of support for Brock Brewster as president and the launching of a congressional probe into the extortionate prices Promethean Pharma demanded for lifesaving drugs.

At the instigation of the Speaker, a drug advocacy group was on its way to throw a picket line around the Meridian Club. With little time remaining until Inauguration Day, Senex vowed the backstabber would never become president.

He telephoned the front desk.

"Have the police arrived?"

"Yes, sir. They've formed a protective line outside the entrance."

The founder of Promethean Pharma poured a single-malt scotch into a snifter of Baccarat crystal for a pick-me-up. He tapped his right heel on the floor and picked up a copy of the *Wall Street Journal* lying atop a coffee table with a built-in aquarium. An angelfish nipped and chased a guppy. He glanced at the headline, read a quarter way down the lead column, and then dropped the newspaper back onto the coffee table.

He closed his eyes in the dim lighting. The unsettling news of the last few days must have unleashed his unpredictable flashes of fatigue. For someone so biologically young, he shouldn't be feeling so strung out. It had to be the stress of the election causing his fatigue. In his mouth he swished the smoky-tasting scotch with the after bite of burnt cork. A wave of relaxation washed through him. Maybe, if he drank more scotch, he'd also slow his weight loss.

Voices startled his eyes open. The bartender pointed him out to a bearded aide from Brewster's campaign headquarters. The aide came over to hand him the judicial opinion of the United States district court. At an expedited hearing, the court had dismissed Brewster's claim that the House Speaker was ineligible to become president. In a note accompanying the opinion, Brock Brewster had the gall to blame him for a drop in the presidential polls because of the dismissed lawsuit filed in Brewster's name. Again, the legal system had failed Promethean Pharma's CEO and the country. It no longer mattered. He had other plans.

The nation was on the verge of a nervous breakdown. The stock market had plummeted. Every country with computer capability was trying to influence the American election. The divisions in the United States had grown so bitter and entrenched that Congress was incapable of coming together even to pass ordinary legislation to keep government functioning . . . let alone pick the next president and vice president of the United States.

China fueled rumors of a looming COVID-28 outbreak by going from denial to no comment. That would have been bad enough, but the fear of COVID-28 had taken hold in the nation's capital. Several congressional staffers had come down with the virus. The Centers for Disease Control and Prevention claimed it had things under control. Informed by its bitter experience with COVID-19, the CDC endorsed involuntary quarantining of infected persons and criminal penalties for noncompliance. Through a high-tech tracing system, it tested those in contact with the infected persons. Additional tests through the DC metropolitan area found no further trace of the infection.

He poured himself another scotch and considered the national confusion. Congress had panicked when it heard the news of COVID-28 in the District of Columbia. It took a recess until it was safe to meet in person. Even with CDC reassurance, the House delayed proceedings until they considered a bill to allow virtual meetings and if so, whether that should apply to the congressional elections of a president and vice president. On and on the anxious and indecisive prattling resounded in the halls of Congress. Until the cowards acted, he would not get his man into the White House.

One bright spot appeared. The armed forces of the United States. Military precautions around the country had become more evident as the Pentagon prepared to forestall any foreign power from exploiting the American political deadlock. By lopsided margins, opinion polls showed that of all the country's institutions, Americans trusted the military the most and Congress the least. If the political situation deteriorated further, the military could be counted on to bring about the law and order the country needed.

Although he could work with the military, it was too by the book for his taste. He preferred a system where he could buy and sell politicians. That wouldn't work so well with the military. They didn't make a career of running for office. But lately even politicians were getting out of hand. They had developed a tendency not to stay bought in a time of crisis. They would eventually follow the mob and turn on him so as to deflect blame for the country's fate. He might have no choice but to play ball with military men to halt creeping anarchy.

All this ruminating was giving him a headache . . . or was it something else? He had skimmed over the medical internet sites only to become more confused. He was playing doctor. He needed answers from the only real doctor who knew. He pecked a text to Dr. Angelo Mora: *Confirming meeting at Kinzie Steel. Symptoms persist. Treatment side effects??? Will this delay termination of transfusion protocol???* He tapped Send.

———

The ping on his smartphone startled Sebastian Senex awake from the twilight nap he had fallen into with images of vampires taking over

Promethean Pharma and sucking him dry. A reply text from Dr. Angelo Mora: *Confirming meeting at Kinzie Steel. Not to worry. Generic symptoms unlikely side effects. Manageable even if.*

*You're the one who should worry, Dr. Mora,* thought Senex. He deleted the text.

The Meridian Club manager entered the room aflutter. "The protestors are coming, Mr. Senex. Would you like to leave out the alley entrance?"

"No agitators will drive me from my home." He set down his snifter. "I want to talk to the police."

On the first floor he pulled back a brocaded drape and peeked outside. A mass of demonstrators with placards depicting an equation of dollar signs and coffins shouted at the police line holding firm before the front door. Another placard showed him as a cartoon spider atop the suburban headquarters of Promethean Pharma with dead bodies dangling from the web of dollar bills he had spun.

The police herded the crowd away from the entrance and spread the demonstrators along the sidewalk across the street from the club. The protestors made room for a procession of women coming down the street holding decorated vases. The women took up a position in a line on the sidewalk in front of the protestors.

These women couldn't intimidate him. He went out to confront them.

"That's him," a woman said. "That's Sebastian Senex . . . the murderer."

A police lieutenant pulled him back. "Stay here. I'll handle it."

The lieutenant swaggered across the street and talked to the women's spokesperson. She handed him her vase. He looked in. He took off his cap and made a slight bow toward the spokesperson. He walked back to the front of the Meridian Club with hat in hand. He smoothed his hair and fitted his gold-checkered lieutenant's cap back on.

The front line of women edged across the street toward the Meridian Club.

"Why are they coming over here?" Senex asked the lieutenant. "What's in those urns?"

"The way I see it, they got every right."

"They could be carrying explosives."

"No explosives. Only the ashes of their loved ones." The police lieutenant fiddled with his riot baton. "They say you killed them with your high drug prices."

———

Sebastian Senex pushed through the gold-colored revolving doors back into the Meridian Club so hard that the doors kept spinning after his entrance. He could hear the muffled shouts of the picketers burning in his ears as he stormed toward the bank of elevators to return to his penthouse refuge. He brushed past the manager asking if club management could help.

The elevator doors opened. A resident with untucked shirt and a dab of shaving foam on his chin exited, saying, "Have you heard what just happened?"

"Vandals are trying to break into this place."

"Not that."

"I don't have time for guessing games." He moved into the elevator and pressed the button for his penthouse floor.

"The Speaker of the House of Representatives died in an explosion."

Senex put his hand on the elevator door to stop it from closing.

"You don't say?"

"Yes, yes . . . he died in an explosion on his way to Capitol Hill from his new office in the Rayburn building. He was riding the underground subway train. The train failed to stop at the end of the line and crashed, setting off a bomb attached to the car."

"My, my." He shook his head. "What's this world coming to?"

Inside his penthouse he texted: *Congratulations Signor M.P. Mission accomplished.*

# CHAPTER THIRTY-SEVEN

Dr. Angelo Mora clumped on his cane toward Daisy Senex as she entered the Lincoln Park Conservatory across from her apartment on Lakeshore Drive. After Vincent Palomba's death, he'd learned that she tried to find solace at the conservatory.

Detective Jim Murphy had cornered him into a meeting later that day to probe about the murder-for-hire contract on the life of Leone. Mora had to find out where he stood with Daisy's father to determine his game plan when he met Murphy.

"Miss Senex, please stop." He touched her shoulder from behind. "I need to talk."

She turned and backed up. "Go away. You turned my father against me."

"I never lied." He leaned on his cane. "I never told him you revealed his secrets to Vincent."

"He blamed me just the same until he found out"—she pointed her finger—"you did it."

"Believe me." He held up his hand. "I deeply regret the pain I caused you."

She scurried away to the Fern Room, empty of other visitors. He lumbered after her until she stopped, allowing him to catch up. "If it hadn't been for me," he said, catching his breath, "you never would have met Vincent."

She moved slowly, without speaking, through a profusion of ferns spilling out from both sides into the narrow pathway as if to grab the intruders. He caught up with her.

"Remember." In the heat of the hothouse, pinheads of perspiration spread across his forehead. "I introduced you to him."

She sat on a white bench nestled in an alcove along the pathway.

"What do you want?"

"I feel uneasy around your father." He removed his hat. "Would you mind if I sit down?"

He sat down, taking her silence for consent.

"He acts irritated when I'm around, even though he tries to conceal it." Mora rested his cane against the bench. "Has he really forgiven me, as he says, for my indiscreet contact with Vincent?"

"He hasn't fired you, has he?" She folded her hands in her lap. "He'll get over it."

"Your father needs me . . . for now." He wrung his hands. "I only wish I could be as certain as you."

"Now you tell me something. Who killed Vince?"

"Are you sure he holds no grudge?"

"My father just needs a little time, like I told you." Her face turned hard and she blushed red. "Vince is dead. My love is dead." She sobbed into her handkerchief. When finished, she raised her face to Mora. "Did you kill Vince?"

"*Me?*" He dropped his cane. "Me?" He paused. "Like I am the animal who tore his heart out?"

"How do I know you didn't order his death?"

"Do I look like a key figure in the Mafia or in the South American cartels?" He picked up his cane and gripped it tight. "How would I, a respected research scientist, ever have such power in a million years?"

"Why don't you answer my question?"

"No. Again no. I had nothing to do with his death."

"Who murdered him?"

"It's all over the media. The Aztec Warriors."

"Puh-lease." She held up the palm of her hand to him. "I'm the expert criminologist. I know all about gangs." She stood up. "Those savages enforce orders, not give them."

He put his hat back on. "Since you know it all, perhaps I should leave."

"I didn't mean to offend you." She patted the space on the bench next to her. "Just tell me who's behind Vince's murder."

"I do not know."

"Why did he have to die that horrible death?" She twisted her handkerchief. "The brutality of it."

He shrugged.

"I must leave." She left him sitting on the bench and walked a few feet away. She turned. "I hope I've reassured you about my father's regard for you."

"I wish you had." Crestfallen, he ran a hand up and down his cane. "I wish you had."

———

Inside Garrett Popcorn Shops at Navy Pier, Detective Jim Murphy gawked at the fastidiously dressed Dr. Angelo Mora licking his thumb stained orangish-yellow with oil from his giant combo bag of caramel-cheese popcorn. He caught a whiff of the cheddar butter enticing him to order his own bag.

"We'd better get started," Murphy said. "But first . . . could you put down the popcorn?"

"Of course." Mora swallowed a final handful. "Sorry." He wiped his hands with several mini-napkins. He took a few more from the napkin holder and wiped his mouth, missing an orange-yellow spot under his lower lip. "This is my comfort food."

"Why do you need comfort food? Your conscience bothering you?"

"Not my conscience. My knee replacement."

"Why did you want to meet here?" Murphy asked.

"I have my reasons."

"Agreeing to meet you here instead of headquarters was a favor. It will shield you from the media . . . for now." Murphy put his elbows on the table. "Now you do me one. Confess what we already know from the Outfit shooter. You put a contract out on the life of a visiting police officer named Commissario Marco Leone."

"If you already know, why are we meeting?" Mora smirked. "You want something from me. What?"

"I figure Sebastian Senex has something to do with the disappearance of gangbangers." He rubbed his chin. "Tell me about that."

"How can I?" Mora drew his thumb and forefinger across his lips. "Senex has a doctor-patient privilege against my testimony."

"Never practice law in this state, Dr. Mora." Murphy shook his head. "The privilege doesn't apply to homicide cases." With a finger Murphy crushed a stray piece of popcorn on the table. "Start talking if you want a break."

Mora looked around and checked the entrance door. "Senex must not know I'm talking to you." Mora shivered as though a chilly wind had blown past him. "He has eyes and ears even in your police headquarters."

"We'll protect you if you play ball."

"What about the state's attorney?"

"Willing to recommend leniency . . . depending on the worth of your information."

"The extradition problem? I don't want to end up in an Italian prison."

"Our federal government controls extradition issues. Not Illinois."

"Either you protect me from extradition or I don't talk."

"I wish we could but we can't."

"Then no deal for what I may know about Senex." Mora stood up. "And I won't confess to solicitation for murder. Prove it in court."

"Wait a minute before you go."

Murphy bristled at the thought but he could see no other way. "I'll talk to my brother. He's a big shot in the Justice Department."

Bryan wouldn't let him forget the favor and would want something in return . . . like agreeing to warehouse their father in a nursing home. "Maybe he can find a way to keep you in the States."

"He'd better." Mora picked up his nearly empty bag of popcorn. "Or you'll get nothing from me."

# CHAPTER THIRTY-EIGHT

The warble of the rusting steam whistle signaled the afternoon shift at the Kinzie Steel mill. In a ramshackle office, Sebastian Senex fretted his next appointment would turn into a no-show. He had a loose end to take care of now that the Speaker had paid for his betrayal with his life. The Sinaloa cartel had settled accounts for him on that occasion. They were ready to help him again.

The appointment was the only reason he left the architectural elegance of Promethean Pharma's suburban campus for this smelly armpit of real estate in the extreme southern part of Cook County. Senex brushed off his desk the fine dust spewed out by a malfunctioning ventilation system.

He'd had to buy Kinzie Steel with the pretext of a tax write-off for reasons more important than the maximization of profits. It was a credible cover. The mill bled losses that reduced record profits over at Promethean Pharma. The dump of a plant had begun a death spiral where it would end up a scrap heap not even capable of producing losses. He liked the tax saving but he didn't have to like the industrial death and defeat that had haunted domestic mills for over thirty years. The United States needed a complete change from top to bottom. He and his kind would provide that change one way or the other. It was looking more like it would be the other.

Sharp knocks on the unlocked office door rousted Senex's reflections on the state of the nation.

With protective goggles raised to his forehead, the Slovak supervisor barged into his private office.

"You?" Senex arched his eyebrows. "I expected someone else."

"This not wait."

"What now?"

"More customer complaints about finished steel." He put his hands on his hips. "Not good."

"I don't have time for this." He only needed to hang on one more month until he could dump the mill at a loss and take the tax credit to offset Promethean Pharma's skyrocketing profits. His greatest fear was that the mill would start earning a profit with pushy eager beavers like the Slovak around. No one was going to deprive him of his financial losses.

"You better have time and listen good."

"Get out. Or I'll call security." Senex brought the receiver of the landline to his ear with one hand and prepared to dial with the other. "You're fired." The Slovak lowered his fist. "I go to union about you," he said, slamming the office door on the way out.

Unlike other steelworkers, the supervisor did not treat him as the white knight they thought he was. They fantasized he had come to save their jobs instead of using them to drive the steel mill further into the ground. The Slovak was one of those union agitators who had brought Kinzie Steel to its knees with their bloodsucking demands. Years ago they should have had a boss who told them to work harder and be grateful they even had a job. He was just putting the mill out of its misery with a mercy killing.

———

An almost inaudible rap on the office door. Dr. Angelo Mora peeked in.

"Come in, Angelo," Senex said. "I was expecting you."

Mora hesitated.

"I won't bite."

"Is everything OK?" Mora entered with hat in hand.

"Absolutely." He offered his hand. "Good to see you again, Angelo."

"Why did you want to see me, Mr. Senex?" Mora shook the outstretched hand.

"To discuss my medical condition, of course, and thank you personally for returning my youth." He took a bottle of prosecco from the minifridge and two tumblers out of the cabinet. He poured the straw-colored prosecco in both glasses and gave one to Mora. "A toast to you, my friend. You have turned back the hands of time." They clinked glasses with rising columns of bubbles.

A smile relaxed Mora's face.

"Will I need further transfusions of the Ponce de León protein?"

"Most likely not." Mora rubbed his goatee. "Even if you did, that would be no problem."

"And you're certain that the Polish assistant with the scar . . . What's that name you gave him?"

"Due."

"You're sure this Due knows the procedure as well as you."

"Absolutely. We think alike."

"Splendid." Senex refilled the tumblers with prosecco. "I'm feeling fine now, but what about those symptoms I told you about?"

"Just your body adjusting to biological change." Mora put down his glass. "Your metabolism will reset. I predict the symptoms will fade away."

"That's wonderful news."

He wanted to ask about his Huntington's but was afraid of the answer.

"I want to show you around my mill."

They went to the platform landing outside his office. Senex gripped the protective railing and pointed to the floor below. "I call that Dante's Inferno." Welding torches spewed sparks into the air. The red glow of flames billowed up through the mill's blast furnace. The yellow lava of molten iron mottled with red blotches spilled from steel ladles. His eyes and skin felt toasty.

On the floor, a dump truck unloaded scrap iron into a well-used vat looking like a gigantic rust bucket into which workers poured a heap of lime. A crane pushed the bucket into an obsolete blast furnace barely able to meet the minimum heat necessary for smelting. Soon after he sold the white elephant of a steel mill, the blast furnace would likely break down.

"Come on." He waved Mora onward. "I have a surprise for you."

"I'm quite hot." Mora fanned himself with his hand. "Maybe another time?"

"Nonsense. I plan to sell this wreck." He guided Mora forward by the shoulders. "There may not be another time." He looked down at the cause of Mora's slow pace. "Still problems with the knee?"

"Unfortunately."

They descended a winding metal staircase into the bowels of Dante's Inferno.

A foreman handed them each a yellow hard hat, a pair of tinted goggles, and a blue cooling vest for protection against environmental dangers. The steelworker advised the blast furnace needed repair. It was losing heat and unable to smelt the metal completely. Senex brushed away the advice and moved on with Mora. He had more important things to think about.

He stopped Mora and raised his voice above the increased decibels of clanging and banging. "I owe you a great deal, Dr. Mora, and I intend to repay you."

"You have been generous enough."

"I can prevent your extradition."

"Really?" Mora clasped his hand. "I'd be so grateful."

"One more thing." He held Mora by the shoulders. "I don't want to be a nervous Nellie, but how confident are you that I'll remain young without further treatment?"

"I'd stake my reputation on it." Mora's voice rang clear and confident above the cacophony. "I jump-started your metabolism. It is now rejuvenating on its own."

"What about my Huntington's?"

"I know it's in remission." Mora stroked his goatee. "It is unlikely the symptoms you experienced signal its return."

"How can you be so confident?" He looked away from Mora to mask his anxiety.

"Take heart, Mr. Senex." Mora paused. "At the university I was good at cards. I had a gift for calculating probabilities." He held the lapels of his suit coat and smiled. "I calculate you will overcome Huntington's because what I did is like fixing a computer. Your body has rejuvenated itself by going back to a point in time before the software malfunction called Huntington's disease took root." He hooked his thumbs in his belt. "I believe I have cured this disease by tricking the software of your DNA."

"If anyone could deceive Huntington's, it would be you, Dr. Mora."

"You are too kind, Mr. Senex."

The foreman had carried out his orders. The area personnel had been temporarily assigned to a make-work project elsewhere.

Senex led Mora under bare light bulbs flickering overhead. They moved past piled-up lumber and broken dump cars into the heart of Dante's Inferno. They walked onto a catwalk overlooking a thirty-five-foot pit belching up the sparking red liquid of molten metal. Bits and scraps of undigested metal bobbed like stew pieces in the witches' brew below. The heat was too low to smelt completely but that was of no consequence.

Before Mora could utter a word, two men sent by Miguel Perez rushed onto the catwalk disguised as workers. They twisted the doctor's arms behind his back and covered his mouth with duct tape. The men dragged him scraping his heels on the catwalk toward the pit. They looked to Senex. He gave the signal. The two pushed the traitor into the pit.

A man's silhouette rippled on the surface of the molten steel for a moment before fading away like the smile of the Cheshire cat.

# CHAPTER THIRTY-NINE

Jim Murphy's eyes opened. Somebody's arm prevented him from sliding off the barstool at Dugan's Irish pub. It was Marco's.

"You need sleep," his partner said.

He yawned and rubbed his eyes. "We all do."

Mondocane awoke from snoozing at the foot of Marco's stool and yapped at a patron down the bar having one too many. The commissario dropped a pretzel to divert Mondocane. The pointer snapped it down and returned to drowsing.

They had responded to an all-hands-on-deck order from the superintendent of police to quell the homicidal mayhem playing out on Chicago streets. Going home when a shift ended was not an option. No one knew how long the lull in the crime wars would last. If innocents hadn't been caught in the cross fire, he might have been tempted to imitate fellow officers who thought it shrewder to let the bad guys blow one another's brains out. It troubled him that every house mouse in the CPD endorsed this excuse.

Jim held his hand over the coffee cup as the bartender readied a nip of Jameson Irish whiskey. "Keep the Irish out of my coffee, or I'll never stay awake." The bartender focused on Marco. "Want a cup?"

"No, no." The Italian detective waved the thought away with his hand. "One does not order coffee at an American bar and expect the taste of coffee at an Italian bar." Marco yawned. "Pardon me . . . but I'd rather fall asleep than drink this caffeinated castor oil."

The flitting images and vocal noise on the overhead TV switched to a breaking-news report that grabbed their attention: A shooting massacre had occurred at the Convention against Ageism in Clearwater, Florida.

Accompanying the breathy staccato of the cable anchor, images of the shooter raced across the screen. An emaciated thirtysomething lay dead on the convention floor with tattooed arms outstretched and a Mohawk-style crest of green hair. The anchor reported that Florida police had found a political screed of over two hundred pages at the shooter's home.

The manifesto threatened revenge on the geriatric generation for throttling the future of the country's youth. The document cited chapter and verse of the ways the generation of senior citizens had messed up the twentieth century and threatened future generations. The extended longevity of what the writer called "The Longest Generation" and its refusal to give up the controlling levers of national power were cited as major social problems. The most promising solution, the manifesto concluded, was for a "happy hour" life termination in cases of excessive longevity, the details of which were to be worked out in a subsequent document. The anchor segued to talking heads debating whether ageism was the new racism.

"Glad that's not our problem," Jim said to the TV. The bartender switched channels to a soap opera. Jim turned to Marco. "Missing Persons is unable to locate Dr. Mora. What do you think happened?"

"He is frightened and hiding somewhere."

"Interpol has reported nothing." Jim choked down frustration and weariness with a handful of bar popcorn and coffee. "My hunch is he's still in the States."

"Does Senex know his location?"

"He claims shock about Mora's disappearance." An intestinal growl made him regret his choice of popcorn and coffee. "He's lying through his teeth but I can't prove it."

"I intended to inform you." Marco handed him a slip. "The Kinzie Steel supervisor . . . someone . . . with an accent worse than mine . . . called again. He demands you interview him about Senex."

"Demands?"

"I think he means . . . requests. Like me, he has a problem with English."

"What for? He refused to talk to me."

"He says he will talk now but only in person."

"He just has a beef with Senex over working conditions. A waste of my time."

"*Manzo?* . . . Beef?"

Jim chuckled at another linguistic pothole in transatlantic relations. It was the only fleeting moment of amusement he'd had in days. "American slang, my friend. It just means a complaint, a quarrel with someone."

"I think you should see him . . . beef . . . or not. Anything negative we learn about Senex we can, as you say, use for . . . leverage . . . against him."

"OK. But you pay the bar tab this time."

———

As Murphy and Leone were leaving Dugan's Irish pub with Mondocane on a leash, two CPD officers were entering, one in plain clothes working undercover and the other in uniform.

They blocked the way out.

The plainclothes cop Leone regretted knowing from police academy days. This loudmouthed acquaintance swayed forward, saying with a slur, "They claim you ratted out Commander Jack Cronin to the feds. Say it's ain't true, Murph."

"They came to me. I didn't go to them. I just told them what I knew."

"You rat fink." Wobbling on his feet, the uniformed officer to the right of Murphy followed up his companion's accusation with a swing.

Murphy ducked. The swing glanced off his shoulder.

Mondocane lunged and snapped at the attacker's leg. Leone heaved the dog back with the leash before he could do more than rip a pant leg with his teeth.

"The commander's a brother. Brothers stick together," the uniformed officer shouted at Murphy. "Only the brotherhood understands the daily shit we put up with."

"You sold out your brother, Murph," the plainclothes officer chimed in. "You betrayed us all when you betrayed our brother."

"The commander's not my brother officer. He would have let the Outfit kill Marco, my partner here, if he had his way." He put his hand on Leone's shoulder. "This foreign cop is my brother. Not the commander."

"Don't call us for backup," said the officer working undercover. He gave Murphy the finger.

Mondocane growled and bared his teeth.

The two stepped back and let them leave Dugan's Pub.

"We won't lift a finger for a snitch," the uniformed officer said. "If I did come, I'd likely shoot you instead of the perp."

Murphy cocked his fist, ready to deck the speaker. Holding back his partner's fist, Leone said, *"La madre degli idioti è sempre incinta."*

"Speak English, not Spanish," said the undercover cop. "Or go back to Mexico where you came from."

Leone led Murphy away. When they had walked a block in silence, Jim asked Marco, "What did you say back there? Trying to figure out what the hell you said cooled me off."

"The Italian saying is translated . . . the mother of idiots is always pregnant."

"You got that right." He threw his arm around Marco. "Thanks, bro."

Jim's cell buzzed inside his peacoat. The first deputy superintendent was on the line.

*It had to be trouble.*

The chief of the Bureau of Detectives informed him that in light of Commander Jack Cronin's abrupt resignation, he was in charge of the Thirteenth District until further notice.

# CHAPTER FORTY

**JANUARY 20, 2029**
**INAUGURATION DAY**
**WASHINGTON, DC**

Off duty, Detectives Jim Murphy and Marco Leone lingered around the donated TV in a corner of the Thirteenth District's roll-call room. Together with district patrol officers, they hooted when an announcement interrupted their favorite TV sitcom.

Dallas Taylor, elected by the Senate as vice president, automatically became president of the United States when the deadlocked House of Representatives failed to elect a president by noontime.

"Thank God, we finally have a president . . . even if it's through the back door of the vice presidency," the desk sergeant blurted out passing through the roll call room.

The newscaster continued: Nine vice presidents before had risen to the Oval Office by the death or resignation of the incumbent president. None before had ever risen because of the failure of the House of Representatives to elect a president before Inauguration Day. Leading constitutional experts affirmed that Dallas Taylor, unlike other vice presidents, only held the presidency until the House of Representatives got around to electing a president sometime after Inauguration Day.

Special programming on the life of interim president Dallas Taylor followed right afterward and preempted the normal January 20 broadcast schedule. A montage of images from Taylor's earlier life flashed across the screen. Baby Dallas in her mother's arms with proud father looking on. Girl Dallas winning tap-dancing contests across the country. Young-adult Dallas undergoing river baptism near her home in Dallas, Texas, and graduating from law school.

From real-life judge to megastar "Judge Dallas" on a nationally syndicated afternoon TV show. From there the charismatic descendant of slaves entered the House of Representatives, then the Senate, the vice presidency, and now bumped up to president of the United States . . . until the House elected a new president of the United States. Only in America.

"What do you know of her?" Marco asked Jim.

"Nothing good." He gritted his teeth, remembering the candidate's anger when he stopped her on Lakeshore Drive for driving a suspected stolen vehicle. "Usual loudmouth politician. She chewed me out for racial profiling and filed a beef with the commander for giving her a speeding ticket."

"What transpired?"

"The commander's a magician. He made the problem disappear without my knowledge." Jim folded his hands as if in prayer. "I pray we never meet again."

The TV programming switched to an update of the breaking-news announcement that Dallas Taylor had become president. As her first act of office, President Dallas Taylor ordered the chairman of the Joint Chiefs of Staff to lower the level of military alertness from DEFCON 3 to DEFCON 4.

Despite her causing trouble for him, he found himself . . . grudgingly . . . admiring her courage in making a four-star general back down from the unprecedented act of raising an alertness level on his own authority.

# CHAPTER FORTY-ONE

"Don't get high and mighty with me," Sebastian Senex shouted into his office telephone. "I didn't ask anything illegal. Just suggest to your head of the environmental division she shouldn't sue Promethean Pharma ... until we have a president of the United States."

"We have one," said Bryan Murphy at the Justice Department. "Dallas Taylor."

"That woman's only an acting president ... a placeholder until the House elects the real one."

"She's not essentially different from the nine previous vice presidents who took over when a president died or resigned."

"No president died or resigned or was unable to perform presidential duties," Senex said. "I can read the Constitution as well as any overpriced lawyer. It doesn't say what her authority is when Congress hasn't selected a president by Inauguration Day."

"Under the Twenty-Fifth Amendment even a vice president taking over as acting president during a president's disability has full presidential power. It shouldn't matter how they got to the Oval Office."

"Stop trying to change the subject." He wasn't going to let Murphy off the hook. "Are you going to protect Promethean from environmental lawsuits ... or not?"

Suffering from a splitting headache, Senex wanted this call over.

"Even if we don't file suit, the Environmental Protection Agency will go after you. Promethean Pharma's Illinois plant emitted methylene chloride in violation of EPA standards for air quality."

"I didn't help you get promoted to deputy attorney general only to hear excuses." Senex's secretary offered him a Tylenol with water. "Put in a good word for me with the EPA, you hear?" He popped the Tylenol.

"I'll see what I can do."

"If you can't see well enough . . . get eyeglasses. I want action."

"Let's get something clear. I can't help you with your Tampa facility. It's leaching ammonia into the Florida aquifer and endangering drinking water."

"That's been clear for a long time . . . too long."

"You admit it, then?"

"When have I ever admitted a violation? Listen more carefully, Bryan. It's been clear you can't do anything."

"Sorry, but the problem's too big and all over the media. The EPA found the stuff winds up in the Gulf of Mexico, poisoning fish."

Bryan Murphy didn't have to tell him. The nineteen-year-old girl near Tampa who set herself afire with kerosene outside the facility in protest had created a firestorm of bad press for Promethean Pharma. As a record number of get-well wishes flooded her hospital room, Promethean was becoming the poster child for corporate pollution.

The echo chamber of news outlets reverberated with the words she proclaimed to bystanders before torching herself . . . *You, the elders who run the world, you are destroying the future of your children on the altar of your money-grubbing materialism.*

"For once I agree with you, Bryan." He waved his secretary out of the office with the empty water glass. "You're not high enough on the totem pole to help with that one."

Either Brock Brewster or Roscoe Corker would deep-six any lawsuits for violation of federal air and water pollution standards when one or the other became president. It didn't look like Murphy would come through. And if he didn't come through, his hope of a political career was over.

"One more thing," Murphy said. "You've offered our best environmental litigators lucrative positions at Promethean Pharma. You did it just when they were ready to bring lawsuits against Promethean and other pharmaceutical companies."

"What a coincidence."

"It doesn't look good, Mr. Senex. It doesn't look good at all."

"This isn't a beauty contest, damn it."

"Did they accept?" Murphy asked.

"Of course. With the salary and prestige I offer, what did you expect?"

"You're open to obstruction of justice."

"There was no court proceeding in progress, or even an active investigation for that matter. My lawyers say I'm in the clear. There's only one question you'll have to answer, sooner or later, if we're to continue our relationship."

"What's that?"

"Are you on my side or not?"

# CHAPTER FORTY-TWO

"I am not Czech. I come from Slovakia." The scowl of the Kinzie Steel supervisor looked fierce behind the Vandyke beard. "Two countries now, not one. Don't you read newspaper?"

Jim Murphy resisted going defensive with the big-biceped steel-worker in Mickey Mouse suspenders and hard hat. Although the steel-worker carried a chip on his shoulder, he didn't want to waste time knocking it off. He pretended to listen so he could get through the useless witness statement as quickly as possible.

The supervisor cracked a hard-boiled egg on the lunchroom bench.

"I'm here, like you wanted. What do you have to say?"

He popped the egg into his mouth and jawed it. Yolk crumbs the color of the hard hat stuck to his chin. Lovely.

"I dunno if I want to talk. You no look like cop."

"These are my street clothes. I'm a detective."

"I dunno. I talk to your boss instead."

He had worked enough domestic abuse cases to know the type. They compensated for inferiority feelings by putting others down. Playing nice-nice would get him nowhere. He knew what might. "OK, Senex warned me not to waste my time with you." He put his notebook back into his pocket. "Said you were a dumb foreigner."

"That crook say that? I talk plenty about that crook." He put down his open-faced sandwich of ham and red peppers on sourdough rye.

"Customers say steel too brittle. They will not pay. They want to know why."

"Why should the police care?"

"One customer think police might care."

"Who?"

"First . . . do me favor."

"What?"

"I have noisy neighbor. Never stops music late at night." He took a bite out of his sandwich. "Can you say to him to stop?"

"Sure." A five-minute phone call was about the right price . . . not a minute more.

"Go-o-o-o-d," the Slovak said, speaking with his mouth full. He swallowed the sandwich bite with the throat contraction of a boa constrictor.

"Contact customer, Ambrose Storage Tank Company. Senex say his tests show steel fine. Company not believe Senex. Company has Vulcan Metallurgy in Chicago do test. Steel failed test."

"Why is that important?"

"Metal expert at Vulcan . . . smart man like me." The Slovak rapped on his hard hat with his knuckles. "He say strange chemicals found in steel. He tell me is suspicious."

"Why?"

"Expert not say. You contact expert at Vulcan Metallurgy." The Slovak removed his hard hat. "I remember. He go on vacation tomorrow. He want to see you today."

He could stop off at Vulcan Metallurgy on the way back to district headquarters.

"Before you go. Here is name and telephone number of neighbor."

The Slovak handed him a slip of paper.

He pocketed the slip.

"Neighbor sleep during day. Angry if people wake him up. He is a police officer like you."

"Just what I need."

"Do not forget to call."

"I wouldn't dream of forgetting."

———

Later that day, a bald-headed man in polyester red pants and orange polo shirt burst through the swinging doors into the reception room of Vulcan Metallurgy. "Hi, I'm Ollie, the chemist. This way, Detective Murphy."

As they walked into the laboratory, Ollie waved him over to the optical spectroscope that analyzed and measured the percentage of chemical elements in steel samples. He explained how the spectrometer recorded the percentages of twenty-three different elements found in steel samples. And then he reexplained it.

The chemist reminded Detective Murphy of his old high school chemistry teacher. He had the same habit of repeating himself as though he were teaching a class of dense adolescents.

"Any questions?"

"No."

"Take a look," Ollie said.

He gave up pretending to understand the chemical symbols running across the screen in various percentages. The high point of his chemistry class had been learning on his own how to make a stink bomb from match heads and ammonia. The prank had earned him a week of detention at Saint Ignatius High School. "What am I looking at?"

Ollie rolled his eyes. "Let me explain. But, please, Detective Murphy, ask a question if you don't understand. There's no such thing as a bad question, only bad answers."

The chemist held forth on how Ambrose Storage Tank Company had asked his employer to do some purity tests on samples of steel it had purchased from Kinzie Steel. Ambrose complained the steel had recently grown harder and more brittle. Kinzie Steel said no problem existed.

"Who was right?"

"Ambrose Storage Tank Company." Ollie bent over to look at the results flickering on the monitor. "Carbon is the most important element in steel production." He scrolled the monitor with his finger to check out the phosphorus percentage. "The levels of carbon and phosphorous are especially elevated when compared to earlier samples." He added, "Got that?"

"Yeah, I got it." He bent down to look at the symbols in a knowing manner. "Any other impurities?"

"Sulfur content is too high." Ollie scratched his bald head. "We ran a different test to confirm these results. Came up the same."

"How's the steel harmed?"

"Sulfur made the steel harder but with a loss of ductility." Falsely assuming he didn't know the meaning of ductility, the chemist continued, "That means the steel got too brittle. It couldn't be stretched like before. Got it?"

"Let's move on, Ollie."

The chemist walked over to a machine clamping the ends of a steel bar. "Watch." He activated the machine, which tested tensile strength up to sixty thousand pounds of pull at each end. "Want me to explain tensile strength?"

"I get it. You should know I did pass chemistry." He failed to add: just barely.

The machine whirred and the bar broke in two. Ollie examined the halves. "Much too brittle compared to earlier samples. Too dangerous for Ambrose to use."

"Anything else?"

"Only that the nitrogen, hydrogen, and oxygen levels were also elevated. The excess nitrogen aggravated the brittleness problem."

"Is that all?"

"Why yes? You can draw your own conclusions."

"Just tell me why you thought I should waste time coming here."

"Waste time? Maybe, maybe not."

"What do you mean?"

"You said you got everything I told you. Can't you figure it out?"

"I don't have time for twenty questions."

"You say you passed chemistry. Remember the acronym called CHNOPS?"

He felt a sweat coming on. On the tip of his tongue.

*What was it?*

"Got it! . . . The six most common elements of life."

"Bingo, Detective Murphy." Ollie gave him a high five. "Carbon, hydrogen, nitrogen, oxygen, phosphorus, and sulfur."

"Why would Kinzie Steel want to add these elements?"

"Beats me." Ollie smiled slyly. "Unless life got into the molten steel."

"Like plants and animals falling . . . or dumped . . . into the vats."

"Yep."

"Say." He stroked his chin. "Are you saying they could even come from—"

"Humans?"

"How about an answer and not a question."

"I only deal with chemicals. Humans are your turf."

# CHAPTER FORTY-THREE

In the community sunroom of Northwestern Hospital, Jim Murphy promised himself he'd only wait fifteen minutes more. He came only because his sister had implored him. Commander Jack Cronin let out word to Katie that he wanted to see his godson. To determine whether he would have felt remorse had he not come, he imagined the commander's death occurring without a hospital visit. No feeling came. Only the same frozen indifference.

Bone-tired from extra shifts triggered by the violent crime wave, he sat down on a brown vinyl sofa next to a forever-green plastic fig tree impaling a wooden container box. Too agitated to sleep, he closed his eyes and rested his head on the corner of the sofa. His free-floating thoughts refused to leave Commander Jack Cronin.

After the Justice Department's prosecution against the commander for public corruption and violation of civil rights went viral, Cronin's closet of sordid secrets tumbled open to public view. Among sundry crimes, he and others under his direction had robbed drug dealers, used bats to beat arrestees on their heads cushioned with Styrofoam to prevent telltale bruises, and dangled suspects out upper-story windows until they confessed. During the constant drumbeat of media revelations and in the midst of his trial, the commander collapsed in the courtroom during the arraignment proceeding. The part of the press corps that knew him best suspected he was faking. He wasn't.

The federal judge postponed the trial until defendant Cronin recovered from a heart attack under hospital care.

Who was this man he thought he knew?

His father and the commander had once been partners, as the commander never ceased to remind him. After Patrick Murphy discovered the commander had slipped his wife money to get the family through hard times, his father ended any relationship with Cronin. Patrick Murphy was not the same afterward. Jim's own relationship with his father tumbled downhill as his father's Alzheimer's spiraled out of control. The dementia patient now stung his son with a denial of paternity.

Jack Cronin escalated up the CPD hierarchy to commander, while Patrick Murphy retired as a patrolman. The meek may inherit the earth, but the date of inheritance remained a long way off. No matter how much municipal corruption the media bloodhounds exposed, a rat who would not rat on other rats had an underground respect in the bars and businesses of the city that an honest cop like his father would never have. After all, this was the city that cheered when Al Capone entered Wrigley Field to watch the Cubs play.

He had rarely seen Katie, his sister, as angry as when he told her of his fatalistic interpretation of city life. *You had better quit if you're burned-out because a self-pitying cop is a useless mope to himself and others. Sign for the team of your choice and play your heart out*, she'd said. *Or get your butt off the playing field. It's called life. The only losers are those who think themselves so. And Dad never did. He was a tough turkey who never cared how others labeled him.*

Sure, the commander was on the take, she said during his meeting with his sister the night before, but he was once a friend to Dad and had helped the family in those days. Whatever he had become, Jack Cronin helped a lot of people in the old neighborhood. *Remember how he took you under his wing and protected you from the blowup over the Millennial assassination? You can't turn your back on him. Love the sinner and not the sin, like Father Malachy used to say.*

The words of their heated conversation had burned into him.

*He would have let Marco be shot to death.*

*Let it go, Jimmy. He denied knowing what the Outfit was up to. You've got to give him the benefit of the doubt. You owe him. Go see him tomorrow.*

Katie had a point. The commander was a Mafia flunky. That didn't mean he knew what they intended. He just followed an order to make his godson leave the Taylor Street area. They didn't have to tell their errand boy the reason why. A good flunky doesn't ask why. Who could say for sure he knew about the hit before it happened?

It didn't matter. He'd had enough of Commander Jack Cronin.

He opened his eyes and shook his head to clear it.

He got up to leave when the commander, stomping along the hallway on a walker, stopped at the sunroom entrance with a peroxide blonde on his arm. Looking half the commander's age, the blonde wore a white smock and black trousers. Her outfit helped him remember her as a Bridgeport manicurist and the commander's on-again, off-again Polish girlfriend. The commander waved.

He couldn't bring himself to either wave back or leave. So he stood glued to the spot until the commander hobbled over in his pajamas and bathrobe. The manicurist girlfriend helped him onto the end of the sofa so he could bask in the sunlight.

The blonde set up her portable manicure table next to the sofa where the commander sat. She unfolded her camp stool and sat down facing him, placing his left hand on a cushioned handrest fastened to the table. They smiled at each other. She unpacked the tools of her trade from a leather kit.

"Thanks for comin', Jim."

"I only came because Katie asked." He folded his arms. "I was about to leave."

"Don't matter none." The commander's right hand trembled. "It does my heart good just to see you . . . and Lord knows, the old ticker needs some good."

"What about your heart?"

"Not good." He rested the trembling hand on his knee. "This trial will be the death of me." The sunlight on the commander's pale face under a shock of silver hair exposed him drained of this life and at the door of the next.

"Why did you want to see me?"

"Is it true you ratted me out to the feds?"

"I told them what I knew when they asked." He clutched the back of the sofa with his hand. "Is that why you wanted me here? To tell me what a rat I am?"

The girlfriend manicurist looked up, startled, with a nail clipper in hand.

"Should she be here?" Murphy asked.

"I've got nothing to hide from her."

She looked at the commander. He pointed to his hand on the cushioned handrest. She went back to clipping his nails.

"I can't blame you." The commander stopped until a fit of coughing ended. "How could you tell them what an angel I was?" He forced a hollow laugh.

"If I'm not here to be chewed out," he said, "tell me why I'm here."

She deposited the fingernail clippings in a gold-spangled toiletry bag.

"Take care of those clippings, honey, like I told you," he said. He shifted back to face Murphy. "You are my son."

"You mean godson."

"No. I mean my son."

"I thought my father was the one with Alzheimer's." Murphy leaned in and raised his voice. "It turns out you're sicker in the head than him."

"Hear me out, lad."

"Before you rave on, get rid of her. I'm not comfortable with her around."

"Honey," the commander said, "you'd best get crackin'." She packed up and left.

"When your father and me were partners, your mother and him were goin' through a rough patch in their marriage. They weren't talkin'. She thought of leavin'. We had a fling, about a month, when she called it off. She found out she was pregnant and came to me, sayin' it was mine. She bein' a good Catholic girl and all, abortion was out of the question. I knew it was mine, so I volunteered to take care of the situation, like financial issues, you see, and—"

"You dirtbag."

With one hand he grabbed the commander by the top of his terrycloth robe. "Take it back."

"I can't." Cronin's eyes reddened. "No one can take back the past."

"It could have been my father's baby." He raised a fist. "You just want to make me your child, because you have no one and no one . . . outside of that blonde bimbo . . . wants you, you pathetic con man."

"Use your head, lad." The commander tapped his temple with a forefinger. "Why would a con man like me slip her money for the tyke if he didn't know it was his?" He stuck out his chin as if it were a dare for Murphy to shoot a jab. "Are you calling your mother, that saint of a woman . . . if ever there was one . . . a liar?"

"Are you calling her a whore?" He pulled himself together. "I don't believe it." He lowered his fist and let go of the robe.

"It's not a matter of belief."

"I don't trust you. How do I know you're not screwing with me?"

"You're looking at the proof and you don't know it yet."

"Enough of the crazy talk."

"Talk to Katie, then." The commander smoothed out the top of his robe and shooed away a visitor who asked if he needed help. "Right before your mother died she told Katie. She said tellin' your father was a big mistake. It killed their marriage. She stayed with him for you kids."

"You bet your ass I'll talk to Katie." He felt numb and struggled for words, but all he could do was say, "You bet your ass."

"I'm sorry for a lot of things, but not that you're my son."

"I'd be as sorry as hell if I were your son." To relieve his turmoil, he sprang up for a complimentary cup of coffee at a self-serve station.

With his back to the commander, he took a deep breath and a swig of stale coffee. Was Cronin losing it? Was he getting even for Murphy talking to the FBI? His head told him what his heart didn't want to hear. The truth and not the motive alone counted. He couldn't head out the door in retreat. He had to shove its falsity into the commander's face. With cup in hand he returned to the sofa.

"I can't be your son." He rotated the coffee cup in his hands. "I'm not like you at all . . . whatever physical likeness we share."

"Do you think I was always what I am?" The commander tightened the robe around his shoulders. "I graduated, bright and shiny, from DePaul University and full of ideas about how the world was supposed to work. I came from a family of Irish cops. By golly, I was goin' to be the best of the best. But I slipped in the slime of the city's underbelly." His forehead wrinkling, he looked down at the floor. "And I couldn't raise myself up."

"Confess to a priest, not me." The commander wanted connection but Murphy felt none.

"If I could change things I would . . . but I can't."

"You could flip and help clean slime from Chicago."

"I'm not a snitch or a rat or whatever you want to call it." Cronin straightened up. "I'm only loyal to family, friends, and tribe in that order . . . and there's no negotiating that."

"Are the mobsters and political hacks your friends?"

"They helped me. So I help them. They don't rat on me; I don't rat on them." The commander tightened the sash on his robe. "The law of reciprocal favors is the currency that makes this city go round. It is the only moral commandment. What the favor is has no more significance than how a robber or a reverend got the dollar bills he uses to pay his debts." Cronin shrugged his shoulders. "Don't ask, don't tell. That's the way it is, lad."

"What civilians call the blue wall of police silence, right?" He rose and buttoned up his leather jacket. "The wall that enclosed your mind before prison walls enclose your body."

"You are my son. Nothin' can change that."

"I don't want to meet again. We can't be related."

"Who's buildin' walls in his mind now?" The commander waved to an orderly who entered the room. "I'm done for. I know that. So, I whispered your name to the superintendent to take over District Thirteen when I'm gone."

"Don't BS me. The captain is next in line."

"That doofus can't do it. He's goin' on medical leave anyway."

The orderly helped the commander up from the sofa onto his walker. "Would you like," the orderly asked, "to share a lunch with Commander Cronin in his private room?"

"Afraid not. I'd get indigestion."

# CHAPTER FORTY-FOUR

"If it is true, why didn't you tell me before?" Jim Murphy asked. "We never hid anything from each other." He slid off the barstool at Dugan's Irish pub. "I'll be back in a minute." Stress made him hungry, or maybe he was afraid of her answer. He walked over to the popcorn machine.

Ever since the commander had taken a protective shine to Katie as a little girl, she had stars in her eyes whenever she mentioned the white knight of Bridgeport. He'd always bring her a treat when their father invited the commander home to share a meal after finishing a police shift together. Jim Murphy thought that where the commander was concerned, his sister was too biased to be believed. He filled the chipped plastic bowl with popcorn to quell his gnawing stomach and returned to the bar.

"I couldn't bring myself to hurt you. That's why I didn't tell." Katie's eyes turned teary. "I knew this would rip your insides up. You and Bryan are at each other's throats, as it is, without making things worse."

"He told you I was his son to get even with me."

"Mom told me."

Spilling some on the counter, he popped a handful of popcorn into his mouth. That had to be it. The commander had every motive to hoodwink him because he had ratted . . . informed . . . really only confirmed what the FBI already knew . . . at least mostly knew about Commander Cronin's trail of corruption. Jack Cronin wanted revenge.

What better way to take revenge on him than to claim he was that douchebag's son?

He swallowed, almost choking, but washed the popcorn down with a bit of Guinness. The commander wanted to stick it to him for being a rat . . . and maybe he was a bit of a rat. He hated doing it, but he had to. The choice was either protecting his career or telling the truth when the FBI came calling. He chose the truth. The truth will set you free, the Gospel reported, but the truth had also made him miserable. He hadn't fully escaped the upside-down ethics of Chicago's DNA.

"He said what he did for revenge. Even if he smeared our mother."

"You're not listening." She tapped her ear. "Or you don't want to." She spoke as though to a child. "I said Mom told me about the affair. He didn't."

"Mom wouldn't do that."

"She said she did. With him. She was human, like you and me."

"I refuse to believe it." He hunched over, resting his elbows on the bar, and ground his knuckles into his cheeks. "Dad never said anything to me."

"Jimmy." She put her hand on his shoulder. "Remember how we couldn't understand why Dad started cold-shouldering you?"

"Not a mystery." His shoulders slumped. "He got tired of his lovable-loser son, first dropping out of the priesthood, then—"

"That wasn't it." She gave him a tap on the arm. "Around that time, Mom told him what she had done. About her pregnancy with you. She told me that aside from her affair with the commander, telling our father was the biggest mistake of her life. He couldn't handle it. It soured him on life, on her . . . and on you, the commander's son."

He grabbed for another handful of popcorn but stopped. The image of Angelo Mora guzzling popcorn, his mouth greasy-yellow with oil, trying to eat his troubles away. He pushed the bowl down the bar counter. It overturned and spilled its contents.

"I could have been Dad's son, even if she was having an affair."

"I suggested that too." She shook her head. "Mom told me they hadn't had conjugal relations, as she put it, for a long time because of their marriage problems. They even slept in separate beds then, Jimmy. You know that."

"Mom wasn't thinking right." He wiped his hand across his forehead. "The cancer—"

"She told me before the cancer."

"They didn't give her enough pain pills. She didn't know what she was saying."

"Are you feeling alright? You're not listening. It was before the pains, before the cancer." Katie picked up the popcorn on the counter and replaced it in the bowl. "It's no use, Jimmy. You've got to accept it."

She took his hands into hers.

"You didn't tell him, did you?" he asked.

"Tell who?"

"Bryan."

"Of course not, you ninny."

Ever since they were kids, she would only call him that when he had pushed her to the limit of her patience. He backed off and turned his attention to the overhead TV.

"Think it over." She buttoned her cloth coat and left a tip for her shandy. "I've got to get back to work at the blood bank."

"I have thought it over. I'm not buying it."

# CHAPTER FORTY-FIVE

Waiting for the telephone call from the Chinese minister of foreign affairs, President Dallas Taylor had never felt more alone than sitting by herself in the Oval Office at seven in the morning on her second day in office and wondering what she had gotten into.

If her formal condolences weren't enough to satisfy him, she'd have an international incident on her hands. The flare-up of COVID-28 in China had angered Chinese citizens against the government for what looked like a repeat of the COVID-19 disaster. The president of the People's Republic of China felt cornered by domestic unrest. He might be tempted to lash out against the United States for the incident and turn the anger against him into xenophobia against Americans.

She shook her head in sorrow at the report on her desk, manufactured from the timbers of the British frigate, HMS *Resolute*. An ex-student armed with semiautomatic weapons had slaughtered five students, including a Chinese exchange student, at the University of Illinois at Chicago and injured three more before taking his own life.

The killing of a Chinese student elevated the domestic tragedy into an international flash point. Sebastian Senex aggravated her discontent by offering free and immediate blood donations to surviving victims in Chicago hospitals. He coupled his offer with public carping about her slowness in organizing a federal response to the tragedy. The man had done everything he could to undercut her bid for high office. He would now do whatever it took to remove her from the Oval Office.

Any minute her staff would connect her to the Chinese Ministry of Foreign Affairs to learn whether she could dissuade the Chinese from blacklisting American communities with high gun-crime rates by not approving universities in those areas for study-abroad programs. The European Union piled on by issuing a travel advisory about gun violence to its students studying in the United States.

She had come to the temporary presidency through the back door of a constitutional crisis, and she'd probably be kicked out the front door in a matter of days by the House of Representatives when they elected a president.

She was unprepared for this crisis. Even when the White House beehive buzzed later in the morning with the full complement of about four hundred White House worker bees, she'd still feel alone and in the dark. She was the isolated queen bee.

Retiring after two terms, the outgoing president had refused to attend her swearing-in ceremony. He declined putting together a transition task force to brief her team on the pretense she was only a transitory president. Aside from his political ties to Roscoe Corker, she suspected the former president couldn't abide her because she was an African American woman in the Oval Office. Maybe he could abide an African American or a woman, but not both at the same time.

Due to his influence, she received only minimal national security briefings from the intelligence community. The secretary of defense and the chairman of the Joint Chiefs of Staff, holdovers like the rest of the cabinet, were happy to support the cold shoulder. They resented what they considered her presumptuousness in lowering the DEFCON level of defense against their advice. The gossip around town was that none planned to resign because they worried she wasn't up to the challenge of the presidency.

"Here's your morning wake-up call, Madam President." In strode Emily James, her chief of staff and longtime friend, with the problems of the day. She plopped down in a chair at the side of the president's desk.

"What's with the 'Madam President,' Emily?" She grimaced. "Call me Dallas in private or Ms. President if we're among others . . . but not Madam President. Sounds like I run a Texas whorehouse."

"Gotcha." James grinned.

"Now, down to business. What's up?"

"Number one. Still no call from the Chinese foreign minister. Number two. The president of the undergraduate student government at UIC is organizing a citywide boycott of all colleges and high schools in Chicago until Congress bans semiautomatic weapons."

"Number two's as welcome as an outhouse breeze." Dallas Taylor rose from her executive chair behind the desk. She looked out the three windows behind her desk with her hands clasped behind her back. "All those kids with nothing to do. It means even more gang shootings and crime in Chicago." Too few kids in Chicago's public school were ready for college, and too many dropped out. That made her mad. A few good teachers and a no-nonsense principal had set her on the right path. "Let's contact the student leaders and invite them to the White House instead to express their concerns . . . if they call off the boycott."

"Number Three. The media—"

"Don't tell me. I know." Taylor twisted her red scarf. "Shooting survivors have been booked on media programs. They'll call for thoughts and prayers on behalf of the victims. There'll be a lot of fuss and feathers, but nothing will happen. Get a bill prepared and find a sponsor for a ban on semiautomatic weapons. We've got to do something."

"I don't advise that. Nothing. Absolutely nothing will happen on this issue, until the House selects a president."

"Who knows when that'll be? We have to act."

"Hold off. Do the photo ops. Meet the students. Prepare the groundwork."

"You're right." She sank back into her executive chair. "Congress can't walk and chew gum at the same time. Let's wait till the election's settled. Can't be long now."

"Number four, I saved for last. You'll love it." The chief of staff shook her head in disbelief. "A breakaway group from the American Gun Association is going around saying Chicago should hire unemployed gang members to protect city schools."

"Should I respond?"

"Not worth it. Even the association thinks that breakaway group is wacky. In fact, the association—"

The chief of staff's cell buzzed.

"What's up?" Taylor asked.

"The Chinese responded."

"Well?"

"For now they're suspending any blacklisting of high-crime American cities."

"Hallelujah! Now—"

James motioned for Taylor to wait a minute while she gave the call her full attention. Her eyes looked at the president in disbelief. She shook her head and disconnected the call.

"What's going on, Emily?"

"Must be a translation problem."

"What's the problem?"

"They decided not to take any action until the House elects what they call a real president."

# CHAPTER FORTY-SIX

Jim Murphy hunched over the hard kneeler in his pew at the requiem Mass. In the center aisle rested a casket covered in a white pall with an embroidered gold crucifix. Inside the casket, newly sprinkled with holy water, lay the corpse of Commander Jack Cronin.

A former police chaplain, the officiating priest eulogized the saintly virtues and stellar accomplishments of the deceased despite the pastor's prohibition of eulogies. A brief homily allowed by church regulation ballooned into what Murphy considered a near plea for canonization. Righteous, generous, law abiding, Irish gift of gab, Knights of Columbus, parish lector, surely with the Lord in heaven, blah, blah, blah, and so it went.

The parishioners and political somebodies from all across the city, numbering in the hundreds, listened enraptured to the idolization of the corrupt cop. Even the pint-sized alderman with the default scowl looked ecstatic. The community had hallucinated its own reality, and in that reality loyalty to clan and kin was the highest virtue. In this reality, not only were all politics local but also the definition of right and wrong.

It was to be expected. The departmental buzz was that years ago the commander had given the chaplain a pass when the reverend got nabbed as a john in a prostitution sting. For once Murphy agreed with his bookish brother. The Latin motto for the city should be *manus manum lavat* . . . one hand washes another . . . instead of *urbs in horto* . . . a city in a garden.

Murphy's ears tingled and his stomach churned. Speak no evil of the dead, Katie said . . . but whitewash them? This figment of haloed imagination called the commander was unknown to those who knew the canny cop. It was as though the commander's arrest for obstruction of justice, police brutality, and lying to the FBI had never happened in the old neighborhood. "Had Commander Jack Cronin not been betrayed and hounded," the ex-chaplain exclaimed, "this exemplary man would have avoided his untimely demise. Instead his enemies tormented him until even the lion heart of this local hero gave out and he passed from us to his reward in heaven. He gave his life to this community just as our Savior, Jesus Christ, gave his life for us."

*Untimely demise?* The priest had airbrushed away the death that dare not be named in the never-never land of communal denial. The commander had in fact blown his brains out with a service revolver. Never-never land could not survive this truth. The suicide did not fit the narrative of this clone of Christ dying on the cross of scandal for the salvation of his community.

Without uttering the name of the Judas who sat among them, the priest paused to stare in Murphy's direction. Craned toward him, familiar and wordless faces accused him of betraying the commander and becoming an enemy of the community. Stumbling over knees and feet and enduring sour glances, Murphy lumbered out of the pew and fast paced down the center aisle toward the exit.

Outside the church he ran into his brother, arriving late for the funeral services due to a flight delay. "What do you think you're doing?" Bryan asked.

"And a brotherly hello to you too." Jim stood in the way of his brother on the church steps. "I'm getting fresh air after all that hot air inside."

"Show some respect."

"Respect is earned, not ordered."

"I shouldn't expect you'd stand up for your own." His brother frowned. "You let him hang out to dry."

"Hang out to dry?" Jim walked down a step to come face-to-face with his brother. "I'm the bad guy for cooperating with the FBI? You're supposed to be on the side of law enforcement. A little hypocrisy going on here, bro?"

"You owe the commander. Before he went down, he pulled strings to put you in charge of the Thirteenth District."

"I didn't ask for it." He put his hands on his hips. "I owe him nothing."

"What game are you playing with Senex?" Bryan asked.

"What do you mean?"

"You know . . . your investigation of him."

"What's it to you? You never took an interest in what I was doing." His brother had been general counsel for Promethean Pharma. "I get it now. You're Senex's errand boy come to get me off his back."

"Don't tempt me, buster." Bryan assumed the tough-guy pose of their early years when he used to intimidate his younger brother. "Leave Senex alone if you have any smarts."

"Or else what, big brother? You gonna wrestle me again into your haunted closet with ghosts . . . like you did when I was a kid?" Jim jiggled his arms and legs. "Look, I'm quaking in fear."

"I'm only looking out for your best interests."

"I heard enough baloney inside without yours. Senex promised you the political moon if you jump through his crooked hoops, didn't he?" He didn't have to listen to Bryan, who told him many years ago that he had to fight his own playground battles. "Aren't you the big brother who told me to take care of myself?"

"Just like you take care of Dad." Bryan stabbed a forefinger at his brother. "I'm suing to remove Dad from your custody."

"Like I don't know." Jim glared at Bryan. "Katie told me. You want him to rot in a loony bin."

"Look, Jim." Bryan backed down a step. "I know we can't get along. But for both our sakes and Dad's, you can't let him continue to drive a car."

"I tried stopping him. He says he'll only listen to you because . . . because I'm not his son." Jim's shoulders sagged. "For his sake . . . not mine . . . talk to him before you leave."

"The only solution is that I get custody. Now let me pass."

# CHAPTER FORTY-SEVEN

With his testimony on prescription drug prices concluded before the Senate Special Committee on Aging, Sebastian Senex hurried from this waste of time to an unexpected meeting. The invitation had come while he was testifying in DC. His first impulse was to refuse. When told the reason for the invitation was unknown, his curiosity got the better of him.

On the way, Senex looked out the limousine window at the darkening DC skyline. More snow and cold weather. Before his biological transformation, his hours-long testimony defending Promethean Pharma would have exhausted him. No longer. As he left the limo, he felt a spring in his step, keeping up with a thirtysomething staffer. The staffer guided him into an enclosed alley on H Street, two blocks away from the White House, and through an underground tunnel to the White House basement.

"Where are we going?"

"She wants to see you in the Oval Office."

They entered the private elevator to the Oval Office.

"She wants this meeting kept confidential."

"Suits me just fine," he said, not wanting his Hinky Dink cronies to think he colluded with Dallas Taylor behind their backs. "It would be bad for my reputation otherwise."

She'd probably invited him for another lecture on the lack of minorities in the upper management of Promethean Pharma. Just like she used to as a Congressional Black Caucus member out to make a name for herself at his expense. It was mutual dislike at first sight. He looked forward to refusing whatever she wanted, except for one request: helping her resign from the presidency. She was in over her head and had to know that by now.

Concealed behind a wall panel when not in use, the elevator opened into the Oval Office. She sat at the Resolute desk, bent over a sheaf of documents, without acknowledging his presence. He was onto her attempt to intimidate him. The elevator door closed behind them. The staffer replaced the wall panel and departed.

Dallas Taylor looked up at him through her reading glasses and nodded to a chair at the side of her desk. He sat down, placing his palms on his thighs and sitting tall and straight. He locked eyes with her, vowing not to be the first to speak or break eye contact. The woman showed no sartorial shame gussied up in her glitzy hoop earrings foreign to the stately décor of the White House. The only redeeming feature was the smart white-knit suit with a pearl necklace worn in place of her trademark hot-pink pantsuit.

"Care to join me in an afternoon glass of bourbon with branch water?" She held up a glass. "I find an occasional drink refreshes me."

"I don't imbibe." Senex sniffed. "I would think it interferes with your work."

"Just about every one of our best presidents did imbibe." She put the glass away. "FDR, JFK, and LBJ . . . and they all did quite well."

"That's your opinion." He shifted in his chair. "Why am I here?"

"One reason only." She removed her reading glasses and let them drop on her lanyard. "To inform you Promethean Pharma must comply with its statutory duty to negotiate with the secretary of Health and Human Services over the sale price of the vaccine called Anoflix." She opened and closed the eyeglass frames hanging from her neck. "Otherwise my attorney general will sue Promethean for an excise tax amounting to seventy percent of the drug's gross sales."

"Go ahead." He leaned in toward her. "The newfangled federal statute is unconstitutional. It's a socialist scheme to destroy the free market."

"What free market?" she asked, her voice rising. "Your company has the patent and is the only one ready to make the upgraded vaccine for COVID-28. The director of the Centers for Disease Control and Prevention tells me the old vaccine is useless for this new strain detected in China." She uncrossed her arms and took in a deep breath. "You don't have to like me, but why not negotiate for the good of the country?"

"Because I spent almost six billion dollars in research and development of new drugs . . . besides an additional two billion for Anoflix. Because I assembled the team of experts and I provided the indispensable leadership. I deserve the fruits of that genius. By refusing to negotiate I am preserving liberty for this country."

"Lordy, you're too modest, Mr. Senex. Your genius doesn't end here." She removed the lanyard from her neck and pointed her eyeglasses at him. "Promethean now charges the Chinese government one thousand dollars each for three doses of Anoflix over a six-month period to protect one individual." She folded her arms. "I won't allow price gouging in the United States."

"If you won't, the Chinese will."

"I'm barring you from exporting Anoflix to China under the Defense Production Act unless you negotiate."

"Do that and I'll move production to China."

"You're still a US citizen subject to our laws."

"You're not thinking straight. Just making trouble for us both." He furrowed his brow. "Think what the United States saves with Anoflix. If COVID-28 infects the United States, the cost to our health-care system will be about five hundred billion dollars over several years, without even considering the catastrophic blow to the economy." He steepled his fingers and smiled. "Look at the big picture. I'm saving the government money."

"I call that an extortion threat."

"I call it hard facts."

"You're entitled to recover costs and a reasonable profit. You're not entitled to hold the country hostage. Negotiate now."

"Never."

"I can't believe you're going to drag this out in court." Taylor closed her eyes and massaged her temples with her fingers. She reopened her eyes. "If the Chinese don't stop COVID, Mr. Senex, and it takes root here, we're talking millions of cases and hundreds of thousands of deaths without a vaccine."

"Is that all?" He got up to leave.

"There's more. Sit down." She pointed to the chair. "I'll also have the Senate Special Committee investigate your refusal to comply."

"Those clowns couldn't find the aspirin bottle in a medicine chest."

"You must think me dumb as a post." She leaned back in her swivel chair and locked her fingers across her chest. "I know you want to drag this dispute out till the House makes your boy the president. He'll then drop any lawsuit I file against you."

"You're out of your league. Resign."

"Want to play tough?" Her head bobbed as she spoke. "I'm fixing to schedule a press conference and call Promethean out on its price-gouging monopoly."

"Monopoly?" He laughed. "That monopoly is called a patent. It is a legal monopoly enshrined in our Constitution to promote innovation. I earned that patent by bringing this blockbuster drug to market. I'm entitled to my profits."

"We'll see about that." She shook her forefinger at him. "Patents shouldn't be used for price gouging and letting the poor suffer and die."

"If you attack me or my company, I'll counterpunch through the media." He clutched the arms of his chair. "There's something more going on here. You've been after me as soon as you got to Congress."

"I'll tell you, mister." She rose from her chair and looked down at him in his. "Years ago my granddaddy worked as a stevedore out of Galveston before he had to retire because of work-related injuries. The pain was so bad he got a prescription from a pill mill for opioids manufactured by Promethean Pharma."

"What does that have to do with me?"

"Plenty. Promethean targeted the neighborhoods of racial minorities with these." She reached into a desk drawer. "Here's a discount coupon from Promethean for their opioid medication." She let the coupon flutter to the desk. "They found a batch of these in the rooming house where my granddaddy passed from an overdose."

"That's unfortunate." He rose from the chair. "However, his bad judgment and lack of willpower are not my fault."

"Get out . . . now."

———

A few days later, Sebastian Senex clapped at the conclusion of a TV advertisement prepared by Habercrum and Hitch Advertising Agency at its Manhattan office. The wunderkind ad executive in a red blazer specializing in political attack ads murmured a thank-you under his wild thatch of jet-black hair as the room lights snapped back on.

"That'll teach her." Senex pushed back in the swivel chair. There was the wet-behind-the-ears congresswoman in all her glory appearing to shake hands with Malik Shakur, leader of the anti-Israeli and anti-white Black Power Movement known as BPM.

"We enhanced the image . . . as you suggested, Mr. Senex." Biting his lower lip, the ad executive young enough to be his son asked, "Think we overdid it?"

"Not at all. You've done a great job with deepfake AI technology." He had the smarts to pressure the executive to change the image of Dallas Taylor shaking her finger at Shakur in disapproval into a handshake and her frown into a smile. The photo had to be adjusted to get at the larger truth. She pretended to disagree with Shakur, but he knew underneath she was on board with his plan for social revolution.

For the next few hours, the inner circle of the creative team at Habercrum and Hitch Advertising Agency wined and dined him at Jean-Georges restaurant. They brainstormed the presentation and marketing of the political attack ad against Dallas Taylor. A somber Habercrum joined the table. The creatives rose in respect. He motioned them down. They sat back down on cue. Habercrum looked at Senex. "This is risky business, Sebastian, risky indeed."

"How so, Harold?" He preened his ego by comparing in his mind the decrepitude of Habercrum, a man of similar age, with his own rejuvenation. "At the snap of my fingers I have photograph experts ready to counterpunch anyone who might dispute the photo. We'll label any objection fake news."

Habercrum asked the creatives to leave. After they left, he continued, "What if Malik Shakur backs Taylor up. Sebastian?"

"I paid Shakur off." Senex wiped his lips with the napkin. "Besides, he hates her guts. He thinks she sold out the brothers and sisters.

Shakur likes the payback of Dallas Taylor appearing to support him."
Senex shook his head. "Would you believe it? That woman not radical
enough for Shakur?"

"What about other witnesses?"

"Stop worrying, Harold. They were alone." He threw the napkin
on the table. "We go back a long way but if you keep this negativity
up, you're going to hurt creative innovation. I wouldn't want to take
Promethean Pharma ads somewhere else."

"Aren't you forgetting the photographer?" With credit card waving
in hand, Habercrum called over the waiter. "Or did you pay him off
too?"

"Better than that," Senex said. "As luck would have it, he died last
year in a car crash." He drew his thumb and forefinger across his lips.
"Zipped silent forever."

# CHAPTER FORTY-EIGHT

"Not now. I'll see him later." Dallas Taylor waved her personal secretary out of the Oval Office. "I need to see what's going on in Chicago." To her left she looked over at the three television sets newly installed alongside one another under the bookshelves, just as her fellow Texan, LBJ, had placed his TV sets. Like him, she could watch all three newscasts simultaneously.

On the TV screens, fires smoldered and flared up through the debris of ruined buildings. It reminded her of the riots after the death of Martin Luther King, Jr. or George Floyd. Cartel gangs and the remnants of the Outfit fought hit-and-run battles on the streets. A growing phalanx of military veterans under the American Patriots banner executed vigilante justice against lone-wolf criminals spawned by the general mayhem.

Snipers shot at human targets from the upper stories of buildings. Increasingly outgunned and stretched thin, the Chicago police husbanded their resources to defend upper-income homes and businesses with periodic offensive actions into the worst of the urban war zones. "They've all gone loco in Chicago," Taylor muttered to herself.

"I must see you now." Like an unwelcome apparition, the secretary of defense, General Horatio A. Harrison, known as "Hard-Ass Harrison" in his active-duty days, stood at the doorway hand on hip and the other holding a stack of papers.

"Retired four-star army general or not, you can't just waltz in here." Taylor shooed him with a wave of her hand. "Vamoose to the waiting area. I have to call the Russian president."

"Your cell phone is not secure."

"I know that." She put away her cell. Truth was she had forgotten President Trump had caused himself problems by giving out his cell phone number to foreign leaders. "I just want to congratulate the Russian president on his birthday." She picked the secure telephone line from the console.

"You should consult the National Security Council. Calls to foreign leaders have national security implications."

Who was he trying to fool? They both knew official eavesdroppers standing by in another room would monitor the call. They'd take notes on the conversation and compare their notes to an electronic recording.

"Wait outside, General, until I call you in."

After the telephone conversation, she kept the secretary of defense cooling his heels and sipped from a glass of bourbon and branch water to gather her thoughts. The former president had loved military men around him and took pride in retired general Horatio A. Harrison. She swirled her drink of bourbon and branch water. A gut check revealed the source of unease.

Generals as secretaries of defense made her nervous. Almost eighty years ago under President Truman, General George Marshall received a Senate congressional waiver of the rule requiring military personnel to wait ten years after retirement before becoming defense secretary. Congress then whittled down the cooling-off period to seven years.

Not long ago, Congress granted a waiver of even that reduced period so that General James Mattis could serve as defense secretary under President Trump and a further waiver to General Lloyd Austin, who had served in the same post under President Biden. Recently, Congress had eroded the waiting period yet again by reducing the interval to only three years. Having been out of active duty only two years, General Harrison could not even meet that low hurdle. So Congress created an exception for this fair-haired boy with ties to the military-industrial complex that President Eisenhower had warned about.

The wall of separation between the military and civilian spheres was turning into a stepping-stone, and Taylor didn't like it. Neither would the framers of the Constitution. It was dangerous for the future of civilian rule. To be fair, Congress only reflected public opinion polls showing Americans far and away trusted the military more than any other social institution. She had to deal with the law and public opinion as it was, not as she would have liked it.

Old Hard-Ass looked like he was going to prove a troublesome cabinet member. She kept him on because he came highly recommended as a Beltway whiz kid. The other reason was that the outgoing administration had delayed her ability to conduct background checks and security clearances for potentially new cabinet members. She overlooked this political pettiness for the big picture: it appeared statesmanlike and bipartisan for her to keep the cabinet holdovers for the time being. That's what John Adams had done in keeping George Washington's cabinet. The country longed for a unifier who would not demonize the opposition in a time of crisis.

At the end of a half hour, she allowed the secretary of defense into the Oval Office. If he proved half as good as his admirers claimed, she'd put up with him even if he turned out to be a yellow jacket in an outhouse.

"Have a seat."

"I prefer to stand."

"What do you want?"

"You had no right to lower the DEFCON level to four from three without consulting us."

"Say what?" She took out a copy of the Constitution from her desk. "My copy says I am the commander in chief."

"You should have taken the advice of the secretary of defense and the chairman of the Joint Chiefs of Staff."

"But then it would have been an order and not advice." She stood up and looked at him straight on. "I'd like us to get along, so remember I don't take orders. I give them . . . understand?"

He gave a curt nod.

"And, by the way, I did get advice . . . just not from you, because I already knew your opinion and that of the Joint Chiefs."

"Madam Acting President, we are in a constitutional crisis."

"Get this straight. I have the full powers of any president."

"I won't argue the point. I have more pressing news." He hovered over the Resolute desk, riffling the papers in his hands. "The latest reports show our enemies taking advantage of our governmental transition. The North Koreans have lobbed another missile over Japan, the closest yet to the Japanese shoreline. The Russians are probing our infrastructure with their computer networks . . . not to mention Chinese warships doing military exercises off Hawaii."

"The combatant commander for the navy supports my decision."

"The others . . . the army, the air force . . . they disagree and want to go back to DEFCON 3." He put his hands on his knees and leaned forward. "You probably don't know it, but DEFCON 3 gets our warplanes into the air within fifteen minutes. We don't have that level of security under DEFCON 4."

"I know what the DEFCON levels mean. Probably, you don't know I was on the Senate Homeland Security Committee." She backed away from more tit for his tat. "The way I see it, General, this whole thing's like a Texas Hold'em poker game. Every escalation of the DEFCON level we've made, the Russians have matched with increased mobilization. This last time they called and raised the stakes as a warning. I got the message."

"They're bluffing."

"You want to take the chance of nuclear annihilation?" She took a deep breath and stopped counting to ten when she reached two. "You know damn well they've reduced their level of preparedness to match the lowered DEFCON level. My decision de-escalated the tensions."

"You have your opinion." He folded her arms. "And I have mine."

"And mine's the only one that counts." She got tired of him standing over her. "Now sit down. I'll tell you something more important on my mind."

He sat down.

"Look at that, General." She swept her hand in an arc toward the row of TV sets. "Chicago is in flames. No DEFCON level will help us if this country starts falling apart."

He looked back at her from his inspection of the ceiling while she was talking. "The Joint Chiefs have asked you before. I ask you again."

He swallowed. "For God's sake, call out the National Guard to put down the violence."

"The Constitution only allows me to call out militia . . . now called National Guard . . . to execute the laws of the United States, suppress insurrections, and repel invasions. We have none of the three here. Only an acute breakdown of law and order."

"That's not what the US attorney general thinks." The retired general handed over a legal memo from his stack of papers. "Drug cartels are involved in the breakdown of law and order. That could implicate the laws of the United States."

"Lookie here, General." Taylor grabbed her reading glasses hanging from the lanyard around her neck and placed them on her nose. She skimmed through two sheets of paper on her desk. "These letters are from the governor of Illinois and the mayor of Chicago. It says here," she said, tapping a letter with her forefinger, "that they don't want the National Guard to come in and lay down martial law. They say they're capable of enforcing state law on murder, robbery, arson . . . all the normal crimes occurring there . . . without the guard. They just want financial aid and body armor, as well as FBI backup."

"Screw 'em." Hard-Ass stuck out his chin and chest. "Congress amended the Insurrection Act. You now have authority to override local officials in calling out the National Guard if you determine they can't handle a public emergency."

"It's never been tested in the courts." She let her eyeglasses dangle from the lanyard and sighed. "But you have a point. The amendment is my backstop if all else fails. But for now, let's wait a bit until the optics are better. If the situation gets worse, they'll beg me to bring in the National Guard. I'll then ride in on my white horse to save the day without stepping on anyone's toes."

"Nero waited while Rome burned. Are you planning to do the same with Chicago?"

"Bless your heart." She toyed with her lanyard around her neck for a few seconds, considering what to say. "Ever since I took over this office you've been as busy . . . and as successful . . . in intimidating me as a one-legged man in an ass-kicking contest." She folded her arms and looked at him. "Just tell me what's sticking in your craw . . . if we're to get on together?"

"What's sticking in my craw is this." He leaned forward in his chair. "You're only sitting in that chair by the skin of your teeth because the country's in crisis. You're only an acting president . . . not a real one. I think you should act like an acting president and not like an elected one."

"I sure don't share that opinion!" She rose up, her head bobbing and eyes diamond hard. "Nine vice presidents have taken over as president when a president died, or in the case of Nixon, resigned. I am the president for now with all the powers of this office, which I need precisely because we are in a national crisis." She put her palms on the table. "You don't have to like me and I don't have to like you . . . but when push comes to shove, I'm the one doing the shoving. Understand?"

"Oh, I understand more than you think."

# CHAPTER FORTY-NINE

Inside the ladies' restroom at the sports arena, Katie Murphy opened up to Nicole Garvey about her brother. Jim hadn't been himself ever since he learned the commander was his real father. The commander's suicide rattled him even more. Katie had held him while he cried. His sister had never seen him cry, and he wouldn't like her mentioning it. Katie trusted Nicole—she was good for her brother. Touched by Katie's expression of trust and approval, she assured Jim's sister she could keep a confidence.

Nicole knew something was wrong with Katie during the battle-of-the-badges basketball game between the Chicago Police Department and the Cook County Sheriff's Office at the arena. Jim's sister shook her head at all the shots her brother didn't make. Her brother was a star basketball player, she insisted, even though he had missed shooting the game-tying basket in the closing seconds.

After they parted outside with hugs, Nicole Garvey walked on alone over the street slush of the Near West Side to Dugan's Irish pub to meet Jim. She had a lot on her mind, trying to absorb the news that Cronin was Jim's real father. That news provided needed context for Jim's callousness when he learned of the commander's death. His attitude and refusal to discuss it had turned her off.

He didn't tell her about the commander's claim of paternity, but then again she couldn't expect that so early in their relationship. He had only recently found out himself. His moodiness had nothing to do with her. For that she was thankful.

Although they had just started dating, she had interpreted his suddenly sullen irritability as dissatisfaction with her. She took it as an early warning that he might be about to dump her. Before she got hurt, she was steeling herself to the possibility of dumping him first. Jim was slumped in a chair at a table next to the wall. *Where's Daisy?* Did her colleague stand them up?

She sat down across from Jim.

Two empty Guinness bottles stood next to the third he was working on. His eyes were bloodshot and his cheeks unshaven.

"What happened to Two-Drink Murph?"

"I don't like being nagged."

Because of Katie's revelations, she cut him some slack. "Is everything OK?"

"Should it be?"

"Things should be more than OK. Katie said the superintendent of police put you in acting command of the Thirteenth District. You can now do things the right way. It's your dream come true."

"Where's Daisy?"

"Must be running late."

"Or wasting my time." He huffed and folded his arms. "An airhead."

"That's not fair." He wasn't himself. *Back off.* "Please hear her out, Jim. I think she has something important to tell you."

"Why didn't she tell you if it's so important?"

"Daisy knew I didn't like Vince Palomba." She twisted a napkin on the table. "When he died, she lost it and blamed me for not liking him. We're not on talking terms . . . at least for now. All I know is that in her emotional outburst, she let slip something about secret experiments to stop her father from aging."

"She's got nothing." He got up. "If preventing old age is a crime, I'd have to lock up most of this city."

"Look, Jim. She thinks something's illegal. Otherwise she wouldn't want to talk to you." She put her hand on his arm. "Daisy was furious when I last saw her . . . not just at me. Something else raged inside her. It frightened me. I'm sure she's got much to say . . . just not to me."

"Fifteen minutes." He checked the time on his cell and sat down. "No more."

"I found out something interesting." She tightened the cardigan around her shoulders. "While doing research on the archaeology of Easter Island, I learned there's a bacterium in the soil that produces rapamycin, a potent antibiotic used to prevent organ rejection and now also used as an antitumor drug—"

"How's that connect to my Senex investigation?"

"I'll answer if you let me." She didn't like being talked over. "Rapamycin, it turns out, lengthens life spans in insects, worms, and mice . . . as much as thirty percent and—"

"Don't you get it?" He ran his fingers down his face. "I can't arrest Senex for taking rapamycin."

"That's not my point . . . if you'd just let me finish." Her patience was running thin. "A footnote in the article mentioned Dr. Angelo Mora had done research on the antibiotic years ago at the University of Padua in the search for what he called the fountain of youth. He rejected rapamycin because it threatened the human immune system. Instead he saw parabiosis . . . joining the blood circulatory systems of two living organisms, one younger and one older . . . as the way forward to rejuvenation and—"

"A pissing match among experts means nothing."

"I'm leaving unless you stop talking over me." She took a deep breath. "I know you've been through a lot with the commander but . . . please . . . hear me out." When he remained silent, she continued. "Mora suggested young convicted criminals be forced into parabiosis before execution, or offered commutation of sentence for agreeing to parabiosis, so their blood didn't go to waste."

"You mean—"

"Exactly. Think about it. Dr. Mora, brought to Chicago by Sebastian Senex, is around when gangbangers disappear and three—" She cut herself off. No need to remind him of Santiago's death.

"I get it." He swallowed hard. "Neofascist comes to Chicago, gang-bangers disappear, three found dead in a truck . . . including my son. Senex must have known the background of his chief medical investigator." He held her hand across the table. "Not much to go on but it's something."

"Why not interrogate Mora?"

"I'd love to." His facial excitement faded to gloom. "But Dr. Mora has gone missing."

"Cheer up. I brought good news."

"Must be a mistake."

"Has Marco's pessimism infected your top-of-the-morning optimism?" She pushed his arm playfully. "Stop imagining the worst." She handed over a business card. "This publisher for my archaeology book heard about you from yours truly. He's interested in publishing a line of children's books and looking for authors. Need I say more?"

"What's this got to do with me?" He dropped the card into his shirt pocket without reading it.

"Sparky the Squirrel. Remember the notes you left behind when we had lunch in the Walnut Room at Macy's?"

"They were just notes to kill time."

"Hold on." She straightened up. "Marco told me you're writing a children's book."

"I didn't ask you to find a publisher."

"You're welcome." She got up and buttoned her coat. "You obviously want to have a pity party for yourself. But you don't need me for that." She picked up her purse. "Daisy just wants to speak to you anyway."

"I'd like you to stay." He looked down at the floor. "They'll laugh at me if they find out."

"Who?"

"District Thirteen cops. They're old-school." He ran his fingers through his hair. "If word gets out I'm writing a children's book . . ."

"I'm not laughing."

"Don't tell anyone."

"Oh yeah." She shook her head in disbelief. "Like I'm going to tell your macho brother cops you're writing a book about a squirrel who lost his nuts."

She put two fingers over her lips and widened her eyes right before they both rocked with belly laughter. His laughter came through like a rushing stream breaking up a logjam of despondency. Color returned to his cheeks. His eyes grew bright and merry.

"I have a soft spot for kids." He shook his head at the waiter offering another Guinness. "Our baby died at birth . . . and then Santiago."

"I know." She came around the back of his chair and kneaded his shoulder with her hand. "Marco told me."

"All I wanted was to help a disabled girl in a wheelchair by tossing her ball back." He took her hand still resting on his shoulder. "Next thing I know I'm responsible for the death of the next president of the United States and the mess the country's in." He shrugged. "As Marco would say . . . 'Mondo cane . . . It's a dog's world.'"

"Dogs don't wallow in the past." She removed her hand and sat back down. "The assassin's responsible for the murder. Maybe someday you feel that as well as know it."

Just then Daisy Senex flung open the front door of Dugan's Pub and came over to their table. She pulled out a chair and sat down without a greeting.

"Do you want me to leave?" Nicole asked.

Daisy shook her head. "Stay."

"Let me get this straight," Murphy said. "You have dirt about your own father?"

Daisy pulled out a letter written to her by Dr. Angelo Mora in his own hand shortly before his disappearance. The doctor's lab assistant told her Mora gave instructions for him to deliver the letter to her in the event of the doctor's death or disappearance. Daisy read the letter like a woman in a trance.

> *My poor Daisy . . . If you are reading these words, know that I am dead at the hands of your father for what he considers my betrayal of him to organized crime. Even though he received from me the gift of youth and a reprieve from death, the ingrate murdered me.*
>
> *My secret blood research on his behalf and of which he availed himself reversed his aging process through parabiosis. My genius even surpassed that landmark breakthrough by my further discovery of the Ponce de León protein that renders parabiosis outmoded.*
>
> *Your father and I agreed that the blood of criminal riffraff should be used for the experimentation. To this*

*end he conspired with organized crime to kidnap and use street criminals as my guinea pigs and sources of youthful blood.*

*The start of my tragedy occurred when what you call the Chicago Outfit refused to assassinate the Democratic candidate, Franklin Dexter Walker, at your father's request. Your father instead recruited the renewed Sinaloa cartel for this enterprise. Because of a business falling-out spawned by my discoveries, he has now declared war on the Chicago Outfit and brought in the cartel to wage that war. Sinaloa brought in the Aztec Warriors as allies. Vincent Palomba learned of this through his informant in the cartel.*

*I lied when I told you in the Lincoln Park Conservatory that I did not know who ordered the killing of Vincent Palomba. The Aztec Warriors who killed and cannibalized the heart of your dear lover, Vincent Palomba, acted at the direction of the Sinaloa cartel. What I didn't tell you was that your father is not only responsible for the death of the missing hoodlums sought by the police. He also retained the cartel to specifically murder your beloved Vincent Palomba. Sources within the Chicago Outfit confirmed all this from captured Sinaloa members.*

*And, finally, I must tell you what I could not tell Detective Murphy during his interrogation. From personal involvement, I know the son of Detective Murphy, Santiago, was rounded up on the street so that I could join his body to that of Sebastian Senex—*

"It can't be," Murphy said.

*—and use the blood of Santiago's body to rejuvenate Sebastian Senex at the threshold of death.*

"My son's blood is in that piece of garbage." He stood up. Garvey hugged him.

*I confess that at the direction of Sebastian Senex and the leader of the Chicago Outfit I ended the life of Santiago, after the parabiosis procedure, with a fatal combination of drugs. I repent my actions and seek my revenge against Sebastian Senex through Detective Murphy. Farewell.*

"Senex will pay," Murphy said. "He murdered my son."

# CHAPTER FIFTY

While gray skies drizzled over New Orleans, Sebastian Senex marveled how much General Horatio A. Harrison had aged. Or maybe it only seemed that way because he himself looked so young. They took a table inside the covered portico of Café Du Monde away from perimeter tables exposed to the windswept rain. He owed much to this friend of the family who, as adjutant general of the Illinois National Guard, had watched over him in the guard.

Senex had shimmied up the greased pole of promotion and retired as a National Guard colonel on inactive status before becoming CEO of Promethean Pharma. Their fast friendship grew distant when General Harrison rose through army ranks until he reached the chairmanship of the Joint Chiefs of Staff and now secretary of defense. In a camouflage jacket, the general sat with hands on the table and fingers interlocked. Furrows ran along his forehead. Rumor was ol' Hard-Ass was having a hard time adjusting to civilian life.

"You look great, Sebastian." The general took a pill with water. "Wish I felt like you look. Working in DC with political blockheads tires me out."

"Sorry about that."

"Civilians dumb as a box of rocks." He signaled for a waiter. "How do you do it?"

"Do what?"

"Look so good."

"Not smoking, eating right, exercise . . . the usual." He didn't want to waste time on chitchat. "You know, you're the reason I came to the National Guard Association Convention." He was set to continue when a waiter interrupted to take their orders.

The waiter started with Senex. "What'll you have?"

"A café au lait and a beignet."

"And I'll have a good ol' cup of plain American coffee . . . black and no sugar."

"Who would have thought you'd be secretary of defense one day . . . and giving the keynote speech at this convention."

The general softened his clamped lips into the semblance of a smile.

"I don't use the word lightly, but you're a true American hero . . . Afghanistan, Iraq, NATO command, and then big shot at Lockheed Martin, reorganizer of the Pentagon—"

"Enough." The general held out his hand with a big grin on his face. "You didn't do so bad yourself."

"Nothing compared to you." He sipped his café au lait. "You should think of running for high office, Horatio."

"Not Horatio." The general's face winced. "I prefer Ray."

"Sorry, Ray." How could he have forgotten? He worried the mistake would set back his plan to butter up the general. At least he remembered not to call him Hard-Ass. Hearing that nickname would have sent H. A. Harrison up the wall. "I forgot your name preference, but you see, I'm distracted with worry about our country." He had heard rumors of friction between Dallas Taylor and the general. He needed to exploit that.

"I'm worried too." Harrison looked around and leaned over. "Can you keep a secret?"

"Of course." Senex offered half of his beignet. The general patted his plump belly and declined.

"Being out of active command grinds on me. I have to play nursemaid to a former television judge and kooky politician. Would you believe she watches TV for hours in the Oval Office? She scares me with her incompetence in these dangerous times. Our foreign enemies are circling around."

"Unless you convince her, Ray, to call up the National Guard . . . Chicago will be in ruins."

"I've tried. She refuses to listen. It's hopeless." He shrugged his shoulders. "With your influence, can't you get the governor to do it?"

"The coward." He crushed the remainder of the beignet with a spoon. "He's afraid he'll lose votes if the guardsmen miss work and are taken from their families. Or if the guardsmen harm protestors and rioters. He's dead meat next election, as far as I'm concerned." He held up his hands. "But these hands are tied for now."

"Not like our old pal, the former governor. He got things done."

"What can we do," Senex asked, "about this accidental president in the White House before things get worse?"

"Somebody should do something. Dallas Taylor is a celebrity imposter. She's likely to sack the current cabinet and install her team of second-raters."

"But if no one else does anything?" He leaned across the table and looked into Harrison's eyes. "How do we get her out?"

The general fidgeted. "Let's hope the House chooses a president soon."

"And if not soon?"

"We'd have to do something."

# CHAPTER FIFTY-ONE

*What would he do?* President Dallas Taylor swung around in her Oval Office swivel chair to contemplate a framed photograph of a scowling LBJ pointing an accusatory forefinger at some unseen target. The man could be a crude sonofabitch but no one doubted he was in charge.

He stayed the course in signing the Civil Rights bill even though it wrecked the Democratic Party in the South. He pushed to eliminate poverty while fighting the Vietnam War even though it ballooned the national debt. Whatever his Texas-sized failings, LBJ had what Texans called double backbone when it came to fighting for the underdogs. So would she.

If a Texan as god-awful mumbly as LBJ could handle the presidency, so could an articulate black woman from a Texas ghetto with a natural flair for media communication.

She looked at the political advertisement on TV. The ad kept popping up all morning on one or more of the three TV sets tuned to different cable networks. This was a low-blow attack ad dressed up in the guise of a public-service ad about terrorism. The ad creator had manipulated a photo of her and Malik Shakur, the leader of BPM, so that she appeared to shake hands with him instead of what really happened: shaking her finger in disapproval of his message.

She had to contend with something her political idol did not. The era of fake images had dawned hand in hand with fake news. Artificial intelligence furthered exploitation of the visual media. Determining the truth in the political arena became more difficult. It wasn't simply that much of the public relied on deepfake images via social media in place of true images. No siree, the problem was worse than that. Many doubted even true images because they thought they could be deepfakes. This cynicism ate away at the cohesiveness of an American society where visual facts were treated as fakes and fakes treated as visual facts.

*Who was behind it?* She put her money on Sebastian Senex. You didn't need artificial intelligence to make that bet. Just half a brain. When she gave her press conference criticizing the price monopoly of Promethean Pharma regarding Anoflix, Senex must have followed through on his threat to smear her as an African American radical in cahoots with domestic terrorists.

Under the legal pretext of being a social welfare organization, the super PAC had used dark money from a 501(c)(4) group whose donor list could legally remain anonymous. She and Sebastian Senex were now at war. She winked at LBJ and strutted off to a meeting in the Cabinet Room with a holdover team of officials from the previous administration.

Inside the room with her fifteen cabinet members gathered around the oval table, she had only one item on her mind. "Give me a status report on the federal court case against Promethean Pharma," she asked the attorney general, "for refusing to negotiate the price of Anoflix."

"We've caught Promethean Pharma off guard," the attorney general said, a smart-as-a-whip woman with Florida roots. "They assumed we'd only try to enforce the excise tax against Promethean Pharma for failing to bargain." She rubbed her hands together as though about to devour a treat. "But I had a better idea."

"You should have informed me of your idea before this meeting," said the silver-haired secretary of health and human services. "The new federal statute designates HHS as the drug-price negotiator."

"The attorney general determines legal strategy," Taylor said. "She reports directly to me. Not to you."

A friend of the former president, the secretary of HHS was on thin ice. Taylor didn't appreciate his jealous turf battles with other agencies.

Worse, the man never saw or offered solutions, only hopeless problems. She'd have to remove him once she settled in.

"Trying to enforce the so-called excise tax is a dead end," the attorney general continued. "Any tax they pay is a drop in the bucket given their profits. They can continue gouging patients as a cost of doing business." The attorney general paused for what seemed to be dramatic effect. "Instead, I'm asking the court to enjoin Promethean Pharma to negotiate in good faith, similar to what happens in labor dispute cases . . . or else risk contempt of court if they don't."

"I like it." Taylor saw her holdover attorney general being nominated to the Supreme Court. She came from the same dirt-poor beginnings as her new boss and made a success of herself as a former Harvard Law professor and federal judge. Right now, though, Taylor needed this legal whiz in court against Promethean Pharma and Senex. "How quickly can we do it?"

"Good news," her legal star responded. "The district court judge fast-tracked the case because of its public health implications. We're moving for an emergency temporary restraining order tomorrow, to be followed by an injunction."

"Excellent." Her legal team would stick it to Senex. She wouldn't have minded so much if he hadn't made his opposition so personal. But how could she forgive him for stirring up his legislative lackeys to bar her from using the Oval Office until the Senate elected a president? The attempt to humiliate her had never gotten off the ground, but it still infuriated her.

"What about the older Bayh-Dole Act?" asked the secretary of homeland security. "Since Promethean Pharma developed Anoflix and obtained a patent with federal funding, the act compels Promethean Pharma to issue a license to other drug companies to produce Anoflix where health concerns justify the move."

She had a fond spot for her inherited secretary of homeland security. An obese ex-CIA deputy director and chain smoker, he knew his stuff. He made it his business to know the ins and outs of whatever came before the cabinet and what bureaucratic wires had to be pulled to make government work. He was an ally who joined her for an occasional bourbon and branch water.

"I like compulsory licensing too," the attorney general said, "but I prefer to hold that big cannon in reserve if we lose on the injunction. Compulsory licensing hasn't been tested in the courts. We don't know how much federal funding is necessary to trigger the compulsory license provision, and we don't have an actual coronavirus outbreak in the United States . . . only a possible threat from China. The issue will raise a hornets' nest of legal and political problems."

"I see your point." The secretary of homeland security cocked his ear. "I can already hear Senex yelling socialism."

"That's it, then. Injunction now, compulsory licensing if needed." Taylor rubbed her hands and picked up her papers. "I'm off to another meeting."

A Justice Department messenger bent over to whisper in the attorney general's ear.

The attorney general reported, "It's about the Promethean Pharma case. Excuse me." She turned her ear back to the messenger.

The whispers back and forth between messenger and the attorney general buzzed louder until the president couldn't stand the suspense. "What's going on? We'd all like to be in on it."

"Sorry, Madam President." The attorney general dismissed the messenger and stood up. She looked at Taylor sitting at the head of the table and then turned to the others in their seats. "I have news."

"Good news?" asked Taylor.

"Afraid not. Senex has just issued a national press release. Promethean Pharma has ceased the production, marketing, and distribution of Anoflix. We can't enjoin them to negotiate the price of a product they no longer produce."

"Senex is playing a game of chicken. And I'm not turning tail," she told her cabinet. "Go get that compulsory license."

# CHAPTER FIFTY-TWO

"I say let's go." Jim Murphy looked over the exterior of the Kinzie Steel mill. Weeds grew around the building. Rust streaks and soot splotched the exterior. Broken windows let in the wind. "The property's abandoned. We don't need a warrant."

"The judge did not think Mora's hearsay death note sufficient for a search warrant." Marco looked away from the mill to his partner. "The mill has a new owner. I do not think we should enter without judicial permission."

"They haven't occupied it yet."

"But they have legal title. They purchased it from Promethean Pharma."

A black Cadillac drove up and pulled to a stop in the parking lot section reserved for management. Out of the luxury sedan came a pair of Chinese men with matching black suits and alligator briefcases.

They introduced themselves as engineers employed by the Chinese corporation that had purchased the mill from Promethean Pharma. With the utmost courtesy they asked permission to enter the mill to prepare its renovation and reopening.

"Where's your identification?" Murphy asked. He had to preserve whatever evidence remained in the steel mill to incriminate Sebastian Senex.

The men showed passports.

"Not good enough." Murphy handed them back. "How do I know you represent the owner? I don't know you from Adam. I need proof of your authority."

They wanted to know who Adam was.

"Not important," he replied.

They showed a document written in Chinese.

"This won't work either. I only speak and read English."

Agitated, the executives spoke to each other in rapid-fire Chinese.

"You'd better go back and check with your boss. I need proof you're who you say you are. Right, partner?"

Leone returned a hesitant nod.

They apologized in English for the inconvenience and departed.

As the detectives watched the Cadillac leave, Marco said, "You have only delayed events. They will return."

"I know but I had to stall. We can't have them disturbing any evidence inside." He shook his head. "If only my rubber-stamp judge hadn't retired, I could have gotten a warrant in a heartbeat."

"Do you still wish to search without a warrant?"

"You convinced me, partner." He patted Marco on the back. "Too risky. If we do find something today, a court might throw it out as an illegal police search."

"So . . . what is our next step?"

"Yes, that's it," he said more to himself than to Marco. His face lit up. "I know what I'm going to do."

————

The next week, after supervising roll call, Jim Murphy received a communication from the legal department of the city of Chicago. Sebastian Senex and the Chinese corporation had obtained a preliminary injunction against the Chicago Police Department from further prohibiting or delaying entry of duly authorized representatives of the Chinese corporation . . . or of Promethean Pharma personnel as agents of the Chinese corporation . . . onto the premises of the Kinzie Steel mill.

The inclusion of Promethean Pharma in the order supported what Murphy suspected. Sebastian Senex had something to hide from the police. Later that day, Murphy received a call from the head of security for Promethean Pharma: Senex himself planned to enter the mill tomorrow and expected no further police interference. Something crucial had to be in the mill. And he had better find out what that something was before Senex got to it first.

He checked cell messages, which had backed up on his phone because of all the crime-wave emergencies he had to resolve. Ollie, the quirky chemist from Vulcan Metallurgy, had returned his call and left a message: *The answer is 5,463°F for Ta and 3,463°F for Zr.*

*Bingo.* Things were falling into place. He remembered a few abbreviations from his high school chemistry class. It was a long shot but he had to go with his gut. He tapped Nicole's telephone number on his cell.

"It's me. You and Daisy have to move today before Senex gets there."

"We're on our way as we speak," Nicole said. "What if it's not in the steel mill?"

"Then check out the slag heap next to the mill. Can you do that?"

"I've examined many ancient slag heaps during my archaeological digs. A modern one should be a breeze."

"Will Daisy testify she entered the mill freely? And not because the police asked her?"

"We've gone through this." He felt the exasperation in her voice. "Daisy wants to take her father down for Vince's murder. It's her choice."

"Good." He rubbed his chin. "And she asked you to come along?"

"Of course. Why is all this so important?"

"Because if she's doing this at the request of the CPD, Senex might exclude any evidence you find as part of an illegal search. If she's doing this without police pressure, we should be clear."

"Here's another reason," Nicole said. "Daisy is temporarily working part-time in the human relations department at Promethean Pharma. Her father wanted her to have a job in the real world, as he put it. She may qualify as a Promethean representative with permission to enter under the judge's order."

"Wonderful."

"The luck of the Irish, right?" He heard Daisy in the background telling Nicole they had arrived. "We're here and ready to enter."

"Here's to more luck inside." He had the luck of the Irish all right. His luck was knowing Nicole.

———

Waiting to hear from Nicole, Murphy thought of the gray, glassy heaps of rocky slag, like a mini moonscape, piled up in the fenced yard next to the steel mill. It was a long shot, but without Daisy he would have had no shot. He could still see the fire in Daisy's eyes as she told him she would help. Love and hate were two complementary emotions, and one of the worst hates was family love gone bad. She wanted vengeance for her father's complicity in the death of Vinnie Palomba.

He took his mind off waiting by reading a report on the latest crime statistics. The special strike force he had organized came to an unwelcome conclusion. Carjackings had spiked mainly because the bad guys needed them to carry out untraceable drive-by shootings. Social media crackled with boastful accounts of which gang had stolen the most expensive car. Even the superintendent of police had his Lexus stolen outside headquarters for use in a gangland murder.

For the rest of the day, Murphy spent his declining energy in the conference room, now turned into a war room, to issue orders to district police about the explosion of gang wars across the city. Afterward they filed out, leaving him alone with half-eaten sandwiches and stale doughnuts together with cold coffee. He wasn't sure the police had the manpower or the firepower to maintain peace in a city convulsing with violence.

*How long can the city hold out without outside help?*

Leone had warned him. He who commands has no rest.

Murphy laid his head in his hands with elbows propped on the conference table. He slumped forward in his chair, trying to fight off sleep. His eyes closed.

His cell buzz jolted him awake. *Nicole.*

"I found it in the slag heap."

# CHAPTER FIFTY-THREE

"If I want another bourbon and branch water, I'll damn well have it." At the head of the conference table in the Situation Room, President Dallas Taylor caught the attention of the waiter. Retired general Horatio A. Harrison, secretary of defense, held his out his hand to stop the approaching waiter.

"Let him pass . . . Hard-Ass."

"I don't appreciate that name."

"And I don't appreciate being told what to drink."

"This is a crisis situation, Madam Acting President." Harrison panned the faces of colleagues in their high-backed leather chairs. "We need sobriety."

"I am the president. Let him pass."

He let the waiter pass.

"Back to business." She opened the daily morning book with the latest intelligence on political hot spots around the world. She had a fight on her hands. If it were just Hard-Ass aching for a military counterstrike, she could handle him.

The military brass in the room were on his side. The director of national intelligence and the director of the CIA were leaning his way. Besides those two, the other civilian members of the National Security Council were lying low to protect their behinds. She had inherited her cabinet from the prior administration with no time to vet them. "What's the current situation?" she asked.

"I have the admiral of the Pacific Fleet on tap to update us." The national security advisor pointed to the videoconferencing screen flickering on the wall at the foot of the table. The admiral's image appeared on the screen in full dress uniform.

"Can you hear me, Admiral?" Taylor asked. "What's going on?"

"Loud and clear," he responded. "No new developments. Naval forces from the People's Republic of China have landed on Taiping Island in the Spratly Islands chain and taken control from Taiwanese personnel. Any orders?"

"Keep me informed on further developments." She waved to the screen. "Thank you, Admiral." The screen want blank.

She looked down the table at the two rows of faces on either side. "The catalyst for this Chinese provocation is Sebastian Senex. He's stopped producing Anoflix both in China and the United States. So they're running out of Anoflix to snuff out their COVID-28 outbreak. They blame me. The Chinese president doesn't understand why we allow his defiance." She crossed her arms. "And frankly neither do I."

"This has nothing to do with Senex," the director of national intelligence said. "Our intelligence sources report Chinese scientists have pirated the Anoflix patent. They'll produce their own vaccine without Promethean Pharma. They just wanted to test our military response in seizing Taiping Island."

"It doesn't change facts," she said. "Sebastian Senex has worsened our relationship with China and held hostage the health of the American people."

"Be that as it may, we can't let personal animosities get in the way of our foreign policy," said the director of national intelligence. "The Chinese Communists are taking advantage of our constitutional crisis. They're exploiting the bitter divisions in the country. They see the inaction of the House of Representatives in picking a president." He turned to Taylor. "No offense, Madam Acting President, but you are not that president."

"I am the president until the House elects one. And where I come from, if it looks like a duck, walks like a duck, and quacks like a duck, we call it a duck." She couldn't afford to appear petty. "But use whatever title you want . . . as long as you all know that I have all the powers of a president. If that's a problem, you're free to resign."

"I say we bomb the hell out of the invasion force." All eyes turned to the speaker, Secretary of Defense Harrison.

"If we do that, we'd better prepare for a full-scale war." She rolled her eyes. "The Chinese won't stand down."

"Yes they will," said General John Klaine, the chairman of the Joint Chiefs of Staff. "They're not ready yet. Hit 'em, I say, before they are. Hit them with overpowering force. This is the perfect time to draw the line."

She respected the chairman. A bionic prosthesis replaced his right leg, which was amputated after bomb fragments ripped apart the leg in Vietnam. He had worked his way to the top through merit and courage. They didn't usually agree, certainly not when she had ordered him to lower DEFCON level three to level four, but at least he was open to what she had to say.

"I can't agree." Taylor folded her hands in front of her. "The Chinese didn't back away in the Korean War. I see your point, but I don't think we should draw the line here and now. Let's wait a bit longer."

"Are you saying," Harrison said, "we should back down? They'll smell our weakness and hit us harder. And then the Russians and North Koreans will move in on the kill . . . as we remain paralyzed . . . like a mouse mesmerized by the rattlesnake ready to pounce."

"This Texas girl, General, knows a thing or two about rattlesnakes." *Just like some rattlesnakes in this room,* she thought. "It's just a myth about rattlesnakes mesmerizing mice." She folded her arms. "Sort of like the myth about the domino theory your predecessors created to rationalize intervention in Vietnam."

"This South China Sea confrontation is no myth." The director of the CIA went on: "The Chinese, North Koreans, and Russians are meeting. They're developing a united strategy against us. The Chinese takeover of Taiping Island is the first step. We should nip it in the bud."

"They're testing us," the secretary of state said. "I suggest we first build an international coalition. Not only Taiwan, but the Philippines and Vietnam have their own claims to the Spratly Islands. Along with other countries, they'll object to the Chinese incursion."

"Incursion? Object to? Wait to build an international coalition?" asked the Homeland Security advisor. "The Chinese are creating irreversible facts on the ground. International handwringing won't stop them. Only force."

"The Chinese claim the Taiwan government intentionally sank their fishing boats near the island," Taylor said. "The Taiwanese claim it was an accident."

"Are you going to believe our enemy over our friend?" asked Harrison.

Taylor opened the morning book. "It says here"—she ran her finger down the page—"the People's Republic claims it will . . . temporarily . . . occupy Taiping Island to settle the incident with the Taiwanese officials."

"And you believe them?" asked the secretary of defense.

"I don't see harm in waiting a bit," the secretary of state said.

"We need time to gather allies," said the director of national intelligence. "I have a plan to freeze the status quo while pursuing that option." He pointed to the dark screen. "May I talk to the admiral of the Pacific Fleet, Madam Acting President?"

She nodded agreement. The admiral materialized on the screen.

"Admiral, this is the director of national intelligence. Could we blockade Taiping Island with the Seventh Fleet?"

"Most certainly." The screen voice sounded eager for action. "Taiping is an insignificant island compared to blockading Cuba. China won't take on the Seventh Fleet just to stay on Taiping."

"That may be true, Admiral." Taylor stood up. "But the Russians had nuclear weapons in Cuba and didn't promise to stay only temporarily."

"I come back to my question," asked Harrison. "Why do you believe the Chinese? They have taken land specks in the ocean and transformed them into artificial islands with military potential. They're relentless, like army ants."

"We can afford to wait," the secretary of state said. "We can always revisit the blockade option later and even set a deadline if they don't withdraw as promised."

"Sounds good to me," Taylor said, glancing at the wall clock. Another crisis awaited. Gathering the morning book into her hands she stood up to leave.

"We should do something now before they reinforce the island."
The secretary of defense crossed his arms and glared at Taylor. "You're
letting the Chinese humiliate us."

"There's a Texas saying. Don't rile the wagon master." She glared at
retired general Horatio A. Harrison. "Back off, Hard-Ass."

# CHAPTER FIFTY-FOUR

From the wall of Dugan's on Halsted, the poster-sized photo of young mayor Richard J. Daley smiled on Jim Murphy, who returned the smile with a lift of his Guinness pint. "Here's to the luck of the Irish. We'll need more of it." He turned to Nicole on the stool next to him. "And to you for your help."

Nicole clinked her hurricane glass of piña colada against his pint. "It was your hunch."

True, but Ollie the chemist had turned hunch into fact. Mora's tantalum-and-zirconium knee implant had a melting point higher than the capacity of the dysfunctional blast furnaces at Kinzie Steel. On behalf of his employer, Vulcan Metallurgy, Ollie had determined the blast furnaces at best reached a temperature of around 1,660 to 2,300 degrees Fahrenheit. But tantalum only melted at 5,463 degrees Fahrenheit and zirconium at 3,463 degrees.

He also was indebted to her. She had found Mora's tantalum-and-zirconium knee implant in the slag heap outside Kinzie Steel. But it didn't feel like a debt. It felt like a gift.

With that evidence, the luck of the Irish got him to first base where he obtained a search warrant for the interior of the Kinzie Steel mill. The unusual replacement joint made it probable the knee implant belonged to Mora. With the warrant, he did a thorough search of Kinzie Steel. Inside the mill he made it to second base when his officers found two tumblers in Senex's office. One bore the partial fingerprints of Angelo Mora and the other those of Sebastian Senex.

The luck of the Irish stopped at the preliminary hearing before trial. At the hearing he was tagged out sliding into third base. The preliminary judge found no probable cause to try Sebastian Senex for the murder of Angelo Mora. Case dismissed.

"Why," Nicole asked, "didn't the judge find probable cause to try him?"

He shrugged without explaining his suspicions. It would sound like sour grapes and who knew? Maybe it was. Maybe his native city had made him overly skeptical. But only the naive wanted express proof of a quid pro quo. Nowadays, the quid and the quo were always understood without being expressed. This wasn't the 1930s where the predetermined bangs of a gavel meant an envelope of cash had changed hands.

The case was transferred twice to two different judges before it wound up before the judge who dismissed the murder charge. The judge socialized with the sleazebag defense attorney who had a fixer reputation. The attorney had made a substantial contribution to the judge's reelection campaign. The case had the smell of a fix. Not sour grapes. Cops had different noses from civilians. They were sommeliers when it came to the subtle aromas of corruption in the Windy City.

"Isn't there anything you can do?"

"It's a heater case. Too much publicity. The state's attorney refuses to refile it without more evidence. He's afraid of appearing to persecute a pillar of the community."

"Strange place, this Chicago."

"Not if you're from here."

"Hold on." She slipped off the stool and put coins into the jukebox. "Just in Time" sung by Sarah Vaughan filled the air. She stopped in front of a mirror to fix her hair.

"Look on the bright side," she said slipping back onto her barstool. "The superintendent is bound to formally appoint you commander."

"Hope so. Being commander is what I want. To shape up the district, I'll need the superintendent's full backing."

"Making you interim was just his way of testing you. You've passed. Crime has gone down in your police district, and Senex is going down soon." She patted his arm. "And you're going up."

"I know I can clean up the Thirteenth District."

"When's the president," she said, "giving her press conference?"

He looked at his cell. "Anytime now."

"Think she'll make good on her threat?"

"Not her." He remembered how she had chewed him out for stopping her Jaguar on Lake Shore Drive. "All talk, no action . . . like most politicians."

"I think you're wrong." She hummed for a moment to the tune of the song on the jukebox and then broke off. "Is the state attorney's office at least going to charge Senex for the gangbanger deaths?"

"If they're not going after Senex for Mora's murder, what do you think?"

"No."

"Bingo."

He had implored the state attorney's office to at least go after Senex for those gangbanger deaths and disappearances. Back off, they told him. They said he was turning his feelings about Senex into a vendetta. He was too involved with the death of his son. They scorned his belief that gangbanger blood was used for parabiosis experimentation to rejuvenate Senex. They turned him out the door and said not to return without more evidence.

Despite their bluster, he knew why no assistant state's attorney wanted to take the case. They wanted records of wins and no losses so their boss, Mr. State's Attorney, would have an election talking point. Taking a long-shot case wasn't in his interest or theirs. They feared being known as losers if they weren't victorious. For too many of them, justice was a zero-sum game where all that mattered was whether you won. Not how hard you tried to get justice.

At Nicole's request, the bartender switched channels to the press conference. "Look." She pointed to the TV set over the bar. "It's already started."

On the TV screen, President Dallas Taylor reminded a reporter that when her attorney general had sought to enforce Promethean Pharma's obligation to negotiate the inflated price of Anoflix, the company ceased producing the drug. It did so to evade its duty to negotiate.

"What is the administration's next step," another reporter asked.

The president replied that her administration had no choice but to invoke the Bayh-Dole Act. That act provided the authority to compel Promethean Pharma to issue licenses to other pharmaceutical companies willing to manufacture and distribute Anoflix at a reasonable price. The patent would still remain the intellectual property of Promethean Pharma.

Hands shot into the air like eager grammar school children wanting recognition. She recognized the CNN reporter. The reporter asked whether any pharmaceutical companies had so far been issued compulsory licenses. Taylor answered in the negative but added that Health and Human Services was engaged in a worldwide search for likely manufacturers.

"Still think she's all talk and no action?" Nicole asked.

"We'll see."

Just then Marco and Katie came through the door of Dugan's to join them. The two crowded around Jim and Nicole on their barstools.

"More good news I hear," Katie said, slapping her brother on the back. "I talked to Bryan last week. He says you two are getting along better."

"Thanks to you, Katie. You're the family glue."

Without his sister there'd be no truce with Bryan. Ever the peacemaker, she had arranged one between them. In return for a trial visitation where the man Jim still considered his father would temporarily stay with Bryan in DC, Bryan would shelve a custody lawsuit for the time being. She took it on herself to chaperone their father to DC until he was in Bryan's safe hands. Bryan would return their father when upcoming Justice Department business required his return to Chicago.

"Time to go to the superintendent's office," Marco reminded him. "He expects us."

"It's in the bag," Katie nudged her brother. "Commander Jim Murphy."

"We have a saying," Marco said. "Never promise the sun before it rises."

———

With Jim Murphy in the passenger seat, Marco Leone turned the squad car into the parking lot of police headquarters at Thirty-Fifth and Michigan. On the way, Marco updated Jim about the investigation into the theft of the superintendent's Lexus and its subsequent use in a gangland killing.

He barely paid attention to Marco's report because that wasn't what the meeting was about. The superintendent would grill him to find out if he had what it took to turn his district into what it should be. He had prepared a wealth of ideas for de-escalating tensions in minority neighborhoods and reforming a stop-and-frisk policy.

As he entered the office, the superintendent looked up from his desk. "Have a seat, Jim. Good to see ya."

The superintendent liked to use a first-name informality in formal situations. The scuttlebutt was he did this out of a desire to be everybody's friend. He was the compromise choice for superintendent between a police board and mayor at odds. As a result, no faction in the city was truly happy with his recent appointment.

The superintendent was a cop's cop rising from the ranks with a knack for keeping his head down and picking the winners in office and city politics. He also had kept his nose clean when it came to the daily temptations every cop faced. From a diversity viewpoint he was perfect. With a father half Irish and Hispanic and a mother of African American heritage, he had for the moment pacified major political constituencies.

"It's a busy day," the superintendent said. "So I'll get down to business."

In his mind Murphy rehearsed his expression of gratitude when the superintendent would tell him he was officially the new commander of the Thirteenth District. He was eager to explain his plans so the superintendent would know he had made the right choice.

The superintendent's smile faded. He asked in a hushed tone lowered almost to a whisper, "Any progress on my stolen Lexus?"

"Wha . . . ?" Murphy recovered in time to remember the briefing Marco had given him in the squad car. "The Lexus was used in an attempted drug buy and in a drive-by shooting after the buy went sideways. One person dead. A patrol car found it in Fuller Park. Torched and now a burned-out shell. Probably gasoline accelerant."

"Je-sus." The superintendent ran his hand through a curly thatch of hair. "They stole it right out there." He pointed out the window behind him. "Right under our noses at police headquarters, in the parking lot. Can you believe the balls?" He hunched over his desk toward Murphy. "It doesn't look good." He cast eyes down on the desk. "Any reporters get wind of it?"

"Not yet. It's bound to break."

"Do what you can to keep it under wraps."

"I'll get right on it."

"We got to spin it. Maybe the car's not mine."

"The secretary of state has your name on the title."

"Come up with something." He scratched his head. "Any leads?"

"A confidential informant fingered the Latin Barons . . . a splinter group from the Latin Kings."

"That's it?"

"No." Murphy squirmed in his seat. "The CI says undercover officers stopped the car after the carjack and before the buy." He rubbed his throat. "The officers . . . according to the CI, mind you . . . skimmed the cash the Latin Barons had taken for the buy . . . and then let them go."

"Je-sus. Dirty cops?" The superintendent looked toward the ceiling. "Cut me a break up there." He lowered his eyes and locked them on Murphy. "Anything to it?"

"The CI's a crackhead with a long rap sheet."

"I need to know one thing . . . Is he reliable?"

"That's why we use him."

"Set up a sting. See if the undercover cops take the bait."

"Right on it."

"Thanks for coming in, Jim. Now back to my inbox." He reached for a stack of papers in the lower part of his two-tiered inbox. "That'll be all."

"Nothing else?" he asked.

"Should there be?" He slapped his forehead with his hand. "Of course." He ran his hand through his thick hair. "I can't appoint you commander of the Thirteenth District. A transfer will be taking over."

"I don't understand."

"Street cops don't like what they call a cheese-eating rat who rats on one of their own." He held out his hands in resignation. "I'm not saying it's right. I'm saying it is . . . and as the super I have to be concerned with CPD morale."

"You're saying I didn't do my duty by cooperating with the FBI." He squeezed the arms of his chair. "Is the FBI now one of the bad guys?"

"Listen up, Detective Murphy." His muscles tightened around his jutting jaw. "I have to run a department in the middle of a crime crisis." He struggled to stand up. Too much time behind a desk had turned his stomach to flab. "I'll give it to you straight." Once up, he held on to the edge of the desk. "Cops are asking for transfers out of your district. They walk the other way when you approach. They don't like you. I need someone else for commander. Case closed."

"I'll clear my things out of Cronin's old office at once."

"Not so fast. We need time to transfer in the new commander. You're still my interim."

"How can I do my job if they know I'm only interim?"

"Just don't rock any boats . . . and don't rely on backup if you're in the field. It might not come." He ran his hand through his hair. "Geez . . . I wish it were otherwise but it's not. Good day, Detective."

Murphy saluted and walked out of the office. *The luck of the Irish.*

# CHAPTER FIFTY-FIVE

"You promised to help, Sebastian. We've tried everything but she's fading."

Sebastian Senex poked at his crab cake sandwich in Bullfeathers restaurant near Capitol Hill. Brock Brewster's refusal to take no for an answer tested his patience.

"If it cured your Huntington's, it might cure my wife."

Senex nodded to the passing lobbyist on his payroll but blew off the lobbyist's attempt at conversation for a more important matter. He had to take Brewster in hand before things spun out of control.

"I don't want to lose her." Brewster closed his eyes and rubbed his forehead. "Without her prodding I wouldn't be where I am today."

With that assessment Senex agreed. She provided the political fire in the belly her husband lacked. Senex and the wife had their extramarital fling without Brewster being the wiser. Why she broke off the affair was beyond belief. She dumped a winner like him for someone like Brewster. And now he was supposed to help her? She had made her bed with Brewster, not him. Let her lie in that deathbed.

"Are you listening, Sebastian?"

"What about your promise to go to court?"

"I kept my promise. I sued to stop the Speaker from becoming president." Brewster put down his forkful of salad. "It's not my fault we got thrown out of district court in record time."

"You didn't appeal."

"Are you serious?" Brewster pushed away the salad bowl. "Clyde Pomeroy died in the explosion on the subway train. A dead man can't be president."

"That's not the point." Brewster motioned the waiter over for the check. "I have my sources. You decided not to appeal before he died."

"What, in God's name, is the point?"

"The point is you planned to disobey me." He dabbed at his lips and chin with the napkin. "How can I trust associates who keep secrets?"

"You baffle me." Brewster stopped talking to sign an autograph for a passerby. "We are without a president. Until the House selects one, we know Dallas Taylor is a danger to the country. And yet your concern is I didn't jump high enough when you whistled?"

"Here's the bottom line, Brewster." Senex left cash on the table for the bill. "The Speaker's dead. You didn't plan to fully keep your part of the deal. So, I don't owe you anything."

"Don't owe me?" His eyes widened. He leaned in toward Senex. "Like you wanted, I've exhausted myself buttonholing and buttering up every congressman I can lay hands on to get elected president."

"Like I wanted?" He expelled air through his teeth and lips. *Pfft.* "You loved doing it. You pleaded for my help, although your wife urged you to stay away from me."

"She and I had our differences." He lowered his head and stared at the table. "But I love her. She needs me now."

"Your devotion is admirable." Senex replaced his wallet inside his jacket. "But it's not just your failure to appeal. If I give you the treatment protocol, the secret will get out before Promethean Pharma can profit from it."

"I can keep a secret." Brewster took Senex's hand. "For my wife's sake."

"Stop begging." He pulled his hand away. "I'll think about it."

# CHAPTER FIFTY-SIX

"We didn't ask you to fly out to DC." The US Capitol Police sergeant wiped pizza grease from his mouth. "We just wanted assistance."

The sergeant tossed the half-eaten pizza slice back into the delivery box on the conference table. It landed on the leftovers of a pepperoni pizza with a pseudo-mozzarella topping the consistency of heart plaque. "Chicago's not the only place, you know, that has telephones, faxes, internet, and mail service."

"I had to be here anyway," Jim Murphy said, "to testify in your superior court."

Styrofoam coffee cups ringed the table with the leavings of unfinished Danish and doughnuts on paper plates. The station-house cuisine made him feel right at home.

"What for?"

"Family business." *None of your business* got no further than the tip of his tongue.

The mad dash by cab from the DC airport to testify in court and then on to the Capitol Police headquarters left him cranky. He had to keep his cool. The Chicago Police Department needed help from the Capitol cops on a multistate drug bust. It wouldn't pay to piss them off.

"Why's it so warm in here?" Murphy popped open the top button of his shirt.

"Thermostat's busted." The sergeant jerked his thumb at a police cadet eyeing a pizza slice. "Make yourself useful. Go find the maintenance guy."

The clamp-jawed DC cops hanging around the table after roll call studied the alien cop from the Windy City with fish eyes reserved for suspects. They looked resentful, as though his appearance were an unspoken criticism of their work. He'd feel the same if his superior called in a stranger cop from across the country to help solve a case. *Can we trust this guy,* he'd say. *Is this gung ho hot dog going to take credit for my work?*

The sergeant washed down the pizza with a cup of industrial-strength coffee. "Our lead dick on the case will be here any minute."

"No problem," Murphy answered. He used the downtime to figure out how things had gone haywire between him and his brother. Bryan started it by reneging on his agreement to return Patrick Murphy to Chicago after the visitation ended. Bryan wanted proof his Chicago brother had a reliable caretaker for their father after Bryan found out from Katie that their father had escaped more times than Jim had told him. Bryan didn't understand that Jim was doing the best he could and was looking for a reliable caretaker. Instead of continuing the family negotiation, Bryan had sued him in the Superior Court of the District of Columbia to take sole custody of their father.

The morning's testimony in superior court had left him exhausted, hearing the accusation of his incompetency and meager resources compared to his big-shot Justice Department brother. What gnawed at him most was hearing Patrick Murphy testify that Bryan was his only son and that the unfamiliar man over there kidnapped him and kept him locked in a room.

The door at the Capitol police station flung open, and a baby-faced detective in T-shirt and jeans hustled in. He took off his raid jacket and crashed in the chair opposite Murphy. "Drug bust" was all he said before taking off the jacket.

Murphy interpreted the words as an explanation for his delay.

"Before we start, let's get straight," the DC detective said. "This is our case, period. Any problem with that?"

"No."

"Why are you here?" he asked Murphy.

"I don't want to be here. Our chief of detectives said your brass wanted help with the assassination investigation of the House Speaker." The heat in the room was getting to him. Baby Face added to the heat under the collar. Murphy fanned himself with a takeout menu from the pizza box to cool off before he and Baby Face got into it. "Any problem with that?"

"We don't need no help," said the Capitol police sergeant.

"The chief says I handle this." Baby Face pointed to the door. "The show's over. Everyone out now, except me and Detective Murphy."

Baby Face watched the last officer slam the door shut.

"I don't mean to bust your balls, Detective Murphy," Baby Face said. "DC has over two dozen law-enforcement agencies with overlapping jurisdiction. We can get a little paranoid about others hogging the limelight." He read an index card he removed from this pocket. "I see your case against Sebastian Senex for the murder of some vic called Dr. Angelo Mora got thrown out of court." He scratched his unshaven chin. "Sure you can help us?"

"Why are you bringing that up?" He stood up. "Just to needle me?"

"No offense, pal. We need your help." Baby Face waved Murphy back down. "Senex is big news in DC." He yawned. "Pulling every string to get the House to elect Brewster president."

"That's old news in Chicago."

"This isn't." The DC detective handed Murphy a grainy black-and-white photograph. "We got this off a security camera. Recognize the guy on the right?"

He held the photo up to the ceiling light. Two men stood side by side on the dimly lit underground walkway between the Capitol Building and the Cannon House Office Building. He studied the man on the right. About six feet tall. The eyes of a predator. Aquiline nose. Elongated head. A pronounced jaw line like a barracuda. "I know him."

"Who is he?"

"Sebastian Senex."

"That's what we thought . . . but Senex is in his seventies. This guy looks too young."

"This is where you owe me." He explained in detail Senex's search for the fountain of youth through blood transfusions and the reversal of his aging noticed by those who knew him. He ended his monologue with a question. "Do you think Senex had the Speaker murdered?"

Before he received an answer, Murphy's phone buzzed. It was his DC lawyer with the decision of the superior court judge. "Excuse me. I've got to take this call."

Baby Face shrugged. "Take it in the hallway. We're through anyway."

The lawyer reported the superior court decided DC had enough connections with the custody case to decide the matter. His brother was a resident of the District and Patrick Murphy, his ward, was physically present in DC. Therefore, the court heard the case.

"I lost, right? The judge was biased in favor a DC resident, right?"

"No and no," the lawyer said. "Because Illinois is the home state for your father, and you as current custodian live there, the judge held that an Illinois court was better positioned to make a final decision."

"What now?"

"Your brother has thirty days to file suit in Illinois for sole custody of your father at which point the DC superior court will relinquish jurisdiction."

"Who gets custody in the meantime?"

"Your brother."

"I do what I can." Murphy rubbed his face with his hand. "I drive by when I'm on duty. My sister helps when she can. The last time he got away I was right on it . . . and friends on the force found him right away. Bryan doesn't have a police department to search when he runs away like I do. I—"

"I feel your pain, but it's not my call. Gotta go."

At least the next round would be in his home court.

# CHAPTER FIFTY-SEVEN

In the study just off the Oval Office, the president of the United States psyched herself up by tap-dancing in rusty rhythm to Trombone Shorty's "Here Come the Girls" on a square plywood board with quarters taped to her shoes. This was how she practiced as a dancing wonder child in a Dallas shack called home with warped wood floors. She revered the tradition of struggling tap dancers who brought along their own boards when working gigs in clubs with uneven flooring.

She was up for a struggle tonight with Sebastian Senex.

Despite the double whammy of racism and sexism, this come-from-behind kid had defied the odds. She had danced her way up the ladder of social success all the way to the White House. If only her mama and papa were around to see how their iron discipline had paid off. They saw how iron discipline worked for Michael Jackson and his dancing. They made it work for Dallas Taylor the dancer and now president.

Her stratospheric rise meant many had to be left behind, her mama and her papa wondering what alien they had created when she went out into the world and came back an enigma. And all the men who passed through her life. They didn't have what it took to keep up. They felt intimidated and fell away. Better one day alone with an ache of emptiness than a thousand with men who couldn't cut it.

She stumbled. Feeling dizzy, she stopped dancing to suck air. She gulped from a water bottle. Her left arm and leg felt sore. Her granny would say she wasn't a spring chicken anymore. At least the endorphin rush eased the headache plaguing her all afternoon. No two ways about it. She had put off medical checkups for too long.

She had been too busy to maintain a physician-patient relationship. The rare emergency doctor took the place of a personal physician. The White House physician she inherited from the outgoing administration had resigned for greener pastures. Emily James, her chief of staff and best friend since college, nagged her to find a new one.

Two staff members and Emily had selected Dr. Bert Gaines, a decorated navy commander, and two others as top-notch candidates for White House physician. The final choice was hers. Only Emily knew that Dr. Gaines and the president had been college sweethearts. Though she broke the relationship off as a hindrance to career ambitions, she wondered if he carried a torch for her, or at least, a candle.

Her chief of staff protested, perhaps too much, that the selection of Dr. Gaines for consideration had nothing to do with her college romance. Staff who didn't know Dr. Gaines also recommended him because of his outstanding record as a navy physician.

Her finger running down the background report had stopped at marital status: divorced. She had convinced herself he had the best qualifications. She looked forward to meeting him again. He was always a straight talker. Living in her presidential bubble of suck-ups, she convinced herself it would be sensible to have him around. She had made an objective choice. That's all there was to it.

"Show time." Emily was at the door. "Don't forget to put away the toys. Won't do to have the press get wind of a Dancing Queen in the White House." Emily always knew how to put a smile on her boss's face.

Taylor primped herself in the floor-to-ceiling mirror. She squared her shoulders and strode to the Resolute desk in the Oval Office. She sat down in front of the flag of the United States and the presidential flag, which flanked three elongated windows.

Taylor closed her eyes before the TV cameras went on and took a deep breath. She was Judge Dallas and they loved her even when she didn't occupy the Oval Office. Energy coursed through her chest. She joked with the gaggle of reporters and technicians tinkering with TV equipment.

Her chief of staff stood in the doorway of the secretary's office and connected her thumb and forefinger in an A-OK to her boss. The little girl from the wrong side of the tracks was on top now. She knew it. And they knew it. With hands folded on the Resolute desk she was poised to take on Sebastian Senex and all he stood for. The red camera light blinked.

"Good evening, my fellow Americans," she said. "As you know, I invoked the provisions of the Bayh-Dole Act to require that Promethean Pharma grant licenses to other pharmaceutical companies willing to manufacture and distribute the Anoflix vaccine. The vaccine is the only hope to prevent any outbreak of the mutated coronavirus from inflicting immense injury to our citizens and our economy. In the past week more instances of what is called COVID-28 have surfaced in China.

"Despite its best efforts, my administration has been unable to license the production of Anoflix to another pharmaceutical company able or willing to produce this lifesaving vaccine in a timely manner. Because Promethean Pharma has stopped producing the Anoflix vaccine to evade its legal duty to negotiate the selling price, I am forced to take further action in the national interest. I declare a national emergency under the National Emergencies Act and invoke the Defense Production Act to implement the following measures.

"Subject to the requirement of just compensation, the United States will temporarily take over the Anoflix patent and the management of Promethean Pharma to continue the uninterrupted production of Anoflix at a price determined unilaterally by the Department of Health and Human Services. This will continue until such time as Promethean agrees to resume production of Anoflix for sale in the United States at a negotiated price as required by law.

"I regret this interference in the business affairs of Promethean Pharma. But the refusal of Sebastian Senex, the CEO and board chairman of Promethean Pharma, to put the good of the country ahead of his financial interests left no other choice. Good night, and God bless y'all."

She rose from her chair but immediately crumpled back into the seat with a hand to her forehead. She braced herself and straightened up.

"Cut the cameras," her chief of staff said, rushing up to her.

She fell into the arms of Emily James. "Get me Dr. Gaines right away."

———

The next day Sebastian Senex turned the temperature of the Meridian Club sauna up to 185 degrees clad only in a Turkish towel wrapped around his loins. He sat down beside General Horatio A. Harrison, the secretary of defense, on a red-cedar bench. Both were stripped down to their essentials. He liked it that way. Mendacity and evasion and pretense all melted away like the toxins steamed from the skin. He never embarked on any serious undertaking without gut testing a potential associate in the sauna.

And for this, the most serious of all his ventures, transparency and trust were essential. The two were like Roman senators in the baths plotting political changes more to their liking. As they looked at the glowing sauna rocks, Harrison said, "What do you think of her performance last night?"

"Looked bad for me at first." He splashed water over the rocks with a wooden ladle. A spurt of steam sizzled into the air. He tightened his towel and sat down. "But her collapse at the end turned it around. The media chatter this morning was about her health and not me." He looked at the beet-red Harrison drinking bottled water. "Time to strike while the iron's hot."

"We shouldn't rush." Harrison rose to stand over the heated sauna rocks and warmed his hands. He returned to his seat. "Maybe something's wrong with her health. Could be something serious. Then she'd be removed for inability to perform her presidential duties."

"Confound it." He tugged at his Turkish towel. "'Maybe' . . . 'could be' . . . won't cut it. Her problem last night might just be low blood sugar." He rubbed his left arm with a bristle brush to improve circulation. "Even if a cabinet majority wanted to remove her, the vice president would have to agree under the Twenty-Fifth Amendment."

"Wait a minute." Harrison scratched his chin. "We don't have a vice president. She shot up to president . . . I mean acting president . . . or whatever the lawyers call her . . . until the House elects the president."

"See the problem?" he asked.

"Ha!" Harrison shook his head. "The law of unintended consequences. We can't remove her because there's no vice president to concur with the cabinet."

"What about impeachment?" Harrison wiped the sweat off his face with a face towel.

"Out of the question." He beat his bare back with a whisk of eucalyptus leaves and twigs. "The House is totally absorbed in just picking the next president. The House censured two members for coming to blows over the election." He applied the whisk to his chest and stomach. "Anyway, the Senate's never removed any president from the Oval Office after House impeachment."

*What's Harrison's problem? How did Mr. Hard-Ass turn into Mr. Softie?*

"Level with me." Senex stood over the seated general. "Are you worried about losing your position as secretary of defense if we go ahead?"

"I'm on thin ice with her." The secretary of defense straightened out his legs and wiggled his toes. "I'm better for the plan inside the tent than outside."

He sipped from his water bottle and poured the remainder over his head, letting it run down his torso in cooling rivulets. "Do you really think she'd risk a political firestorm by firing you?"

"She might."

"Come on, Harrison." He threw the empty bottle on the floor. "Buck up. You're supposed to be secretary of defense."

"Precisely." Harrison headed for the sauna door followed by Senex. "I want to stay secretary of defense."

After showering, they changed clothes in the locker room. Harrison's cell buzzed.

"Is that right?" Harrison pressed the cell against his ear. "No mistake? OK. Let me know of any developments." He disconnected the call. "Let's move on the plan . . . now."

"Why the change of heart?"

"She wants from me a signed and undated letter of resignation." He shook Senex's outstretched hand to seal the deal. "My days are numbered. We have to strike first."

# CHAPTER FIFTY-EIGHT

The black limousine pulled up outside the Robert F. Kennedy Justice Department Building. Sebastian Senex looked out the tinted windows from the back seat. The person he needed to set straight hadn't arrived. Sebastian Senex resented waiting. Through the intercom he ordered the chauffeur to keep the motor running and leave after ten minutes if he didn't show up. While waiting, he reread the *Washington Times* headline: **CORKER DIES IN AIRPLANE BATHROOM**. In disbelief he reread the account of the tragic farce.

On a fact-finding boondoggle to Ukraine, the substitute Democratic presidential candidate suffered a fatal heart attack while having sex with a twenty-eight-year-old female aide trapped behind a malfunctioning bathroom door on a Lufthansa aircraft. In Kiev, firefighters pried open the door and released both corpse and aide. Corker always wanted to be a member of the mile-high club, the aide said.

Senex's Plan B had gone up in smoke along with Corker. Brock Brewster was his only plan now. He had to make sure Brewster kept his head screwed on straight in the race for the Oval Office.

As the limousine pulled away, Bryan Murphy yanked on the door handle.

He looked to his left and his right before hopping into the rear seat next to Senex.

The CEO of Promethean Pharma ordered the chauffeur to keep driving around the block.

"You're late," he said. "It shows a lack of respect."

"Sorry, but Justice lawyers are in a tizzy about Corker's death. The Twelfth Amendment restricts the House choice to the top three contenders in the Electoral College. With Corker dead, Dallas Taylor moves into third place behind Brock Brewster and Frank Hammer for consideration as president."

"Get serious, man. Taylor only received five votes for president in the Electoral College. She doesn't have the chance of a snowball in hell. And Hammer only got seventy-six votes."

"Sure looks that way."

"Great news for my boy, Brewster. He's a shoo-in for president with a hundred and ninety-two electoral votes."

Things worked out for the best. Plan B-Corker was too reckless to be an effective president. He'd go all out for Brock Brewster.

"Keep in mind," Murphy said. "The House vote alone counts. Not the electoral vote."

"The handwriting is on the wall. Brewster's going to be president, I tell you."

"If you say so, that must be right." Murphy checked the time. "Now that I'm the acting attorney general, I have a lot of work to do. Got to get back to Justice. Why'd you want to see me?"

No thanks for all he had done to get Murphy promoted to acting attorney general. Without the dirt he had dug up on the attorney general, Bryan would not have the promotion. The feminist attorney general suing Promethean Pharma for environmental violations and defending against Senex's lawsuit challenging the takeover of Promethean Pharma had resigned her office in disgrace. Opposition researchers funded secretly by Promethean Pharma sniffed out proof that in her earlier years as a prosecutor she had withheld information from an African American defendant that would have exonerated the man. Instead, a death sentence was carried out.

"Why did you look around before getting in? Afraid of being seen with me?"

"Afraid of being seen with someone arrested for murder," Murphy said through clenched teeth. "It wouldn't look good for you or me if it hit the news."

"Don't get high and mighty with me. The case was dismissed." He fiddled with his seat belt. "Your brother tried to nail me. What are you doing to keep him off my back?"

"My brother and I aren't talking. Nothing I can do with the state murder charge . . . even if I wanted." Murphy took a water bottle from the backseat cooler. "Weak case anyway. They don't have Mora's body." He swigged from the bottle. "All circumstantial."

"Let's discuss things you can do." He made sure the privacy partition was closed tight. "As acting attorney general, you have control over the environmental cases and federal eminent domain case against Promethean Pharma."

"I'm listening."

"Good." He ordered the driver to turn up the background stereo music for added precaution. "I want that methylene chloride pollution case in Illinois to go away."

"Sorry." He wrung his hands and peeked out the window. "I can't do anything. She filed the case the day before her resignation."

"You can dismiss it, damn it."

"Hey, Sebastian. I wasn't Dallas Taylor's first choice. I'm only acting. She could can me if I did something so obvious . . . and where would that leave you?" He snapped his fingers. "I've got it. Make a lowball offer to settle the case. I'll see if we can accept close to your offer and dismiss the case. It looks better that way."

"I fully expect the case to be settled for the dollar amount I suggest. The Justice Department won't nickel-and-dime me."

"Let's not get ahead of ourselves. Make an offer."

"And what about the Tampa facility case? That hasn't been filed yet."

"No way." Murphy squared his shoulders. "It's a heater case. The media would crucify me if I didn't file suit. You agreed."

"When I agreed my exact words were . . . 'you aren't high enough on the totem pole to help.'" He raised his voice. "You're on top of the totem pole now. I expect you not to sue."

The chauffeur turned his head to look through the rearview mirror. Senex waited until the chauffeur faced forward. "If you want my support when you run for the Senate, you'd better remember who brung ya to the dance. I made you and I can break you. Once the House picks

Brewster . . . any day now . . . Taylor'll be out on her ear." He jabbed Murphy in the shoulder with his forefinger. "And so will you, sonny boy, unless I put a good word in with President Brewster."

"Back off, Sebastian." He rolled down the rear window and took a deep breath. "I'm not your errand boy."

"Just do what I tell you."

"Screw you." Murphy scrambled out of the limousine. "Get another errand boy."

# CHAPTER FIFTY-NINE

"I rule as follows," Judge Pomo declared, fingering the white cane propped up against the bench in the Circuit Court of Cook County. He adjusted sunglasses on his nose. "Although I acknowledge Jim Murphy, the current custodian, has grown up believing Patrick Murphy was his father, the DNA results from the fingernail samples left by the deceased Jack Cronin lead to only one conclusion. Jim Murphy is the biological son of Commander Jack Cronin."

Standing next to his brother before the judge's bench, Jim Murphy now knew what the commander meant when he had said at Northwestern Hospital: *You're looking at the proof and you don't know it yet.*

This wily rogue cop called Mr. Billy Club had outfoxed him.

Jim Murphy didn't buy the testimony of the commander's manicurist-girlfriend that she hung on to the toiletry bag with his fingernail clippings for sentimental reasons . . . despite the slip of a teardrop or two on the stand. The commander must have instructed her to hang on to the bag once he heard Bryan was starting a custody battle.

He cursed himself for agreeing to the DNA testing for himself and his . . . or what he thought was . . . his father and letting the results be compared with those of his brother and the commander. The DNA tests had ripped apart the family story that was part and parcel of who he thought he was. The truth had left him angry and confused.

"However," Judge Pomo continued, "because of the strong family bond created between Jim and Bryan Murphy and the man they considered their father, I further rule that they be appointed plenary co-guardians over Patrick Murphy, and that until otherwise adjudicated or agreed to by Jim and Bryan Murphy, Patrick Murphy remain in the custody of Bryan Murphy."

His instinctive reaction was to assume some hidden incompetency or the corruption of the judge for letting Bryan keep physical custody in Washington, DC. But his conscience wouldn't let him. The judge had a reputation as an exceptionally honest and fair jurist.

He had to face facts and look at himself. Law and science said Patrick Murphy was not his father. Jim Murphy couldn't match the same quality of home care Mr. Hotshot could provide for Patrick Murphy. He just wasn't the success Bryan was. His head told him to give up the battle, but his heart hadn't caught up with his head.

"We don't get along," Jim said to the judge preparing to leave the bench. "How can we cooperate as co-guardians?" His attorney tugged on his sleeve to silence him. "Your decision won't work."

"I believe," the judge said, "you two will work it out. You are bound to the man who was the biological father of only one but the real father of both."

Patrick Murphy remained seated at the counsel's table, murmuring singsong to himself. In his hands he kneaded the patrolman's service cap he had worn after joining the CPD.

"You both care about him. In caring for him you will learn to work together."

"And if we don't?" Jim asked.

"My door's always open. I'll decide for you."

"But we have nothing in common . . . not even a father."

"Detective Murphy," he said, rising from the bench with his white cane. "Take it from an only child. As the years roll by, I predict you'll come to cherish the one person with whom you share a history needing no explanation. The court is now adjourned." He tapped his way down the bench stairs and back into chambers.

Jim bolted out of the courtroom into the eighteenth-floor corridor of the Daley Center. The wall of reinforced window glass overlooking the rusted Picasso sculpture in the Daley Plaza below brought him to a stop. He pressed his head against the glass and closed his eyes.

His family had fallen apart. His wife and Santiago were dead. He and Bryan were at each other's throats. And the man he thought was his father wasn't. Patrick Murphy had denied paternity and he, the would-be son, was the demented one for refusing to believe it. His dear sister had tied herself into emotional knots trying to keep things together between him and his brother . . . no, his half brother.

The man who was his biological father was everything he despised. He had lost one relationship he loved and gained another he loathed. Life was absurd, just like his lawyer's admonition that he wear his police uniform to court to make a good impression, even though a blind judge heard the case. Maybe Marco was right . . . *Mondo cane* . . . It's a dog's world.

A tap on his shoulder. "Katie. What do you want?"

"I want you and Bryan to work this out."

"Still believing in miracles, is that it?" Jim asked. Over her shoulder he saw his own lawyer and Bryan's conferring outside the courtroom. "Like the time you prayed for money to buy a Supergirl doll and found twenty-five dollars on the floor of your closet when I was the one who put it there."

With his arm around Patrick Murphy, who wore a nobody-inside smile, Bryan stood next to the lawyers and a popular journalist covering the custody hearing. The journalist took down every word falling from Bryan's mouth, as though words from an oracle. The only reason for that had to be Bryan's promotion to the position of acting attorney general of the United States.

"Maybe you were the miracle I prayed for." She brushed the hair away from her eyes. They looked swollen and red. "Just try to work it out, Jimmy . . . for my sake."

"OK, sis . . . for your sake." Bryan stared back at him with a stone face. "But no promises." He averted the stare to avoid getting into it with Mr. Hotshot.

She kissed him on the neck, whispering, "Thanks, little brother."

"I'm only one year littler." He touched her cheek as she pulled back.

"Bryan stopped me outside the courtroom," she said. "He wants to talk to you."

"Not now." He turned his back to her and stared out the window with arms folded. A pack of kids raced around the Picasso sculpture like a troupe of monkeys. "I'm in no mood to make nice-nice with Mr. Hotshot about . . . what do I call that man now?"

"How about Dad, like always? He acted like a father. Isn't that what counts?"

"Until he turned on me."

"Forgiveness came hard to him." She held his hand. "He couldn't handle the cheating by both his wife and best friend."

"I'm not talking to Mr. Hotshot about Patrick Murphy."

"That's not what he wants. He wants to help you against Senex."

# CHAPTER SIXTY

"Why's he here?" asked Dallas Taylor. She pointed to Sebastian Senex sitting in a corner of the rustic conference room at the Camp David presidential retreat.

"I invited him because you weren't available to ask," Horatio A. Harrison said. "The rest of the cabinet agreed. He has sensitive information you may want to challenge directly."

Seated at a round oak table in the center of the room, she let him stay and skimmed the petition asking for her resignation from the presidency. A little over half of her cabinet had signed it. "Do you seriously expect me to resign?"

"We do," continued the secretary of defense. He turned to the director of national intelligence and the chairman of the Joint Chiefs of Staff seated to his right. "Gentlemen?"

"We agree," said the director of national intelligence. The chairman of the Joint Chiefs added, "And so do the others not here today."

"For the record," the national security advisor said, "the secretary of state and I don't agree with the petition." The secretary of state nodded agreement.

"You're not a cabinet official," Harrison said to national security advisor. "Why are you here?"

"Neither is the chairman of the Joint Chiefs," the secretary of state said. "But he's here."

"General Harrison." Taylor turned to her secretary of defense. "We have irreconcilable differences. I intend to act on the signed but undated letter of resignation you gave me."

"I withdraw my offer of resignation and will confirm my withdrawal in writing after this meeting." Harrison looked to Sebastian Senex nodding support.

"If you don't resign, I'll have to dismiss you."

"I wouldn't advise that," the director of national intelligence said. "The existing cabinet is in charge." He avoided Taylor's eyes and shifted his feet. "A majority of your cabinet has signed that petition. You lack the votes to dismiss General Harrison."

"Hogwash. My acting attorney general, Bryan Murphy, assures me my powers as president are full and complete until the House selects a president."

Sebastian Senex now knew on what side Bryan Murphy stood. He'd see to it that Murphy had no future in politics. He poured a glass of water from a silver pitcher near the fireplace and swallowed an aspirin. He glanced out the window at the wooded hills. Green buds were breaking out on the tree branches swaying above melting islands of snow. For now he would stay silent in the background with his ace in the hole unless he had to play it.

"For the good of the country, we ask you to resign," said General John Klaine, the chairman of the Joint Chiefs of Staff. "I bear you no ill will."

"For the good of the country?" She shook her head, looking puzzled. "If I resign, that means a crucial delay for the presidential election in the House of Representatives. We have no vice president now. So the Speaker becomes president. Until the House elects a new Speaker to direct the presidential vote, the country remains in a dangerous uncertainty."

"You have failed to protect us against our enemies." Harrison spread out a map of the South China Sea. "Look here." He tapped a spot on the map with his finger. "During a military drill, a Chinese warship fired on one of the Spratly Islands. A Taiwanese garrison was hit. Two soldiers died, four wounded. And you have done nothing. This is an escalation, beyond probing by fishing boats and building artificial islands."

"Aren't you the folks who told me the Chinese wouldn't withdraw from Taiping Island. But they did. Not one of you acknowledged I was right. But I was." No one responded to her accusation. She had caught them off balance. "I just learned the Chinese ordered the warship to return home. Our secretary of state has demanded an explanation."

"And how far has that gotten you?" Harrison asked, turning to the secretary of state.

"No response yet." The secretary rubbed his wrist. "But we're working on it."

"Meanwhile," the national director of intelligence said, "a Russian brigade supported by tanks blitzkrieged yesterday out from Kaliningrad along the sixty-mile border between Poland and Lithuania, and you've again done nothing."

"Problem solved." Taylor called on her secretary of state.

"We received word this morning," the secretary said. "The Russians explained it as a military exercise gone wrong. Their troops are on the way back to Kaliningrad."

"I respectfully disagree, Madam President," objected General Klaine. "They're testing us. The Chinese have convinced the Russians to join them by using Oriental psychological warfare. Their feint-and-withdraw tactics are designed to mess with our heads when we're vulnerable without a president. When they've demoralized and divided us enough, they'll attack for real if we don't hit back hard now."

"No one else in the Pentagon is buying that theory," she said. "The important point is that they've stood down."

"And then there's this," the director of national intelligence said. He took out a document from his briefcase and handed it to her. "Several prominent neurologists observed you on television when you collapsed in the Oval Office. They concluded that you possibly suffered a stroke, potentially rendering you unfit for the office of president."

"You know it's unethical for physicians to diagnose persons they never examined," Taylor said. "The White House physician, Bert Gaines, did examine me and concluded that what I experienced was a transient ischemic attack, what's called a TIA, with no residual effects."

"You want us to take the word of Dr. Bert Gaines," the director of national intelligence said, "a college boyfriend? How is he less biased?"

"Dr. Gaines is a friend and social companion. I'm in the unusual position of being an unmarried woman president. I needed to attend several public functions, and he was simply my escort."

"You're evading the issue," Harrison said. "Do you have a romantic relationship with him?"

"Even if I had one, that's none of your business."

"What do you say about this?" Harrison held up a copy of the *International Enquirer.*

"I say your reading habits leave something to be desired."

"Do you deny an intimate relationship?"

"I said all I'm going to say."

"Let's not get sidetracked," the director of national intelligence said, shooting a frown at his colleagues. "A TIA significantly increases your odds of getting a full-blown stroke."

"You boys are a few pickles short of a barrel if you think I'm going to resign because of this," she said. "I'm not disabled and even if I were, you can't make me resign without the concurrence of a vice president. And we don't have a vice president. You won't remove me under the Twenty-Fifth Amendment because you can't."

"That's not all we have," Harrison said, looking over at Senex.

Sebastian Senex felt his restraint at an end. She had taken over Promethean Pharma and humiliated him on all the news networks. The news clips of him being escorted out of his office by US Marshals when he refused to cooperate with the occupation of his company had gone viral. No matter the outcome of his judicial appeal, the media humiliation cried out for revenge. He could never forget or forgive Dallas Taylor. He would have to play his ace in the hole.

"Resign," Sebastian Senex said.

Everyone at the table faced him.

"Why should I?"

"Let me give you another reason," Senex said, going over to the table and sitting down. "Your birth certificate."

"My what?" Taylor's jaw dropped and her eyes widened. "Are you going to push the fake news I wasn't born in the United States? That didn't work in the Obama years, and it won't work now."

"Let me tell you a fairy tale." Senex eased back in the seat and wrapped his hands around the back of his head. "There once was a girl born by midwife in a backwater town in Texas. Her parents had the midwife, who now lives in Austin, backdate the birth certificate by a year . . . in return for a little sweetener, of course.

"By affidavit the midwife claimed the parents did so because of a fierce desire for their girl to succeed in becoming the female Michael Jackson. To do that they needed her to meet minimum age requirements to enter tap-dancing contests around the country at the earliest opportunity."

"Where are you going with this?" she asked.

"It's truly a fairy tale of Cinderella proportions." Senex touched his fingertips together. "The girl became a tap-dancing wonder, then a lawyer, a TV judge, a member of the House of Representatives, a senator, a vice-presidential candidate . . . and now an accidental president who is acting until a real one takes over any day now."

Senex passed copies of the birth certificate and the midwife's affidavit around the table.

"Why are you whistling up the wind?" Taylor fingered the birth certificate. "You're going after my parents for lying about my birth. You can't. They're dead."

"We're going after you." Senex pointed his finger straight out at her. "The Constitution requires a vice president and president to be at least thirty-five years of age." Senex waved a copy of the Constitution. "You weren't thirty-five when you became an accidental president."

She bit her lower lip.

"What do you have to say?" Harrison asked.

She stiffened up as if struck. "Even if this document is genuine," she said and stopped for a moment. She placed her hand on her throat and removed it. "I had absolutely no idea my parents had done this."

"That's what you would say," Senex said.

"Prove I knew."

"Let us stay on track," the national director of intelligence cut in. "It's irrelevant either way. Your state of mind has nothing to do with the objective age requirement set out in the Constitution."

Taylor sprang from her chair and went over to the fireplace. She looked at the fading embers while wringing her hands and found the answer in the embers. She returned to the table. "Let me finish your fairy tale, Mr. Senex, with an omitted fact. I turned thirty-five a week ago."

She returned to her seat and looked Senex in the eye. "I am now thirty-five and eligible to be president."

"You weren't thirty-five when you took office." Senex's voice rasped. "It doesn't matter how old you are now."

"We'll see what my acting attorney general says about that."

"She's wrong, isn't she?" Senex nudged the director of national intelligence.

The director shrugged. "It's for the courts. But I have to wonder why anyone would drag their parents through the mud."

"I beg you to resign," Harrison said. "Spare the nation a legal battle over this. Look at the facts. Chicago is in flames and you won't call out the National Guard. Our foreign enemies are circling us in the middle of a perfect storm of constitutional crises."

"I wanted to be president of the United States," she said in a whisper, slumping her shoulders, "to take necessary action. I knew it would be hard. But you have all made things much harder. I never expected to see the den of vipers we have become."

"Then resign," Senex demanded.

# CHAPTER SIXTY-ONE

"What are you doing here?" Bryan Murphy's jaw went slack. "You're the guy who didn't want to see me." He put down the corned beef sandwich he bought at the Berghoff Cafe in O'Hare International Airport. "Now that you're here, have a seat."

"I'll stand." Jim Murphy clutched the back of a chair across from Bryan. "Katie said you had something to say."

"Jim, do you think he knew?"

"Do I think Senex knew what?"

"Not Senex." Bryan wiped his hand with the napkin. "Dad."

"Sis promised you'd talk only about Senex . . . not your father."

"Our father."

"That's not what the DNA says."

"You were always his favorite."

"Until he turned on me."

"He always loved you, but he had a vision problem. When he looked at you, he saw the commander." Bryan wrapped the sandwich remainder in a to-go bag. "Our dad had a hard time living in the present."

"Another word about your father and I'm gone." Jim noticed a man looking at them from two tables over. Lowering his voice, he gave a nod in the man's direction. "Know that guy?"

"FBI security." Bryan lifted his small glass of dark beer in a mock toast. "I've been promoted to acting attorney general." He took a drink of water from a plastic cup. "It comes with the territory."

"I can read the newspapers about your promotion," Jim said, waving away a waiter asking if he wanted anything. "Pin a rose on you . . . as Mom would say."

"Don't go prickly on me just because you didn't make commander."

"Kiss my tuchus." Katie had blabbed about another of his failures. He about-faced and strode back down the concourse away from Berghoff's.

A hand gripped his shoulder.

If he stopped and turned, things could get ugly. If he didn't, he wouldn't hear what Bryan might have to say about Senex. He turned. "Stick to business. I only want to hear what you have on Senex . . . and no more needling."

"Agreed. I'm sorry you took offense."

"Sure you are." He motioned to a couple of unoccupied plastic bucket chairs at the nearby United Airlines gate. "Let's talk there . . . and stick to Senex."

Bryan laid out how DEA agents during a routine raid of a Sinaloa-funded meth lab in Texas had found an ephedrine stash. Similar raids in the southwest also uncovered other large quantities. The meth labs were about to close for lack of the drug. As if by magic, they now had all the ephedrine they needed. During the latest raid, DEA agents extracted an invoice from the mouth of a Sinaloa chemist before he could swallow it. The invoice showed the ephedrine came from a subsidiary company controlled by Promethean Pharma.

"This is tip of the iceberg," Bryan said. "I thought you'd like to know."

Bryan's account confirmed Outfit rumors that Jim had wrongly discounted as vendetta badmouthing of Promethean Pharma and the Sinaloa cartel.

"Why are you telling me this?" Jim asked. "Senex gave you your break as general counsel for Promethean Pharma. Why turn on him?"

"I have my reasons." He pulled a roller carry-on closer to his seat. "My question is why you came if you thought I was in Senex's pocket?"

"Even thieves fall out." Jim looked at a plane taking off outside the window. "That's the only reason."

"Sure it is." Bryan reached for his roller carry-on. "You're going to get a lot more dirt on Senex, bro."

"Half bro."

"Whatever." Bryan opened the carry-on and pulled out a directive he had issued to the FBI.

After reading it, Jim scratched his head. "So you're really going full bore against the old bastard. I wouldn't have believed it." He was going to shake Bryan's hand but pulled away. Too many teasing pranks and put-downs for that. "Time to level. Why did you turn on Senex?"

"Let me count the ways." Bryan shook his head. "He wouldn't stop pressuring me to take a dive on litigation involving Promethean Pharma." He paused to check the flight-information monitor. "He even fantasized I might influence you to back off the murder rap against him." Bryan scoffed. "Shows how little he knows."

"I have to thank you for the information."

"No thanks needed. Strictly business, remember?" He checked the airline ticket in his breast pocket. "I'm doing this not just because it helps bring down Senex. It advances my goal of being appointed attorney general, instead of just an acting one . . . and then who knows?"

"Upward and onward." Jim shook his head. "That's you alright . . . but thanks anyway. You didn't have to give it to me."

"It's not about you." Bryan raised the retractable handle for his roller carry-on. "The man's a menace to the United States."

"Welcome to the anti-Senex fan club."

"I have a favor to ask."

"I might have known."

"Surprised? We're from Bridgeport, ain't we?" Bryan snickered, holding on to his carry-on handle. "This is only the beginning. I know a lot about Senex and the way he operates. I'm willing to share." He ran his free hand over his slick black hair. "All I want is to make your CPD investigation of Senex in Chicago part of a joint task force with the FBI."

"Whoa, pal." Jim sprang from his seat. "I do that and the FBI will hog all the credit. The Fibbies have burned us too many times."

"Not this time . . . not with your brother overseeing things."

"How can I trust you? You went off with your buddies when the neighborhood bully beat the crap out of me." He rubbed his hands down his sides. "When did you ever look out for me?"

*Final boarding call for United Airlines Flight 1633 to Washington, DC.*

"Are you going to live in the past like him?" Bryan got up from his seat. "You were always his favorite. Remember when the three of us got tight at the local tavern. You and I traded some punches and you ran off. The old man ran after you to see if you were hurt. Never asked about me."

"Whaddaya talking about?" Jim walked beside him to the gate. "You always got the grades. He was proud of you. I can't forget how he turned on me when he found out about the affair."

"But he and I were never close . . . not like you and him . . . until he turned on you."

"You and I were never close either, you know."

"How could we be? I excelled in school to get his attention but still hadn't until he became demented. Great compliment, no? You got it without trying while he had all his marbles." He got into line to board. "Why are we bickering over the past? Do you want to live there?" Bryan held out his hand. "Want to get closer?"

Jim took the hand and shook it. Not Bryan's usual bone-crusher grip. "I'm in, bro." He walked away a few feet and stopped to ask, "What's our joint operation called?"

"Let's call it . . ." Bryan caught himself and smiled. "You name it, bro."

"Me? Something wrong with you today?" Jim cracked a return smile. "I name it Operation Big Shoulders."

# CHAPTER SIXTY-TWO

From the stage President Dallas Taylor squinted at the sunlit gold buttons of West Point cadets seated in white trousers and white bandoliers over gray jackets. On this, their graduation day, they sat up ramrod straight with military parade hats on their knees and eyes trained on her.

The earlier discovery of an explosive device where she now stood to deliver the West Point commencement address had Secret Service agents turning the stadium upside down in the search for others. They found none . . . at least none they could detect. The agents fingered white supremacists, neo-Nazis, or radical skinheads as the probable culprits.

Myriad hate groups and individuals had communicated to her their assassination threats if she did not resign. Any one of them could be responsible for the device. She had already received as many death threats as most modern presidents in their entire first term. Until now, no actual attempt had been made.

This attempt, however, crossed a red line. Every twisted copycat in the country would be out to assassinate her. The assassination of her running mate, Franklin Dexter Walker, had blooded the political waters. The predators would rise from dark depths in their frenzy to take her down.

The assortment of bigots and nutjobs and political fanatics worried her less than the disciplined phalanx of military brass seated on the dais behind her. Her spine tingled with the thought of their hostile glares drilling into her back. Many distrusted her administration and disliked her unorthodox entry into the Oval Office.

But they were ambitious military men familiar with the fine art of being political while not appearing so. The uncertain extent of their displeasure fermented below the surface of the DC political swamp. The ambiguity of the forces against her and how far they might go to expel her from the White House worried her. She would not let it panic her into paranoia.

About to speak, she turned to an aide rushing onstage to report a military unit had stationed itself near the White House. She pulled herself together at this puzzling news. The commander claimed the unit was ordered there to protect the White House against a bomb threat and would remain in place for twenty-four hours. Something wasn't right.

Would they bar her from reentering the White House on some pretext when she returned to DC? Like the landlord did to her parents when the rent was overdue? She took deep breaths and reined in her suspicions. She'd see what actually happened when she returned to the White House.

Unfettered imagination was indispensable for artists but an unreliable guide for politicians. The fate of the republic might come down to the sober decisions of an African American woman, the descendant of slaves in that same republic, navigating the ship of state through the treacherous narrows of political upheaval and constitutional turmoil.

*Have I made the right decision? Is it what LBJ would have done?*

Taylor released her death grip on the lectern and stood tall for her commencement address. After a perfunctory recognition of the VIPs in attendance, she followed the tradition of using presidential authority to pardon West Point cadets for their minor disciplinary infractions.

She tried joking that she could have used such a pardon for antics she had committed in college. Few responded to the warm-up line that had worked for past presidents. The country was as tense as a trapeze wire about to snap. And she was doing the high-wire act on stage without a net with many wondering if she would jump off or be pushed.

When Taylor turned the page of her text, Sebastian Senex and General H. A. Harrison, about to be fired when she returned to DC, slipped through the stage wing into two chairs to the immediate left of the lectern. Harrison and Senex came to preside over her humiliation. A West Point alumnus, General Harrison had turned cadets and faculty against her. The military academy would have canceled her appearance if she hadn't already accepted its invitation to deliver the commencement address.

She and Senex made eye contact for a moment before breaking away. His eyes told her what he expected as she began her speech.

She spoke of political courage as a virtue that no republic could survive without. Most often courage was equated with playing one's cards even with a deck stacked against you. Often overlooked, she said, peeking down at her text, was another aspect of courage pointed out by the songwriter Kenny Rogers, useful advice for politicians as well as card players: the courage of knowing when to fold them. There was, for example, the courage of LBJ in refusing to run for reelection when he had become a divisive figure in the country.

Senex and Harrison smirked.

She wanted to rub the smirks off their faces.

She wandered more and more from her set speech with increasing passion and improvisation. When asked what type of constitution the framers had devised, she reminded her audience that Benjamin Franklin had replied: "A republic if you can keep it."

She implored the cadets to shun the purveyors of political gloom and doom, the pessimists, the naysayers who panic in times of crisis and yearn for the rule of a strongman over the rule of law. Even as we talk here, she said, the House of Representatives has elected a new Speaker.

"The new Speaker has taken charge, and she is ready to take a vote that, according to my best sources, is practically certain to give us the next president of the United States within days. We don't need anyone on a white horse to ride in and save this country. We only need the House of Representatives to do its job."

She clung to the glimmer of hope in a call from her acting attorney general, Bryan Murphy.

He and his brother were on their way to a hearing conducted by the Senate Committee on Finance. Armed with a search warrant for Promethean Pharma headquarters, a joint task force of the FBI and the Chicago Police Department called Operation Big Shoulders had uncovered reams of documentary evidence incriminating Sebastian Senex in kidnapping and murder in collusion with Chicago criminal elements and in the distribution of illegal drugs in collusion with the Sinaloa cartel. The evidence revealed a lurid type of blood procedure inflicted on kidnapped victims by a neofascist named Dr. Angelo Mora for whose death an Illinois grand jury had been summoned. She expected more complete information when she met the Murphy brothers after her return to DC.

Exhorting the cadets to go forth and learn the lessons of leadership while mastering the complicated machinery of modern warfare, she recited the motto of West Point . . . Duty . . . Honor . . . Country . . . while conflicting thoughts raced through her mind.

"Go forth and pledge your lives, your fortunes, and your sacred honor for the good of the United States."

*Do it or don't do it for the good of the United States?*

She didn't know what LBJ would do.

"Thank you, and may God bless all you brave cadets."

She knew what she would not do. And that was all that mattered.

She sat down amid polite applause.

"What are you doing?" Sebastian Senex rushed over to her. "You're supposed to announce your resignation."

"I've changed my mind," she said. "Read my lips. No resignation."

# CHAPTER SIXTY-THREE

Air Force One had landed President Taylor at the Corpus Christi International Airport less than twenty miles away from a longed-for R & R on San José Island. While the Marine One helicopter underwent unexpected repairs at the airport before transporting her to the island, she would use the down time to meet the professor who changed the course of her life.

Surrounded by Secret Service agents, Taylor took her seat in the rear of the auditorium on the campus of Texas A&M University at Corpus Christi. Despite fuming by the agents at the itinerary change, she had made the right decision in stopping off to meet her former political science professor. She'd have to wait until he finished his debate in the Performing Arts Center with a law professor from Harvard Law School. The debate topic emblazoned across the stage read: IS THE HOUSE OF REPRESENTATIVES LIMITED TO BROCK BREWSTER OR FRANK HAMMER?

Professor Chang and the Harvard professor sat at separate tables, each with a water pitcher and a glass. A lectern separated the two tables. Behind the lectern hung a screen imaging the inconclusive results of the presidential election in the Electoral College:

*TOTAL ELECTORAL VOTES: 538*    *WINNING VOTES: 270*
**ROSCOE CORKER 265**
**BROCK BREWSTER 192**

**FRANK HAMMER 76**
**DALLAS TAYLOR 5**
**ELECTION GOES TO HOUSE: HOUSE LIMITED TO TOP**
**THREE CANDIDATES**
**CORKER IS DEAD: IS DALLAS TAYLOR ELIGIBLE?**

The sound of Chang's voice brought back college days when Taylor had listened enraptured to his lectures as he introduced her to the world of politics. Her classmates also loved listening to this man whose ancestors had a long history as civil servants and court advisors to Chinese emperors. They immigrated to the United States during the Gold Rush to escape the political repression of the Qing Dynasty.

In after-class discussions, he had moved from the subject matter to her future goals. Chang stilled the rage roiling within her at the injustices committed against African Americans. With his help, she transformed that rage into a constructive dynamo that powered her to the highest office in the land.

After the university provost introduced the speakers and acknowledged the presence of President Dallas Taylor, Chang moved over to the screen to explain that with Roscoe Corker now dead, the House of Representatives should consider Dallas Taylor, along with Brock Brewster and Frank Hammer, for official election to the presidency. He supported his conclusion by noting that she already exercised the powers of that office as a former vice president elected by the Senate.

In rebuttal, the Harvard Law professor commented that the precise wording of the Twelfth Amendment only stated the House was limited to electoral candidates "not exceeding three." The language did not literally require the House to consider the three candidates with the highest electoral votes. The House should exclude Dallas Taylor from consideration for the presidency, he said, because even her insignificant five electoral votes were procured by five "faithless" electors from Illinois. Without permission from Illinois voters, who expected them to vote for Roscoe Corker, these faithless electors switched their votes to her.

Taylor chuckled to herself. The whole debate was the type of impractical speculation that academics thrived on. Even if the House did consider her for president, her odds of winning the presidency were worse than finding a mole on a chigger.

Brock Brewster was going to be the next president. With the House choice realistically limited to Brewster and Frank Hammer of the National Independent Party, she didn't see Hammer as a serious threat. Hammer's only smart move had been picking Professor Chang as the vice-presidential candidate for the National Independent Party.

Even that smart play for the rising Asian American vote went sour when Hammer's hacked email described Chang as a running mate who should be seen but not heard. A man with intellectual pretensions, Hammer nursed a jealousy of Chang's credentials and achievements. The tension between Hammer and his wife during the campaign also didn't help the National Independent Party. A week ago, the tension erupted into a messy divorce proceeding. For good reason, all the smart money was on Brock Brewster to win the House election for president.

At the debate's conclusion, the Secret Service hustled Taylor out of the Performing Arts Center. She yielded to their insistence that she confine the meeting with Chang to a farewell conversation inside the armored Cadillac One.

Only seconds after she entered the rear seat of the Beast, as it was known, Chang joined her with a dozen red roses in hand.

"What are these for?"

"To the winner belong the spoils," he joked. "You beat me fair and square for vice president in the Senate election."

What other rival, she thought, would have kept their friendship intact after losing the vice presidency to her? His views of himself and others did not depend on gaining political office at all costs. He was in the right political party. The National Independent Party. He was his own man, win or lose.

"I should give you a gift for your advice on how to negotiate the South China Sea dispute with the Chinese. I'm ready to sign an executive agreement with them to resolve the major problems."

"It was nothing."

Modest man that he was, Chang had agreed to Hammer as the presidential candidate for the National Independent Party rather than risk splitting the party. In a fair world, Chang would have been at the head of the ticket and Hammer collecting tickets at the door. Hammer couldn't see beyond the political utility of Chang's ethnicity to her beloved mentor's merits.

"Your advice was crucial." She smelled the roses and passed them to the Secret Service driver up front. "Thanks, David, for supporting me tonight as a candidate for House election to the presidency. But you didn't have to play Don Quixote for me."

"What I said in the debate is what I believe. It doesn't depend on you being the candidate."

"Guess I never have to worry about you licking my boots." She gave him a hug. "Never change. My boots at the White House are already sopping wet."

"Goodbye, Madam President. Professors are rewarded by the successful careers of students like you. Be well."

As the Beast zoomed away, she wondered when and if they would ever meet again.

# CHAPTER SIXTY-FOUR

With a drink of bourbon and branch water, Dallas Taylor settled down in the rattan chair before the bay window overlooking the Texas shoreline of San José Island. Terns drifted on air currents over the Gulf, while two pelicans bobbed on the water like fishing floats. Dolphin fins broke the water and resubmerged just as quickly to make their way along the shore. Hundreds of miles away from presidential turmoil and worries, she felt at peace for the first time in a long time.

Thanks to the mansion's new owner, an international philanthropist and political supporter, she had the run of the place for much-needed R & R. The sun glittering off the foaming crests of waves breaking on the sand lifted her spirit. She craved rest after the near-death experience at West Point.

Why all the fussing and the feuding in her life? Wasn't this what she always wanted? Peace and joy. She didn't want to end up dead like Roscoe Corker, flaming out in scandal under the pressure-cooker stresses of national politics. No need to worry. In a few days Brock Brewster would evict her from the Oval Office and force her to pursue peace and joy.

The sweet smell of the roses on a nearby table recalled the visit with Chang at her alma mater and his advice on how to approach the Chinese. Until Brewster turned her out of the presidency, she'd hunker down like a jackrabbit in a Texas dust storm and fight for her upcoming executive agreement with the Chinese to resolve their major disputes in the South China Sea. The Republicans had the votes to block any treaty, but they couldn't block an executive agreement.

She wouldn't have to worry for long about her backdoor maneuver around the treaty power because she was a backdoor president with a temporary term in the White House. Once the House of Representatives elected Brock Brewster, he would likely reverse the agreement with his own executive order. But at least she'd give the deal a chance.

"Madam President," said an aide, breaking into her thoughts. "Our phones are dead."

"What about TV, radio?"

"All jammed."

"What's Joe say?" Her secret service agent would know what was going on.

"He's using an emergency texting apparatus to find out. He checked the ferry. It's not working."

Joe rushed into the room. "We must leave. Now."

"What's happening?" Taylor asked.

"Nothing good." He looked out the bay window, right and left. "Communications across the country have been disrupted or shut down. The National Military Command Center at the Pentagon thinks it's a foreign cyberattack."

"Who?"

"Don't know yet."

"What are we doing about it?"

"A marine platoon has moved out from Quantico to guard key buildings in DC. A unit from the Tenth Mountain Division at Fort Drum in New York took a position outside the New York Stock Exchange."

"That's strange. Who gave the orders?"

"Why, General H. A. Harrison. Your secretary of defense."

"He's not my . . ." *Damn.* He had withdrawn his resignation. She had planned to announce his dismissal when she returned to the White House in a few days. It was too late to get into a legal battle over his authority. She had been asleep at the switch.

"What is it, Madam President?"

"Nothing." She sprang from her chair. "I must get to DC pronto. Is the copter ready?"

"Marine One's on the helipad for takeoff to Corpus Christi where Air Force One will fly you back to DC. The decoy chopper is also operative." He did a final check out the bay window. "All clear. Let's go, Madam President."

Aloft in Marine One on her way to Corpus Christi International Airport, she received a report from the secretary of state. He had patched into Marine One's communications system, immune to cyberattacks. She heard him without the drumbeat of background noise. What he said confirmed her suspicions.

"You're telling me the whole thing's a deception?"

"All I know," the secretary said, "is that a trusted source inside the National Military Command Center claims that's the situation. A foreign actor is not the origin of the cyberattack."

"How would your source know?"

"He's part of a special team that oversees the technology securing the military's communications network."

"Where's the cyberattack coming from?"

"The United States."

"Our military?"

"Unclear. General John Klaine, chairman of the Joint Chiefs of Staff, will join you when you transfer to Air Force One at Corpus Christi. I suspect he knows something."

"Without my permission to join me?"

"He's fired up to see you. Will you see him?"

"If I want to find out what's going on, I'd better."

"Any instructions?"

"Don't let foreign countries think anything unusual is happening. Business as usual till I return to DC . . . and find out what the hell's going on. Bye."

She sat back and let the brown and green patches of land out the window chill her out for a few minutes. The movement of military units without explanation merited suspicion. Hard-Ass wasn't the real problem even though she messed up in delaying his dismissal. Whenever he was together with Sebastian Senex, his speech and body language deferred to the pharmaceutical tycoon. Her instincts screamed Senex was behind it all. She hoped it was just another bluff to pressure her into resigning. Her blood ran cold at another possibility: an attempt to take over the United States by a coup d'état.

She had to use judgment without letting imagination run wild. No one and no group claimed responsibility for the cyberattack. Might this be a top-secret military test of American cyber defense without any sinister intent to seize control of the government?

If so, she wasn't informed and that bothered her. But maybe the boys at the Pentagon figured the test would be more accurate if she didn't know at first what was up. That might be why the chairman of the Joint Chiefs was meeting her in Corpus Christi. Or was it magical thinking on her part? Everything was maybes and mights until she had a heart-to-heart with the chairman of the Joint Chiefs.

———

Aboard Air Force One on the tarmac, President Dallas Taylor had barely sat down behind the desk in the "Oval Office in the sky" to meet the chairman of the Joint Chiefs of Staff when he appeared grim faced at the door.

Light streamed in from a cabin window to her left onto a star-studded floor marking the president's personal space. With the Presidential Seal on the wall behind her, she waved him in. Leaning heavily on the metal prosthetic of his right leg, he stood in front of the desk.

"The cyberattack. That's why you're here, right?"

"There's been a cyberattack on selected infrastructure."

"Everyone in the country's quite aware of that, General Klaine," she snapped. "The only question is what you know about it."

"I know that unless you resign the cyberattacks will continue. So will military protection of key installations in Washington, DC."

"What I most feared." She gathered her thoughts. "Who's in on this coup? General Horatio A. Harrison? Sebastian Senex?"

"Among others. By the way, they call it . . . transitory emergency measure." He looked like he needed sleep. "I haven't made up my mind whether to join them."

"You know they're guilty of serious crimes . . . and so are you."

"I didn't know about it until they put the plan in motion."

"But you're not stopping it."

"My decision depends on what you do." Klaine shifted to his other leg. Pain seemed to ripple across his face. "They asked me as a neutral go-between to report back your choice . . . immediate resignation or temporary military control."

"Neutral?" She spat out the word, resting her clenched hands on the desk. "What about your duty to the president of the United States?"

"I took an oath to support and defend the Constitution of the United States . . . not you. You're violating the Constitution by entering into an executive agreement with China. You need a treaty."

"Isn't that above your pay grade, General Klaine? That's something for me, the Justice Department, and the courts. You're supposed to protect this country, not sit on the sidelines and play constitutional scholar." She pointed at herself. "I'm in charge. Not Senex. Not Harrison. Not you."

"Yes, you civilians have been in charge alright. Ever since Vietnam you civilians, presidents and Congress alike, have erased the need for a declaration of war from the Constitution while the Supreme Court looks the other way. You fight wars all over the world but never finish them."

He leaned over the desk into her space.

She prepared to summon the Secret Service agents sitting outside.

He stepped back.

"That's how I got this lovely-looking bionic limb. They amputated my leg after a chopper crash in Nam." He pointed to his prosthetic. "Ever since then, young men and women like I was, kids from society's margins, fight our wars out of sight for everybody else while everyone else gets a pass from military duty."

"Have you studied my political record?" She tapped the desk with her forefinger. "I've opposed these military interventions."

"You miss my point. I'm not against use of the military." He shifted back to his prosthetic leg. "I'm against pointless wars not in our national interest. They sap our strength, plunge the country into spiraling debt, and swell the ranks of vets with PTSD who cause unrest at home. We should stand firm with our real enemy and concentrate all our force on that enemy."

"And who might that be this time?"

"China."

"The Russians will resent the downgrade."

"Your sarcasm doesn't change geopolitical facts. China will take us down unless something is done to focus on the real enemy. And that's where you are weak. You're letting them loose in the South China Sea. You're wrecking the Constitution to appease them."

"I am the commander in chief under the Constitution you claim to support and defend." She poked her finger at him. "You owe me loyalty."

"This is getting us nowhere. Will you resign?"

"If I resign, the new Speaker of the House, Madison Malone, will take over as president under the Presidential Succession Act. Presidential selection will be further delayed until the House elects another Speaker." Taylor shook her head in bewilderment. "How does installation of someone basically ignorant of foreign affairs accomplish what you want?"

"Senex and General Harrison have their own vendettas against you." Klaine sat down on the sofa across the room. "I don't dislike you . . . personally. But I agree with General Harrison that you are about to make a catastrophic mistake by signing that executive agreement. The new Speaker also agrees and says it's unconstitutional. She promises to stop appeasing China. That's good enough for me."

"Let the Supreme Court decide if it's constitutional."

"The Supreme Court? It's become seesaw politics in legal robes."

A Secret Service agent knocked on the door.

"Come in," she said.

The agent poked his head inside and cold-eyed the chairman of the Joint Chiefs before speaking. "Air Force One is ready to go. We need to return to Washington, Madam President."

She nodded. The Secret Service agent closed the door behind him.

"There's an easy way out of this, General Klaine," she said. "Those in the know say the House will elect Brewster president this week. He's Senex's boy, so he'll do whatever the plotters want. No one need know what went on behind the scenes. The United States will be spared an attempted coup. I will take no action against you and the others." She placed her hands on the desk and leaned forward. "I hold off reprisals and they halt the military takeover during the week."

She folded her arms.

"On the other hand, if the conspirators aren't willing to wait a week, I'll address the nation from the Oval Office about the coup attempt. I'll mobilize against them whatever part of the military hasn't gone over to the traitors. I'll also have Senex and the others prosecuted for insurrection, sedition, treason, whatever law my acting attorney general can throw at them." She placed her palms on the desk. "Wait a week and hold off until then. That's my offer."

"What if Brewster's not elected this week?"

"What if pigs flew?" she asked. "Let's cross that fantasy bridge when we come to it."

"I'll take your offer back to Senex and General Harrison."

# CHAPTER SIXTY-FIVE

Upon her return to the White House, a reinvigorated President Dallas Taylor dismissed General Horatio A. Harrison from the cabinet without public explanation. Unless the plotters refused her offer of a one-week delay until Brock Brewster took over, she wouldn't inflame the nation's turmoil by disclosing Hard-Ass's mad attempt to overthrow the government. She stifled her urge to exact payback for his treachery toward her and the country. He was only Sebastian Senex's tool. To publicly humiliate him would only lock the general tighter in Senex's embrace.

She next rang up General John Klaine, chairman of the Joint Chiefs of Staff. He told her what she wanted to hear. After a bitter disagreement, General Horatio A. Harrison and Sebastian Senex agreed to the one-week truce. Harrison feared she was playing them for suckers. Senex thought they had nothing to lose by accepting her offer.

Because of their disagreement, General Harrison was waffling on his commitment to any coup. The chairman of the Joint Chiefs also informed her that the marine platoon was moving back to its base at Quantico from DC, but the Tenth Mountain unit maintained its guard position around the New York Stock Exchange.

In a play for Klaine's allegiance, she confided to him that the Chinese had backed off their agreement on the South China Sea because of their domestic politics and her insecure tenure as president. She would sign no executive agreement after all with the People's Republic of China.

As she expected, the chairman of the Joint Chiefs was delighted the Chinese had backed away from a deal they now doubted was in their interest even though the chairman thought it a giveaway to the Chinese. The secretary of state must have worked out a reasonable South Sea compromise if the war hawks on each side didn't like it.

The upside of the collapsed negotiations with the Chinese was that the chairman's delight in the collapse of the executive agreement provided the opportunity to offer him the position of secretary of defense on condition he thwart the coup attempt if it became necessary. In agreeing, he confided that his distrust of the conspirators had only grown since he met with her on Air Force One.

The next call was to her press secretary to get a cover story out to a public on the verge of panic. The public would be told the cyberattacks were part of an unannounced military preparedness program to test for weaknesses in the country's infrastructure. To get the most from the tests, the story would go, they had to be a surprise to best simulate the effects of foreign cyberattacks. The tests were at an end, so the public should go back to its daily business without fear. The military unit outside the New York Stock Exchange and the marine guards in the District of Columbia were explained away as a prescheduled military exercise program.

She was cooking on the front burner now. LBJ would be proud of her.

"Madam President," her appointments secretary announced through the half-open door of the Oval Office. "The Murphys are here for their appointment."

"Send them in."

"Sorry we're late, Madam President," Bryan Murphy said. "Marines held up traffic heading back to their base at Quantico."

"I'm running behind anyway." She brushed aside what she had been reading and looked at Bryan. "I'm ready to rock and roll against Senex's criminal enterprises."

"This is my brother, Detective Jim Murphy of the Chicago Police."

Jim stood at attention before the president's desk with hands clasped in front like a truant schoolboy.

"We've met previously." Taylor tapped a pen on her desk. "Under less pleasant circumstances."

The Chicago detective started apologizing.

She held up her hand. "No need, Detective Murphy. Those were trying times for us both." She laid the pen on her desk. "Bygones are bygones. Agreed?"

"Agreed."

"I've learned," President Taylor said, "a grand jury in Chicago has been convened to hear evidence against Senex for Dr. Angelo Mora's murder. But didn't a judge dismiss the charge at a preliminary hearing?"

"In Illinois," the Chicago detective said, "we allow a criminal indictment even though a judge released a defendant at a preliminary hearing. The mountain of evidence uncovered by Operation Big Shoulders forced the state's attorney to seek an indictment."

"Hallelujah." She clapped her hands. "We're going after Senex in court after all. Not just the court of public opinion in the Senate hearing."

"Not just state court," Bryan Murphy said. "I've directed Justice's lawyers to throw the book at him in federal court. We're going after him for environmental violations. We're also suing for criminal violation of the RICO statute by running Promethean Pharma as a criminal enterprise."

She looked at Bryan. "You and the FBI have done great work with Operation Big Shoulders."

"My team at Justice should share the credit."

Jim elbowed his brother.

"And, of course, my brother, Jim. Without Jim's search warrant and consent to a joint investigation we wouldn't have Operation Big Shoulders."

She rested her chin on a hand. "If I were an elected president and not just this temporary one, I'd put your name up for attorney general right now." She held up her hands. "But I'll be gone in a matter of days when Brock Brewster takes over the Oval Office."

"I understand," Bryan said.

"Let's go over the game plan for my White House press conference." Taylor stood up. "I want you boys to stay on either side of me like silent spear bearers in an opera. I, the prima donna, will report on the Operation Big Shoulders investigation of Promethean Pharma and Sebastian Senex. The press conference will be a suspenseful overture to the opera of your testimony before the Senate Committee on Finance. I'm not going into any details of Operation Big Shoulders. My goal is only to whet the appetite of the media sharks for your testimony."

The press secretary popped her head in through the Oval Office door. "The media's waiting."

The time on the Seymour grandfather clock near the door caught her eye. She came around her desk. "Got to get ready, gentlemen." She motioned the brothers to take a seat on the sofa opposite hers. She tugged off her pink Western-fringed boots and rested her feet on the coffee table separating the sofas. She wiggled her toes. "What a morning," she said, slipping on a pair of burgundy Ferragamo flats. She stood up and smoothed down the sides of her gray pantsuit. "I'm ready and rarin' to nail Senex's hide to the barn door."

In the James S. Brady Briefing Room, acting president Dallas Taylor took a position behind the lectern flanked by acting attorney general Bryan Murphy and his brother, Detective Jim Murphy, who was spiffed up in his freshly cleaned and pressed CPD uniform. Behind each of her human props stood an American flag.

She began with a lavish introduction of the brothers Murphy that made Jim blush. Taylor skirted the topic of Operation Big Shoulders with praise for the joint investigation conducted by the FBI and the Chicago Police Department united by their unbreakable bonds of law-enforcement brotherhood in fighting crime.

It was time to throw the press corps a juicy morsel to perk up their appetite for the testimony of the Murphy brothers before the Senate Committee on Finance. She discussed the extent and seriousness of Operation Big Shoulders while leaving any further information to the congressional testimony of the Murphy brothers. Negative insinuations involving Sebastian Senex were left dangling. She was enjoying herself fending off answers to questions begging for a preview of the Murphy testimony. She entertained one last question before leaving to take care of the nation's business.

"I've just been informed that the wife of Governor Brock Brewster has died. Do you have a comment?"

"I'm deeply saddened." And for once her political role aligned perfectly with her inner feelings. Brewster's wife had welcomed her with open arms to DC soirees hosted by the Brewsters when the other District's socialites shunned the new Texas congresswoman from the wrong side of the tracks. "She was a kind woman in a town too often unkind. My sympathies go out to her husband, Governor Brock Brewster."

# CHAPTER SIXTY-SIX

"What a genius," said Dr. Grzegorz Wojciechowski, the former researcher at Promethean Pharma. "My latest research confirms his pioneering work with parabiosis."

"Scz . . . Scz . . . I can't pronounce your twin's first name."

"Call him Uno. Mine is Due. Those are the nicknames Dr. Angelo Mora gave us."

Senex had more than a hard time with their names. He also had a difficult time telling them apart, except for the scar on Due's face.

"Uno didn't think Mora was a genius. He claims Mora stole the discovery of the Ponce de León protein from him."

An MD with a PhD in hematology from Cambridge University, Due flipped his hand as though brushing away a fly. "My twin brother is an idiot. He only set the stage for Dr. Mora's discovery. He envied the doctor's genius and even my superior abilities."

"You're supposed to be a top MD researcher at the Undiagnosed Diseases Network. Not some eulogist for Dr. Mora." Seated on a medical exam table in a patient's examination gown, Senex kicked his heel against the side of the table. "Forget Mora. Find out what's going on with me."

Due dipped his head and clicked his heels. "Forgive me."

Was the Polish foreigner with aristocratic airs mocking him?

Due ran his hands over and around Senex's throat and chest with the deft movement of a masseur. "A little swollen under your armpit."

"That started two days ago." He coughed.

"How long have you had the fatigue, sore throat, and fever?"

"Almost two weeks." He coughed again. "Sometimes I stop to catch my breath."

"Open your mouth." Due inserted a tongue depressor and peered in. "You were accused of Dr. Mora's death after I left Promethean Pharma, were you not?"

Gagging in an attempt to speak, he pushed the probing hand away. The tongue depressor fell to the floor. "The judge dismissed the case. That means I didn't do it. Don't you follow the news?" He slid off the exam table and stood eye to eye with the medical researcher. "I don't want to hear that man's name again. Understand?"

"I am not your servant," Due answered. He grabbed Senex's medical record off a worktable, knocking over a container of cotton swabs. "I shall return when your tantrum ceases." He slammed the door on the way out.

If Senex alienated Due, he jeopardized his own health. He couldn't afford to alienate more people. Convinced he had murdered her lover based on Mora's death note, Daisy would not talk to him. Bryan Murphy had also turned against him.

What calmed him was the control he still had over Brock Brewster. If worse came to worst, Brewster as president could pardon him for federal crimes. Illinois political and legal issues were not insurmountable. He knew the right fixers.

Waiting for Due's return, he clicked on the TV in the examination room to see if the House had selected Brewster as president. Brewster's image appeared on a news program. He emerged shattered from the deathwatch at the hospice where his wife had just passed away. He'd probably carry a grudge for failing to receive the Ponce de León protein protocol for his wife.

That problem could also be finessed. Once Brewster tasted the presidency, he would buck up and carry on. Actually, the wife's death was a good thing. The poor widower could do no wrong. The public and Congress would sympathize with Brewster's loss and grant him an extended honeymoon period to implement political programs for the benefit of Promethean Pharma.

Due swung open the door. "Are we feeling better?" he asked with one hand still on the doorknob.

Senex gritted his teeth and feigned mock penitence.

"Good." He closed the door and came in.

"Are you sure about my Huntington's?"

"Absolutely." Due raised his fist in a victory pump. "It's amazing. Your Huntington's is in remission."

"How do you explain it?"

"Dr. Mora had an explanation," he said, as though daring him to challenge mention of the name. "It was my honor to be his assistant."

"I want your explanation."

"It's the same. The parabiosis treatment and the later Ponce de León protein injections reversed the aging process. Like Dr. Mora told you, the resetting of a computer to a time before the malfunction occurred."

Due sat down. "There's a market for the Ponce de León protein." His eyes brightened. "Clinics across the United States for those willing to pay. With my help—"

"Whoa." He put out his hand. "You're getting ahead of yourself." The sawbones was impertinent, but he admired how Due sized up an opportunity. They saw something in common. Dollar signs.

"Remember me if you need a medical consultant to market this."

"Sure."

Due excused himself to confer in the hallway with his physician assistant.

He returned with a jack-o'-lantern smile. "I have your test results." He read through the printouts. "No sign of Huntington's." He put the printouts on the worktable. "Based on a new blood test from Sweden and our RNA genetic profiling, we determined your biological age to be forty-four years."

"What about the symptoms? Don't tell me fibromyalgia like my Chicago doc. I'm not buying it."

"Do not confuse my expertise with that of a mere internist." He waved his hand with a dismissive air. "I have ruled out fibromyalgia."

"So?"

"You have mononucleosis." He smiled and wagged a forefinger at his patient. "Nothing to do with your anti-aging procedures, unless it rejuvenated your libido." Due winked. "That is why Americans call it the kissing disease."

"That's all? Just mono?" He rubbed his hands together in relief. "Will I need Ponce de León injections to maintain my youth? My deceased researcher didn't think so."

"Deceased researcher?" Due stared down Senex. "You must mean Dr. Angelo Mora . . . the great Dr. Angelo Mora."

He swallowed the urge to lash out at Due for mentioning Mora's name. He had to focus on the big picture. "Do I need continued injections of the Ponce de León protein?"

"That's the only point on which I differ with Dr. Mora." He rubbed his hand across the scar on his cheek. "I think you will eventually need booster injections, but I cannot say when you may need them. This is unknown territory."

Of course he would say that. He saw dollars signs in keeping close to his patient. But maybe Due was right. He had to be careful not to push away the one person who could keep him alive.

"Your research with that deceased Italian researcher, your knowledge of the parabiosis procedure, and the Ponce de León protein . . . that's all confidential. Right?"

"Naturally. I am bound by physician-patient confidentiality and privacy laws as well as the ironclad confidentiality contract I signed with Promethean Pharma." Due picked up the printouts off the table and prepared to leave. "I appreciate your letting me know the real purpose behind that so-called artificial blood project at Promethean Pharma."

"My life depends on your knowing the truth about my medical history." Well, mostly the truth. Due didn't need to know how he got the young blood. "One other thing," he said buttoning up his shirt. "Are you sure there are no side effects from parabiosis and the Ponce de León protein?"

"None whatsoever." Due put his hand on the doorknob to leave. "Of that I am certain."

# CHAPTER SIXTY-SEVEN

Like a swarm of discombobulated bees, a crowd milled about the Senate hearing room awaiting a surprise witness before the Senate Committee on Finance in its investigation of Promethean Pharma and its CEO. To maximize security, the chairman ruled that the identity of the witness would remain confidential until called to testify.

Jim Murphy had his testimony postponed until after that of the unknown witness. He gathered his papers and left the witness table to settle in the first row of spectators beside his brother, who insisted on being present to provide moral and legal support.

Jim looked at the wall clock. The hearing should have started at eleven. It was already 11:10 a.m. with no sign of the mystery witness. The chairman appeared eager to move on but agreed to wait five more minutes.

Despite Bryan's upbeat chatter, Jim doubted his testimony or the efforts of President Dallas Taylor would be enough to take down Sebastian Senex. Ever since President Harry Truman had tried to take over the steel mills, the Supreme Court took a dim view of emergency powers as justification for appropriating private property. He also had no assurance the Illinois grand jury would indict Senex for the murder of Dr. Angelo Mora. If necessary, Senex wouldn't hesitate to tamper with the grand jury.

Above all else, the in-the-bag selection of Brock Brewster as the next president of the United States would bring the full power of the office of president to Senex's side. Brewster would certainly pressure the Justice Department to withdraw environmental lawsuits and the RICO criminal prosecution against Sebastian Senex. He feared the taunt of "Murphy's Law" dogging him around if Senex once again escaped justice.

The wall clock read 11:15 a.m. Just as the chairman asked Jim to return to the witness table, the doors of the committee room swung open. A US Secret Service detail preceded the entry of Brock Brewster with his personal retinue.

A line of reporters and camera operators sat on the floor with their backs against the raised platform on which the committee sat. Some knelt on one knee with cameras aimed and clicking. They jockeyed for the best position to snap a picture of Brewster.

Baggy-eyed, Brewster shuffled past Jim down the center aisle with a deadpan look to take his seat at the witness table.

In the hours of monotonic testimony that followed, Brewster wound a verbal noose of unethical behavior and criminality around the neck of Sebastian Senex. To Jim's astonishment, Brewster revealed the complex web of Senex's violations of campaign laws and pharmaceutical regulations. The riveting nature of the testimony silenced the shifting of feet, the muffled whispers among spectators, and the rustle of papers.

"How could you possibly know of these violations, Governor Brewster?" The chairman shed his deferential tone.

"Because he told me about them."

"Hearsay," the chairman said. "Mr. Senex is not here to defend himself."

"I had personal knowledge. Some involved my campaign."

A committee member intervened. "Governor Brewster, I admonish you to consider your right to remain silent under the Fifth Amendment."

"I am perfectly aware of my right against self-incrimination. But I am past the point of covering up for Sebastian Senex . . . or myself."

He watched the reporters dash up the side aisles and out the door to report the damning testimony of the leading presidential candidate for the Oval Office.

Brewster moved on to the long conversations Senex had with him about the need to save the United States from itself. He had told Brewster often about the need to eliminate gangbangers from the streets of Chicago.

"What did Senex mean by the word . . . *eliminate*?" asked a junior member of the committee.

"When I asked him, he did this." Brewster drew his forefinger across his throat. "That's what he meant."

"That's what you say it meant," the chairman said. "It could just as easily be interpreted as exaggerated hyperbole to show displeasure."

"Not the way I interpreted it."

Brewster testified that for Senex the rush of illegal immigrants across the border and the rise of a dangerous and criminal underclass within the United States required a strongman to save and rejuvenate the country, just as he was saving and rejuvenating himself with the parabiosis protocol. He expected Brewster to be that strongman and do things the Chicago way, as he called it.

The chairman pounded his gavel to stop Brewster's testimony. "Putting aside this wild and inflammatory language, Governor Brewster, do you have any direct knowledge that Sebastian Senex planned to take any illegal actions to accomplish his alleged goals to save the republic from itself?"

"No. But I know he applauded the assassination of Franklin Dexter Walker."

More reporters rushed out of the room.

"That will do, Governor Brewster." The chairman pounded the gavel. "We are getting way off topic. The concern of this committee is the pharmaceutical industry, not the suppression of free speech by a distinguished and philanthropic citizen. Unless you have relevant information concerning Sebastian Senex, I will dismiss you as a witness."

"I do indeed have such information." Brewster described his suspicions that Senex was using Promethean Pharma as a front to engage in secret procedures to find the fountain of youth without the knowledge of the Food and Drug Administration. When he confronted Senex over lunch at Bullfeathers restaurant in DC, Senex admitted using what he called the fountain-of-youth protocol without FDA approval. He promised to provide the protocol to cure Brewster's wife but reneged on the promise.

"Why would he do that?" the chairman asked.

"He said I had failed to obey his orders and couldn't keep a secret. But I found out the real reason."

"And what is that?" a committee member asked.

"Before she died . . ." Brewster choked up. "Before she died . . . my wife confessed the real reason. Unknown to me, she and Sebastian Senex had a relationship years ago. My wife terminated it. He threatened to take his revenge against her. She believed that he withheld the fountain-of-youth protocol out of revenge. This testimony is now my revenge."

"I suggest you watch your words, Mr. Brewster." The chairman banged his gavel as more reporters left the hearing room. "This vindictiveness does not befit a candidate for the office of United States president."

"That won't be a problem." He stood up at the witness table. "I hereby announce the withdrawal of my name from consideration by the House of Representatives for the office of president of the United States."

# CHAPTER SIXTY-EIGHT

Sebastian Senex glared through the outside glass door into the foyer of Senex Community Hospital on Chicago's North Side. The enclosed atrium glittered with festive lighting decked out for the annual fundraiser dinner. Under the sparkle of the steel-and-glass dome, donors in the distance chatted over champagne glasses and filet mignon at linen-clothed tables supporting vases of white roses nestled in ivy and fern. As board chairman of the hospital, he had the brilliant idea of hiring ten top chefs to personally offer donors their culinary creations at ten candlelit cooking stations within the hospital to show off its facilities.

A security guard opened the door halfway.

"You can't come in."

"Do you know who I am, junior?"

"Sebastian Senex."

"The board chairman and hospital CEO."

"Not anymore." He came outside and stood between Senex and the door. "You're the former chairman and CEO. I'm under orders to keep you out."

"Call the dragon lady." He backed away from the door. "You'll regret this."

The guard fingered numbers on his cell. "It's me. I stopped Sebastian Senex at the front door. He says I made a mistake." He listened to the response, nodded, and hung up. "No mistake. She says you have to leave. You're an embarrassment." He cleared his throat. "Her words, not mine."

"Embarrassment?" Senex stamped his foot. "I cultivated those fat cats in there for the hospital. It bears my name. Without me it's nothing."

"I do what I'm told." The guard shrugged and ran a hand over his spiked hair. "You can't enter."

Senex fumbled for his cell in his tuxedo trousers under a velvet-collared black chesterfield coat and left a voice mail for his lawyer. "Call me at once."

He never liked the Ivy League shrew born and bred in Minnesota. No one who counted in Chicago knew anything about her. He had made a fatal mistake by agreeing to put her on the board for the sake of gender diversity. The board needed a woman, they said. They said she was demure and congenial.

Once on the board, she rallied board members to her side and forced him to abandon what she called a conflict of interest in selling Promethean Pharma drugs to the hospital. He should have gotten rid of her then. Instead she wrested control of the board away from him. This collection of backstabbing wusses ousted him first as CEO and board chair and then as a board member. To stick the knife in further, they made her CEO and board chair out of spite.

She was just a prissy schoolmarm trapped in a CEO's body. No wonder the private dick he hired couldn't find any dirt on her. He couldn't let a pushy woman like her get the best of him. He strode forward and opened the foyer door.

"The board acted illegally in dismissing me." Senex moved through the open door. "Get out of the way."

The guard stood scowling at the door and balled his fists.

"I'm not leaving until I talk to her." Senex moved back outside. "Tell her that."

The guard closed the glass door in his face and made a cell call.

In a black cocktail dress she strode over to the door with her trademark Wonder Woman logo earrings and a gem-studded clutch purse. She exchanged words with the security guard and went outside.

"You're not coming in."

"You can't stop me. It's my hospital."

"No it's not. You're not a board member or a CEO."

"I've called my lawyer."

"Good." She stepped toward him. "Tell him an internal investigation shows you and the hospital administrator finagled the organ transplant list to jump your favored patients to the front."

The administrator must have cracked. He listened to her rant about the illegal and unethical nature of what he had done. She understood nothing about friendship or the way the world worked.

"We did it for the good of the hospital." He pointed to the upper floors of the building. "Without the donations of those well-heeled patients, this palace of glass and shimmering steel wouldn't exist."

"Meanwhile, some poor SOB dies because someone else jumps the line."

"You wouldn't understand. You're not from here." He tightened his white silk scarf around his neck. "We help our own."

"Your own means anyone with big bucks."

"Some patients never gave a dime."

"You're right about that." She looked him in the eye. "They were political hacks and businessmen you needed to keep obligated to you."

"One hand washes the other. It's the Chicago way."

"It's crooked and unethical."

She knew nothing. The Chicago way made things work. One favor for another. Tit for tat. What inhumane times did he now live in if you couldn't wrap your arms around your friends? It wasn't illegal unless you got caught. And it wasn't unethical because the Chicago way had a higher ethic. The Chicago way was the grease that made the machinery of government work and get things done. She wasn't from Chicago. She'd never understand.

"Let's work this out," he said. "Man to—person to person."

The security guard advised her the award ceremony was about to begin.

"Nothing to work out." She looked at her wristwatch. "Go, Sebastian, to avoid further embarrassment to yourself."

"Don't play dragon lady with me."

"Leave at once or I'll call the police." She walked back to the entrance.

She opened the door but turned before going in. "Oh, at the next board meeting I'm having the hospital renamed."

She entered and spoke something to the guard with her finger pointed at him. He watched her walk back like a queen to the festivities. Rage and fear roiled through and left him out of control and defenseless. Daisy avoided him. Angelo Mora had betrayed him. Bryan Murphy had abandoned him. Brock Brewster had blown his plans into smithereens by backstabbing him and withdrawing from the presidential race.

Numb, Senex looked up at the stars. He found no answer there except for Plan B. The buzz of his cell startled him. His lawyer would know what to do.

"What's going on, Sebastian?"

"She wouldn't let me in."

"We had this conversation before. I advised you to stay away."

"She's making a fuss about organ transplants."

"You have bigger problems."

"What do you mean?"

"The grand jury indicted you today for the murder of Dr. Angelo Mora."

"You know the Plan B hypothetical I put to you?"

"I advised against it."

"I've made up my mind."

"I don't want to hear any more about it."

"You won't."

# CHAPTER SIXTY-NINE

"You did it, girl." Her chief of staff gave Dallas Taylor a high five in the Oval Office for officially becoming president of the United States by vote of the House of Representatives. "I have a few minutes free, so I brought these." Emily James put down two champagne flutes and a champagne split. The longtime friends embraced. She clinked her flute with Taylor's. "You have it all now. The leader of the free world and Dr. Bert Gaines. I'm so happy you two are back together."

Emily had stood by her from the first step Taylor took into the political arena. The president's chief of staff gave up her other clients and worked exclusively for Taylor all the way up to the Oval Office. Taylor had confided in Emily about Taylor's affair with Al Tweed, the chairman of the Democratic National Committee. She'd never forget her friend's understanding and consolation. The bad times were past. Emily was right. She finally found her man and reached the pinnacle of her political career.

The new Speaker had called earlier to relay the results of the vote in the House of Representatives. It was all the more delicious because of the resentment in the Speaker's voice. They might both be women in a man's world, but they sure didn't belong to the same political sorority. Taylor and the new Speaker had a stormy relationship ever since they represented different Texas congressional districts. They came from the same state but worlds apart. Republican versus Democrat. White versus Black. Wealthy versus impoverished. Rancher's daughter versus janitor's daughter.

She leaned back in her chair with a smile across her face. The scrawny dancer girl from Dallas was now the most powerful woman in the world. A surge of pride welled up in her for reaching the top of the political ladder, even if it was through a squeaker election in the House. It didn't matter how you got to the dance as long as you arrived.

After her chief of staff left the room, she imagined Abraham Lincoln must have felt the same way after his underdog election as she did now. No matter how she examined it, the weird way she became president felt like the finger of God touching her.

How could she have predicted the political suicide of Brock Brewster in taking down Sebastian Senex with him before the Senate committee? Brewster's testimony recalled the preacher's Bible story of Samson pulling down the temple pillars of the Philistines in an enraged act of mutual self-destruction. His withdrawal from the campaign for the presidency in the House shattered any organized Republican opposition to her candidacy.

No more than she could have predicted Roscoe Corker dying in a sky-high scandal on the way to Ukraine. And who could have predicted the assassination of Franklin Dexter Walker and the election in the House of Representatives? A perfect constitutional storm swept her into the highest office.

For House members opposed to her, only an unpalatable choice had remained—Frank Hammer, the National Independent Party candidate. The Senate had already elected her as vice president. She had experience in government. Frank Hammer had none. His arrogance and marital problems alienated representatives when they had to choose between the only two candidates left standing.

And then there was the nagging question: If they elected Hammer, did she go back to being vice president or did Hammer have the right as president to nominate his own choice for vice president?

The country had only two House elections for president in its history, and both caused unrest and bitterness in the defeated candidates. No matter which way she looked at it, Congress had to elect her to avoid putting the country through more constitutional uncertainty. For House members opposed to her, she became the lesser evil.

Taylor emerged from the chaos as the default leader of the United States through some mysterious destiny. The experience called to mind the aphorism sometimes attributed to Otto von Bismarck, chancellor of nineteenth-century Germany, so often quoted by her beloved professor of political science, David Chang: There is a Providence that protects idiots, drunkards, children, and the United States of America.

With hindsight one could see the cause and effect of how her pitifully small five votes in the Electoral College cast by maverick electors had grown incrementally but steadily with each vote in the House. With foresight at the time, however, no one could have predicted those five votes by so-called faithless electors would have mushroomed into a majority of votes. It was like the multiplication of loaves and fishes.

Her heart called it a miracle, though her mind refused. Whether by coincidence in an indifferent universe or the grace of the Lord, one clear fact remained: she had clawed and scratched her way into the Oval Office. She knew what to do with that power. She would make the federal government work for the benefit of all citizens. She would begin with a complete overhaul of the—

The telephone rang. *It was Al Tweed.*

"Why are you calling again?"

"David Chang's not a Democrat. The party won't accept it."

"You don't speak for Democrats. I'm the party leader."

"I'm sure Chang's good at math. But you need people skills to be a VP."

"He doesn't do math." Talking to him gave her a headache. "He's a professor of political science with more skills than the losers you've backed."

"Want me to resign as DNC chairman?"

"Go, stay. I don't care. Just don't get in my way."

"I've not always done right by you, Dallas, but—"

"To you, it's not Dallas anymore. It's Ms. President or Madam President. Got it?"

"We know each other, Madam President."

"I don't think so."

"I want to work with you."

"I don't want to work with you."

"You made a mistake picking Chang for veep."

"Then so did Congress," she said. "They approved him for vice president of the United States by an overwhelming bipartisan vote." He had no response. "He's not a Democrat but he's what the country needs. We're done. Goodbye."

The speed of congressional approval for her choice to fill the vacant office of vice president didn't come as a surprise. Congress and the country were exhausted after the roller-coaster events following the assassination of FDW. Picking David Chang, a political rival from another party, also gave her brownie points with voters for tamping down the partisanship now a clear and present danger to the future of the United States.

She had let word out that unless Congress approved Chang, she would submit no other name to fill the vacant office. Congress got the message. If something happened to her, the United States would lack a VP ready to take over. No one wanted to risk another crisis. Republicans voted for Chang because he wasn't a Democrat, and Democrats voted for him because he wasn't a Republican.

David Chang was part of her solution to the complex puzzle of putting the United States back together in working order. His nomination symbolized that she would not allow the two-party system to turn into two packs of mad dogs tearing the country apart as well as themselves. In unifying the nation behind her programs, she would signal the blinkered vision of party partisanship was over. She was a Democrat but an American first.

Chang would make an excellent vice president. He brought to the table a broad-minded view of the world that only an academic like him could offer. He would be her Henry Kissinger with a Chinese heritage. Chang knew both Chinese and American cultures and could bring them closer together for the sake of world peace.

It wasn't just his friendship, his brilliance, and his polish that made him a distinguished choice. He had the further endearing trait of not being a potential rival. She didn't want a team of rivals waiting to stab her in the back. More than just his integrity protected her from his betrayal. He and the National Independent Party were novices when it came to the brass knuckles of American politics. He couldn't rival her political infighting skills even if he had wanted to. Chang would be more than a figurehead vice president without being a political danger. A win-win all the way around.

To relieve her excitement, she went over to the three windows facing the twilight creeping over the south lawn of the White House. So much good news had washed over her in the past week, it was no wonder she felt woozy but happy. Champagne was known to do that to her. Even more than bourbon and branch water.

She looked out, beginning to sense the impending burden of her new office. Through relentless efforts she had achieved the dream goal of the presidency. She fretted that her next goal would be using whatever means it took to stay in power. Over her life, it struck her that goals faded with increasing rapidity and became only means to other ends that faded equally into mere means.

Would pedaling faster on the cycle of ambition bring her closer to the promised land of peace and joy that tap dancing had given her? She aborted her inconvenient reflection. Navel-gazing might undermine her drive to prove she was no longer a little girl from the wrong side of town with the wrong skin color.

She scurried from the windows to bury her gray thoughts in a whirlwind of work set before her on the Resolute desk. Dropping into the executive chair, she took a document from the pile.

Fatigue flooded her body. The chairs and sofas wore halos. Something shook her like a rag doll. Unseen pins and needles pricked up and down her left arm as heavy as bricks. Her thoughts swirled in pain. She hit the panic button concealed under the desk. The room tuned blindingly white before fading to black.

# CHAPTER SEVENTY

Sebastian Senex executed his Plan B as the guest of a Cuban government lacking an extradition treaty with the United States. From his Havana safe house with a clanking air conditioner, he called Daisy on the secure phone system the Cuban Intelligence Directorate had set up to prevent gringo wiretaps. Maybe she'd answer this time. The ringing turned into voice mail. *"You have reached—"* "Hello?"

"It's me. Please don't hang up?"

"I won't, Daddy. Where are you?"

"Cuba."

She'd called him Daddy. *He had a chance.* "I need you."

Fanning himself with a tattered *Playboy*, his Cuban handler pierced him with coal-black eyes. The stare set off the shakes plaguing him in mind and body ever since his arrival. Cuban suspicion made him wonder how long the safe house would remain safe.

"Of course. Your needs come first," she said. A pause. "Are you OK?"

"I've been better."

The mononucleosis had grown worse or become something else. Pain ran up and down his spine like fingers on a piano keyboard. Black spots had broken out along his back and chest. He felt exposed and alone. He had to confess and seek absolution like those Papists. He had no choice but to go through the ritual.

"I'm sorry about Vinnie . . . but I had to do it. I need you to forgive me."

"I understand your need." A pause. "There's nothing to forgive."

"Your words make me so happy, Princess, so happy." The sweat rolled down his forehead over his closed eyes. "What changed your mind?"

"What a bubblehead I was. I didn't see things clearly."

His handler ordered him to wind up the call.

"I need you to come to Cuba with money. The Cubans say they'll protect me. But they want my financial connections . . . and US dollars, plenty of them."

"It's the least I can do for not seeing things as they were."

"The Cubans will contact you with instructions. Keep this confidential. Understand?"

"Oh, I understand fine."

His handler came toward him with a finger drawn across his throat.

"Hafta go now. Miss you, Princess."

The handler wrenched the receiver from his hand.

———

"What news, Bert?" The mental fog lifted from Dallas Taylor's head at Walter Reed National Military Medical Center. Out the window of the acute-care room, treetops swayed in the morning wind as gray clouds scudded across the sky. A nurse in blue scrubs ran past the open door. Beeps and buzzes sounded from unknown locations. Taylor's left arm tugged on an IV. At the foot of the bed, two doctors in white lab coats with stethoscopes coiled around their necks spoke in medical jargon. Dr. Bert Gaines nodded to them. They left.

"No news from the stroke team," Dr. Gaines said. "Stroke's tricky."

"Aren't you going to stay . . ." *Stay* wasn't the word. She struggled to find it. "Say . . . I told you s-so?"

"I'm your doc and then some." He smiled. "Not your accuser."

"I have hard time speaking."

"It's the stroke. It's called aphasia." He caressed her right cheek. "There's a weakness here."

She traced a forefinger down a sag on her face.

"Your stroke did that."

"How long the poop?" *Droop* was the word she wanted. Her laughter collapsed into worry.

"I know what you mean." He took her hand and squeezed it. "As you recover, the droop should fade away." He let the hand go. "Speech problems aren't unusual."

"I . . . I . . . must go back to building . . . the office. I"—she forced out the rest of the words in an explosion—"must work to do."

"You can't, Dallas." He pulled a chair over to the bed and sat. "You're lucky the stroke team administered a clot-buster drug right away. But you're in danger of another stroke."

"How long here?"

"It depends on test results. Earliest would be a day or two." He ignored the heartbeat ringtone of his cell. "Whatever it is, you'll need rehab therapy."

"They will make me . . . leave office."

"No one knows how bad this is. We'll know more soon."

"Does he . . . they . . . know I have stroke?"

"Your press secretary put out a cover story. You're here for observation after exhaustion from work stress."

"It buys time."

"You know it's all coming out, eventually, don't you?"

She said nothing. *Maybe it won't.*

He stood up. "Can you lift your right arm?"

She lifted it up a few feet. It collapsed on the bed like a dead branch.

She looked away from the arm to his face. "Pretty bad?"

"Bad enough."

"Say I am doing well."

"Look, Dallas. I love you and I'll stall until we know more." He pulled his shoulders into a military posture. "But I'm not going to lie. This wasn't just a TIA, like the last time."

"You look." She took his hand. "I will be fine."

He kissed her on the forehead. "Dallas dear, will you marry me?"

# CHAPTER SEVENTY-ONE

Disguised as tourists, Jim Murphy and Marco Leone waited inside the José Martí International Airport on red plastic chairs for the Miami flight to arrive in Havana. A man in a yellow T-shirt with a taxi service logo sat down on a chair facing them. He tapped his Cuban straw hat three times. Jim touched his Cuban straw hat in the same way. "That's our contact," he said to Marco.

Although Daisy had denied knowing her father's whereabouts, Nicole tipped him off that Daisy was . . . supposedly . . . going to visit Miami's beaches to unwind. FBI agents uncovered her plan to hop a flight from Miami to Havana where her father had contacts in Cuban pharma.

Things would go smoothly with the help of this Cuban double agent provided by Bryan's CIA connections. When Daisy arrived on American Airlines, the agent would find out her destination even if she refused his offer of taxi service. They'd then tail her to Sebastian Senex's hideout.

The double agent's operatives would snatch Senex with as little force as possible and, if they were lucky, with just deception or bribery. They'd secure his hands with zip ties and cover his head with a black bag before handing him off to an undercover fishing boat off the coast. Jim's brother called the international kidnapping an involuntary rendition with a matter-of-factness that made him uncomfortable.

"There she is." Jim nodded toward a statuesque blonde strolling in a stream of arrivals with a pink suitcase on wheels. Right on script, the double agent sauntered over to Daisy. She stopped. They talked. She smiled and shook his hand as though she knew him. Daisy and the double agent starting walking toward an airport exit reserved for VIP pickups.

"Let's follow," he said to Marco. "Something's not right."

At curbside, the double agent helped her through the rear door of a black Mercedes. The agent took a seat next to the driver. The Mercedes squealed out of the airport to an unknown destination.

"Do you know what I conclude?" Marco asked.

"We've been conned." Jim smashed his fist into the palm of his hand. "Our double agent is a triple agent."

"Precisely." Marco rubbed his chin. "I have an idea. Let's go to the Italian embassy."

———

The chief of staff poked her head inside the Oval Office. "Dallas, your congressional execution squad is here."

President Taylor examined her face in a pocket mirror. The facial droop had diminished. She sat back in her executive chair and gripped the edge of the Resolute desk with her left hand as if she were flying through air turbulence. She kept the cold and numb right hand under the desk. She struggled to keep the fingers from curling.

Madison Malone, the new Republican Speaker of the House; the Republican majority leader; and the Democratic minority leader filed into the Oval Office with pallbearer faces. They stopped at the front of the president's desk. In the middle of the three stood Malone, with hands on hips and dressed in her power ensemble of a lavender pantsuit over a white blouse.

"You know why we're here," the Speaker said. She wore a twenty-two-karat gold necklace nestled on the blouse. The bling signaled she was top gun in the legislative bloc of multimillionaire representatives bored with making money and eager for a political career.

"Why do you want me . . . to go?" she said to Malone. *To go? What was the word she really wanted?* "You missed the boat. Congress made

David Chang vice president. You are not next . . . in line . . . to take over."

She enjoyed the if-looks-could-kill face of the Speaker.

"Sorry about that," Taylor said, sticking the knife in a little further. The Speaker was a Vassar-educated snob who had blackballed her when she tried to join the Chevy Chase Country Club.

The Democratic minority leader stepped forward. "Madam President, with all due respect, you're overreacting. We all want your medical results from Walter Reed hospital."

By provoking an unnecessary catfight with the Speaker, she caused self-inflicted damage. She was even antagonizing the minority leader, a trusted ally. *What had come over her?* It wasn't like her to lose her cool when political stakes required winning friends and influencing people.

"Sorry, I was short. I've been working over . . . overworking."

"Are you OK?" the minority leader asked.

"A little tired. That's all."

She had better control her words.

"I went to . . . the . . . hospital for observation. Exhaustion from work stress. I feel fine now."

"Walter Reed referred us to the White House physician for further information," the minority leader said. "What does Dr. Gaines say?"

"Dr. Gaines resigned this morning," she said. "Our social relationship is now personal. Medical ethics prevent him from being my doctor."

"When do we get your test results?" the Republican majority leader asked.

"Soon . . . if relevant."

"You don't decide that," the Speaker said. "We do." She stood with feet apart and hands on her hips. Toes and fingers aimed at the president like knives. "We want all your other medical records in the meantime."

"You have the medical notes from Dr. Gaines."

"That's not enough," the majority leader said.

"What are you hiding?" the Speaker tapped her foot. "Give us all your medical records."

Taylor rubbed her cold and numb right hand with her left under the desk.

"Why should I? No president has done that."

If she didn't release all her medical records, there'd be political hell to pay. If she did, they'd find out about the abortion she had and there'd be political hell to pay.

"We don't want another disabled Woodrow Wilson in that chair," the Republican majority leader said. "Will you allow us to examine all your medical records?"

"Over my dead body."

"That's exactly what we fear," the Speaker retorted. The majority leader snickered, and the minority leader looked at the floor and shook his head.

The Speaker stepped toward the desk. "We'll use the Twenty-Fifth Amendment to remove you for inability to do your job."

"You're bluffing," Taylor said. "Even if you have enough cabinet votes, you need the vice president to . . . go along. *Concur.* Do you think David Chang, my former professor, the new vice president, will concur?"

*He might,* she worried. David Chang would do what he thought right. And if the medical tests showed a problem, he'd be another problem. The trouble with philosopher kings like Chang was that they put the general welfare above friendship, family, and personal interests.

"He might like the idea of becoming acting president," the Speaker said. "Politics has its addictive magic."

"Even if Chang concurs," Taylor said, "you need two-thirds vote of the Senate and the House to over . . . overrule my objection to your finding of disability." She pointed at the Speaker with her left forefinger. "You know you don't have the votes. Why waste my time with scarecrow tactics?" She was rolling now. "I'm president. Get over it."

"We'll return when you're feeling better," said the Democratic minority leader.

After they left, she took her cold and numb right hand out from under the desk.

# CHAPTER SEVENTY-TWO

The beat-up Cubataxi bounced to a stop at the corner. Jim Murphy piled out of the rear seat and rubbed his butt. Marco Leone paid the cab driver off meter while a passing teenager belted out a salsa beat from his boom box.

"Your idea won't work," Jim said.

"Do you have a superior one?" Marco pointed to the Italian embassy. *"Andiamo."*

They wove their way through a swarm of Cubans checking and scrolling their cell phones near a Wi-Fi hotspot. At the gates of the Italian embassy, a security guard called on his cell. He opened the gates and escorted them toward the embassy entrance. A slender man walked out in a blue seersucker suit and a yellow bow tie as if an oversized butterfly had mistaken his throat for a flower. The man and Marco hugged on the pathway between gate and entrance.

He had been around Marco and the Taylor Street ethnics long enough to understand some Italian words flying between the stranger and his partner. The diplomat had met Marco at the Italian police academy before joining the Italian secret service. He reached the pinnacle of that cloak-and-dagger career by exposing the CIA's kidnapping of Muslims on Italian streets in broad daylight with the collusion of higher-ups. For his unwelcome vigilance, they put Marco's friend out to pasture as a security attaché at the Italian embassy in Cuba. The yellow bow tie would have been reason enough for the tropical exile.

Their host ushered them into a conference room of cinnamon-colored wood glistening with lacquer. A waiter appeared with three wineglasses of Aperol Spritz. The attaché lifted his glass in a *salute* toast before huddling with Marco in rapid-fire Italian.

From what he understood, Marco and the attaché were catching up on old times. Marco switched to English to discuss his idea for countering the double-cross by their double agent. The attaché's face lit up when he heard the idea. *"Un momento,"* he said. The attaché and the butterfly on his throat flew off to another room.

"My idea advances," Marco said.

"You only got to first base."

"How is that?"

"It's like you told me. Never promise the sun before it rises."

While Marco flipped through a newspaper, Jim examined a mosaic of chocolate-brown wood chips set into a wall of cinnamon-colored wood. A mosaic of Che Guevara in his beret and beard kept watch over the room with brooding eyes. He had been a detective long enough not to wonder whether the dark-chocolate eyes concealed electronic surveillance.

"It is done," the attaché said in English. He looked at the Che Guevara image and lowered his voice. "The ambassador approves."

The attaché took them to the foyer where he explained the Italian embassy would facilitate a meeting between the Cuban Intelligence Directorate, commonly known as G2, and the detectives. A G2 agent would contact them at the Hotel Capri where they stayed if the Cubans wished to discuss a deal. The G2 wanted the attaché to inform the foreigners that Cuba might do this only as a favor to the Italian government and not for the *Yanquis*. Whatever, Murphy thought, as long as we get our man and go home.

"The ambassador received this daily news summary from Rome," the attaché said with a smile. "It concerns the commissario." He handed it to Marco.

Marco's face grew somber.

"Who died?" Jim asked.

"I have been appointed chief of police . . . the *questore* . . . for Rome."

In a White House medical examination room, Dr. Bert Gaines laid the medical report from Walter Reed hospital on the crash cart.

"The MRI confirms you had a stroke. There's a small lesion in your temporal lobe."

"Is there some way—"

"To spin this?" He came to the examination table where Dallas Taylor sat with legs dangling over the side. "No, my dear. You can't spin this. You're lucky to be alive."

He caressed her cheek.

*Does he want an answer?*

"One last check before I hand you over to another doc." He winked. "I'm much too involved to be yours." He took off his navy-blue jacket. "Close your eyes and raise both arms."

She raised her right arm to almost the same level as the left one. Hope surged. She was still in the game.

"Good," he said. "Hold your arms out and resist while I push them up and down."

She resisted with all her strength. She hated losing, whatever the game. Her right arm gave way earlier than she expected. "Not so good, right?"

"A little better." He took her right hand and splayed the fingers, stretching them one way and then another. "The finger curling's almost gone. How's your hand?"

"The chill's gone but still a little numb. I can write with it."

"Your speech?"

"Back to normal."

"Really?" He raised his eyebrows. "That's not the White House scuttlebutt."

"I get tired reading and don't always find the right words. So what? I can do without the fancy words."

"Too bad, Dallas, but your duties require a lot of reading and fancy words." He took out his iPad. "I'm making a note to have a speech-language pathologist see you."

"Everything will get back to normal . . . eventually . . . right?"

"For the next three months at least, you'll need intensive rehabilitation."

"I can work that into my schedule."

"I don't think you should continue as president." He folded his arms. "You're at high risk for another stroke. You've been letting yourself go. You need medication for your cholesterol. You have an irregular heartbeat. And, to top it off, there's a small aneurysm, or bulge, in your abdominal aorta. If that rips open . . . well, I don't have to spell it out."

"What's your answer?" he asked.

"I want to be president."

"That's not the question I asked you at Walter Reed."

"I want to marry you. But I also want to be president."

"And I want to marry you." He put his jacket back on. "But I don't want to be a first gentleman . . . lounging around the White House . . . worried about a wife who ignores her husband's medical advice."

"The country needs me."

"The cemeteries are full of needed people." He walked to the door. "And the country sure doesn't need a dead or disabled president."

"Think it over, Bert."

"I have. Me or the White House."

# CHAPTER SEVENTY-THREE

Marco Leone and Jim Murphy finished dinner in the Hotel Capri restaurant. With no contact from the Cuban Intelligence Directorate, they decided to cut their losses and leave the island the following morning before the Cubans arrested them. Operation Big Shoulders had morphed into Operation Bummer. Jim waved good night as Marco entered his room down the hall. He then opened the door to his own room. In the dark, a window air conditioner sputtered its death throes.

A table lamp switched on.

An intruder wearing a New York Yankees baseball cap sat in the corner. About to light a cigar, he asked, "May I?"

"Who the hell are you?"

"I assume that's a no." He put the cigar down. "Let's say I'm called"—he touched his forefinger to his lips—"Hmmm. Raoul . . . or Roberto if you like."

"You're from G2."

"Possibly." He raised a folder. "You've had quite an up-and-down career, Detective Murphy. My condolences for your son's death." He placed the folder down. "Not surprising. Your country is known for its violent crime."

Bryan had warned him that Cuban spies knew their trade.

"Why are you here?"

"I'd rather not be. I don't like Uncle Sam."

"You sure like his baseball caps."

The Cuban agent scowled.

Murphy took a chair and placed it opposite the intruder's. "Down to business." He sat backward facing the Cuban over the rear of the chair. He refused to be cowed by the intelligence agency's intimate knowledge of him. "We want Sebastian Senex returned for trial."

"And you want us to just hand him over?"

"What do you want in return?"

"We want Edel Montez."

The feds had caught the Cuban spy working at the National Security Agency. They gave him an early retirement in federal prison.

"I don't have authority to exchange him."

"Then I'm wasting my time."

"Even if I could, how do I arrange that from Cuba?"

"Use that." The agent pointed to the telephone. "It'll be charged to your room. Uncle Sam always has money for foreign meddling."

Murphy dialed his brother with the private number Bryan had given him. Bryan had emphasized that President Taylor would do her utmost to bring Senex back. When Bryan heard of his brother's plight, he promised to contact the president and call back within the hour.

"Thanks, bro." Jim hung up. "My brother said—"

"We already know." The agent smiled. "I was told to wait for the answer."

"Your big brother knows all," Murphy said. "How comforting."

"I understand why you want Senex. For murder in Chicago. But why does the FBI?"

"Economic and environmental crimes."

"What did you expect? He's a success in your robber-baron system."

"I'm not here to argue politics." He checked to confirm the presence of the return airline ticket in the nightstand drawer. "Why do you guys always blame us for your problems? We left seventy years ago."

"You understand nothing. You don't know how my peasant parents lived before the revolution." The agent put the dossier on Murphy back into his briefcase and sighed. "The problem is you never left. You remain stuck in our national consciousness like a chicken bone in the throat."

"Whoa." Murphy held up his hand. "Let's stick to business."

The Cuban sulked while they waited for Bryan's call. Murphy killed time by leafing through a tourist magazine as the minutes dragged on. The background Afro-Cuban jazz from the rooftop band stopped for an intermission. That meant an hour had now gone by without Bryan's call.

Had his brother abandoned him again?

The agent received a call that woke him out of his doze.

"Here's the situation," the Cuban said afterward. "If the deal goes through, we give you the location of Senex. You wait a day before you come for him. There is no need for force. It will be arranged to appear you Yankees kidnapped him."

"Why wait a day?"

The agent hesitated before answering.

"His daughter is coming tomorrow."

Murphy put two and two together. "Wow. She brings protection money and you guys—"

"Betray him. Is that what you think?" The agent took off his Yankees cap and fanned himself. He put the cap back on. "Whatever you call it, you are responsible with your embargo. We are a proud people who will do whatever we must to live as we wish." He shrugged. "And you are a proud people who will do whatever you must to make us live the way you wish."

"Why do you hate us so?"

"I don't hate you. And I don't love you. I both hate and love you Americans."

The telephone rang. He heard his brother's voice say, "It's a go."

———

Vice President David Chang stood in the doorway of the Oval Office.

"You can beat this, Ms. President," said Emily James sitting next to Dallas Taylor on an Oval Office sofa.

Her friend's encouragement simmered her competitive juices.

The press secretary nodded. "The optics are doable."

"Don't be shy, David. Enter." She waved him in, to any empty chair next to the sofa. "Any thoughts about this political mess, Mr. Vice President?"

Chang sat down. He took off his glasses and rubbed his eyes with his knuckles. "Excuse me. I arrived late last night." He replaced the glasses and said, "The situation reminds me of President Truman. When he ran in 1948, the polls were against him in a four-person election. The pundits predicted he'd lose, but he didn't."

"Exactly," said Emily. "Truman was a bigger comeback kid than Bill Clinton."

"I can see it now," said the White House communications director. "We wage a Trumanesque give-'em-hell campaign against the do-nothing Republicans in the House. Teddy Roosevelt had his Square Deal. FDR had his New Deal. And Truman his Fair Deal. What you need, Madam President, is a Real Deal campaign slogan."

"John Kerry already used Real Deal." Emily wrinkled her nose. "Kerry lost."

"Hold on you." She waved her hand. "You all are counting your chickens before they hatch. They want to boot me out with the Twenty-Fifth Amendment, not an election."

She eyed Chang to see if he'd pledge his undying loyalty and say *I'll refuse to concur with the cabinet in declaring you unable to perform your duties of office, no matter what your medical records show.* He remained silent. Hurt erupted inside her at his failure to say anything. She checked herself in time before venting her pique.

"You're right, Madam President. Your medical condition is the immediate problem." Chang looked down, shaking his head. "Your advisors and I don't like prying." He looked back up. "But if we want to hatch those chickens, we'd better know your medical condition for an effective response."

"The medical records before I became vice president are off limits. Period." She grabbed the edge of the sofa with her right hand to prevent the fingers from curling. "I should have the same medical privacy as every other citizen." She didn't have to hang out her teenage abortion like dirty linen for the whole world to poke their noses into.

"Then what about the Walter Reed test results?" Emily asked.

"I've been thinking hard about that." She had almost lashed out at David Chang because of irrational suspicions about his loyalty. *What has come over me?* She had kept the depth of her medical condition to herself. It wasn't fair to David or her staff.

Her fear was that David wouldn't equate the good of a friend with that of the country. She was ashamed of her fear, but there it was. And this integrity was a key reason she had picked him for vice president in the first place. He was the same person as always. Was she? They said it was the stroke, and the mood swings would tend to fade away. The word *tend* worried her.

An aide broke in with news. A super PAC and individuals fronting for Sebastian Senex were running ads and preparing a lawsuit to challenge her qualifications to be president. They claimed she failed to meet the minimum age qualification of thirty-five years under the Constitution.

"It's the Obama birther issue all over again in another form," the White House communications director said. "It won't hold up. Bryan Murphy at Justice agrees."

Chang added, "You clearly were thirty-five when the House voted you in as president. I don't see the relevancy of your age when you occupied a temporary caretaker position until the House election of a president."

"No so fast." The press secretary tapped a pen against his lips. "Sure, a court might dismiss the lawsuit. But for some, President Taylor has to be an illegitimate president. They can't accept that an African American woman could have attained the highest office in the land. Obama had to fight the issue over and over again." He stuck the pen in the breast pocket of his jacket. "Don't underestimate its dog-whistle appeal."

"They're going to drag the names of my mama and papa through the mud. They're going to say my parents bribed the midwife, they committed fraud on the birth certificate, probably murdered the midwife before they're through."

She shook her head. A sob came up uninvited from her chest. She pulled herself together. "I know what I'm going to do." She had to be careful. If she gave her emotions free rein, she might have another stroke.

"You're going to produce your test results, right?" the White House communications director said. "Good decision. Once they're public we can do damage control. Otherwise it looks like you're hiding something."

"I'm going to resign as president of the United States."

"Why on earth?" asked the director of communications.

"You'll understand once you see my hospital test results. I had a stroke."

"We already suspected something like that. The message can be massaged," the director of communications said, "before the results go public."

"Still in shock, I see." She looked at them all. "I've had it. The stroke has forced me, kicking and screaming, to look at myself. I simply have to admit I'm not up to the job anymore. The public isn't going to want another Woodrow Wilson in the White Home . . . I mean House."

She burned with embarrassment at an erroneous choice of words that her advisors pretended not to notice.

"Fact is I do want to go home . . . back to Texas."

The director of communications cleared his throat. The press secretary studied his fingers. Their silence told her they understood her decision whatever their objections.

"Consider this," Chang said. "The Twenty-Fifth Amendment allows me to be acting president until you are capable of resuming your duties as president."

"That's kind of you, David. But when you see the medical records and talk to Dr. Gaines, you'll find my disabilities are serious and probably going to last beyond my term of office."

"That means, Ms. President, I shall become president once you resign."

"Exactly as I intend." She patted his hand. "The United States could not be in better hands."

The chief of staff waited until the men left the Oval Office.

"In my bones, I knew this would happen." Emily James hugged her best friend. "Good for you, Dallas. Get out of this pressure cooker and get well." Tears fell down her cheeks. "Without you here, I don't know what I'm going to do next."

"How'd you like to be my bridesmaid?"

# CHAPTER SEVENTY-FOUR

Sebastian Senex, who would live forever, lay dying within the walls of a plaster-peeling bedroom in a seedy part of Havana. Sunlight streamed through warped window shutters. It wasn't supposed to be this way. He was supposed to have the best medical talent money could buy. Their only task would be to keep him young.

Seized by delirium, he harangued the uncomprehending maid for stealing his pink bunny slippers. With a toothless grin, she wiped his forehead drenched in sweat with a wet rag. Three Cubans from the Intelligence Directorate and a medical doctor played dominoes at the kitchen table through the open door of the bedroom.

Burning with fever he reached for a glass of water, knocking it over, sores marching up his ulcerated arm like black widow spiders. The white-haired maid mopped up the mess. "Give me my slippers. I need to go the bathroom . . . *el baño.*"

The doctor came to Senex and reached under the bed. "Here are your slippers. Where you left them."

The maid helped him up to a sitting position on the side of the bed. She went to place a slipper on his foot. He grabbed it away and snuggled his foot into it. The other dropped from his hands. The maid put on the remaining slipper without further objection.

She helped him to his feet and stuck a cigar in her mouth. Senex fussed about the health dangers of tobacco. She went outside to smoke. An angry-hornet pain gnawed at his stomach.

"Am I going to die?" he asked the doctor.

"We all are."

"You know what I mean." He grabbed the physician's arm. "How could the American doctors have been so wrong?"

"Your condition is extraordinary. Multiple cancers present simultaneously in your body. Every major organ is affected." The doctor put his arm around Senex and guided him to the bathroom. "Our specialists theorize your blood procedures caused your cells to multiply wildly. Your elixir of life brought you both youth and ravenous cancer."

"Will I die from this?"

"Yes."

"When?"

"Soon."

"How could this happen?" He put his hand to his feverish forehead. "The United States has the best medical system in the world."

"For people like you, no doubt."

The doctor held him up when he staggered.

"But your wealth and social position," the doctor said, "mean nothing to these cancers."

"Any hope at all?"

"The determination of research physicians, like ours, freed of capitalistic—"

"Spare me the communist catechism." He squeezed the doctor's arm. "Are there any long-shot options?"

"We have advanced cancer treatments in Cuba." The doctor opened the bathroom door for him. "But for you," he said, shrugging, "nothing works."

The doctor had that right. Nothing worked in Cuba when he needed it. The electric lighting didn't work in the bathroom. The toilet bowl lacked a seat. Mold ran along the baseboards. Taking a rusty straight razor from the medicine chest, he held it to his throat. He studied the razor and put it back. Not even the razors looked like they worked.

When Daisy brought the money, he could pay the Cubans. They were holding back treatment until they got paid. That had to be it.

*Where is Daisy? Has she abandoned me after all?*

The cracked mirror over the sink showed tears streaming down his cheeks. He put hand to mouth so they couldn't hear his weeping. Never had he cried so hard since his mother died. He washed away the tears and pulled himself together before leaving the bathroom.

The doctor gave him a pill. He fell into a deep sleep.

———

The drilling sensation in his bones startled him awake. The Cuban guards and the doctor were eating dinner in the kitchen. The dimness of the room and the meager light from the exposed bulb now lit in the bedroom announced evening.

He shivered and pulled the blanket to his chin. Fatigue chained him to the bed. The long sleep and return of the fever had clouded his vision and mind. He heard the entrance door to the apartment open. English. Her voice.

*Daisy has arrived.*

In the open doorway of the bedroom stood Daisy like a shimmering specter with a carry-on bag. A rodent scurried across the floor and under the dresser. He rubbed his eyes to make sure it was his daughter. "My angel has arrived."

"I'm not the angel you're expecting."

The Cuban agent with a bandolier strapped across his chest took her pink suitcase back into the kitchen.

"Did you bring the US dollars in large denominations like I asked?"

"Don't I always follow orders?"

The doctor entered. He took Senex's pulse and watched him from the foot of the bed.

"I can pay . . . whatever you want," he said to the doctor. He forced himself into a sitting position. "She brought the money . . . *mucho dinero.* I can pay for the cure."

"We have none."

His coughing erupted. Mucus slid up into his mouth. He asked his daughter for a box of facial tissues lying on the dresser. She didn't respond. The doctor brought the box to his bed. He coughed into the tissues and threw them into the wastebasket.

Something within was pinning him down, down until he collapsed flat on his back. He imagined a hand pulling him through the mattress, through the floor, through the earth, and heaping dirt on him. He screamed. "There must be something to save me."

"There was," Daisy said.

"What do you mean . . . there was?" He raised himself onto his elbows. He fell back to the bed. "I need to know."

"Well." She put a forefinger to her lips. "If you really want to know."

"I do, I do."

"Dr. Mora told me the day before he died that he had foreseen the possibility of cells turning cancerous. He had a solution."

"What?"

"He never told me. We were supposed to meet later." She leaned over to him. "But you had him killed before he could tell me."

"He said my symptoms were just the body adjusting. He told me not to worry." His eyes questioned her. "Why would he say that?"

"Exactly, Daddy." She hovered over him. "He didn't want to worry you about possible cancer. He just said he had the remedy in case you needed it."

"Where?" He raised his hands toward her. His body shook in a spasm of coughing. "Go back and find it in his apartment, his lab, his—" He slid out of the bed onto the floor. "I order you."

Daisy coaxed him back into bed. The doctor gave him another pill. He closed his eyes and drifted off. They went back to the kitchen and waited. "It won't be long now," the doctor said.

———

Within the hour, Daisy and the doctor returned to the bedroom. The doctor examined the body and pronounced Senex dead. "What a pity . . . Dr. Mora died before revealing his remedy."

"That would have been impossible." A tight smirk stretched across her lips. "I made the story up."

"Why do such a thing to your father?"

"To see his expression."

"He was your flesh and blood. How could you?"

"Because I was his angel . . . the angel of death." She handed the doctor a bottle of white powder. "I won't need this after all to take care of my father. You might want it for your rat problem."

# CHAPTER SEVENTY-FIVE

After her wedding on the beach on San José Island, Dallas Taylor sauntered barefoot in a midlength bridal gown of chiffon lace and tulle along the surf with President David Chang. The Gulf of Mexico swirled over her feet. She squished seaweed under her toes, like the feel of strawberry jam squeezed between her fingers as a child. She was grounded to life then. Her stroke had set off a wake-up call before she sleepwalked through the rest of life.

The president's cell phone buzzed. After confirming David's use of a secure smartphone, the Secret Service agent dropped back again behind them so Chang could answer the call. Her former professor looked like he was sucking lemon while cutting short the call.

"The DNC chairman called."

"What's that man want?"

"To hustle me for a cabinet position."

"Careful. He's a sidewinder."

"Excuse me for a minute. I must talk to the agent."

Whatever doubts she had about David vanished after his negotiations with the Chinese. Because she banned the export of Anoflix to China in her battle with Sebastian Senex, the Chinese developed their own COVID-28 vaccine in record time. They snuffed out eruptions of COVID-28 before it became another world scourge. The suspicion, which the Chinese publicly denied, was that they had developed their vaccine by infringing on the Anoflix patent controlled by the United

States. The Chinese countered that the export ban represented hostility toward China.

As national pride and profit hurtled both countries toward confrontation over patent rights, David allowed the Chinese to save face. He had proposed and China agreed that both nations would relinquish COVID-28 vaccine patent claims against each other and pool their COVID-28 vaccine patents for the benefit of all nations under an open licensing arrangement. License fees would be graduated according to the wealth of the country or other entity seeking a license. The agreement transformed the United States from villain into hero.

Looking like her father long ago, a man walked along the beach with a toddler girl full of glee riding high around his neck with legs dangling.

The president came up alongside her after talking to the agent.

"I wish my parents were alive for the wedding," Taylor said.

The orange sun of a lazy afternoon filtered through sparse clouds floating like coral islands in the blue sky. A stray gull darted down at her wedding headband of roses and seashells and veered back upward.

"They'd be proud of you," he said, brushing away a bug. "What about my offer?"

Down the beach the sound of a harp broke through the chatter of guests in the wedding tent from which they had come. She loved her freshly minted husband for keeping her aunties and uncles occupied, so she and the president could take care of business.

"I've considered your offer," she said. A young woman gathered seashells ahead. "I think a cabinet position would be risky, given my stroke."

"Not even attorney general? You could go after the bad actors in big pharma."

"Bryan Murphy deserves it. Give him the position."

"I suspected you'd say that." Chang smiled.

It was so typical of the man. He offered her a position, even though she came from a different political party and considered his ideas impractical in the blood sport of American politics.

He had already brought back a tone of civility to politics, almost forgotten, like pay phones and carbon paper. With him in office, the National Independent Party expanded its membership across the country. From its newly established think tank of innovative Gen-Xers and millennials, the NIP proposed amending the Constitution to model gun control on the Twenty-First Amendment, which had overturned the amendment establishing Prohibition.

The premise of the proposal was that in twenty-first-century America, the cultural values of each state differed radically on the role of guns. Each state should, therefore, decide for itself how to regulate or not regulate guns. Any transport of guns into another state in violation of its laws would be prohibited, just like the transport of intoxicating liquor was under the Twenty-First Amendment. She didn't think it had a chance of getting passed. Most folks considered the Constitution like the Bible and you didn't amend the Bible.

That said, the country was seeking compromise instead of conflict as the default position. People were thinking outside the box instead of fighting like trapped scorpions inside. The country was big and diverse. It didn't have to march in lockstep. That's the way the country was set up. The secular bible of the Constitution provided for change by amendment.

"You know," she said. "I doubt I'd have resigned, despite my health and Bert, if I didn't have you to succeed me."

"I'm grateful, Dallas." He tossed a stone, skipping the surface of the water. "But I need you nearby to avoid political booby traps."

"Why?"

"I have a vision of the possible but you know the art of the possible."

"My life comes first now." They stopped walking. "It took me a while. But I think the purpose of life is life. And I don't want to lose what I found."

A woman and young girl walked in the distance. The woman pointed to the mansion hidden from the beach. *Someday you, too, can be president, like Dallas Taylor, and be a guest there,* she imagined the woman saying. *Tell her the price of the presidency, lady . . . first tell her the price to be paid . . .* she wanted to warn the pair.

"What if I had a position that wouldn't stress your health?"

"I don't know, David." They resumed walking. "I've lost my taste for the bickering, the posturing, the conniving, the plain cussedness of politics."

"How'd you like to be head of my proposed National Youth Corps?" He stepped around a sandcastle crumbling into the surf. "All the forces in this wonderful, diverse nation have lately been focused on the individual . . . me, me and not the community.

"I want a counterforce that will take the rich kid from the suburb, the rural kid from the farm, and the poor kid from the inner city, youths from every part of the country and from every religious, racial, and ethnic background. I want them to live and work together and to see how others live . . . or barely live . . . in this country.

"Among the young, I want to create a sense of common purpose with peace instead of conflict. I want them to be for something and not just against something." He stopped her with his arm and locked her eyes with his. "I want to heal the deep divisions based more on mutual ignorance than malice."

"Amen, Professor." She looked out to sea. "But be prepared to battle those who will call you a fascist, an Uncle Tong, an authoritarian, a Maoist hell-bent on cultural revolution. They'll use every racist innuendo in the book against you, like they did me. You threaten those whose importance depends on stirring up division. I wouldn't go to bat for half the things you want. I respect the limits of things as they are." She smiled. "But you have an advantage."

"What's that?"

"You're what JFK said he was . . . an idealist without illusions."

The Secret Service agent caught up. "Mr. President, we need to get you back to the White House."

"What do you say, Dallas?"

"One condition." She folded her arms and smiled. "Only if I can include tap dancing as part of the program."

"You've got a deal."

They fist-bumped and headed back to the merriment of the marriage tent.

# CHAPTER SEVENTY-SIX

"Delivery for Jim Murphy and Marco Le . . . Lion." A gum-chewing delivery boy in a Cubs baseball cap laid the cake box from Ferrara Bakery on the table in the back of Dugan's on Halsted. He almost tripped over Leone's suitcase on the way back out. Mondocane fretted on a leash at Marco's feet before flopping on the floor in a heap.

A banner ran across the wall beside the table: CONGRATULATIONS COMMANDER JIM MURPHY AND QUESTORE MARCO LEONE! . . . DUGAN'S BARTENDERS AND BARFLIES.

"What's this?" Jim said to Nicole.

"Something Katie and I ordered to celebrate your promotion to commander and Marco's to questore."

"Marco gets the first slice," Katie said. "He's leaving when the cab comes."

Marco opened the box. *What goes wrong can go right . . . Murphy's Law Amended* appeared in colored frosting on Ferrara's classic cake of fresh strawberries, custard, and cannoli cream.

"What is this strange con-coc-tion?" Marco said.

Nicole gave a slice to Marco. "For the skeptic."

Mondocane whined in vain for cake. He dozed off at Marco's feet with his muzzle resting on Bruno Magli shoes.

Marco tasted a sample of the cake. *"Perfetto!"* He formed a ring in the air with thumb and index finger.

"Hey," Jim said, "look at that handsome mug up there."

On the TV screen overhead, Commander Jim Murphy of the Chicago PD announced from the lectern of the Dirksen Building conference room the successful conclusion of Operation Big Shoulders at both the federal and state levels. He thanked the new CEO of Promethean Pharma for full cooperation with governmental authorities. Because of a plea deal, including admissions of guilt, all legal actions against Promethean Pharma ended. Bryan Murphy, the nominee for attorney general, stood in the background up against a line of governmental flags with other strike-force participants.

"I agree. Not a bad-looking mug," Nicole said kissing Jim on the cheek. "You told me your brother always upstaged you. I'm not seeing it."

"Not like him," Jim said. "Beats me why he's changed."

"Did you not also agree to let Bryan place your fath—" Marco caught himself. "Forgive me. I know you do not wish to call him father."

"It's OK, Marco." Jim rubbed his cheek warmed by memories of the man. "Being a father is more than blood. It's about a man's commitment to protect a new life. And he did that for me. He was my father."

"Bryan's changed attitude beats you?" Nicole's eyebrows shot up. "Katie said you let Bryan place your father in the Taj Mahal of senior assisted care in Arlington, Virginia." She took his hand. "I think you both changed."

"Could be," Jim said. He pointed to the inscription on the cake. "We agreed to close the book on the past."

"Regarding books," Marco said, "will you allow Nicole's publisher to examine your child's . . . children's book?"

"Sure thing." He snapped on his peaked commander's cap with its navy-and-gold checkerboard pattern. "With this hat, what copper's going to needle me about a children's book?"

While Nicole discussed with Marco his return to Italy from O'Hare Airport, Jim watched the TV news program switch from the Dirksen Building to a reporter standing outside the new headquarters of the National Independent Party.

The reporter rattled off statistics proving the party was growing by leaps and bounds. Conservatives wished it were more liberal and liberals wished it were more conservative, though its innovative policies introduced by President Chang could often be interpreted either way.

It provided a Goldilocks political diet for nonideological Americans starved by the stale fare of the two-party system. The energy of this third political party had taken the pundits by surprise.

President David Chang had federalized the Illinois National Guard to assist Chicago police in crushing the turf war between the Outfit and the Sinaloa drug cartel. The gangland killings in broad daylight had come to a quick end. Citizens felt safe again on the streets.

It was as though the city, like the country, was emerging from a drunken hangover. A grateful public rewarded the political party they considered responsible for not letting politics get in the way of the general welfare. The duopoly of Republicans and Democrats had loosened its stranglehold on the nation's political life.

"I have to get to work," Katie said coming back from the restroom. She whispered in her brother's ear, "Thanks for making up with Bryan for my sake."

"Don't mean to be rude but I did it for both our sakes."

"Works for me." She gave him a kiss and left Dugan's.

After a commercial break, the TV screen panned to workmen installing a nameplate on the door of the top executive office at Promethean Pharma and removing one with Sebastian Senex's name.

The new CEO and board chairperson smiled and pointed to the nameplate: DAISY SENEX.

"It's a new day at Promethean Pharma," said Daisy into the reporter's microphone. She lowered her finger from the nameplate. "From now on this company will be operated with the strictest adherence to corporate integrity and the public good."

"I don't get it," Jim said to no one in particular. "She was supposed to be a ditz."

"She never was," Nicole said, her cheeks flushing. "I knew her. You didn't. Her father brainwashed her into believing she was a ditz. She woke up after the murder of Palomba."

"I wonder what happened between her and her father in Havana?" Jim asked no one in particular. "Guess we'll never know."

The bartender pointed to the cell in his hand. "Hey, Marco, your cab's outside for O'Hare," he yelled over the din of bar chatter and TV sound bites.

Marco herded Mondocane into his pet carrier. Jim picked up his partner's suitcases and walked him to the entrance door with Nicole. Outside the bar Jim handed over Marco's suitcases to the cab driver, who stuffed them in the trunk. Jim was going to miss Rome's new superintendent of police. "So, Marco, what have you learned in America?"

"We are all in the same leaky boat called the world. The alteration of seats on the boat does not stop the leaks." He hugged Jim. "We have to repair the leaks together."

"I draw the line at cheek kisses," Jim said, pulling away. "You want to ruin my reputation with Chicago coppers?"

Nicole kissed Marco goodbye on the cheeks.

"I wish I could go with you," she said, "but my research project is here."

"Is that what you call this police officer?" Marco asked with a smile. "A research project?"

"Get out," Jim said, "before I have you arrested."

"I shall see you in the hereafter in Rome."

"You got a deal," Jim said. It wasn't a linguistic lapse he wanted to correct.

# ACKNOWLEDGMENTS

In writing this novel I had the good fortune of assembling team members from Girl Friday Productions who launched my first novel, *The Mithras Conspiracy* (Lido Press: 2019). I thank Sara Spees Addicott, senior editor, for again keeping the unruly machinery of book production chugging along to a timely result. Thanks also to Bethany Davis, production editor and new team member, for making my life easier by coordinating the copyediting and proofreading. Although at opposite ends of the country, I had the pleasure of meeting Sara and Bethany (even if virtually) for the first time via Zoom conference.

And how could I forget to express my gratitude to Scott Calamar, the copyeditor, and Wanda Zimba, the proofreader? They skillfully did the nitty-gritty work of tightening up the nuts and bolts that I had failed to tighten.

Just as he did in my first novel, Paul Barrett, art director, worked his artistic magic on this novel's cover and interior to make attractively real what I only vaguely visualized. I am also indebted to all the unknown resource partners of Girl Friday Productions who behind the scenes have added their expertise to a publication I could not have achieved on my own. A shout-out also to Victor Salas of the University of Illinois Chicago School of Law library for his research assistance.

Finally, to this author writing in a year of COVID-19 house arrest, I could not have asked for a better companion than Donna, my wife. She not only endured a writer's travails but made the ultimate sacrifice of listening to the recitation of a husband's manuscript and providing suggestions. The spirited back-and-forth of those sessions improved earlier drafts and helped us get through a time of coronavirus.

# ABOUT THE AUTHOR

M.J. Polelle is a Harvard Law School graduate and an emeritus professor from the University of Illinois Chicago School of Law where he taught constitutional law. A native of Chicago, he was a special assistant state's attorney of Cook County and a Cook County judicial candidate. He has visited Italy many times, both for professional reasons and for pure pleasure. Polelle is the author of *The Mithras Conspiracy* (Lido Press: 2019). He now lives in Sarasota, Florida, with Donna, his wife. Visit the author's website at www.mjpolelle.com.